TORN
IN EXILE

A.L. MCDONNELL

Published in Australia by Thestel Books
First published in Australia 2021
This edition published 2021

Copyright A.L. McDonnell 2021

ISBN:
978-0-6450821-2-8 (paperback)
978-0-6450821-3-5 (ebook)

Cover design, typesetting: Working Type

McDonnell, A.L.

Torn: In Exile

pp410

almcdonnell.com

ABOUT THE AUTHOR

The author, **A.L. McDonnell** is a medical practitioner and psychologist who lives in Queensland's Lockyer Valley. She has written many scientific pieces and articles for lifestyle magazines and, as a medical practitioner, has worked extensively throughout the outback which is home to some of life's most colourful characters. Odd experiences are often the norm in the remote far west, and she was fascinated by the way individuals could spin their yarns, in pubs or around the campfire, turning ordinary events into something beyond this world and, even more, the many methods they claimed to have used to confront their bizarre encounters. The In Exile series grew from such a tale when she was asked what she would do if a spaceship landed in one of her own paddocks ...

For more **https://almcdonnell.com**

*This book is dedicated to all
those who dare to dream.*

ACKNOWLEDGMENTS

Without Barry, this novel would still be gathering dust in the bottom drawer of my desk.

My thanks to my lovely writers' group for all their help and encouragement – Jill, Kate, Jan, Danae, Bryce, Ruth, Barbara, Claire and Jo– and all the editors and instructors who helped with early drafts.

Thanks to Mark Griffiths for his military knowledge, and my apologies to Mark for the number of times I ignored his sound advice for the sake of a good story.

CONTENTS

CHAPTER 1

Planet – Condona; Galaxy – Strenata; IPL Sector – 1

They were stranded, millions of light years from home, and the only way Jemma could stop herself from sinking into the depths of despair was the belief that someone would find a means of getting them back to Earth. She continually reminded herself that the mission that brought her here had achieved a positive outcome. They'd rescued Sean, her husband, from an extraordinarily dismal place in which he'd been held captive. Now he was back with her, and safe, which had been anything but certain a few weeks ago.

Condona, a planet on the other side of the universe from Earth, had been sympathetic to their plight and provided refuge, asking for nothing in return. Werrimen, Supreme Commander-in-Chief of the Inter-Planetary League came from Sidlow, a planet not far from Condona, and she knew the Condonans well. She had assured Jemma that the Condonans never would seek any form of recompense.

Jemma sighed as she walked hand-in-hand with Sean through the big, open Condonan parkland. Their life here was more than comfortable, and if they were to be stranded on Condona for the rest of their days, which was still a possibility, they'd be fine.

Like all the other refugees she'd been allocated a job, mostly menial tasks like paperwork and running messages. She didn't mind, so long as it kept her busy and didn't allow too much time to worry. Still, in the early hours of the morning, often after lying awake most of the night thinking, the gloom would set in. She knew there was nothing she could have done to change the past, yet she felt guilty that she'd dragged Sean, and so many others, into her nightmare.

She was the one the rebels were after because she'd inherited the role of Supreme Ruler of Anders Major, a planet close to Earth. That had made her the target of multiple abductions and assassination attempts. Yet she had no memory of Anders. Her grandfather had sent her family to Earth before she was a year old, and her parents had failed to fill her in on her heritage before they were murdered. Still deep in thought, she started when something flashed past overhead, so close that it blew her long dark hair across her face.

'Holy Moley,' Jemma cried, raising her hands to protect her head.

Sean's brother, Dan, grinned down at her and waved.

'Delinquent,' she yelled, shaking her fist at him.

Dan had taken to riding the little one, or at a stretch, two-person aerial scooters that were popular among Condonan youth. He reminded her of a ten-year-old kid on red cordial as he swooped down again, laughing as he skimmed close.

'You're old enough to know better,' she shouted, glaring at Dan. But she did secretly understand his need to let off steam. Sean had been abducted first by the Zants, a group of hostile aliens from the planet Ailazant. Then Dan had led the first rescue mission, but he'd failed, and in the process, he and their friend Matt had also been abducted. Their treatment by the Zants had been savage and Jemma had no doubt that all three men had suffered unspeakable cruelty during their captivity.

Her gaze drifted to the dozens of brightly coloured transporters that flew overhead as hundreds of people made their way to work. Most adults used four-person transporters which were also airborne, but much more comfortable. In Jemma's experience, on Earth, in the early twenty-first century, people mainly travelled in motorcars, or occasionally in an aeroplane or helicopter. And, after the IPL had moved them forward eighty years to the late twenty-first century, she'd become accustomed to transporters zipping past overhead. Those transporters had been uniformly grey in colour and subtle in their shapes. Here, all sorts of shades and patterns were used, often with decorative add-ons like fake wings or animal shapes. Some had big smiles, others bared teeth. It was quite a spectacle.

'Ignore him,' said Sean, laughing. 'Did you see poor Nik sitting behind him? She was hanging on for dear life. Looked like she'd rather be anywhere but there.'

'Yeah, but he looks so happy, and given what you all endured, that's so good to see.' Still gazing at the aerial craft,

Jemma didn't notice that Sean had stopped dead in front of her until she had to pull up to avoid walking into him.

His arms were crossed, and his head was tilted to one side. 'You seem a long way away.'

'No, just thinking.' She tilted her head in the opposite direction which made him laugh, and that warmed her heart. There was a period of time after arriving on Condona that he'd been so stressed she hadn't been able to get him to so much as smile. She'd been worried that he might have suffered too much, both physically and mentally, from his ordeal to ever fully recover. Post-traumatic stress had to be a very real possibility, for all of them.

'Alright, I'll bite. What were you thinking about?' Sean picked her up and swung her around.

'Put me down. Everyone's looking at us,' Jemma exclaimed. Although tall herself, Sean towered above her, so when he eased her back to the ground she had to stand on her toes to extend her arms around his neck.

'Let them,' he murmured, drawing her into him.

Condonans, who were human just like the refugees from Earth, hurried past in every direction on their way to work. Even now, she struggled to get her mind around the fact that so many planets throughout the universe, including Condona, were populated by humans. She slipped her hand back into Sean's as he turned towards the large open space that was surrounded by the town's major building. On Earth she'd have called it a central park. Yet, it was different from Earth's parks. The greyish-brown plant matter underfoot consisted

4

of a thick mat of tiny plants with long leaves that crinkled and curled back towards the centre, making it feel like a plush pile carpet. Many people walked on it barefoot, but she always wore shoes. The first time she'd come out here, an insect that looked remarkably like a green ant had stung her, leaving a painful welt that had lasted for several days.

'We're going home,' murmured Sean. 'I can feel it. Werrimen's going to make it happen.'

Jemma was delighted to see him so happy and energetic, but she remained wary herself. There'd been so many times since they'd arrived here that her hopes had been raised only to be dashed again.

On every occasion something had gone wrong.

To get home to Earth, they'd need a spaceship capable of traversing the transport zones which used the folds in the universe to reduce vast distances to something more manageable. She didn't pretend to understand it, but that was how they'd arrived here from Earth, so she knew it was viable. Condona was one of only two planets in the known universe with the capability of building such craft. The other planet was Ailazant, sworn enemy of both the IPL and Condona. The Zants had systematically destroyed Condona's fleet, despite the IPL's best attempts to stop them. Somehow, the Zants had repeatedly managed to slip through the heaviest security unnoticed. Or worse, they'd used mind altering techniques on local people to manipulate them into infiltrating and wreaking havoc on the fleet.

The people of Condona had already started to build new

ships, and the IPL had amassed a massive security force, made up mostly of Sidlowns, the only non-humans officially present on Condona. The Sidlowns were easily distinguishable from the general population. They stood at least thirty to forty centimetres above the tallest of the humans, including Sean with his 192 centimetre, heavily muscled frame. The Sidlowns also had disproportionately large heads and hands, although some of them had human DNA and were otherwise not particularly different from humans. They mostly had fair skin and brown hair. The native Sidlowns had a more reptilian skin with very little hair, and generally appeared to be more frail.

Jemma desperately wanted to believe the Condonans could come through with their shipbuilding. They sounded confident, but she knew that they'd struggled to amass sufficient resources, and she wasn't convinced they had everything they'd need, even now. Yesterday though, Werrimen had informed her that the first two ships were almost ready. Still, Jemma was afraid to let herself believe it could be true even though she trusted both the Condonans and Werrimen. Yet she wouldn't dash Sean's hopes.

'I so hope you're right and we really are going home,' she said, unable to prevent the shiver brought on by the chill breeze that cut across her face. Condona had seasons, just like Earth, and they were currently heading into the winter phase. Days were becoming shorter and colder and the Den, Condona's equivalent of Earth's sun, was now slow to rise above the horizon. From first light to full daylight took around two hours, and in that time the temperatures would drop, sometimes too well below zero.

Sean put his arm back around her. 'Won't be long and we'll be inside. Walk a bit quicker; it'll warm us up.'

They both wore IPL uniforms which looked something like a pilot's jump-suit. Theirs were light grey and reflected their status as junior Prehlings, as Werrimen called them, which roughly translated to 'apprentice'. Senior Prehlings wore a mid-grey, while Trustees, the most senior of the apprentices wore a dark grey. Supreme Trustees like Werrimen, wore black. All the uniforms were made from a light fabric, not unlike parachute silk. It seemed to firm up in the cold air and cling to their skin not unlike good quality thermal underwear. On hot days, the same material would soften and keep the wearer cool, although Jemma had no idea how.

She smiled at Sean who was bouncing with enthusiasm. Whatever the situation or the temperature, he was so good at staying positive. Back in their day, before they'd moved forward in time, he could have graced the cover of any high-quality fashion magazine with his high cheekbones and finely sculpted face. His body was as honed as an elite athlete, and those piercing green eyes would sway the heart of any girl.

Jemma sighed. 'Do you really believe in your heart of hearts that Werrimen has a solution?'

'Sweetheart, I know it's hard, but I have to hold onto that hope. If there's anyone in the universe who can help us, it's Werrimen.'

'I guess you're right. And if she can't, Condona's not so

bad. The countryside is beautiful, and they've given us a great house.' While it was different from anything Jemma had known on Earth, it was comfortable, and as far as the Condonans were concerned, it was theirs for as long as they needed it.

'Come on.' Sean shook his head and marched off, obviously not pleased that she would contemplate anything other than their imminent departure. She had to run to keep up with his long strides.

Sean had a presence about him that made people follow, including her at times, although it did irk her when he threw orders her way. He presumed people would do as he said without question. Usually they did, but this time she stopped and decided to stand her ground. She was grinning when he turned back.

His brow creased as he looked at her. 'What?'

'Oh nothing. Just enjoying the view.' Whenever Jemma had told him how much she admired him, he'd been embarrassed. She usually made light of it, but she was sure he knew.

'Yeah, right. Let's go.'

Jemma smiled and jogged up to him.

He wrapped his arms around her again. 'Werrimen will be waiting for us. I don't know what she's got planned, but I'm hoping she's set a date and, whatever she says, I think we're about to get seriously busy.'

'If she can get us home, I don't care.'

'Good,' he said, grinning as he released his hold. 'Now, be a good girl and try to look cheerful as we head in.'

Before she had a chance to formulate a decent sarcastic response, Sean's grin vanished.

His arms came around her like a pair of fast-moving steel bars. Jemma instinctively raised her arms and tried to resist as he hurled her to the ground, crying out as she crashed face-first into the grass. He slammed his body down over hers, expelling all the air from her lungs.

Jemma hadn't heard the explosion or felt the ground shake beneath them until she'd hit the grass. Sean clearly had. He raised an arm to shield them both from the mass of debris that hurtled through the air in their direction. Something smashed onto her legs, crushing them, but she was too afraid to move when she heard Sean cry out. He seemed to be batting things away with his free arm and she heard him swear several times.

The whole thing seemed to go on for a long time, although she suspected it wasn't. Finally, Sean relaxed his grip ever so slightly, allowing her to cautiously raise her head. She gasped when she saw blood dripping down Sean's face and arms. There was a deep cut above his left bicep and a large gash on his head. Looking down at her own body, she was shocked to see that she was also covered in lacerations and grazes. Their clothes were torn, and a thick crust of soot and dust covered them both which Jemma suspected was controlling some of the bleeding.

'What the hell was that?' exclaimed Sean, carefully hauling himself up onto his knees, although ensuring that he still shielded her with his body.

Jemma didn't move. 'Could it have been an earthquake, or whatever they call it here?' She waited for him to shift, but when he didn't she kicked a large panel that looked like wood from her legs, then wriggled out of his hold and pushed herself up to look around.

'No, too sudden for an earthquake.' He jumped to his feet. 'Oh, sorry. Here, let me help you up.'

She brushed ash, bits of concrete and other materials she couldn't identify from her hair and clothes before turning to look in the direction of the explosion. 'It's the factory,' she cried. 'The one where they're building the spaceship!'

'Yeah, it is,' muttered Sean, also staring at the inferno.

'Jesus, Sean, a few minutes more and we'd have been there. God, almighty.' Jemma winced as sirens screamed overhead. She could hardly breathe, and it wasn't because of the rubbish flying through the air, but the realisation of how close they'd come to being inside that building when it exploded.

They'd almost certainly have died.

Jemma stared at the flames that shot dozens of metres into the air, licking through the structure in front of them as if it were made of paper, and consuming everything in their path. People ran in every direction, screaming and cursing.

A siren directly overhead seemed to galvanise Sean into action. 'We've got to get closer.' he shouted, over the noise of ongoing smaller explosions. 'Werrimen planned to meet us there. Jesus, she might have been inside. We've got to find her!'

'Oh, Jesus. Dan, Nik and Matt were meeting us there too!'

cried Jemma. 'We saw Dan and Nik heading that way a few minutes ago. They might be inside.'

'We're okay,' yelled Dan, as he and Nik emerged through the thick smoke and ran towards them. 'What in hell's happened? That building had more security than Fort Knox!'

'Must have been an accident,' shouted Sean over his shoulder as he continued to run through the wreckage, 'although I can't see how. The Condonans are so careful. They had all sorts of precautions in place to prevent accidents.' He shoved through the dense throng of people who mostly surged in the opposite direction, desperate to get away from the inferno. 'Keep up with me. We've got to find Werrimen and Matt.'

Dan tore past Jemma, and although both she and Nik were close to 180 centimetres tall, and fit, they couldn't keep up.

'We'll go left,' called Jemma. 'Sean and Dan are heading towards the front of the building. We can use the laneway that's two buildings up and get to the other side of the fire. Werrimen and Matt might be there.'

'I'm behind you,' Nik shouted in response.

Condonans dressed in a variety of styles, but the most popular was a long, loose garment, like a kaftan. It had trousers underneath that were made of a heavy fabric designed to protect the wearer from the cold. As people rushed to escape, many had tripped over the fabric of their skirts and, in their struggle to get up, knocked others over, creating a squirming tangle of bodies. Jemma and Nik did their best to weave around those on the ground and to avoid others who were

11

fleeing the fire. It was a relief to get through without being trampled underfoot.

Jemma stopped to catch her breath and caught sight of Werrimen, standing as close to the fire as any living being could tolerate, pacing, shouting and gesticulating to a Sidlown colleague.

'Are you two alright?' yelled Matt, as he charged past. 'Where are Sean and Dan?'

'We're fine,' replied Jemma, as she headed towards Werrimen. 'They're round the other side.'

Nik held up her communicator. 'Quiet. I'm talking to them.'

'Alright,' said Matt. 'Tell them to come here. We'll stick with Werrimen until they get here. Best to stay together.'

Jemma was still too numb to argue. All she could do was trust in Sean's ingenuity to find a way past the fire, given it had now spread well beyond the laneway she and Nik had used to get through. She sighed when she noticed that Matt and Nik had quietly positioned themselves to flank her, as they so often did. It used to annoy her, but she now accepted that everyone in her group was focussed on her protection. Given the current circumstances, she appreciated it. She couldn't see how this explosion could have been aimed at harming her, but there'd been so many attempts on her life over the last year she couldn't deny the possibility that Fredrick Pritchard, the man who'd killed her parents and her grandfather, was behind it.

When Sean finally got through, she ran to him, grateful

to feel his arms come around her, but even as he murmured reassurances he continued to push forward towards Werrimen, a grim look on his face.

'There is nothing we can do,' said Werrimen. 'We must wait until the fire is under control.'

'Any idea what happened?' asked Sean.

'No.' Werrimen ran her big hand through her hair. 'There was no combustible fuel in there. An electrical fault may have resulted in flames, but there should not have been anything that could explode. The fire must be brought under control before anyone can investigate. I have been asked to proceed to the arena on the other side of town to await information.'

Jemma barely heard their conversation. She couldn't take her eyes off the inferno. Flames continued to shoot into the still dark sky, illuminating everything in the vicinity, while small crafts with sirens blaring rushed overhead. Some dropped loads of water directly onto the fire.

She edged closer to Sean, hoping others wouldn't hear what she had to say. 'Something strange just occurred to me. This is out of left field, and I probably shouldn't even be thinking about it now, but those sirens are just like the ones we use on Earth. It's making me wonder if people from here, or maybe the IPL, introduced them to Earth. That would mean aliens have been present on Earth for centuries.'

'Yeah, I guess. If you'd told me a year ago that humans were scattered across the universe, I'd have told you not to be so ridiculous, but nothing seems all that far-fetched now. Maybe they've been guiding us all along.' His body sagged as he stared at the burning warehouse. 'Jesus, Jem. Who could do something like this?'

'Could it be Pritchard?' she murmured. 'Or maybe the Zants?'

'God help us. Even here?'

Alarmed by his inability to move, she grabbed his hand. 'Come on. We can't do anything yet. We might as well head to the arena now.' He didn't resist, so she led him towards the others and repeated her message.

The Den was now well above the horizon. As they discussed what to do, she stopped and took a deep breath. A plethora of brilliant colours shone through the early morning sky, like a rainbow that spread from horizon to horizon. Surrounded by a soft mauve haze, the Den had risen far enough to reveal a rich golden centre. Red and yellow rims extended out well beyond the surrounding clouds, their edges blending perfectly with the shimmering mauve. Even the plants and trees took on a different hue, a silvery grey against the brilliantly lit sky. As the colours faded, the familiar blue of the sky peeped through, but the Den never went to the clear yellow of Earth's sun. It always maintained a purplish rim and haze. It was a magical experience, and Jemma encouraged Sean to stand and watch in the hope it might help him relax.

With a deep sigh he wrapped his arms around her, resting his chin on the top of her head. Transfixed by the light show as the Den continued to rise higher in the sky, a soft breeze caressed her skin and she relaxed into his arms.

But her relief was short-lived.

Another explosion, further away this time, rocked the ground. They both struggled to maintain their balance as debris again flew around them.

'Jesus,' yelled Sean, pulling Jemma close to him, and turning so that his back would take the brunt of flying rubble. 'What the hell's going on?'

Jemma was first to steady herself. The new inferno exploding into the atmosphere had changed the Den's brilliant light show from a magical experience to a sinister collage of debris and ash.

'God, Sean, you're hurt!' His head wound had opened up and he had even more cuts and grazes on his arms.

'No, I'm okay. Are you injured?'

'I'm fine,' said Jemma.

Sean ran a bloodied hand through his hair. 'I need to get there.'

'You go,' she shouted, above the noise from the new explosion and people screaming. 'You'll be quicker. I'll follow.'

*　　*　　*

Sean needed every bit of energy he could muster to run toward the second fire. He felt, rather than saw, Dan and Matt run up behind him. When he reached the second factory, all the breath seemed to have been sucked from his body. The external walls of the building were well alight. He couldn't see through to the interior or to the spacecraft that was under construction inside. He was vaguely aware that Werrimen was now beside him, but he couldn't tear his eyes from the flames, even as he felt her hand rest on his shoulder. Neither of them spoke. What was there to say? Utter helplessness coursed through his body, and he vehemently cursed whoever had done this. Two fires in two factories several kilometres apart couldn't possibly be an accident.

'It's a disaster,' he muttered to Jemma as she and Nik caught up, 'a fucking disaster.'

The Condonans had placed the factories on opposite sides of the town. Someone had explained to him early on that if something went wrong in one factory the other was far enough away to be safe. He doubted they'd envisaged anything like this though. On his last tour of both factories, he'd not seen anything explosive in either. This had to be arson, and the grim look on Werrimen's face confirmed his thinking.

'Dear God,' murmured Jemma. 'What could anyone hope to gain by doing this?'

'Do not try to apply logic,' said Werrimen. 'We will find them, and when we do their reasons will most likely not make sense. All we can do now is wait for the Fire Chief and the Security Chief to do their jobs.'

Sean stood back and pulled Jemma with him, but he continued to stare past the barriers, desperately hoping to see the extent of the damage. Jemma's question had cut to the crux.

What could anyone possibly hope to gain by doing this?

He couldn't come up with any sensible answer. If someone on Condona wanted to be rid of the group from Earth, why destroy their only chance to leave? The ships had been close to finished, and Werrimen had been confident they'd soon be on their way. She'd confided in him that she was ready to set a date for their test flight and had intended to reveal it at their meeting today. Obviously, it wouldn't happen now. Condona had poured everything they could scrounge into building these ships, partly because they'd pledged to help the stranded refugee group from Earth. But also because they hoped to rekindle the business that they'd run for centuries, probably longer if the truth be known, of transporting people around the universe. That included the IPL. Once they had their ships operational, he was sure they'd make their investment back in no time.

It was around three hours after the first explosion that a commanding voice ordered them to go to the arena for further instructions. Holding onto Jemma, Sean motioned to the others to join him, then turned to walk with the crowd. He presumed that Jemma would think he was doing his best to reassure her. In truth, he needed contact with her to steady his nerves, probably much more than she needed him.

Although a short distance away, Werrimen strode in the same direction, deep in conversation with the Fire Chief. She looked angrier than he'd ever seen her. A large crowd, already assembled in the arena, was absolutely silent as people huddled together waiting for information. He expected bad news, yet the lack of almost any sound from all those people chilled him to the bone. Even the birds, which on Condona were normally quite raucous, had gone quiet.

Most eyes followed Werrimen and the Fire Chief as they

positioned themselves on a platform which rose onto a small stage. Soft murmurs broke the silence as Werrimen stepped forward. People didn't seem antagonistic. It was more of a pervading fear.

'My friends,' said Werrimen, her voice breaking. 'It is my painful duty to inform you that explosive devices were secreted into both of the spaceship factories and placed under each of the craft under construction. Combustible fuels were scattered around each craft. The first factory and everything within it has been destroyed. There is no hope of salvage. We have concluded that the culprits had inside knowledge of the building process because all the doors of that craft had been left open overnight to disperse toxic fumes from fixings in the interior. Usually, those doors are closed. Had that been the case, the skin could have protected the craft. The perpetrators must have known that the craft would be vulnerable last night.'

There were gasps across the room and someone yelled, 'Are you suggesting that someone from Condona did this?'

'No, I am not,' she replied. 'There are people here from many different planets. Any one of them may have passed for a Condonan or, alternatively, may have had permission to work on the craft. It is far too early to cast blame in any direction.'

'Do you think she suspects one of us?' whispered Jemma.

'I doubt it,' replied Sean, softly. 'But from here on, we're going to have to be on our guard. We won't know who we can trust. Hopefully, the Condonans won't turn on us.'

Werrimen raised her hand for quiet which quickly

dampened the rush of whispered conversations. 'I have slightly better news from the second factory. The only exposed area of this craft was the landing equipment, mainly the balance legs, although the blue light has suffered some damage. We believe that we will be able to salvage this ship. It will set us back a little on our timeline, but that is unavoidable. This is a far better outcome than I had expected.

'The IPL, and several other planets, have this morning pledged to assist Condona with resources so the rebuilding can go ahead as planned. I will hand over now to Giareto, your Fire Chief, who will give you more complete details. Thank you.'

Werrimen left the stage and strode across to Sean and his team. 'This is a setback. Our plans are delayed, but testing will go ahead. Would you all, except Jemma, head to the security office? They are expecting you.' She smiled at the look on Jemma's face. 'I am not excluding you. There is something I wish to discuss. I must finish up with the officials here, then I will come to your house, if you would wait for me there. After that, you may join the others in the security office.'

CHAPTER 2

With no idea why Werrimen had separated her out, Jemma headed home.

Home. If only.

She'd worked hard with Sean to make their house here feel like home, adding personal touches and sprucing up the yard, yet it was so different from anything she'd known on Earth. Early on, Sean had found some bright yellow paint and decorated the front door, so it stood out against the off-white external house colours that graced every house on Condona. It was just a little thing, but it made them both feel happy and people walking past would often stop and smile.

When they'd first arrived on Condona, the property next door was bare except for a neatly excavated and flattened house pad waiting for builders to start construction. She'd watched, fascinated, when six people had arrived. They'd constructed a kind of metal mould, in the shape of a house, beside the pad. They'd poured in two different substances from containers that were the size of large paint cans on Earth. Nothing happened for several minutes but then the liquids combined, and a vapour began to rise before thickening and expanding. Eventually a solid-looking opaque substance filled the mould. The builders tested the substance and then carefully removed the metal structure from all the exposed surfaces. The completed shell of a house was revealed, but Jemma was puzzled because the shell wasn't on the house pad and the metal mould was still intact underneath. She'd walked across to look and was surprised to find that the walls and floor were half a metre thick and felt like a cross between cement and polystyrene. She stood back when the builders brought in pulleys and rollers and began to shift the now solid building off the metal base and onto its final site.

A couple of them adjusted the structure, still using the pulleys, until they were satisfied the house was level. The others set about constructing a different mould in the shape of a semi-gabled roof and poured in another liquid which also set in minutes. Four flying craft hovered overhead. Each craft dropped down a kind of heavy metal rope. The builders attached one to each corner of the roof. They weren't gentle as they lined the roof up above the house, literally dropping it on. Yet it remained solid, with not so much as a crack or chip from the rough treatment. Once the external structure was completed, the builders moved inside. They poured in similar substances to those they'd used for the external walls to form internal walls, kitchen cupboards, wardrobes and even beds. The whole thing had taken less than half a day and people had moved in just hours later.

Jemma smiled as she walked past that house and up to her bright yellow front door. She stood under the bead – a miniscule computer used throughout the universe by the

IPL. It checked twenty-five personal identification points, taking just seconds to get a match and for the door to open. Lights turned on automatically as she entered, which was a relief as Condonan houses didn't have windows. Although the roof was semi-transparent, it only allowed in small amounts of natural light, so the interior was quite dark, even in the middle of the day. She'd been shown a way to close the roof and make it opaque when they'd first arrived, but without another source of light a closed roof meant total darkness. She didn't like to admit it, but the darkness was so complete that it left her more than a little claustrophobic. For all his bravado, Sean didn't push the idea of closing it either.

They hadn't tidied up when they left that morning because Sean had been anxious to get going, and it looked a bit like a bomb had gone off inside. She shrugged and set about rectifying the mess, running through every room to pick up clothing, wash plates and make beds. Next, she grabbed the sweeper, which was something like a cross between a broom and a rake and ran through the house for a quick sweep. Finally, she stood back to survey her work, and decided that a nice bunch of flowers would be a good finishing touch.

Condonan people took pride in their gardens and she'd been so impressed by the well-established plants and flowers in other gardens that she'd set about developing her own patch soon after they'd moved in. She'd thoroughly enjoyed the process and, if truth be known, it had stopped her from going mad before they'd been allocated to jobs. It'd also been a great way to meet the neighbours as she'd sought their advice on plants and growing conditions.

Strangely, the most common flower colour on Condona was blue, in varying shades from the softest to the most vibrant. Her mother had once told her that a genuinely blue flower was very hard to find on Earth. As she thought about it, she realised that there was a lot that was strange about that statement. Those had been her mother's exact words, *hard to find on Earth*.

Obviously, the signs had been there all along that her family had come from another planet. Perhaps she should have picked up on it, but she'd had no reason to contemplate the possibility that they were refugees on Earth. She still couldn't understand why her parents hadn't told her, or that she was expected to return to Anders, particularly now that she knew she was supposed to take over the role of Supreme Ruler.

And that was just ridiculous.

She was a scientist, a university academic, not the leader of an entire planet and really, it didn't matter where she was born, her home was Earth. But which Earth? The one she'd known in 2020, or the one they'd moved to in late 2021?

'Cut it out,' Jemma snapped, as she picked up a pair of scissors and walked out into the front garden. 'You'll send yourself mad if you keep that nonsense up.'

She took a few deep breaths and bent over the first bush. Picking her flowers relaxed her as she breathed in the perfume, carefully arranging the blooms until she had enough to fill a large vase. Satisfied, she straightened up to head back inside, but a flicker of movement to her right made her freeze. She automatically shifted the scissors in her hand to turn them into a weapon as General Hunt had taught her.

A blonde woman ran towards the far side of the house.

'Stop,' yelled Jemma.

The woman faltered and turned back. She stared at Jemma for a few seconds then picked up her pace and raced around the corner of the house.

Jemma dropped her flowers and ran after the woman, but she reeled back when she reached the corner around which the woman had disappeared. A small black box was stuck halfway up the side wall. Jemma hadn't seen anything like it before, but she was sure that it hadn't been there earlier. Backing away, she almost collided with Werrimen.

'Is there a problem, Jemma?'

'Yes.' She pointed to the wall. 'There's something there.'

Werrimen followed her gaze. 'By all the stars.' She picked up her communicator. 'I need a full security team immediately.'

'What is it?' Jemma realised she was trembling as Werrimen took hold of her arms and led her away to stand well outside the yard to wait.

'Similar devices were used in the factories, my dear. We must stand back. They have the capacity to be ignited from a remote source. We do not want to be anywhere near if that should happen now. The Fire Chief is bringing a containment box.'

'God help us,' murmured Jemma. 'What next?'

'Nothing, I hope,' replied Werrimen.

'There was a woman,' said Jemma, still breathing hard. 'She ran. I gave chase, but I couldn't reach her.'

'Did you recognise her?' asked Werrimen.

Jemma shook her head. 'No, she didn't look familiar at all, but I did get a good look. I'm sure I can give a decent description.'

'Good. Keep that image clear in your mind,' replied Werrimen, hustling Jemma away from the house as a siren sounded behind them. 'Fire Chief Giareto is here now. We will stay well out of his way.'

Jemma watched as the black box was enclosed in a larger container, but she looked away when Giareto glared at her.

'The device has been neutralised and we can't see any others,' he said to Werrimen although he was still gazing intensely at Jemma. 'It is the same type as those used in the factories.'

'Jemma saw a woman running from the house,' said Werrimen. 'I will work with her to get an image of the woman.'

'Who was the woman?' snapped Giareto. 'Why would she want to do you harm?'

'I have no idea on either count,' replied Jemma, as it dawned on her that he might consider her a suspect.

'Jemma is not involved,' said Werrimen, softly. 'But it is possible that someone did want to harm her.'

'Why would that be? exclaimed Giareto. 'If there is a risk to Jemma, or if it places others at risk, I need to know.'

Before Werrimen could answer, Jemma touched her arm.

'I've just realised that I heard something as I got home. I didn't take much notice of it at the time because there's always noise around the building sites, but the sound was familiar. Do you remember you used an electrometer to identify which planet I came from? The noise I heard had the same high-pitched sound as an electrometer.'

'Oh dear,' said Werrimen. 'If that is the case, we must take this very seriously. We will find Sean and discuss it with your group.'

'I need more explanation,' snapped Giareto.

'Yes, you do,' replied Werrimen. 'I will meet with you shortly, but first I would like to move to a safer location.'

Jemma felt small and vulnerable as she walked quietly beside Werrimen. Rebels from Anders Major remained determined to stop her from returning there. But how could they be here? Anders was in the same galaxy as Earth. Both were on the other side of the universe. She didn't even know for sure that it was them. Yet, they were the most likely to have an electrometer, the device that could pick up on the fragments in the tattoo on her hip. Shattered, she could almost hear Sean's boss, General Hunt, telling her what to do.

Calm down, put the emotion aside and think through the facts. What do you actually know, and what are you surmising?

If only he were here, now.

'I know you are worried, my dear,' said Werrimen. 'I am too, but think about it. If there is someone here who is antagonistic to you, they must have come through with the group

26

we rescued from the Zants. It should not be too hard to track such a person down.'

'I guess.' The IPL mission that had rescued Sean, Dan and Matt had, ultimately, rescued over seventeen hundred other people who came from all corners of the universe, and all of them had been temporarily relocated to Condona. Everyone had been interviewed though, and medically checked before they were settled, so if the blonde woman she'd chased from her yard had been from Anders Major there should be an official record.

When they walked inside the second factory, Sean came across and wrapped his arms around her. 'What's happened? God, Jemma, you look like you've seen a ghost.'

'No, not a ghost,' she said, forcing herself to smile. 'She was flesh and blood.'

'What? Tell me about it.'

Jemma sighed, then told him about the woman. 'I would recognise her, I think, if I saw her again, but she wasn't someone I know.'

'Describe her,' said Dan, frowning as he edged out from behind Sean.

'Medium height, maybe a hundred and seventy centimetres; blonde mid-length hair in a bob, two strands from the front pulled into a band at the back of her head; slim and quite fit. I couldn't see her eye colour, but she was pretty. Looked really intense when she stared at me.'

'And Jemma heard an electrometer just before this happened,' said Werrimen.

Sean gently turned Jemma, so she looked only at him. 'Shit, sweetheart. Are you sure?'

'When I thought back about it, yeah. It's a unique sound, really high-pitched, hurts the ears.'

'Any idea who she could have been?' said Sean, looking at Werrimen.

'No, not at this stage. We will have to mount a search,' said Werrimen.

'I've got an idea,' said Dan. 'It's so bizarre, I'm not even sure if it should say it, but it sounds like Lena.'

'Couldn't be,' said Sean. 'She was a gentle soul. I can't credit she'd do something so violent. And why would she be after Jemma?'

'Yes, indeed,' said a male voice in the doorway. No-one had noticed Giareto walk in. 'If Jemma creates a threat, or is under threat herself, we need that information.'

'Yes, of course.' Werrimen showed the Chief to a chair and walked around to the other side of the main desk. She waited until everyone was seated. 'We did not think there would be any risk here, and I cannot state with certainty that there is a threat. Let me tell you the story.'

'Thank you,' said Giareto. 'You must understand that my priority is the safety of the citizens of Condona.'

'Most certainly,' said Werrimen, with the slight bow of her head that Jemma now recognised as a mark of respect. 'If Jemma should take up her birthright, she would be the next Supreme Ruler of the planet Anders Major. Sadly, the rebel leader, Fredrick Pritchard, who is also known as Drick, murdered both her grandfather and her parents, among others, and he will do anything to stop her from accepting the position. He has tried to abduct her on numerous occasions. The problem is that Jemma was taken to Earth as a baby, and she has no memory of Anders Major. She sees herself as belonging to Earth, but the rebels will not leave her be. I am at a loss as to how they have tracked her here.'

'That is very difficult,' said the Chief. 'I will organise extra protection immediately while we search for the person responsible. We do not want trouble here, but we will not stand by and allow Jemma to be hunted either.'

'Thank you,' said Werrimen. 'I will also organise more protection.'

'While you are here, Jemma, we will do our best to protect you,' said Giareto as he headed to the door. 'I'll let you know when I have arrangements in place.'

Werrimen had walked with him, and now stood in the doorway. 'I've called Emilrad to join us. He would know the woman, Lena, better than any of us. I will have him work with security to find her. If it is her, Jemma, and you can identify her, we should be able to get to the bottom of all this.'

'Okay.' Jemma sat quietly, resting her head on Sean's shoulder as she waited for Werrimen to formulate her plans.

'My intention today had been to start all of you on flight training,' said Werrimen. 'Although the transport zone craft are unavailable now, there are other Condonan craft we can use. The more experience you can get, the better. It is my intention that you will all be part of the flight crew to get us home. Jemma, I had planned to let you work with Sean, but I think after today's events it would be better if you, Dan and Matt work as a team. Sean and Nikola can work together. Jemma's team will start working on transporters, Sean's team on spaceships. When you are proficient you will reverse your roles. Dan, Matt, under no circumstances is Jemma to ever be left on her own. One of you will accompany her at all times. Is everyone clear?'

Werrimen waited for them to agree, then smiled. 'Don't look so horrified, Sean. Your instructors know that you dislike flying. Take the rest of the day to relax. If I hear anything from Emilrad, I will let you know. Otherwise, I will see you here in the morning.'

CHAPTER 3

Late that afternoon, Giareto called Jemma and her group to a meeting of Trustees and Condonan officials. Aware that everyone from Werrimen down was convinced the fires had been set to stop her from returning to Earth, Jemma was hesitant about attending. She knew Werrimen would expect her to be there, but that didn't make her feel any easier about it. Sean insisted, so she gave in and walked with him to Werrimen's office.

Emilrad was with Werrimen when they arrived and both were deep in conversation with another Supreme Trustee, not someone Jemma had met. All Supreme Trustees wore a black uniform with a crest on the right shoulder. The central feature of every crest was a pair of swords pointing downwards and crossed at the tips. Two hands were clasped together in a handshake at the top of the crest and four palm fronds framed it, two on either side. As a Prehling, or junior Trustee, she didn't have any palm fronds. The first two would be awarded on elevation to senior Prehling, and the others, along with a dark grey uniform, to those who made Trustee. All Supreme Trustees, and some of the more junior Trustees, had a bar at the bottom which held a number of stars. Most of them had

31

one bar, often with only one or two stars, but Werrimen and the man with her had two bars.

Nineteen stars filled the bars on Werrimen's uniform. She'd earned the last one for her daring rescue of Sean, Dan and Matt. But this fellow had twenty stars.

Giareto and the Condonan Security Chief stood behind the Supreme Trustees, waiting quietly, until the man with the twenty stars nodded. The Condonan dignitaries both bowed their heads ever so slightly, then the Security Chief walked forward to start the meeting.

Jemma was astonished to see that the most senior people on Condona had just deferred to this fellow! He was clearly accepted as superior despite his power base being from another planet.

'Thank you all for coming,' said the Security Chief. 'First, for those of you who don't know the IPL dignitaries standing with me, let me introduce Kelberren, First Supreme Commander-in-Chief of the IPL, Werrimen, third Supreme Commander-in-Chief and Emilrad, Supreme Trustee Commander. They are here to help us move forward following the devastating loss of one of our spacecraft factories and severe damage to the other. Buildings are easy to replace, but the destruction of a spacecraft is a severe setback. Recognising our vulnerability, Condona's Council of Leaders has accepted an invitation to join the Inter-Planetary League. We have previously resisted, determined to remain independent, but we now accept that we need help. I will hand over to Kelberren to discuss our plans.'

Kelberren bowed his head to the Security Chief as he walked forward. 'I am at some disadvantage as I have not met most of you. I would appreciate the opportunity to address that deficit over the next few days. Emilrad has just informed me that a woman has been detained. She is suspected of being the one who set the explosions in the factories. Is Jemma here?' He looked around the room.

Jemma slowly raised her hand to shoulder height, albeit with a little help from Sean. 'I'm Jemma.'

'Don't be shy, Jemma,' said Werrimen. 'Stand up.'

She stood but didn't let go of Sean's hand, even as he whispered, 'It's okay.'

'Thank you, Jemma,' said Kelberren. 'Would you go with Emilrad after the meeting? You are the only one who has seen this woman's face. Our hope is that you can confirm we have the right person.'

'Okay,' said Jemma, and sank back into her seat.

'I will leave security to determine if there is further risk.' Kelberren nodded to the Security and Fire Chiefs. 'Our other pressing issue is the recovery of the spacecraft factories. Condona has the greatest expertise in building spaceships and, apart from the Zants, the only expertise in the universe for building ships that can cross transport zones. We have now reached an agreement between the Condonan Council of Leaders and the IPL that we, and our associated planets, will provide the resources and financial support to enable you to rebuild. This is on the understanding that you will, in turn, help us set up factories on a number of other planets and pass on your expertise to the people managing those factories.' He looked to Werrimen. 'We have already agreed that one of those factories will be on Earth. The Earth contingent should avail themselves of as much experience as possible, while they are here.'

'Holy hell,' muttered Sean.

Jemma smiled. The first contact she and Sean had of aliens and space flight had happened less than two years ago from their perspective. Now they were being told they were to learn to build ships. Matt and Nik had degrees in engineering, but she was a biologist. Sean and Dan had both studied law, international relations and military strategy. The whole concept was so far out of her comfort zone she had no idea how to process it.

The room was utterly silent for some minutes after Kelberren closed the meeting until Emilrad beckoned to Jemma to follow him.

'Were you happy with the meeting?' asked Emilrad, as he led Jemma away.

'I'm happy that Condona will move ahead, even happier that Earth will get a factory to build spaceships, but I'm terrified that I'm going to be asked to do things that are outside my expertise.'

Emilrad smiled. 'You will be asked to do many things that you have not done before, but you will have plenty of support. Do not panic. We are all here to help you.'

They entered a large building with which Jemma wasn't familiar, although it was obviously something to do with policing. There were people confined in small glass enclosures with just enough room to sit on a small bench or to stand in front of it. Most sat quietly but a couple stood, punching the walls and yelling. Thankfully, no sound emerged because she doubted it would have been anything she'd want to hear.

After speaking to the officer on the reception desk, Emilrad sat with Jemma to wait for an escort. She stiffened when she saw two armed officers head to the enclosure nearest to where she sat. They opened it and spoke quietly to the occupant who shouted something back at them and threw a punch at the nearest officer. He was stopped by some kind of invisible barrier. The prisoner was asked again to sit quietly, but he declined, so the door was again shut. A whitish mist flowed through the enclosure. The man slumped back on the seat and became quiet, although he appeared to be conscious. This time when the enclosure was opened, the man accompanied the officers without resisting.

Jemma gaped, then looked at Emilrad. 'What did they do to him?'

'Just a mild sedative. He will be fine, but it is safer for him as well as the guards to stop him from fighting.'

She struggled to take her eyes off the enclosures even as another officer arrived to take them to an interview room. He explained that the woman they wanted Jemma to view would be shown on a screen, so there would be no need for direct contact.

As the image came up, she stiffened. 'That's her.'

'Are you sure, Jemma?' asked Emilrad quietly.

'Yes, I'm sure.'

Emilrad sighed. 'That is the woman we knew as Lena. We were imprisoned with her. I would like to interview her, if I may.'

'I'd like to be there too,' said Jemma. 'I need to know why she would do this.'

Emilrad touched the back of her neck, smiling when she jumped. 'I'm sorry, Jemma. I have been told you are sensitive to our methods, but I must know the truth.'

Jemma glared at him. She'd experienced the Trustee's touch before. It was their way of ensuring that there could be no deception. 'I don't lie.'

'I understand,' said Emilrad kindly, 'but you have been through a great deal. You would have every right to be angry enough to seek revenge. I must know your intention is honourable.'

'I am angry,' snapped Jemma. She slumped back in her chair, aware that he retained his contact with her. 'I'm not after revenge. I want to know why someone who has never met me is prepared to try to kill me.'

'We know that she is an Ander's rebel,' said Emilrad. 'That is reason enough.'

'No, not for me.' Jemma sighed. 'I know they are antagonistic to my ancestors, and now to me, but I really don't know why. I need to know what my ancestors did to cause this level of hate.'

'I see.' Emilrad removed his hand. 'I am sorry I had to do that. I am happy to agree now that you should meet with her. Bear in mind that she might not have the answers you seek. Such hate has been passed from generation to generation.'

'Maybe she can give me something,' said Jemma. 'Anything would be better than what I have now.'

'Yes, I see. We will go together to the cell.'

Jemma stood quietly by his side as they waited for the door to open, her mind in turmoil. If Emilrad was right and the attacks were due to blind, unreasoning hate, there would be nothing she could do to fix it. The next few minutes could potentially provide her with information that might change the entire course of her life.

As they were shown into the room, the woman Emilrad had identified as Lena sat behind a table writing in a worn notebook. She wasn't shackled and appeared to be free to move around.

'That woman is my sworn enemy,' said Lena, calmly and without lifting her head from her writing.

Jemma felt her stomach clench. 'How can I be your enemy? We've never met.'

'You are from the house of Kilkinan. Your family destroyed our society.'

'How did they do that?' Jemma slipped into a chair opposite. The woman looked worn down and somehow smaller than she'd appeared while planting the explosive device on the house.

'You don't know what your own family did?'

'I know nothing of Anders Major,' said Jemma. 'I only

learned of my heritage a few months ago. I believed that I was born on Earth.'

'So, to hide their shame, they hid the truth. That is consistent with their reputation.'

'Tell me about their reputation,' said Jemma.

'Why? So you can go back and enjoy their debauchery and arrogance?'

'No. I have to determine if I want to go back at all and if there would be anything I could do to improve the situation. Can you tell me about their *debauchery and arrogance?* How did it affect you and your family?'

Lena sat forward, staring at Jemma. 'I think you're speaking the truth.' She held out her hand as though to take hold of Jemma's hand, but something blocked her before she reached Jemma. Lena withdrew, shaking her fingers as thought they'd been stung. It had to be some sort of invisible force field, probably the same as the enclosures she'd seen downstairs.

Jemma flashed an annoyed look at the guard. 'Can you remove that?'

'You are an exulted person, Jemma,' said Emilrad. 'It is for your protection.'

'Oh crap. She wasn't going to hurt me. If I'm so exulted, do as I say. Take it down and let me speak properly to Lena.'

Emilrad nodded and the guard shrugged and keyed a sequence into a small screen.

'Impressive,' muttered Lena.

'Not intentionally,' replied Jemma. 'I simply need information.'

'Alright.' Lena tentatively stretched her hand forward again and this time made contact with Jemma. 'You are not what I expected.'

'I'll take that as a compliment. Now, please tell me what you know about the *debauchery and arrogance*.'

'They cared only about themselves. Partied all the time. Used young women and young men from my people for their pleasure.'

'You mean they raped them?' exclaimed Jemma.

'Sometimes it was with consent,' said Lena. 'They offered food, which was scarce in our villages, let them live in their mansions, promised all sorts of rewards.'

'That doesn't really mean consent if the young people agreed because they were desperate.'

'No, I agree.' Lena tightened her grip on Jemma's hand. 'You honestly didn't know about this?'

The guard pushed Lena roughly back into her chair.

'Back off,' snapped Jemma, leaning forward over the table and taking hold of Lena's hand again. 'No, I honestly didn't know. Tell me what else.'

Lena sighed. 'I can't believe you don't know this. Alright. Nobody outside the ruling classes was permitted to own anything. Every house was theirs. We paid rent. If we did something to displease them, we paid more rent, sometimes until there was nothing left. My people were there for their use. We were slaves.'

'Dear God,' said Jemma. 'I don't know what to say. Even worse, I have no idea what to do.'

'It is time to leave,' said Emilrad. 'This is not something I knew about. We must all discuss it.'

Jemma rose but before she left, she turned back to Lena. 'Thank you for telling me all this. I think I understand your anger now, but I can't condone what you did. People could have been killed and there is no excuse for that.'

Lena spat on the table. 'You're just like all the rest of them.'

CHAPTER 4

Sean was unable to get it through his head that the woman he knew as Lena could have had anything to do with the explosions. He'd already received advice that Jemma had identified her and Emilrad had confirmed her as Lena. Even so, he waited outside the building to hear it directly from Jemma, although he hadn't expected her to tear out of the building and launch herself into his arms as though she hadn't seen him for months. It was a struggle to remain on his feet.

'Oh God, Sean,' she cried. 'That was awful.'

'I can only imagine,' he murmured, easing her back a little. 'Tell me about it.'

Emilrad cleared his throat behind them. 'I will leave Jemma to explain, Sean. When you are ready, would you please both join us in Werrimen's office?'

'Thanks.' Sean nodded to Emilrad, then led Jemma to a bench outside the building. 'You'd better give me a quick run down.'

She tripped over her words as she tried to explain but finally got it all out.

'Oh boy.' Sean paused and sat back to think. 'Sounds like

our ancestors might have been seriously bad news, if what she says is true.'

Jemma nodded. 'That was my first thought, but I can't reconcile it with what I know. My mother used to always say there are two sides to every story, and you shouldn't judge until you know both. We really can't be sure that Lena's viewpoint is accurate, and Emilrad made the comment that he hadn't heard anything like her story before.' Jemma rubbed her eyes and sighed. 'I so wish Mary was here. She's experienced both cultures now. She could compare.'

'Agreed, and my mother too, but for the moment we're going to have to form our own judgement. Mary and Eric aren't anything like she suggested, nor was my father, and Dan and Nik both speak positively about their guardians. It's possible that they all changed their ways after arriving on Earth, although I doubt that they could have changed so much. But we've got no way of working it out now and Werrimen wants to talk to us about how we're going to get back to Earth, so we should go.'

Sean kept his arm around Jemma as they walked to the office. It wasn't a long distance, but it did give him time to think about Lena. She hadn't seemed antagonistic when they were incarcerated, but she didn't know then that he was from Anders Major. He'd said he was from Earth and, from his perspective at the time, that had been the truth. He was sure he'd have heard an electrometer if she'd had one, which meant she must have acquired one since arriving on Condona. So, she wasn't operating alone, and that was something Werrimen needed to know.

Werrimen's office was already crowded when they got there, not just with Werrimen and Emilrad, but Dan, Nik and Matt, along with Rodeg and Dragile, who both stood aside to allow them access.

'I presume Jemma has told you about Lena, Sean,' said Werrimen.

'She has but we both suspect there's more to this story. The problem is there's no-one here who can give us the other side.'

'Emilrad and I have also discussed it and reached the same conclusion,' said Werrimen. 'The IPL had a presence on Anders Major at that time and, I believe, would have intervened if the situation were as dire as Lena portrays. I suppose it is possible that such things could have happened without the Trustees being aware, but I cannot see it.'

'So maybe Lena has it wrong,' said Sean.

'Possibly. We will investigate further when we are in a position to do so. Emilrad tells me that Lena has admitted her guilt with the explosions. We must leave it to the Condonan people to determine her fate, although we will continue to observe. We will not tolerate unfair treatment, even under these circumstances.'

'That's fine,' replied Sean, and he went on to explain his belief that she couldn't be working alone. 'She didn't have an electrometer in the Zant prison. We'd have heard it, and she'd have immediately known our origin. That means there are others here with her, now.'

'That is a good point,' said Emilrad. 'I agree with you she could not have had one. I will speak to Condonan security and advise them to broaden their search.'

'Sit down please,' said Werrimen. 'We are here to discuss other matters.'

As Sean turned, he noticed Matt staring at some far distant point, his back ramrod straight. Nik was leaning back in her chair, her hands covering her mouth. Dan sat forward and stared at Werrimen, his hands fisted on his knees as he looked between Werrimen, Emilrad and Rodeg, all of whom were smiling.

'Okay,' said Sean. 'Something's clearly happened while we've been away?'

'I have laid out our plans,' said Werrimen, laughing. 'There is much work ahead of us. It may be a little daunting, but we must get started.'

'Understood. What do you need us to do?'

'The fire in the second spacecraft factory has caused a minor setback, but I am told the delay will only be minimal,' said Werrimen. 'We must prepare for the flight back to Earth. Emilrad informs me that the transport zone craft will be ready in twelve to fourteen weeks.'

Emilrad bowed his head. 'That is the information I have been given, Madam.'

'Good. Everyone in this room must be ready to be part of the flight crew,' said Werrimen.

'Okay.' Sean was aware that Jemma, Matt and Nik had each done some very basic training on transporters already, and Matt had been about to start larger craft. That was before they were abducted, but they should be able to pick it back up quickly. They wouldn't need much more than that just to help out on their way home. He and Dan would have a sharper learning curve, but they'd just have to deal with it.

'Each morning,' continued Werrimen, 'you will participate in flight training. As you know, we are to build a factory on Earth when we get back. Each of you will work in the factories at other times to learn all you can before we leave.'

Three months to learn to fly and also learn how to build the damn things. Sean sighed. 'I can't see that we can become proficient in that timeframe.'

'You can,' said Werrimen. 'Sean, as we've already discussed, you will work with Nikola.'

'I'm not confident in my capacity to learn to fly,' said Sean, aware that Jemma had taken hold of his hand and was now squeezing it.

'Why is that?' said Emilrad.

'Oh God.' Sean blanched.

'Would you like me to explain?' asked Jemma. When he nodded, she turned to Emilrad. 'Sean's father was leader of the Anders security house, Bellear. After they moved to Earth, he was given a high rank in the Australian Army. On Sean's ninth birthday, his father took him up in a transporter. We don't know how his father had access to such craft, but something happened in flight and the craft dropped heavily. Sean vomited and aspirated. He spent time in the medical centre of a spacecraft afterwards, but he only regained that memory a few months ago.'

'By the stars,' said Emilrad. 'Someone erased his memory?'

'That was our impression,' said Werrimen. 'Sean, we will work together on this. You must learn to fly these craft. It is not just about getting home. You will need these skills for your future. Do not worry. We will talk after this meeting is concluded, and you will have all the help you need.'

Sean had to fight his instinct to run. Perhaps Jemma was right, and they could be happy here on Condona. But if he ever wanted to get back to Earth, he had to recognise that he was in Werrimen's world which meant he'd have to find a way to deal with his fear. If only his father had told him the truth at the time.

'Jemma, Matt and Dan, you will work with Emilrad to commence your training on transporters,' said Werrimen, ignoring Sean's reaction. 'Sean and Nikola, you will start on spaceships with Rodeg. In the afternoon you will present to the factory where tasks will be allocated. Your Trustee training will continue outside those hours. We will work it out as we proceed.'

Nobody moved, and Sean realised he wasn't the only one to be stunned by Werrimen's expectations. He simply couldn't see how they'd be ready in the time frame she suggested.

'Please do not allow yourselves to be overwhelmed by what is ahead of us,' said Werrimen. 'We will get through this together. Now, since we have finished here, we shall get started. You should join your Trustees and discuss your program. Sean, would you stay behind please? Jemma, I will call you when we have finished so we can discuss your next step.'

*   *   *

Dan, Matt and Nik left with their Trustees, leaving Jemma by herself, leaning on the wall outside the building, not quite sure what to do. And Werrimen had said she was never to be alone.

She felt so lost.

Born on a planet she'd never seen, attacked by people she'd never met. Somehow, she had to work out how to deal with it all. She pushed herself away from the wall. If she was to work anything out, she couldn't stand here feeling sorry for herself. If she were to follow Werrimen's directive, she should probably head back inside and find someone she trusted to wait with her. But it was only a short distance back to their house. She could run there, check the house and then lock herself inside. Werrimen and Giareto had rushed her away as soon as they knew about Lena's explosive. It couldn't hurt to have a look. If the security and fire personnel were still there, she'd just turn around and go back to Werrimen's office.

Lost in her own thoughts, she wasn't aware that someone had come up behind her until she felt a hand on her shoulder. Her reaction was automatic. She simultaneously twisted and dropped, forcing the man to release his grip, then she slammed her knee into his groin.

The man cried out, doubling over. He raised his hand to indicate she should stop before her fist connected with his jaw.

She jumped back but remained ready to defend herself if he tried anything further.

Once he got his breath back, he looked up apologetically. 'I'm sorry. By everything holy, I didn't mean to scare you.'

'Who the hell are you?' demanded Jemma.

'I was incarcerated with your husband. He pointed you out the other day, so I thought I'd say hello.'

'Are you telling me that you were abducted by the Zants, too?' snapped Jemma.

'Yes, I was. We were deeply grateful for your search and determination to find him. Without you, most of us would have eventually died there.'

'I'm glad we managed to help so many people,' said Jemma, relaxing her stance but still alert and ready. 'You must realise we're all jumpy.'

'Yes, I do,' he said, attempting to straighten up, although he remained bent slightly forward.

Seeing his discomfort, she was embarrassed she'd reacted so strongly. 'Are you from Earth?'

'No, but not far away.'

'Oh God. I take it you're from Anders Major, then?' A large rock fashioned into seats was nestled beside the path. Jemma sighed and sat down. 'Why can't you people leave me alone?'

'Because you are our Supreme Ruler.'

'No, I don't believe so,' said Jemma. 'My grandfather was Supreme Ruler, but I know nothing about it. I have made it clear that I will not be going back there. I belong to Earth now.'

'The people of the ruling houses will not allow you to refuse. If you continue, they will find a way to take you. You won't be able to keep your high moral ground.'

'They don't have a choice,' exclaimed Jemma. 'The decision is mine. What's your name?'

'They call me Ryan.'

Jemma doubted that really was his name, but at least it gave her something she could call him. 'Ryan, the people of the ruling houses don't have any say in my decision. I have repeatedly advised everyone who'll listen that I will not go back. Lena told me stories of rape and abuse of the people by those in the ruling houses. I could not abide that, and don't wish to be any part of it.'

'I'm not sure I believe you, but if you are telling the truth they will corrupt you soon enough and everything will return to the way it was.'

She stood and glared at him. 'How did you know I was from Anders? Do you have an electrometer?'

'No, I do not. Several of my people are here. One of them had an electrometer when we were taken and the Zants didn't find it. He was in a different building from ours.'

'I thought the Zants were your allies on Anders? Why would they have taken you?'

'We thought they were, too,' said Ryan, 'but they can't be trusted.'

'No,' said Jemma, 'they can't. So, what do you want from me?'

'You identified Lena. If you care at all about our people, you will tell security that you were wrong.'

'She has admitted to planting the explosives,' replied Jemma. 'It's too late for that.'

'Then I am sorry, we have nothing to talk about,' said Ryan.

Jemma shook her head. 'What's your relationship to Lena?'

'She is my sister.'

'Oh, dear God.' Jemma stared at him. If they were related, there might also be other links. 'What do you know of Fredrick Pritchard?'

'I do not know that name,' said Ryan, looking puzzled.

'You may know him as Drick.'

'Oh, yes I know Drick,' said Ryan. 'He is my great-grandfather, a noble man. His only interest is to save Anders Major and return the power to the people.'

'Ryan, I realise that you will probably not believe me, but I must say it. Pritchard ... Drick ... is an inter-galactic terrorist. He cares nothing for human life or the people of Anders Major. His only interest is money and power. He has not told you the truth.'

Ryan started to back away. 'You have just validated our belief. Drick is a good, caring, decent man and you would besmirch him. Hear this. We will not allow you to return to our galaxy. Tell your people that you plan to stay here. Otherwise, we will take action.'

As Ryan turned on his heel and walked away from her, Jemma struggled to decide what to do. Given that the people from Anders were human and could not be distinguished from humans from Earth, there was no way to identify her enemies. For most of her life since her parents died, she'd relished being on her own. But now, alone meant vulnerable. She hated the idea of always having to rely on someone to accompany her, but as she scrutinised the shadows and laneways that lay ahead, she knew she needed that help. Sitting back on the rock, she pulled out her communicator and contacted Sean.

When he answered, she couldn't think of anything to say.

'Jem, are you okay?'

'Yeah, I think so. I've just been threatened. Can I come to you?'

'No. Stay where you are. I'll come to you.'

*   *   *

'Is there a problem?' asked Werrimen as Sean closed his communicator.

'Someone threatened Jemma. I'm going.'

'Of course. I will notify security and follow.'

Already outside the door, Sean didn't fully hear the rest of her answer and didn't plan to delay long enough to find out. He ran to the disc, tapping at his thigh as he waited for his surroundings to clear, then tore out the front door and onto the path towards their house. The couple of minutes it took to reach Jemma felt like hours, his fear for her safety increasing with every step. When he saw her, sitting on the rock with no obvious injury, he paused to steady himself. It wouldn't do her any good to see him panicking. He focussed on clearing his mind of all the worst-case scenarios he'd been imagining so he could determine what had actually occurred. As he approached, she jumped up ready to defend herself before relaxing enough to run to him.

'It's okay,' he murmured, wrapping his arms around her. 'Can you tell me about it?'

'Your house is close,' said Werrimen softly behind him. 'We should go there.'

Sean forced himself to hide his surprise at hearing Werrimen's voice. In spite of her size, she could get within centimetres of him without triggering any of his senses, something no-one else could do.

'I don't know if it's been cleared,' said Jemma.

'I will check as we walk.' Werrimen opened her communicator. 'It is better not to be out in the open if there is a threat.'

'Let's go then,' said Sean, holding his hand out to Jemma. He continually cast his eyes around as they walked, ready to spring at the slightest sound.

At the house he left Jemma with Werrimen so he could walk around and check outside. It was hard to tell if there'd been anyone there since Giareto had left, his people had left so many footprints, but Sean couldn't see any new black boxes, so he turned to go back. By the time he reached the front entrance Werrimen had already gone inside with Jemma, so he allowed himself a moment to settle down before joining them.

'Oh, there you are, Sean,' said Werrimen as he walked in. 'Would you fill us in now please, Jemma?'

As Jemma recounted her ordeal, Sean's frustration boiled over. Although he felt Werrimen's hand on his arm, he was too angry to be distracted now. 'I don't suppose he told you where he lived?'

Jemma shook her head.

'Would you recognise him again, Jemma?' said Werrimen.

'Oh yes. I wish I knew how to download the image from my brain. It's very clear.'

'May I try?' Werrimen smiled. 'Sometimes I can see the image you see. I know that Zadrus is more attuned to you, but we are close enough that I might succeed.'

'Sure.'

Werrimen gently placed her hands on either side of Jemma's neck. 'I have a very clear image of a young man, around Sean's age, but shorter by about ten centimetres, mid-brown hair, fair skin, blue eyes.'

Jemma stared at Sean, then Werrimen. 'That's him.'

'Good, I now have an image too. Sean, we have been practicing this. I would like you to try.' She placed his hands on Jemma's shoulders, not in quite the same position but he supposed his smaller hands would have to be set differently. 'Now relax, clear your mind and allow the image to emerge.'

'That's strange,' he muttered. 'I'm getting an image of Lena.'

'Oops, sorry,' said Jemma, blushing. 'I didn't think you were ready. I let my mind wander. I'll focus on Ryan now.'

'Are you saying you really were thinking of Lena?' exclaimed Sean.

'I was,' replied Jemma.

'Jesus,' said Sean. 'I saw Lena as clear as day, clearer than I usually see my own thoughts.'

'Very good,' said Werrimen. 'Now both of you clear

your minds again, then Jemma concentrate on the man who accosted you.'

'Okay, I think I'm getting that image. As you described Werrimen. Wow. That's incredible.'

'Not really,' said Werrimen. 'You two are in tune with each other, so once you know what to do it is relatively easy. Do you know the man?'

'No,' said Sean. 'Not someone I recognise.'

'Very well,' said Werrimen. 'Rodeg is an exceptional artist, so if he can see the image and capture it, we may be able to identify this person.'

'Right, but I would like to speak to Lena first, please,' said Sean, softly.

'Why?' Werrimen pointed to a chair and sat beside him.

'I'd like to see if I can get some more information. If she is Ryan's sister, as he claims, she might know where he's living.'

'Even if she does, she won't tell you,' said Jemma. 'She thinks we're scum and that they're the righteous.'

Sean stared back at her, then turned to Werrimen. 'Before we were taken by the Zants, we discovered small silver bars implanted in the necks of a group of people who called themselves the Rescue Earth Group. They also believed they were on the righteous path.'

'That's right,' said Jemma. 'Lena's statements were just like theirs. The overthrow of the ruling houses happened not long after I was born, as I understand it. There's no way Lena could have seen the behaviours she describes from our ancestors.

We travelled forward eighty years in time, so the things she describes happened at least a hundred years ago!'

Werrimen nodded thoughtfully. 'Yes, I see. You are both thinking that someone has control of them?'

'Is it possible?' said Jemma.

'Well, yes, I suppose it is,' said Werrimen. 'Sean, I will organise for you to talk to Lena, but first I will take Emilrad with me and check her for implanted devices. It is also possible that she has simply been misled. If your ancestors were the monsters she describes the IPL would have been aware, yet I have never heard anything of this. There may be some elements of truth, but I suspect the facts have been misconstrued. I can only guess at who would do that, or why.'

'That makes me feel a bit better, I guess,' said Jemma.

'Good.' Werrimen stood and started towards the door. 'Sean, I will call you when I am ready for you to join us with Lena. Jemma, I will see you in the morning to start your flight training and talk about how we can manage your Trustee training until we get back to Zadrus.'

'Well, what do you think of that?' said Sean, after closing the door behind Werrimen.

Jemma patted the seat beside her and waited until he'd settled. 'I've been confused since the night we first saw that blue light on Springbrook Mountain. My parents, my guardians, your mother are all normal people. I can't believe Lena is right.'

'I know what you mean. My father was so strait-laced he made General Hunt look soft and cuddly.'

Jemma laughed. 'Oh dear, I can't get that image. Let's have a bit of lunch while we wait for Werrimen to call you. I can't go with you. Lena won't talk to me. She sees me as the enemy.'

'Understood,' said Sean. 'She probably won't talk to me either, but I have to try.'

He sat opposite Jemma at the table. Neither of them said much, but even so, he didn't want to drag himself away from her, even when the call finally came for him to join Werrimen. He knew that Jemma was more capable than any woman he'd ever met, more capable than most men, yet he felt so helpless when it came to keeping her safe. They'd grown so close over the last couple of years, and they'd thrived despite all the obstacles that had been thrown in their way. The loss of their unborn child was still heavy in their hearts. Somehow, he had to find a way to make it right.

He stood, kissed her, and left. On his way to the security building, he mentally dared Ryan to cross his path and attempt to confront him. Then they could have it out. He could force the truth from the man. But no-one came near.

Emilrad met him at the entrance to the security building. 'We could not find any implants but when Werrimen touched Lena's neck, she became confused. I am not sure if she was trying to lie and could not, or if she was trying to tell the truth but has been so brainwashed that she could not access it from her own memory. I favour the latter.'

Sean frowned. 'It's more than someone feeding her a pack of lies. You're saying that her memory has been manipulated, and the truth erased. But who would do that? And why?'

'Those are the important questions. Unfortunately, I do not have answers. We will continue to work on her to find out. Be gentle as you speak to her, please. She is very distressed.'

'I have no desire to do her any harm,' said Sean. 'She was good to us while we were in captivity. It doesn't sound like she can give me much information, but she might be able to tell me where her people are living. Maybe I can do something to change her mind. I don't know, Emilrad, but I have to try.'

'I understand.'

Sean followed Emilrad into the interview room. It was bleak and cold. Two chairs were placed on either side of the table and Lena sat on the side opposite the door. Sean slid into a chair alongside Emilrad. He thought his heart might break when he saw the woman he'd known as so strong and capable slumped forward, her elbows leaning on the desk so her hands could support her head.

'What do you want?' asked Lena. Her voice was barely audible.

'Oh, Lena. What's happened to you?'

'Ask your wife,' snapped Lena. 'She's the one who organised it.'

'I need to understand,' said Sean. 'Can you tell me why you planted those explosive devices?'

'As I said, ask your wife.'

Sean paused for a moment, desperate to find a way to get through to her. 'A man called Ryan stopped her yesterday on her way home. I'd like to talk to him, too. Can you tell me where to find him?'

'Ryan? Is he alright?' Her eyes showed the first spark of life he'd seen since he walked into the room, but it quickly faded.

'He seemed to be fine,' said Sean. 'So, his name really is Ryan?'

'Of course,' exclaimed Lena. 'My brother is a good man.'

'Maybe he can help me understand. Do you know where he is?'

'Why? So you can have your goons capture him, too?'

'No,' said Sean. 'I don't even need to know his location, just a way to contact him.'

Lena spat on the table. 'I will not help you harm my people any further.' She turned her chair so her back was to Sean.

Emilrad stood. 'I think you have achieved all you can here. We should go.'

Sean nodded and stood himself. 'It's wretched to see Lena like this. Can you help her?'

'I do not know,' replied Emilrad, 'but we will most certainly try.'

As Sean turned to leave, he saw Lena move slightly to look up at him. Her brows were furrowed. Perhaps, somewhere deep within her mind, he had got through to her.

CHAPTER 5

Jemma didn't expect Sean to glean any more information from Lena, but when he came back to the house disappointed that he'd learnt nothing, she made up her mind to forget all about Anders Major and get on with learning to fly the spacecraft. And that excited her, although she was aware that Sean didn't feel the same. He hadn't been able to overcome his childhood experience, even though in every other facet of his life, he was the bravest man she knew. Despite his assurances that he was fine, he tossed and turned most nights. There wasn't much she could do to help; Werrimen was hell bent on separating them for their training. She made up her mind to have a quiet word to Nik, but on their way to Werrimen's office in the morning Rodeg intercepted them and, steering Sean and Nik away, removed her opportunity.

'Looks like it's just the three of us,' said Dan, resting his hand on Jemma's shoulder. 'He'll be fine. Stop worrying about him.'

'I can't,' she muttered, but she didn't resist Dan's gentle push as they continued on towards Werrimen's office.

'Focus on what we have to do,' said Dan. 'Nik'll help him.'

A few seconds later, Emilrad ran towards them and called Dan and Matt.

'Hmm. Looks like it's just you, then,' said Dan.

'Fine,' she muttered. 'If I don't survive, it was nice knowing you.'

Dan laughed. 'Buck up. I suspect Werrimen's organised this so she can chat. She's worried about you. We all are.'

'I know, but I'd rather everyone stopped worrying about me. Sometimes I wish I could go back to my safe and ordered life at the university. There were times I was bored, but right now I'm finding the concept of boredom, seriously attractive.'

'You wouldn't for long. We'd better go. I'll see you shortly. We're in this together, kiddo.'

Jemma slapped his arm. 'You're only two years older than me, old boy, and don't you forget it.' She watched him walk away, then continued on to Werrimen's office. She was surprised to find Dragile there, chatting to Werrimen and sipping a highly coloured drink that had an opaque steam rising from it.

'Good morning, Jemma,' said Werrimen. 'Are you excited about today?'

Jemma grinned. 'Yes, I am, but I'm worried about Sean.'

'I understand. Leave him to me. I cannot allow him to back away from skills that he needs. I am aware of his background, but it is not in his interests to allow his fear to stop him. I will get him through it.'

'Not much else I can do,' said Jemma. 'Good morning, Dragile. It's good to see you again.'

'Thank you,' replied Dragile. 'I understand we'll be seeing a lot more of each other.'

Jemma's eyes narrowed as she looked at Werrimen. Clearly the woman was up to something.

'Let us begin, then,' said Werrimen. 'Jemma, I know you connected with Dragile when we searched for Sean. I also know that you saw him at his worst. He has done a lot of soul searching since then and, I believe, has come out much stronger for it. I have asked him to take over as your Trustee instructor while we are here. Would that be acceptable to you?'

Jemma couldn't think of anything sensible to say and couldn't hold back the laugh. 'You've never before asked me if I was okay about anything to do with training. Dragile and I got along very well, and I suspect we saw the worst of each other.'

'That settles it then. I will leave you with Dragile to go to the spaceship factory. He will show you what is happening. I believe Dan and Matt will be waiting for you there. After that you will go to the transporter landing zone and begin your instruction with Emilrad.'

Dragile steered her out of the room. 'Werrimen is testing you. She sees something special in you, but she is worried about how you will determine your future. We will discuss it later. Talk to Emilrad about your training and let me know when you are finished.'

'Yeah, sure.' She looked up at Dragile as they entered the

factory. He was still smiling so, with a shrug of her shoulders, she turned and ran to join Dan and Matt.

Although the second factory still showed signs of damage from the fire, reconstruction of the craft was in full swing. People buzzed about in every direction. Walls had been erected around the spaceship and an internal roof was about to be lifted over the top. Jemma couldn't see any sign of damage to the spaceship itself, but they'd been told there was, so she assumed it'd either been fixed, or it was somewhere she couldn't see.

Emilrad smiled and nodded. 'Work here is progressing well. Do any of you have any questions regarding the progress?'

'Only how long it will take,' said Dan. 'Translate that to, how long will we have to prepare for this flight?'

'As we said yesterday, the engineers here have estimated twelve to fourteen weeks, which is roughly the same as twelve to fourteen Earth weeks, but it could be sooner, or it may take a little longer. That is your guide. Do not worry, you will be ready.'

Dan shrugged. 'I can't see it,' he muttered.

Jemma gave his hand a quick squeeze. 'Come on, brother-in-law. As you've so often told me, we don't have a choice. Let's just get on with it.'

'Cheer up, Dan,' said Matt. 'We'll find a way to do what they want. It won't be the first time we've done the impossible.'

Together, they followed Emilrad, but the slight slump in Dan's shoulders worried Jemma. For so much of the time they'd known each other, Dan and Sean had been the strong ones and she'd needed their help to fight multiple demons. The tables might have been turned now, and if so she'd just have to motivate both the men to do what they had to do. At least Matt seemed to have remained cheerful.

The morning passed quickly as they were shown the transporter. Emilrad ran through all the controls and explained how the thing worked. By the time he'd finished, Jemma's head was so muddled she couldn't remember the difference between take-off and landing, or which part of the engine was the critical bit that she *must always remember to check*.

Emilrad laughed at the look on her face. 'That was just an overview. We go out for our first flight tomorrow. By the end of the week, you will be proficient.'

'No way,' muttered Dan.

*   *   *

When the week did end, Emilrad proved to be correct. Jemma wouldn't have called herself fully proficient, but she was comfortable with take-off, landing and managing the craft through the air. She wasn't confident that she knew what to do if something went wrong, although Emilrad assured her week two would sort out all her issues.

Sean had coped better than she'd expected. The large ship seemed to have given him some confidence, but the big test would come in week three when they swapped. He'd have to deal with the more confined space of the transporters. Conversely, she'd found it far better to start on the transporters.

Managing an entire spaceship struck her as a much more daunting task. Dan had also settled down and both Matt and Nik were, like her, champing at the bit to take charge of any flying machine, whatever the size. Nik had wanted to learn to fly helicopters on Earth but hadn't had the chance before they left. Matt didn't say much but Jemma could see from his expression that he was in his element flying and couldn't wait for the next phase, which would be learning to fly the transport zone craft.

On the first day of the following week, which the Condonans called Firstday, although she'd have called it Monday, she'd completed her pre-flight procedures and commenced lift-off when a loud clanging noise reverberated through the craft. Emilrad stood behind her at the controls. Matt was in charge of communications. Dan was navigating.

'What's that noise?' she said, attempting to sound confident.

Emilrad shrugged. 'Perhaps you should investigate.'

She turned to Dan. 'Would you take over here, please?' She looked around frantically, but given Emilrad wasn't the least bit perturbed, she forced herself to calm down. Presumably, the noise was a set-up for their training. 'It appears to be coming from under the floor.'

'Very good,' said Emilrad. 'Remember, you are a long way from the ground. You must identify the source of the noise. Jemma, you are in charge of this flight. Can you think of anything else to do?'

'I guess I could ask Matt to contact the controller and

explain the problem,' she said.

'Yes, I suggest you do that.'

'Won't they be annoyed that a training flight is calling them when you clearly know what the problem is?'

'You are astute,' he replied, laughing. 'We are set up to go to a training coordinator to make this as realistic as possible for you.'

'Thanks, I think. How does Matt announce himself?'

'He will use his name, provide the current coordinates, then explain the problem.'

'Shit.' Jemma ran her fingers through the various screens, looked under the control desk and then back at Emilrad, feeling hopeless. 'How do we find the coordinates?'

'Do not panic,' said Emilrad. 'Who in your team should know the coordinates?'

'Oh God. The navigator, I guess. Dan, would you ask your screen for the coordinates, please?'

Three screens were arranged in front of the control panel, although they were more images than screens as there was nothing solid about them. Each of them showed a variation of the course they had taken. When Dan asked for the coordinates, the first screen quickly changed its image to show a line of numbers. Relieved, she looked back to Emilrad, but he stood there saying nothing.

'Damn it.' She turned to Matt. 'Contact the coordinator, please.' When Dragile's smiling face came on the screen, she had to laugh.

'What is the problem?' he said.

As she explained, it struck her how much of her current situation involved family. Dragile and Emilrad were brothers. Sean and Dan were brothers. She and Nik were cousins. Matt was the general's great-grandson. 'We heard a loud clanging noise. I have located the source.'

'Describe it please,' said Dragile.

'There is something that looks like a fan with four wings. One of the wings appears to be bent.'

'You must ask the transporter controls to stall the anti-gravity mechanism. You will easily remove the bent wing, as you call it. The transporter can fly with as little as two of those wings.'

She started to move back to the open space, then stopped. 'What will happen if we turn off the anti-gravity? Are we going to float?'

'Well done,' replied Dragile. 'Everyone should secure themselves to their seats. Emilrad will show you how. Jemma, you should wear the harness that sits just inside the engine section. The loss of gravity will only be for a couple of minutes. As soon as you are finished, tell control to restart the anti-gravity mechanism.'

Jemma followed his instructions to the letter. Sweat trickled down her forehead as she grasped strategically placed handholds. Her arms felt like they'd lost all their strength. After she'd removed the wing and ordered control to re-apply the anti-gravity mechanism, her legs almost buckled beneath her, but she was determined not to let either Dragile or Emilrad see how frightened she felt.

'Well done,' said Emilrad, as she slipped back into her chair. 'You may begin your descent.

When they finally arrived back on solid ground, Jemma's relief was palpable, and the look in Dan's eyes suggested he felt much the same, but neither of them was prepared to admit it to Emilrad.

The next few days followed the same pattern. Either she, Matt or Dan had the controls, and something would happen that they had to investigate. Finally, at the end of the week, Emilrad said he was prepared to certify them to fly transporters. She'd hoped for a day off at the end of this phase, but Werrimen told them to swap for the next round of training that would start the next day.

Jemma and Sean walked home in silence, both too tired to do anything other than eat dinner and fall into bed.

The following morning, Jemma rose early enough to prepare breakfast and to have time to sit and chat. When Sean joined her at the table, she slid across a cup of the hot drink that was popular on Condona, known as Target. She had no idea why they called it that, and suspected she didn't want to know, but it tasted like a cross between coffee and hot chocolate and had just enough zip in it to be a decent heart-starter for the day.

'How do you feel about starting on the transporters?' asked Jemma, tentatively.

'Not keen,' said Sean, 'but I don't have a choice. Don't worry about me. I learnt very early in my military career how to manage my fear, so I've just got to put all that training into play and get through it.'

'What can I do to help?' asked Jemma.

'You could grow a few centimetres, cut your hair short and pretend to be me.'

'If only,' murmured Jemma.

'Don't 'spect there's much you can do, then. I'll get through by focusing on our end point - getting home to Earth. Now, how do you feel about going to the big ships?'

'A bit nervous.' Jemma looked at him, not sure how much to say.

'And ...' Sean reached across for her hand.

'I didn't like to say anything because I know how hard this is for you. But Sean, I'm loving it.'

Sean smiled. 'Just say it.'

'I've never known freedom like it, sailing across the skies – above the houses, out over oceans. Knowing I can go wherever I want. Oh God, Sean, I'm sorry.'

'Why on Earth would you be sorry? Jem, I've never seen you this excited about anything, not even your scientific research, and I know you love that. Just because I don't enjoy flying doesn't mean I can't be happy for you.'

'Do you think ...' Jemma stood and shook her head. 'No, that's silly.'

'Come on,' said Sean. 'Do I think what?'

'That maybe my future could lie in flying spacecraft.'

'I don't think that's silly at all,' said Sean, smiling. 'Talk to Werrimen about it. You know, I think your excitement's catching. Let's get down there and get started.'

When they arrived at the landing pad, Werrimen headed

Sean towards the blue light under his transporter, wrapping her arm around his shoulders and chatting to him as they walked.

Dan was waiting for Jemma underneath the larger spaceship. 'You can't afford to worry about him. You've got to have your mind on the job here. These craft will be a lot tougher than the transporters.'

'Yeah, I know, and I'll do what's needed, but you can't expect me not to be concerned about Sean.' Jemma wasn't at all convinced these ships would be tougher. She'd helped Zadrus with navigation on the spaceship that had rescued them on Earth, and she'd enjoyed that once she'd understood what to do. The control panels in this spaceship looked much the same as those, and not much different from the transporters.

When Emilrad arrived, he didn't wait give them any time to settle in. 'We have much to cover. There are many aspects to these ships. Flying and navigating are straight-forward, and I don't expect any of you to have any difficulty. The difference is in the ship's power system. You see, it not only flies the craft, but it must sustain food and water and all the facilities on board. So, with this type of craft, you must have an overall knowledge of every aspect because even though you will have a large maintenance crew, you must know how to locate the problem and then understand the solution that maintenance suggests. Additionally, we will be going outside Condona's atmosphere, and you must be aware of everything out there that could cause a problem.'

'And we're going to achieve all that in two weeks,' said Jemma, her heart sinking.

'Managing the craft, and a broad overview, yes.'

As they followed Emilrad to the control room, Jemma shook her head. Werrimen had said they'd be working in the factory in the afternoons to learn all they could, but there hadn't been time so far, and she couldn't see that changing in this rotation. Still, she couldn't afford to waste her energy thinking about it. She was relieved to be allocated to the navigating job first, given that she had a minute amount of experience with it. She organised her screens, requested the destination Emilrad had given her, then waited for Matt, on communications, to get permission to begin. Dan, as pilot, commenced lift-off. Emilrad stood beside them, two other Trustees behind him, presumably to jump in if Dan lost control.

The morning passed quickly, and after a brief lunch stop they changed roles so that Jemma was now at the controls. Her nerves threatened to get the better of her, but she forced her mind to clear so she could concentrate on her task. Within minutes they were heading into the upper atmosphere which was, thankfully, as far as Emilrad wanted to go for their first flight. Pleased with herself, she didn't expect her level of disappointment when he told her to take the craft down and land it, but there was no time to fret about it. Landing turned out to be considerably harder than taking off.

The rest of the two weeks followed the same pattern, although they moved further out into space and a new

problem was thrown at them each day, from asteroid show-
ers to enemy craft. On the final day, Werrimen called the
group into her office and advised them that they were all to
undergo their final proficiency testing on the large craft the
following morning.

*　　*　　*

After a fitful night's sleep, Jemma made her way, with Sean, to
the spaceship in which they were to complete their test. They
stood together, staring up at it. The thing was enormous —
at least two hundred metres in diameter and the height of a
thirty storey early twenty-first century skyscraper.

'I can't believe we're doing this,' she said, grinning. 'We're
about to qualify as spaceship pilots, cleared to fly anywhere
in the galaxy. We're a hair's breadth away from learning to
fly the transport zone craft. Then we're on our way home.'

'Yeah great,' muttered Sean. 'Home? Excellent. The way
we're about to get there, not my preferred option, but here we
are, and this is what we have to do.'

Jemma smiled. Sean had said he would control his fear,
and he was doing a damned good job of it on the surface,
but she knew he was still churning inside. 'Sean, I'll be right
there, beside you. Will you please let me know if you're getting worried?'

'I'll be right. Come on. They're calling us up.'

She took his hand and walked with him into the blue light
underneath the craft. She felt him tremble as they floated up

to the landing bay, but he said nothing, so she did the same. It always amazed her that she felt perfectly supported on the way up, yet the only thing touching her was the light. In fact, she felt confident all round in these craft, and she wondered what she could do to make Sean feel the same.

Emilrad introduced them to the commander of the spaceship, Dielter, also a Supreme Trustee and also from Sidlow. The group was silent as Dielter led them to the control floor.

'You will take turns in each of three roles, pilot, navigator, and communications.'

Jemma winced when Sean was directed to the pilot's chair, although she suspected it was pre-arranged to throw him straight in. Dan took communications and she started as navigator. Nik and Matt waited behind them. After she'd requested coordinates for the required destination, she set up her screens to show the area surrounding the craft. Dan spoke to the controller to say they were ready to go, then Sean had the craft in the air, as smooth a lift-off as she'd encountered.

Everything went to plan and after two hours they were advised to swap roles. Sean was given a break, while Jemma moved to communications, Dan to pilot and Matt began on navigation. After each of them had performed in all three roles, they began their rotations again. Jemma had just stepped into the pilot's seat for the second time when she heard Nik report an unusual speck on the navigation screen.

The entire front wall of the control room, which was fifty metres wide and three metres high, formed the screen that showed the pilot the surrounding conditions. She knew from previous experience that it wasn't a window, but in fact projected images to make it look like one. Seconds later, Matt alerted Dielter to a weak distress signal. Jemma was ready to dismiss it as part of their test until she noticed that the examiners, all senior Trustees, had crowded around them.

'It is a spaceship. Similar size to the one we are on. This is not something we planned,' said Dielter, turning away so he could report to Condonan command.

From the pilot's seat, Jemma could see that the other craft was on a set course. It appeared to be in orbit around one of Condona's moons.

'Maintain your positions for the moment,' said Dielter.

'There's another ship approaching it at high speed,' yelled Matt. 'Oh my God, they're firing on it!'

'Enhance,' Dielter yelled back. 'Identify the craft.'

Jemma clenched her hands together to stop them shaking as Emilrad leant over Matt to adjust some of his controls.

The image was immediately enlarged, and its quality enhanced. 'I'm not sure of the first craft, Dielter,' said Emilrad. 'The second is definitely Zant.'

'Increase speed,' Dielter said to Jemma. 'Make sure the Zant craft sees us. Our Trustee light sequence provides a clear identification. I doubt even those monsters would dare to fire once they recognise us, but be ready to activate the force field.'

'Any further signal, Matt?' asked Emilrad, quietly.

Another Trustee eased in between Jemma and Matt. He answered before Matt had a chance. 'There's something coming through. It sounds like one of our distress signals, but it is faint and I cannot enhance it further. I have transmitted it to the command on Condona. Hopefully, they can make something of it.'

Everyone jumped when Dielter bellowed. 'By the stars, activate the force field now. The devils have fired.'

Jemma reached for the controls to do as he ordered, but Dielter pushed past her and keyed in the sequence. Even then, the few seconds it took were barely sufficient.

'Brace yourselves,' yelled Dielter. 'We are about to be hit!'

The impact felt to Jemma as if they'd just slammed into a brick wall. Lights went out, and several people lost balance, but as far as she could see when the dim emergency light came on no-one had been seriously hurt.

One of the instructors was first to speak as he peered at the enhanced image. 'The first craft we saw is Sidlown. It is severely disabled. There is a gaping hole in the side. I cannot see any sign of life, but we must check for survivors. If even one of the sectors has remained intact, there is a possibility that someone might have survived.'

Dielter stared at the screen. 'Where is the Zant craft? Are they still a danger?'

'They're getting smaller on our screen. Moving towards Ailazant, by the look of it,' said Matt.

'Remove the force field. Set a course to bring us parallel to the disabled craft.' Dielter assembled the three most senior Trustees. 'Take a transporter and board the ship. We must not assume there are no survivors. Pilot, lock our coordinates onto the pattern of the other craft.'

Jemma thought she should know how to do as he asked, but she couldn't make her mind function, everything had happened so quickly, so she requested help. She didn't care if they failed her now. Getting to that ship and rescuing survivors was all the mattered and she couldn't do it alone.

'Nikola,' said Emilrad. 'Link your screen with the transporter so we can see everything they see.'

Jemma was amazed when Nik spoke to the navigation screen and linked the screens as he'd asked.

'How the hell did you do that?' said Jemma.

'I'll explain later. Dielter, do you want me to link another screen to the Commander's communicator?'

'Yes, good idea.'

Once the ship was on course, Jemma leaned over Nik's shoulder to see the image of the transporter as it docked in the other ship's landing bay.

'We are activating personal mobility equipment,' said a voice through the communicator. 'We are leaving our transported now.'

Jemma, along with everyone else on board the main spacecraft stared at the screen as they waited to hear. She jumped when she heard one of the landing party cry out.

'By the stars!'

'What is it? What have you found?' Dielter leaned even closer to the screen.

'Several bodies. Not recently dead. The Zant attack did not kill them. The bodies are emaciated, must have been starving for some time. The odour here is incredible. There's a sealed sector. Mostly wreckage around it, but there is a panel that appears to be accessible. We're going to try.'

'All our craft are designed in sections,' said Dielter. 'After a craft is disabled, the non-damaged sectors automatically seal, enabling those within to survive. If the control room is intact, even the most severely damaged ships can land safely. I doubt we will find that here. We must wait now until they report.'

Finally, one of the landing party spoke again. 'We've found someone. Low, but still alive. A Sidlown woman and ... by the stars ... a half-Sidlown, half-human child. Stay with them, my Prehling. I will keep looking.'

When the senior Trustee spoke again, Jemma could hear the anguish in his voice. 'I do not think there is anyone else ... wait, I just saw movement.' A long pause followed. 'A human female here. Badly injured. She is hiding a human female child. The woman has lost consciousness. She has severe abdominal wounds. I will stem her haemorrhage as best I can. We must evacuate her immediately.' He called another Trustee to help. 'Take care of the child. Treat her gently, she is in terror. I will use my auxiliary equipment to transport the mother out. Bring the Sidlown woman with us. We will return to assess further once these people are safely in our ship.'

Jemma felt Sean behind her as she watched Nik zoom in on the image of the woman who the rescuers had just found.

'Jesus!' exclaimed Matt.

Although puzzled by the horrified look on Matt's face, Jemma had to concentrate as she was still in the pilot's seat.

She was more than a little pleased with herself that after some initial help she'd been able to maintain the ship in the holding pattern. She was even more pleased that Dielter had left her in control so he could head down to meet the transporter as it docked. There was plenty of help to call on if she needed it, but it was a compliment that he hadn't told someone to stand behind her and check everything she did.

When Dielter returned to the flight deck, her attention was drawn back to Matt when he asked after the survivors.

'Adequate, but they will need hospital care soon,' replied Dielter. 'The human mother is the most severely injured. I would estimate she is around forty years of age, although so emaciated she may be younger. The child is seven or eight earth years and seems healthy. The two Sidlowns are in good health although very thin. We have given them food and water and told them to rest. The Sidlown mother is also looking after the human child, and they seem to know each other well.'

Matt took hold of Dielter's arm. 'I saw them on the screen. Could I be relieved from here, and go down to check on them?'

Jemma didn't expect Dielter to agree until she saw Matt's face. She touched Dielter's arm, 'May I go with him?'

Dielter ordered one of the instructors to take the pilot's seat. 'We will both go.'

Jemma had to run beside Dielter as he strode to catch up with Matt before he stepped onto the disc that would take him up to the medical centre which, in the spaceships, was always on the seventeenth floor. She tried to get Matt's attention and speak to him, but he was hell-bent on getting to the woman who'd been rescued.

As they entered the medical centre, Matt shook Jemma away and rushed to the woman's bedside. He was shaking as he leaned over and gently took hold of one of the woman's hands. 'Oh God, Dana, it is you! Can you open your eyes? Look at me. Please don't leave me now.'

Dielter turned to Jemma. 'Tell me what this is about?'

'I think this might be Matt's wife, Dana. She was taken during the war on Earth before the Inter-Planetary League revealed themselves. None of us thought there was any chance of finding her.'

Matt had lost all the colour in his face as he looked at the child hiding behind the Sidlown woman. 'Hello. Are you Susan? Is this your mother?'

The Sidlown woman gently eased the child out from behind her. 'It's all right, dear. I think this may be your father.' She smiled at Matt. 'Susan has been through a lot. I suspect it will take some time for her to trust you. I can take care of her for now. Dana needs you most.'

'Yes, Matt, you focus on Dana,' said Jemma. 'I'll help this lady and Susan if they need it.'

Matt nodded, then turned to Dielter before moving back to his wife's side. 'Fail me if you wish, but I can't leave her. When are we heading back to Condona?'

'Very soon. The transporter has gone back for a final check of the other craft. We will head home on their return. Do not worry about passing or failing. Stay with your wife.'

'Home,' muttered Jemma. 'If only that were possible.'

'A Trustee ship will be here within thirty minutes,' continued Dielter. 'We will hand all the investigation and surveillance over to them as soon as they arrive. I realise this is difficult for you.'

Dana remained unconscious although her breathing had stabilised according to the medical team on board, but Matt refused to leave her side. Jemma sought permission to stay with them but was relieved when Sean came down to join her.

'Dielter told me about Dana,' said Sean. 'Dan and Nik are at the controls with two of the instructors. I thought you might need some support.'

'I'm fine,' said Jemma. 'It's Matt I'm worried about. You might be better at helping him.'

Sean nodded and moved closer to the bedside. He said nothing, just put his hand on Matt's shoulder.

Jemma headed across to Merrilam, the Sidlown woman, to help settle the children. There was little solace any of them could offer Matt as he stood vigil by his desperately ill wife. It would be unspeakably cruel if Matt were to lose her now, and Jemma couldn't imagine how he'd cope.

The minutes ticked by extraordinarily slowly before Dielter advised that they were about to land.

'An equipped transporter will be waiting to transfer Dana to the hospital,' said Dielter. 'You will go with her, Matt. Another transporter will take Jemma, Dan, Nik and Sean with Susan, Merrilam and her daughter, Lexie, to the hospital. I believe Werrimen will join you there.'

'Thanks,' said Jemma.

There was a slight bump as they touched down. Their tense wait exploded into activity as doors burst open and medical staff ran into the sick bay. Orders were shouted, equipment removed and added, and a passage cleared to shift Dana out.

After a quick check of Dana's wounds, the doctor addressed Matt. 'She's bleeding internally which has caused a hypovolaemic shock, but I think you have retrieved her in time. We must move quickly now; operating rooms are on stand-by.'

Seconds later, they were gone. Jemma found the silence in the medical centre stifling as they all stood around and looked at each other. It was a relief when they were finally directed to the second transporter. Jemma had barely sat down when the blue light snapped off and the transporter began to move. It rose quickly above the city, then shot down to the other side and landed in the hospital grounds. Jemma was first out of the craft and she didn't wait for anyone else before running into the building. Matt was in the surgical waiting room when she found him, his head cradled in his hands. She sat beside him, rubbed his back, and whispered calming words until a man wearing a surgical mask and a loose white overall walked in and squatted in front of them.

'I am Athon, the surgeon,' said the man. 'Are you Dana's husband?'

'Yes,' said Matt.

'I have repaired your wife's bowel and spleen,' said Athon.

'She should make a good recovery, although it will take some time. Nobody knows how long she was in shock, so I cannot guarantee there will be no long-term damage from the lack of oxygen to her brain.'

'She was injured when that other craft fired on us,' said Merrilam. 'Dana was trying to move Susan to a more protected spot on the craft, but she was not quick enough.'

'Well, that is encouraging,' said the surgeon. 'I must return to her now.'

Matt slumped onto a large soft sofa and Jemma sat beside him. Werrimen pulled a chair in front of them and took hold of Matt's hands.

'Merrilam, you told Matt that Susan had been through a lot,' said Werrimen. 'What did you mean?'

'She was born in captivity before they left Earth, I believe,' said Merrilam. 'Dana told me that she received good care on Earth, but when they were taken to Yelteg, which is where we were incarcerated, our captors were not impressed at being landed with a human child. So, while Susan was fed and clothed, she was very aware that she was different from the other children and was made to feel unwelcome. I think I should explain this to you properly at another time. Dana is priority for all of us today.'

Jemma took hold of Matt's hand when she noticed him rub his eyes. He stared first at Merrilam, then at Susan, then steadfastly at the wall as though he was trying to erase any thoughts of his family's suffering from his mind.

A couple of hours passed before the surgeon returned.

'Dana is doing well. For the moment, we are keeping her unconscious to allow her body to recover. When we are sure that every organ and system is stable, we will bring her around, probably in the next couple of hours. You may see her for a few minutes.'

Jemma kept her arm around Matt as she walked with him to the bedside. 'She's got some colour back in her cheeks. She looks more comfortable.'

'Yeah,' replied Matt, with a sigh. 'Thanks.'

When they returned to the waiting room, Susan sat up and stared at her father. With some encouragement from Merrilam, she approached Matt, gently taking his hands in hers.

It was Jemma's turn to struggle to contain her tears. There could be no doubt this was Matt's child, as he drew her close. Maybe, at long last, Matt would find some peace with his wife and child by his side.

CHAPTER 6

Early the next morning, Jemma detoured to the hospital. Dana was now considered stable, but it was Matt who concerned Jemma. She didn't begrudge him the time to get his head around his wife's condition or his newfound responsibility for his seven-year-old daughter, a child he'd not previously met. As far as she was concerned, he could stay with Dana for the duration, but given the circumstances she suspected Werrimen would not allow that. They'd all passed their flight tests, but there was still a lot to learn, particularly once they started on the transport zone craft. Matt would need those skills too.

When she pushed open the door to Dana's hospital room, Matt didn't move. He was slumped in a chair, his gaze fixed on his wife, and he looked exhausted. Susan jumped when she saw Jemma, glaring ferociously before climbing onto Matt's knee. Perhaps the child was trying to protect her father or maybe she was seeking his protection. Jemma suspected it would be years before Susan would feel entirely safe, if that were ever to be possible. Merrilam smiled at Jemma, most likely recognising Susan's disquiet.

'Just popped in to see if any of you need anything,' said Jemma.

Matt and Merrilam both shook their heads. Susan continued to glare at her.

'I'm sorry,' said Matt. 'She's been through too much.'

'It's okay,' said Jemma. 'She's a little girl with no reason to trust me. All that matters is that she gets to know you. Everything else can happen over time.'

'Thanks,' said Matt, wiping something from his eye.

'I've got to go,' said Jemma. 'I'll come back later with news.'

Outside again, she took her time walking through the open square, reasonably confident that Ryan and his cronies wouldn't bother her there in broad daylight. She wanted to appear calm when she fronted Werrimen. Unable to delay any longer, she took a few deep breaths, then headed in to find out whatever it was that Werrimen had planned next.

'Good morning, everyone.' Werrimen looked up with, Jemma thought, a hint of annoyance. 'Now that you're all here, I have much to tell you. The transport zone craft is not yet ready for a flight, but it is sufficiently advanced that you can go inside to familiarise yourself with the controls and operating systems.'

Nik jumped up. 'We really are on our last leg of preparation to go home. I just can't believe it. We're nearly there.'

Werrimen smiled at her reaction. 'We will go to the factory now and work out a program for you. I know some of you are struggling with this. Keep in mind that we must all master these lessons. None of the Trustees who are involved with you have ever flown these craft either.'

Jemma slipped her arm through Sean's as they followed

Werrimen to the factory. 'You'll be fine. It's a big craft. You'll be better there than on the transporters.'

'It pisses me off that I can't get over it, but there it is,' said Sean. 'Don't worry, I'll do whatever I have to. The general used to always say, "keep your end-goal in mind." I can do that.'

'I know, and don't forget I'm there if you need support.'

'I won't. Jem, I'm thrilled that you've found something that excites you. If that's what you want to do when we get back, I'll back you all the way. I'd just rather not go with you.'

'I hope you'll get to a point that you won't feel like that but forget about it for now. We're here.'

'Oh, I get it. You were distracting me.' He turned to her before they reached the door and drew her into his arms. 'I love you so much. I don't know how I'd deal with any of this without you.'

Jemma laughed. 'You wouldn't even be here if you hadn't rescued me from that rainforest way back when. I'm sorry I've done this to you, but I'm not sorry I met you.'

Jemma and Sean were both smiling as they stepped up to the door, but they had to concentrate as Werrimen called them over to explain the entry measures. Security at the factory had been tightened and multiple barriers were now in place before they could get anywhere near the internal spacecraft hangar. Thankfully, the bead recognised them which enabled entry into the main foyer. Werrimen waited while they were each provided with a kind of magnetic key and a password generator which would change every few minutes.

They were told to hold the key against a dark bar beside the door, then quickly check for a password. If they didn't key it in within twenty seconds, they would be trapped in the secure compartment until security arrived.

Jemma's palms sweated as she used her key, and the password generator slipped out of her hand. She grabbed it and managed to input the password with just two seconds to spare. When the door finally opened, she almost fell into the next chamber. The final door was secured by another bead which, she'd been told, also retained an image as the person walked through. As they were required to proceed through one at a time, she then had to wait for the others.

Rather than stand around, she approached the nearly finished transport zone craft. It rested on a metal framework that resembled scaffolding. Ignoring everyone, she walked the length of the craft, taking in everything she could see. Most of its two hundred metre length was cylindrical and it was around fifteen metres in diameter, except for a section twenty metres from the front tip, where a large disc extended out horizontally, fifty metres either side of the cylinder. The height of the disc was the same as the cylinder and it looked like it held three levels.

In many ways it was similar to the Zant craft that had brought them here, although there were differences, some of them quite subtle. This craft was somehow cleaner. Windows were evenly spaced; the paintwork was consistent throughout; and there were no jagged bits hanging off the exterior. While the differences were largely cosmetic, they gave her a greater feeling of confidence that the Condonans had built a superior craft.

The crew were still hard at work on everything from the engines to the outer skin, even the doors and windows. This bright, shiny, new craft that was to get them home had felt like a fairy story while it was under construction, but now, parked in front of her, it was breath-taking. Sean wrapped his arm around her, but the look on his face suggested he didn't share her wonderment.

'Come on, Sean, let's go inside.' Turning, Jemma grabbed his arm and dragged him to the base of the craft to wait for the blue light.

Sean shook his head, but he didn't resist. The bottom floor was clearly the landing bay. It had eight segregated landing pads, each of which would hold two or three transporters. Emilrad, who she hadn't noticed join them, explained that each of the segments reflected a sector of the craft. Every individual sector could be locked down in an emergency. She already knew the sectors were a safety feature in case any part of the craft was disabled, but the thought that they might need to use them made her shudder.

Still dragging Sean along with her, she followed Werrimen onto the disc to head up to the second level which was set up for passengers. Cabins were arranged right around the outside of the disc, and the centre of the floor had multiple rows of comfortable-looking reclining lounge chairs, similar to those on all the IPL crafts.

The top floor was much more spartan. More than half of

it was taken up with the control room itself. Manual controls were more prominent here than in the usual spacecraft, but unlike other IPL craft there was no viewing window. Information used by the pilot came from equipment at the front of the craft which was then relayed to small navigation screens.

The only cabin on the control floor was for the ship's commander, who would not leave this level until the ship emerged from the transport zone. Tucked in the back were a lounge, an eatery, and a small dormitory which was essentially a row of stretcher beds that pilots and crew could use if needed. Mostly though, everyone other than the commander would retire to their own cabin on the middle level when they needed a break.

These craft weren't set up for the comfort of passengers, as they weren't expected to be in them for long. They'd be transferred to local craft near their destination, and the crew would move on to their next job.

Jemma didn't care about the lack of creature comforts. All that mattered now was that it would get them home. She chose not to dwell too much on the logistics of their proposed journey, even though Emilrad had painstakingly explained it to her.

The area that the IPL defined as the universe was divided into ten sectors. Condona and Sidlow were in sector one. Earth and Anders Major were in sector seven, which meant they had millions of light years through which they had to travel.

'Who's going to fly it?' Jemma ran her fingers over the

controls. They were different from the controls she'd come to know in other craft. It had to be a lot more complicated to fly.

'You are,' replied Werrimen.

'No way!' said Jemma, reeling back to stare at her. 'I'm champing at the bit to learn, but there's no way I could take charge yet.'

'You were all trained on spaceships so you would be ready to fly these once one was available. It soon will be.' She laughed at Jemma's reaction. 'Don't worry, you won't be by yourselves, but you must become proficient.'

'Can we do that in time?'

'Of course you can, if you believe in yourselves.' She turned on her heel and walked back to the entry point, leaving Jemma, Sean, Dan and Nik to stare after her.

'God, I wish she wouldn't do that,' muttered Dan.

'Guess we'd better follow her,' said Sean, 'find out what's coming next.'

'A Condonan crew will be here in one hour to commence your instruction,' said Werrimen, as they fell into step behind her. 'The first test flight is scheduled four weeks from today. It will be within Condona's atmosphere. The second test is a week later and will extend outside the atmosphere. If everything is positive, we will enter a transport zone and head for Earth two weeks after that.'

Jemma had to steady herself. 'Seven weeks. Are you saying we could be home in two months?'

'Provided everything goes to plan,' said Werrimen, 'that is exactly what I am saying.'

Jemma didn't have time to think much more about going home to Earth. Once the Condonan pilots arrived, the amount of information that flowed from them needed every bit of her concentration to absorb.

At the end of the day, Jemma's mind swam. By the time they were to take off for their first test flight, she had to understand every instrument, how to access the manual override if needed, how to manage the take-off and landing, how to control the thing mid-air, and how to handle any mishap that could potentially occur.

After floating down to the factory floor through the blue light, Jemma and the others stood staring at each other. No one spoke.

Werrimen waited for them, smiling. 'Are you ready to fly?'

'You can't be serious!' said Jemma. 'There's no chance any of us will be capable of flying that craft in a month.'

'Hmm. I do not accept that, Jemma. I expect you to succeed.'

Jemma shook her head. 'I want to, but I don't think we can do it.' Surely Werrimen didn't genuinely believe they could learn enough within a month, to actually fly the ship? She'd try her hardest, but there just wasn't enough time.

'Do not let me down, any of you,' said Werrimen, as she strode away.

Dan was first to find his voice. 'We can't afford to panic. I suspect she's just decided to push us to see how we deal with it. We're a great team when we work together. Let's show her what we're made of.'

Jemma reached up and kissed his cheek. 'You're more confident than I am, but I know you're right.' If he wasn't, they were in for a difficult time, and the last thing Jemma wanted was to face Werrimen to tell her she'd failed.

* * *

The flight education was gruelling, full of facts, demonstrations, questions and tests, but it was still a shock when, halfway through the third week, Werrimen handed Jemma a pre-flight checklist and told her she would be expected to demonstrate competence with it by herself, the next day. The thing was ten pages long and she had to memorise it.

Jemma could only stare at Werrimen. Perfection with less than twenty-four hours of study was impossible.

Sean took hold of her hand and led her away before she could object. 'It's okay. We can do this. We'll work together.'

'Oh God, Sean. I don't think I can.'

'Come on, Jem. We'll give it our best shot. If you go down, it won't be for the want of trying.'

'Of course I'll try ... but Jesus.' She felt sick to the stomach. She couldn't afford to fail, yet she wasn't at all convinced that she could meet Werrimen's expectations within the time frame.

Sean sat with her until late into the night, questioning her on every point. In the early hours of the morning, they decided they'd have to get some sleep, but she tossed and turned, worrying about all the things that could go wrong.

Jemma forgot to set her alarm and didn't wake until after 7:30 am. She yelled at Sean, who swore when he saw the time. They dressed and ran for the door. No time for breakfast. That would have to come later. It was a little after 8 am when they arrived.

'You are late. Have you slept, Jemma?' Werrimen stood with her arms folded in front of her chest.

'Sorry. I did get a couple of hours.'

Werrimen growled something and strode off.

Jemma wasn't given any time to settle down, but once she started, she fell into the swing of the exercise, and was almost through it before she stumbled. Her instructor tried to calm her. There were only four items left. She was aware of Sean, Dan and Nik doing their best to encourage her, but it didn't seem to help. She'd remembered to check the engines, the compressor for oxygen, the imaging equipment, but there was something else. Finally, she had to admit that she couldn't remember the last one. Her instructor waited a few more minutes, before telling her to ensure all doors, including the transporter bays were shut because even a tiny breach would almost certainly cause them to implode in the transport zone. Jemma cursed herself that she could have forgotten something so obvious. Sean pushed her outside to give her time to recover, but Werrimen stopped them.

'Did you pass?'

'Yes,' said Jemma, 'but I forgot the last item.'

'What would happen if you forgot that item before a real flight?'

'Potentially crash. I'm sorry, I tried very hard.'

'Sorry isn't good enough. You potentially killed a craft full of people.'

Jemma stared at her in disbelief, then ran out through the door.

* * *

Sean charged after Werrimen and shouted, 'She didn't kill a craft of people.' He felt himself losing control, but he couldn't stop. 'We told you we couldn't do this in time. You knew it was too much to ask. Your expectations are too high. You set her up to fail. None of us are as special as you think we are.'

He heard her sigh, but he couldn't cope with anymore either. Turning away, he walked quickly to the front of the factory. Outside, he leaned up against the wall, then slowly slid down into a squat. His head in his hands, he sensed Werrimen's presence before looking up. He was surprised by the concern in her eyes. Jemma's failure was his failure. He knew that. They were a team. He'd let her down, and that was something he'd promised himself he'd never do.

'You have ten minutes to cool down. Come to my office within that time.' As she walked away, she looked hunched. The normal spring in her step was absent. With no option but to pick himself up and follow her, he started walking. He'd have to front up some time. There was no point in delaying it. Perhaps he could find a way to make up for the failure.

Werrimen sat behind her desk and stared at him as he entered her office.

'I'm very sorry, we let you down, ma'am.'

'Yes, but more importantly, you've let yourselves down.'

'Yes ma'am.' His voice now was no more than a whisper.

'Do you know why I'm angry with you?' asked Werrimen.

'We failed. I should have worked harder to prepare Jemma.'

'No, I am pleased you understand that you failed as a team, but that is not why I am angry. Try again.'

'I let you down.'

'No,' replied Werrimen.

'I yelled at you.'

'All of those things are true, but they do not explain my anger.'

What else could it be? He'd failed and lost his temper. He hadn't ever before shouted at Werrimen nor, did he expect, he would ever do so again.

Werrimen sighed. 'You blamed me for pushing you too hard. You did not take responsibility for your own failure.'

'The responsibility is mine.' He dropped his head down. 'I'm sorry, I didn't realise I'd done that.'

'Yes, the responsibility is yours, and Jemma's. You are not just her husband, you are her superior on Earth, in your army, and must take more of the responsibility.'

'Yes, ma'am.'

'I appreciate you are in a very difficult situation, but you lost control. Is this what you do, when it gets too rough? You run away?'

'It could look that way,' said Sean, 'but no that isn't what I do. I snapped in the crisis. I'm sorry. You tell me I'm special and you've pushed me into situations that are so far out of my understanding that I don't have any idea how to deal with them. I don't have your capacity to adapt.'

'It is something we have all learnt,' said Werrimen. 'It did not come naturally to any of us, and all of us fail at times. Let me assure you that you are every bit as special as I believe you are, but you have to prove that to yourself, before you can prove it to me.'

'I will do my best.'

'It is up to me to ensure that you do.' Her shoulders were still hunched forward as though she carried a heavy weight. She didn't appear to want to do whatever it was she had planned.

'I am going to show you the consequences of your failure.' She placed her hands on his shoulders and while he had the normal warm feeling as she transferred her energy, there was something else. A series of visions floated through his mind, spaceships crashing, people screaming, torture on the faces of rescuers as they sifted through the ruins. He felt the physical pain of each of the victims in his own body. But worse, he felt, somewhere deep within his soul, the fear, the grief and the anguish of the rescue teams as people died around them.

After he left Werrimen's office, Sean found a quiet café. He needed time to sit and collect himself, to stop the trembling. No way would he ever throw another tantrum with Werrimen around, he wasn't even sure why he'd thrown the first one, probably exhaustion. But now he knew why the IPL Trustees were all so controlled with their emotions. He smiled to himself as he thought about disciplinary action in his own army. It normally involved extra work, hard exercise, or a senior officer swearing at you, but never anything like this. Still, there was no point in self-pity. He was in this situation now, and whatever happened, he had to find a way to lift himself and deal with it. He didn't want to go through that ever again.

'Are you feeling sorry for yourself, Sean?' He lifted his eyes to find Werrimen standing in front of him.

'No. I was to start with. Now I'm trying to work out how to raise myself above that and start again.'

'Good, I believe in you,' said Werrimen. 'In time, you will understand why.'

'Thank you. Can I ask you a question?'

'Of course. You know you can.'

'I don't want you to think I'm whinging, although it might sound that way,' said Sean. 'I need to understand why you've singled me out. Jemma failed. She's devastated, and I know she'll work on it until she gets it right, but you've left her alone. And you've left Nik and Dan alone. Why?'

'Do you want me to punish them too?' Werrimen leaned on the back of a chair and looked down at him.

'God, no,' exclaimed Sean. 'I need to understand why you're treating me differently.'

'Ah, I see. They will all answer to me, but our interaction is different. I try to make my response to every person appropriate for them, and you know that, at times, I have been even harder on Jemma. You are my Prehling, and I expect more of you than anyone else, including Jemma.'

Sean sighed. 'I'm sorry. It seems I'm being pulled fifty different ways at once, and my head can't seem to process it all.'

'Trust me a bit more, Sean. Ask me the questions, seek my help. We will get through this together.'

'Yes, ma'am.'

'Now get back to that factory and learn how to fly that ship. Do it properly this time.' Werrimen strode away, but this time he caught a glimpse of a smile before she turned her back.

He didn't hurry back to the factory, he wanted time to shake off the horrors Werrimen had shown him. As he walked back in, the Condonan instructor, flicked an appraising look at Sean, then smiled as though he knew what had happened with Werrimen. Condona hadn't been a member of the IPL before the fire, so the instructor wasn't a Trustee, but he seemed to know quite a lot about them. He informed Sean that once the pressure was off, Jemma had gone through the pre-flight procedure with no difficulty. Nik had been allocated the take-off and landing processes, to be tested the next day.

With only a few days left until the first test flight, Sean was acutely aware that they had to get on top of their game. Nik had to pass her test to Werrimen's satisfaction, and it was up to him to ensure she was ready. It was then that it sank in. Werrimen had just effectively placed him squarely back in the command position. So, for the rest of the afternoon and into the night, he had the whole group work together until he was satisfied that Nik knew all she needed to know to get through her test.

In the morning, Werrimen was already inside the craft waiting for the group to arrive. She listened while Nik was tested. It was easy to see that Nik was nervous, but Sean was determined not to let her falter. He stood beside her, reassuring her, while she ran through the procedures for the examiner. Towards the end, just as Jemma had done the previous day, Nik lost her train of thought. She looked like she was about to burst into tears, and there was no way he was going to have that happen, at least not in front of Werrimen.

'It's okay, Nik,' said Sean, turning her to look directly at him. 'Just think of the next step. You can do it. Remember we're a team. Focus on me. Ignore everyone else. You've got this. Now, what's the next step?'

'Jesus, Sean,' muttered Nik. 'I can't think.'

'Yes, you can. You're overthinking. Take a deep breath, shut your eyes, and let yourself relax.' He paused for a few seconds. 'Now, the last item was to call up the navigation screens. What's next?'

'Oh, I know. Check all the instruments are working.' Once she got that step, Nik gained in confidence and, with not much more encouragement, got through to the end.

'Well done,' said Werrimen, but she was looking at Sean as she turned on her heel and left.

Sean smiled at the collective sigh of relief. He called the group to gather around him. 'Alright, Dan got it right yesterday. We're a team. If any of us falter, someone else steps in. Deal?'

'Deal,' they responded together.

'The first test flight is scheduled for tomorrow,' said Sean. 'Let's all get some rest tonight and try to be fresh for that.'

'Yes, boss,' said Dan, although he made sure he was well out of the way when Sean threw a pretend punch.

'And don't you forget it.' Sean grinned as he walked out with Jemma. But the sentiment didn't pass him by. They'd all recognised he was again in charge, and it felt like a particularly heavy responsibility, given what they were training to do.

'Happy, Jem?' he murmured, as they left.

'Yeah, as happy as I can be. We'll get through this, Sean. One day we'll look back and wonder why we were so worried.'

He nodded. 'I suspect you're right. Let's go and check on Matt.'

'Agreed,' said, Jemma. 'I was planning to do that at some point this evening anyway.'

'Great.' He slipped his arm around her shoulders as they walked towards the hospital, surprised at how relaxed he felt, given the flight in a totally untested spacecraft was scheduled for the next day. He stood in the doorway to Dana's hospital room, his arm still around Jemma. He'd have liked to bring flowers, but they didn't seem to do that on Condona. He held his finger to his lips as Jemma went to move around him. Susan was curled up beside Dana on the bed and both were asleep. Matt sat beside with his head on the bed covers and his arm wrapped around both his girls.

Somehow, seeing Matt like that, with his wife and daughter, made Sean realise how much Jemma mattered to him and how lucky he was that they were together again. It could have all turned out so differently. 'We'd better go,' he whispered. 'God, they look good. What a fabulous end to that terrible story.'

Dan and Nik met them on the way out, so he turned them around and led them to a small café he knew, not far from the hospital building. They spent a good hour enjoying a meal as the family that they were. By the time they left, all four were more relaxed than he'd seen any of them for a long time.

CHAPTER 7

When Sean assembled his team at the factory for the first test flight, he found Werrimen pacing around the base of the craft, issuing instructions to the Condonan crew. They were listening politely, although it was obvious they didn't feel the need for her advice. It sank into Sean then that Werrimen was as stressed as the rest of them. She also had to wait through the tests to find out whether or not this craft would hold up to the pressure of space and be good enough to take them all the way to Earth and reunite her with Zadrus, her life partner.

One of the Condonan pilots invited the group to come on board. Two other Condonans, who Sean didn't recognise, were already there and ready to commence the pre-flight procedures.

'Your role today is to listen and learn,' said Werrimen, pointing to a row of chairs behind the pilots.

Sean nodded. He was happy to be an observer on this first flight, no doubt he'd be out of his depth if there was a major problem. Hell, he was out of his depth even being there, and given the silence in his group, he suspected the others probably felt the same.

'Please watch the screens and notify me if you see any-thing of concern,' said Werrimen. 'I have been advised this morning that two Zant craft have been sighted just outside the declared Condonan air space. They have not attempted to enter but have not responded to signals from IPL craft either.'

'Then, why are they there?' asked Jemma.

'We do not know. It is possible they are just curious to see if our craft will fly, but we are all on alert.'

Sean sat rigidly in his chair as the pilot commenced the lift-off, not at all happy with this latest piece of information. His only experience of a transport zone craft was the one the Zants had used when they'd abducted him. That craft had rattled and shaken from the moment it started to move, but this craft, as it lifted into the atmosphere, was distinctly different. The Condonan workmanship was clearly superior. Perhaps it was that the skill of the pilots was superior, but in any case, this flight was far more comfortable than anything he'd been subjected to by the Zants.

He was aware that the Condonans didn't intend to go outside their planet's atmosphere on this maiden flight, but nobody had mentioned the manoeuvres they planned to use to test both the engine and the controls. Sean clutched the edge of his seat when the pilot dived vertically down. Jemma and Dan, on either side, both had a hand on one of his arms, but he couldn't take a breath until the craft had levelled out. His relief was enormous when the pilots announced that they were about to head back down. Once on the ground he jumped down as quickly as he could, happy to plant his feet back on the solid surface.

'That was a very good test,' said Werrimen, smiling at Sean. 'Tomorrow the test will go outside Condona's atmosphere. Two of you will be designated as pilots. The Condonan pilots who flew today will stand behind you and provide direction should it be needed. Sean and Nikola, you will undertake the pre-flight procedures and navigation. Dan and Jemma will take command and manage communications. Are we all clear?' She didn't wait for an answer.

Sean forced himself to focus. He was determined not to let Werrimen down again, so he ordered the team to reassemble at his house to revise the protocols and procedures. He didn't miss the look that passed between Nik and Jemma but decided it was best to let it go. They were much more confident than he but getting the team to operate as a coherent unit and not leave any room for criticism was his responsibility. Werrimen had made that abundantly clear.

Next morning, Sean commenced the pre-flight procedure with Nik an hour before the second flight was scheduled to lift off. They really didn't need the pilot who was on hand to supervise, but it was comforting to have him there. Once they'd checked and cleared all the systems, the new spacecraft was declared ready for its first flight outside the atmosphere. Sean had been informed that a dedicated controller would be in the Condonan operations centre to take their flight instructions and to assist should there be a problem. Even so, he was happy that Dan and Jemma were in the pilots' seats.

Standing behind Jemma, as he'd been instructed, a slight jolt on take-off made him grab the back of her chair.

'It is fine,' said Werrimen. 'Such movements are normal in this kind of craft. Their design is very different from the spaceships you are used to.'

Sean smiled. *Spaceships he was used to.* Hell, he hadn't known spaceships existed until a couple of years ago. He forced himself to focus on everything that Dan and Jemma did, very aware that it would be his turn tomorrow. After the initial jolt, the flight was smooth. Instruments all worked well, and their Condonan instructor was happy with the controls. Sean had begun to relax as they levelled off at 50,000 feet, still well within Condona's atmosphere, until it was announced that they were about to move outside. Still holding onto the back of Jemma's chair, he stared rigidly at the screen, praying that nothing would go wrong.

'It is only for a few minutes, Sean,' said Werrimen, quietly. 'It is the ultimate test, to be sure that we will be ready for the transport zone.'

'I'm fine,' he snapped, annoyed at his own reaction. He'd been into space often enough now to know that he was safe, yet he couldn't get that innate fear out of his head. Impressed by how well Jemma was managing in the pilot's seat, he forced himself to focus on her.

Werrimen was true to her word. Ten minutes in space satisfied the pilots that the craft would stand up to the pressure and they turned back towards Condona. After they landed, he suggested to the others that they meet in the café where they'd had dinner the previous night. It was just a short walk from there to the hospital, so he could visit Matt afterwards to check on his progress before going home, but he'd only just completed his meal when Werrimen's face popped up on his communicator, calling him to join her in her office. It was clear she wanted to talk to him alone, so he walked briskly across, despite his trepidation at what she was about to come up with now.

'Good evening, Sean,' she said cheerfully, as he entered, but the look on her face belied her words. 'I would like to talk to you about Matt. I visited him in the hospital after our return. Dana is doing very well. Susan is starting to form an attachment to him too, which is a delight to see.'

'Yes, they seem to be progressing well,' said Sean. 'But there's something else.'

'I am concerned,' said Werrimen. 'Matt is terrified to leave his family. For the first few days he would not leave the hospital. Merrilam cared for Susan overnight and brought her back in the morning. Now he is at least taking Susan home, but he is at the hospital every waking hour.'

'That's understandable after all he's been through,' said Sean. 'What is it that has you worried?'

'It is not that I do not understand.' Werrimen sighed. 'But, if we allow this to go on too long, his fear of leaving Dana might take over. We must get him back into a more normal pattern for his own sake. Our flight back to Earth is not far away and he is going to have to manage Dana and Susan through that flight, no matter what we encounter.'

'Matt has asked Merrilam to come with them,' said Sean, 'which would be a big help if she's happy to do that.'

'She has told me that she is considering it,' said Werrimen. 'Even so, he must play a role in helping his family through the flight. I would prefer to see him lift himself enough to participate with your team, either in navigation or communications, but first he must regain his self-confidence.'

'Okay, I get what you're saying,' said Sean. 'It's about him. But Werrimen, his fear of losing them again has to be astronomical.'

'Agreed, yet he must move past that.' Werrimen sighed again. 'Allowing him to wallow in self-pity will not help him in the future. He will hate us for pushing, but that will pass. Eventually, he will understand.'

'I guess that means you want me to have a quiet chat with him.'

'I think that would be best. On Earth, you will again be his commander. He may accept direction better from you than he will from me. If he resists you, I will intervene and let him turn his anger on me rather than you, which would be preferable.'

'Understood,' said Sean. 'It's up to me to get him going.'

Werrimen stood and walked around her desk to stand in front of Sean. 'I am pleased to hear you say that. I will be there if you need me, and I fear you might. It is only a few weeks now and we will be back on Earth.'

'That's so hard to comprehend,' said Sean. 'Alright, I'll tackle Matt now.'

But Sean realised as he left Werrimen that something had subtly changed. She'd directed his thoughts back to his leadership role with his team, perhaps a reminder that his responsibilities would expand once more. Clever, but daunting all the same. Pushing everything out of his head except Matt, he strode towards the hospital, wondering what General Hunt would do in this situation.

In Dana's hospital room he found a similar scenario to the previous night, but this time he interrupted, gently touching Matt on the shoulder.

Matt rubbed his eyes as he raised his head. 'Hello, Sean. Sorry, just dosed off. What's happening?'

'Pretty much everything,' said Sean, doing his best to smile. He wanted to keep this as low key as possible, and outside would be best, so he pointed to the door. 'We need to talk. I don't want to disturb Dana.'

'Yeah, sure.'

Sean found a lounge chair away from any other visitors and sat, pointing to the chair opposite for Matt. 'How's it all going with Dana?'

'Good. Long way to go though,' said Matt. 'They assure me she's going to pull through. She doesn't say anything, but I can see pain in her face. It's going to be a long road.'

'God, mate,' said Sean, putting his hand on Matt's shoulder. 'I can't even imagine what she's going through. Or you, for that matter. How's Susan coping?'

'She's amazing,' Matt's face lit up in a way Sean hadn't seen since they'd found Dana. 'It's like she's known me all her life, which, of course, she should have. I'll do anything to get those bastards. I can't stop wondering how many more Danas and Susans are out there. It was going on for years on Earth, and the IPL investigators tell me on dozens of other planets too.'

Sean saw his opening. 'I've been told the same. Mate, we're all committed to the fight and I want you there beside me. Is that where you want to be?'

'Damned right I do. As soon as we get back to Earth and I've got Dana settled, I'll be right into it.'

'You've no idea how it pleases me to hear you say that, but I'd like to see you start to do a few things now. Dana's getting the best of care and Merrilam will look after Susan. Even a few hours a day would let me get you up to speed.'

'Fucking hell, Sean. I'm so scared to leave her. What if she took a turn for the worse?'

'Mate, that much I do understand. Do you remember what I told you about rescuing Jemma from a bushfire? Bloody Pritchard damn near killed her. I was terrified to leave her bedside. General Hunt forced me too, and bit by bit, I realised it was the best thing he could have done.'

'Are you going to force me, Sean?' Matt stared back at him, steel glinting through his eyes.

'Don't want to,' said Sean, with a sigh. 'Here's my proposal. We're going on our second training flight tomorrow. I'd like you to join us on that flight, just to get a feel for it. Two or three hours is all it should take. Then you can come straight back here.'

'And if I say no?'

'Then I might have to pull rank, but I'd rather you were happy about it.'

Matt leaned back in his seat, closed his eyes and sighed. 'I don't suppose a couple of hours could hurt.'

'Fantastic. Be at the factory at 8 am.'

'Yeah. Alright, I'll be there,' said Matt. 'You're as manipulative as the old man.'

Sean laughed. 'I'll take that as a compliment. He was a good teacher.'

Leaving the hospital, Sean turned to head towards home, presuming that Jemma would have done the same, so he was surprised to find her seated outside. 'Hi, sweetheart. You didn't have to wait for me.'

'Yeah, I did. After Werrimen called you, I thought something was up. Did she tell you to reel Matt in?'

Sean nodded. 'That was the gist of it. I want to ease him back in though. Hopefully, she'll be happy with that. He's agreed to come with us on the test flight tomorrow. Just to observe, and then straight back to the hospital. Seemed reasonably happy about it.'

'Did you ask or order?'

'I asked,' he said, a bit disappointed that she had to check, 'but I think he understood that if he didn't do as we agreed that it would turn into an order.'

She smiled as she slipped her hand into his. 'You've changed.'

'Yeah, I'm aware of that. Werrimen's been pushing me for

a while. I'm not sure if I'm happy with it, but I guess that's what's going to happen when we get home anyway.

'Okay, boss. Let's make the most of the bit of freedom we've got while we can,' said Jemma, laughing. She took off, running, towards their house.

Sean had no choice but to give chase.

* * *

Jemma woke to light filtering through the roof. She had to untangle herself from the sheets and ease out from under Sean's arm, which was draped across her. Rubbing her eyes, she reached down to check her watch and squealed.

'Sean, wake up!' She shook him hard when all he did was groan. 'Damn it, Sean, wake up.'

'What's the emergency?' he growled.

'It's 7:30 am,' she cried. 'We're late again.'

'Holy snapping duck shit!' He jumped out of bed and grabbed his clothes.

'No need to swear at me,' she growled, throwing a pillow at him.

'Wasn't swearing at you. I was swearing with you. There's a difference. You get in the shower. I'll find something for breakfast. We'll have to eat on the run.'

'Yes, boss,' she muttered.

'Cut the crap. We're late.'

'I think *I* told you that.' Jemma picked up her clothes and brushed past him into the bathroom. 'Don't forget, I'm the one who has to fly that damned thing today.' She didn't add that she was secretly excited about her chance to get into the pilot's seat and test herself. It was fast becoming her dream to learn to fly every kind of craft the IPL could throw at her.

He muttered something she didn't hear, so she glared back at him and kept going. Once she'd showered, she ate the pre-prepared block that Sean had put on the table. They were the staple food on Condona, much like an energy bar on Earth, although they tasted a lot better. She scoffed down the hot drink of Target, hoping it would give her enough of a lift to get going, then ran out the door as soon as Sean was ready, and jogged with him towards the factory, aware that he'd slowed his pace for her. Without Hunt's perpetual demands for fitness training, she'd slackened off and had lost quite a bit of her speed. She guessed that would have to pick up again when they got back to Earth.

They arrived at 8:01 to a disapproving look from Werrimen, but nothing was said and they were directed into the transport zone craft.

Jemma was thrilled to be greeted by Matt who was already inside. She ran to him and pulled him into a hug. 'It's so good to see you.'

'Thanks, mate. I'm a bit shaky being away from Dana, but she should be okay.'

'She will.' Jemma didn't have time to say more as Werrimen ordered her to the pilot's chair, beside Dan who was already seated, to get prepared.

Sean and Nik set about the pre-flight checks, but Jemma

looked around anxiously for their Condonan instructors. Her breath hitched when the thought crossed her mind, for one dreadful moment, that they might have been left to their own devices for this flight until she suddenly caught sight of them talking to Werrimen.

'Yeah, I thought the same,' said Dan, with a twinkle in his eye.

'Thought what?' She didn't think she'd get away with feigning innocence, but it was worth a try.

'That they'd dumped us and run,' said Dan.

'As if they'd do that,' said Jemma.

'No, they wouldn't. Concentrate now, we're not far off starting. You take communications to start. We'll swap later.'

'Sure thing, boss.' She looked at him and smiled. Sean was openly resuming command, but she suspected that Dan, without his conscious realisation, was doing the same thing. She didn't mind. Despite what everyone said, she didn't see herself as a leader and didn't really want to be cast in that role.

Sean's voice broke into her thoughts. 'Pre-flight checks completed. Ready to go.'

She turned to the screens that floated in front of her, checked her coordinates then spoke into the main communicator. 'Transport Zone Craft, Earth 1 to Condonan Control, seeking permission to depart.'

'Emilrad to Earth 1. You are cleared for lift-off.'

'Proceeding now.' She looked at Dan. 'You can go, boss.'

'"Sir" would do just fine,' he murmured.

'In your dreams, brother-in-law.' Jemma laughed when

he screwed up his nose, but he was instantly serious as he focussed on the lift-off. Although everything was essentially automatic, half the control desk was taken up with manual controls. They had to be able to switch over, and quickly, if they got into the transport zone and something went wrong.

He provided the coordinates that he'd been given for the first stage of the flight, then sat back and glared at her while she did her best to appear demure and ready to obey orders.

'Problem, boss?' she murmured, as sweetly as she could muster.

'You do realise things will change once we get home, don't you?' asked Dan.

'I do, but I also realise how much I've changed. I won't knuckle under quite so readily.'

'God, Jem. Don't set yourself up,' replied Dan. 'The general will be really pissed off at what's happened, not just to us but all those missing people. He's going to want us to shape up and to get things moving pretty quickly. Might have already started.'

'Probably has, but that doesn't mean I have to go along with him. He won't let Sean be my boss, or you, or even Matt. So, I don't fit in. Maybe I'd be better placed with the IPL.'

'Maybe. We'll see when we get there.'

'Do not plan ahead,' said Werrimen. She'd moved in quietly behind them. 'Whatever is happening on Earth is irrelevant right now. Our attention must be on this flight. Check with Emilrad that we are cleared to leave the atmosphere.'

Jemma dutifully obeyed, then looked up a Werrimen. 'Do we always need permission to go outside the atmosphere?'

'No, this is a training flight so we must be in close contact with the controller at all times. They are also checking for any unapproved craft out there. You may now change roles. Jemma, you will take the controls.'

After giving the order to go higher, Jemma sat back and watched, fascinated, as Condona seemed to shrink below them. She was aware from her previous training that they were about to enter the level that contained most of the space junk from the millennia of flights in this sector. She concentrated on searching for any speck in the distance that could mean trouble, aware that Dan was doing the same thing. A few items headed towards them, but nothing of concern. With no further direction from Werrimen or the pilots, when she reached the designated height she allowed the craft to flow into an orbital pattern.

Matt had been sitting behind her since they'd lifted off, but now he came forward and pointed to the screen. 'What's that?'

'Don't know,' she murmured. 'I only noticed it a few seconds ago. It's not moving in the same direction as the other stuff. Would you call Werrimen for me, please? Dan, can you enhance it?'

'No, ma'am,' he said, grinning. 'Not yet. We'll have to get closer to get a decent image on the screen. At the moment, it seems to be moving away from us.'

'Yes,' said Werrimen. 'That is definitely something that

is under conscious control. It is not a random object. Dan, notify Emilrad please. Ask for a security vessel to investigate.'

'Jesus,' muttered Matt. 'Don't tell me it's another prison ship.'

Werrimen shook her head. 'Do not jump to conclusions. There is no way of knowing what it is yet.'

'Of course we do. Those bastards are at it again.'

'Matthew,' said Werrimen, firmly. 'Return to your seat. We will investigate.'

Jemma turned back and fixed her eyes to the screen. She noticed Dan do the same. She'd hadn't heard Werrimen use Matt's full name before.

'Another ship approaching us from below,' said Dan. 'Would that be ours?'

Werrimen leaned over to enhance the screen. 'Yes, it is ours.'

'Are we going with it?' asked Jemma.

'No, that is not our role.'

'We did investigate when we found Dana's ship,' said Jemma.

'Yes. That was because there were no other ships in the vicinity. We are close to Condona, so we will leave it to them to investigate. I am happy with our flight today. You may head back down now, Jemma, and land the vessel.'

Jemma noticed Dan frown, but she waited for Werrimen to move out of hearing range before she spoke. 'What's up?'

'You got more flying time than me. Now you're going to land it.'

She laughed. 'Are you jealous? Don't forget, you got to take off and did the first part of the flying.'

'You took it out of the atmosphere. Now you're going back in and landing as well,' muttered Dan.

'Stop pouting,' said Jemma. 'You can do all the flying next time.'

She didn't have time to worry any further about his little tantrum because as she re-entered the atmosphere, she saw another flying craft. It seemed, at first, to be a simple transporter, but as it came closer she realised it was a Norellian sphere. The type that Frederick Pritchard flew.

'Oh Jesus! Werrimen, quickly!' Jemma yelled.

Dan was already on the communicator to the controller.

'By all the stars,' said Werrimen. 'What is that doing here?'

'Don't know,' said Jemma, 'but it's coming our way.'

'I've notified Emilrad,' said Dan. 'He said security will be here in a few minutes.'

'Yes, we must stay calm.' Werrimen leaned over to enhance the image. 'Definitely Norellian. Many planets have these, not just Anders. However, we do know there are people here from Anders. Security will intercept and find out. Maintain a holding pattern until then.'

Just three minutes later, two security transporters from Condona raced between the transport zone craft and the sphere.

'Continue to hold,' said Werrimen.

A few more tense minutes followed, then two additional transporters arrived and took up positions in front and behind their ship.

'You are cleared to go now,' said Werrimen. 'Follow the lead transporter.'

Jemma gave directions to her control panel to follow the transporter. She wondered if she should have shifted into manual control, but the ship seemed to respond. It was with great relief that she set the craft down, and as she did the security transporters took off at high speed, she presumed to help chase the sphere. Once the craft was powered down and the controls secured, she accepted Sean's hand to stand and then maintained a grip on him as they floated down in the blue light.

'You okay?' asked Sean, leaning close to her, so only she could hear.

'Yeah, a bit shaken, but fine,' replied Jemma.

'I shouldn't say this,' said Sean, 'but I'm glad it wasn't me in charge.'

Jemma smiled. 'You'd have done exactly what I did. I was grateful Werrimen was there, but I realised then that we're never going to be asked to do any of this without her, or Emilrad, or someone like them alongside. Despite all the bluff, they recognise we're not ready.'

'You're right,' said Sean. 'I'm just going to check on Matt.'

Jemma looked up to see Matt still standing almost directly underneath the craft and looking as though he might pass out. 'I'll join you.'

Sean looked back and nodded. 'Matt, I think you should join us in Werrimen's office so we can find out together what those craft were.'

'We know what they were.'

'No, we actually don't,' said Sean. 'You're surmising. Let's get the reports.'

'Yeah, fine.' Matt marched off towards Werrimen's office.

Jemma followed, her arm intertwined with Sean's. Dan and Nik trailed behind them.

Werrimen waved them in but continued to speak to someone on her communicator. When she shut it down, she sighed, 'The transporter that came close to us was a Norellian sphere of the type used by Anders Major. The ship you saw in the distance was also of a type used by Anders, but ...' She held up her hand as Matt went to interrupt. 'But many other planets use the same sort of spaceship, so we cannot be sure. However, the sphere that approached our craft managed to evade security and was taken in by the Anders style spaceship. They set a course to Ailazant and were escorted by two Zant craft. Our security crafts had to let them go. As you know we cannot enter Ailazant's air space, and we were not prepared to shoot them down.'

'We know Pritchard's in bed with the Zants,' said Jemma, 'so, the most likely scenario is that it was an Anders Major spaceship.'

'I agree,' said Werrimen. 'Matt, I am sorry that your first flight in the transport zone craft was marred by such an event. If you can put that aside for a moment, how did you find the flight?'

'I was actually enjoying it until then,' said Matt. 'But those bastards wrecked everything. How can you be sure they won't try to blast us out of the sky on the way home?'

'You have great fear in you, Matthew. I understand why, but we must move beyond that.' Werrimen turned to the others. 'We will have another practice flight tomorrow. Jemma and Dan will take pre-flight procedures. Sean and Nikola, you will be pilot and communications. Go back to the factory now and familiarise yourselves with every aspect of the craft. Emilrad will help you. Matt, stay with me, please.'

'I have to get back to the hospital,' snapped Matt.

'Yes, you do, but you need to speak to me first.'

Jemma led the way out, suspecting that Matt was about to melt down. As she walked through the door, she heard Werrimen instruct him to place his hands on hers.

Jemma hoped with all her heart that he would accept Werrimen's help, but she didn't have time to think about it as Dragile intercepted her.

'Jemma, I would like to speak to you about the Norellian Sphere,' said Dragile. 'What is your worst fear about it?

Jemma shuddered. 'Surely Pritchard isn't here?'

'I see,' replied Dragile. 'Come to my office. We will discuss the possibilities and how to deal with this.'

CHAPTER 8

After she left Dragile, Jemma couldn't decide if she was excited, nervous, apprehensive or just desperate to get started. He'd helped her come to grips with the fact that if Pritchard were around, she would have all the might of the IPL to deal with him. Her focus had to be on the test flight which was to happen at 8 am the next morning. She was to be in charge of the pre-flight procedures. Dan had been told to stand back. Dragile had agreed with her that Werrimen was most likely testing her to make sure she could stand up to the pressure.

Sean was to be first pilot and Matt was to sit beside him with Nik as navigator and on communications. Matt had been told to remain working with Sean so that by the end of the day he'd have received some knowledge of all the roles. Jemma assumed that was another spoke in the wheel of turning Sean back into their commander.

Although Sean set the alarm, neither of them could sleep. Around 5 am, Jemma decided she'd had enough and headed for the shower. When she came out, Sean had fixed her a hot drink of target and put out some breakfast food cubes.

'It's early,' said Sean, 'but I think we should make sure we get adequate nourishment before this flight.'

'Are you worried that Norellian sphere might try to intercept us again?' asked Jemma.

'Yeah, a bit. I know Werrimen's planning something to stop them, but I don't know what that'll involve. I'd like to be alert and ready if anything does happen.'

'Okay. We've just got to get through it.' Jemma was fairly confident that whatever Werrimen organised would keep them safe, but who knew what these rebels might get up to next? The whole group would have to be on full alert for their own safety.

It was just after 6 am when Jemma suggested they head out. That way they could take their time getting to the factory, and hopefully be more relaxed when the time came to commence the test flight. She wasn't surprised to find Dan and Nik already there and waiting. But Matt was nowhere to be seen.

'Do you reckon he's coming?' she whispered to Sean.

'I think he will. He won't want to get on the wrong side of Werrimen.'

'Or you for that matter,' she whispered, laughing.

'Yep, or me. If he's not here by 7:30, I'll go looking.'

'Hope you don't have to.'

'So do I,' said Sean. 'Let's go back through the safety procedures while we wait.'

Jemma groaned. She felt like telling him to go away, but she knew that he had to assert his leadership, so she went through all ten points with Dan and Nik standing beside her, ready to help fill in the gaps. Fortunately, there weren't any, and even Sean seemed relieved.

It was already 7:30 by the time Sean was satisfied that everyone was ready for their first task, although Jemma suspected it was more to do with his own uncertainty than any real concern about the capacity of the others.

'Sean,' she said quietly. 'I think you might need to find Matt.'

'Yeah, I guess.' He sighed. 'I just hope I don't have to be hard on him.'

'I know, but if you don't push him, Werrimen will, and I suspect she'll be a whole lot harder.'

Sean nodded and left.

Jemma chatted to Dan and Nik while she waited, but it didn't allay her fear for Matt's welfare.

'Guess who I found lurking outside,' said Sean, as he returned. Matt walked alongside him, looking sheepish.

'I couldn't get the password right,' said Matt. 'Just as well Sean came looking or I think I'd be in the slammer by now.'

'Doubt it,' said Jemma. 'It's good to see you, Matt. Ready for the big test?'

'No, not really,' said Matt. 'I doubt anyone could really be ready, but given it's our only way home we just need to get on with it.'

She smiled, thinking he sounded better than he had for some time. 'Is everything organised for Dana and Susan?'

'It is. We checked it all out yesterday, and there's a full medical team coming with us. Hopefully, they won't get stuck on Earth for too long. Apparently, the craft will wait until the engineers have trained enough people to build both the factory and the spacecraft before they return to Condona.'

Sean called them over, so any further questions for Matt had to wait.

'Everyone inside,' said Sean. 'Take up your positions. We need to be ready to go when Werrimen gets here.'

'I suspect she's waiting until eight o'clock to avoid stressing us,' said Nik.

Sean nodded. 'You're probably right. So, let's be ready and prove to her that we're capable of this.'

Jemma was pleased to see Sean's confident presentation, but she knew that inside his fear hadn't abated and probably never would. She waited next to the entry for Werrimen and the experienced pilots to come up through the blue light, so she could begin the safety checks and hand over to Sean.

'Good morning, everyone,' said Werrimen. 'Are we ready to proceed?'

'We are,' said Sean.

Nik contacted control to request permission to leave. For the first time, it was the formal Condonan control that answered. Apparently, this was no longer just a simple exercise managed by Emilrad. Sean took off smoothly, going straight outside Condona's atmosphere, as he'd been directed. Jemma looked over his shoulder, surprised to see multiple Condonan and IPL craft around them, and suspected that both Dragile and Emilrad had been diverted to that task.

'We are taking no chances,' said Werrimen, as she edged in beside Jemma. 'You must all be alert for anything that is out of place.'

'On that note, I can see something in the distance on my screen,' said Nik. 'It doesn't seem to be moving randomly. It could be a craft.'

'I agree,' said Werrimen. 'What should you do?'

Sean jumped in before she could answer. 'Nik, notify Condonan control. Werrimen, is there any way we can contact our escorts?'

'Good thinking, Sean. Nikola, use the Condonan security frequency and send out a warning.'

'Ma'am, what if the approaching craft is antagonistic to us and they hear the warning?' asked Dan.

'That is a possibility,' said Werrimen. 'I do not think it matters. Their approach is quite brazen, so there are three possibilities: one, they don't care; two, they are a decoy, and the real attack is coming from elsewhere; three, they are not the enemy.'

Dan nodded and waited while Nik sent out the warning. She'd just finished when her equipment indicated an incoming message.

'It's not ours,' said Nik. 'Werrimen, I'm having trouble clearing the screen. They're trying to send an image through. I just can't quite get it.'

One of the Condonan pilots sat beside her and fiddled with the controls. 'Coming through,' he called.

Jemma, Dan and Matt crowded in behind Sean. The screen, which was relatively small by IPL standards, sat horizontally on Nik's console.

As the image cleared, Jemma cried out. 'No ... No ... It

can't be. Please God, tell me it isn't.' She clutched the back of Sean's chair.

'Fredrick Pritchard,' spat Dan.

'How the hell could he have got here?' demanded Sean.

'We know that he is cavorting with the Zants,' said Werrimen. 'Everyone be quiet now and hear what he has to say.'

'Good morning, ladies and gentlemen,' said Pritchard. 'I believe one of my people advised you that you would not be permitted to return to Earth.'

'That threat was made,' said Sean.

'My colleagues from Ailazant assure me that they can stop you leaving, and if you sneak past them they can intercept you in the transport zone.'

'Go on,' replied Sean.

'It is in your interests to stay on Condona. If you agree to transfer all my people to my custody, I will leave you in peace so long as you do not attempt to leave.'

'One moment, I will confer with my colleagues.' Sean requested one of the Condonan pilots to take his seat, then beckoned his team and Werrimen to follow him to the other side of the control room which he thought would be far enough away to avoid being seen or heard by Pritchard. 'How do I respond?'

'We cannot acquiesce to his demands,' said Werrimen. 'However, we must find out whether he can intercept us within the zone. I did not think that was possible, so I must seek advice.'

'I can't take that risk,' said Matt, 'not with my wife and child on board.'

'Yes, Matt, I understand,' said Werrimen. 'Please give me the time to investigate his threat. In the meantime, I am going to suggest a counterproposal. Offer to take his people with us. We will say they may then be returned to Anders Major from Earth. We will, of course, detain and treat them on Earth.'

'So you want to offer something that we wouldn't consider doing?' exclaimed Jemma.

'In the immediate sense, yes,' replied Werrimen. 'If we can work out how to help them recover their memories, then we could return them to Anders Major. In just won't happen straight away.'

'I guess that's fair enough,' said Jemma. 'And that would force him to ensure our safety too.'

Sean looked at both women. 'I doubt he'll accept it. What's my fallback?'

Werrimen stared at him for a moment. 'All his people on Condona will be rounded up and spend the rest of their lives in an IPL prison.'

'Dear God,' muttered Jemma.

Werrimen sighed. 'I do not like this any more than you do, however I must consider not just your safety but the future risk to the people of Condona. I cannot leave these people free if they are going to be an ongoing threat.'

'Okay,' replied Sean, with a shrug. 'Let's go do it.'

Jemma smiled as he walked back to the console, his back straight and his head held high. His penetrating gaze would make most people back down. The problem was that Pritchard wasn't most people.

As he took his seat back from the Condonan pilot, Sean leaned forward to make sure that he would be seen by the other craft. 'Alright, Mr Pritchard, here is what I propose. We will take all your people back to Earth with us. They can be returned to Anders Major from there.'

'Don't be ridiculous,' snapped Pritchard. 'I will not allow you, or your people, to get hold of my people.'

Jemma stared intently at the screen and was quite sure that Pritchard still believed he had the upper hand.

'That is your choice Mr Pritchard,' said Sean. 'If you do not agree to my proposal, the IPL will round up all your people and they will be incarcerated in an IPL prison for the rest of their lives. It is your choice.'

'You would not dare,' snapped Pritchard. 'Your IPL insists on trials and transparency.'

'Yes,' said Sean. 'Under most circumstances that is true. However, these circumstances are not normal and will require extraordinary measures. As I understand it, the IPL has already started to identify your people and is about to commence taking them into custody anyway. They already have Lena and, I believe ...' He looked up at Werrimen who nodded, 'Yes, they have also located the man who identified himself as Ryan. It is your choice whether they come with us or are transported to an IPL prison.'

Jemma was impressed by Sean's capacity to maintain his composure during this exchange. She was quite sure that he shared her anxiety and wouldn't be at all comfortable to trust Pritchard no matter what he promised.

It took some time for Pritchard to respond, and he appeared to be conferring with someone in the background. 'I will consider your proposal,' he said, finally.

'Thank you,' replied Sean, with no hint of fear in his voice. 'Would you kindly remove your craft now so that we can continue our test flight?'

'I will contact you tonight.' The image on the screen snapped off and Pritchard's craft moved away at high speed.

Werrimen signalled to them to say nothing as she asked the Condonan pilots to take over and ushered the crew from Earth out of the control room. 'What do you think?'

'Have you found Ryan?' asked Dan, frowning.

'I do not believe so,' said Werrimen.

Jemma shook her head. 'Any prisoners belong to Condona, and rightly so. Will the Condonans be prepared to allow us to take them if Pritchard agrees?'

Werrimen nodded. 'The fate of the Anders prisoners, including Lena, has been discussed with the Condonan council. We are all in agreement that it would be better for Condona if the Anders prisoners were to be taken off their planet and either returned to Anders or taken to a neutral facility. Emilrad will contact them again to ensure that agreement stands.'

'So they're expecting us to take most of the Anders people with us, anyway?' asked Jemma.

'That is my impression. We must accept that a strong IPL

contingent will have to accompany us if we are to take the rebels. Be aware that no matter what we promise Pritchard, my people will not simply release the prisoners when we get back to Earth. We will attempt to deprogram them, and hopefully enable them to make up their own minds as to where they want to be. The Condonan Council is aware of our plans.'

'Understood,' said Jemma, 'but Pritchard won't accept that.'

'He will be asked to join us when we get there to discuss the matter. I agree he will be angered by our move and may attempt an attack. That is why we will need the IPL contingent with us.'

'Dear God, will we ever be rid of him?' muttered Jemma.

'I certainly hope so,' said Werrimen. 'In the meantime, we must act strategically, and part of that involves all of you becoming comfortable with flying this craft. You may do your first rotation. Jemma take the pilot's seat. Dan, take over from Nikola. Matthew, I will check on whether we will be safe in the transport zone and talk to you later. For now, you may sit with Dan. Is everyone clear?'

It was obvious to Jemma that Werrimen wasn't about to brook any opposition and she shook her head at Matt when he looked like he might argue. Fortunately, he seemed to get the message and slid into a chair beside Dan. In truth, like Nik, Matt probably didn't need as much training as the rest of them given his engineering background. He'd easily picked up everything they'd learnt on the smaller spaceships, despite having a fraction of the training.

The rest of the day ran smoothly and once each of them had had a turn in every role, Werrimen asked where they felt most comfortable. 'You will need to be proficient in all roles,' said Werrimen, 'but if you like one more than the others, I will try to place you mostly in that role. So, what do you think?'

'Pilot,' said Jemma. 'Definitely. And navigator second.'

'Opposite for me,' said Dan. 'Navigator first, pilot second.'

'I'm easy,' said Nik. 'I've enjoyed learning each role.'

'I understand that Nikola, but does one stand out more?' asked Werrimen.

'Hmm. I like fiddling with the tech best, so navigator first maybe, then pilot. But I like setting up communications too. So, whatever you need really.'

'Good. Sean?' Werrimen turned to him, smiling, and Jemma had no doubt he'd be thinking any role that didn't involve a spaceship.

'Probably communications,' he said, finally. 'I'm happy to take a management role.'

'In my world,' said Werrimen, 'you can't take a management role unless you are competent in all the tasks you would ask your people to undertake.'

'I understand, and I'm prepared to learn,' replied Sean, his face blank.

Werrimen turned to Matt. 'And what about you? What would your preference be do you think? I understand you've had less time to think about it than everyone else.'

'Yeah, I have been thinking about it, though. The

Condonans are going to set up a factory on Earth. I'd like to take charge of that, if it's okay with everyone else. I'd need to learn how to be a test pilot too, so I guess pilot's my first choice here.'

'That's a fabulous idea,' said Sean. 'I think you'll probably have to take a role in the army too, but yeah, I like your thinking.'

'I do too,' said Nik. 'I hadn't thought of that either, but I'd really like to work with you in the factory, and on the test runs.'

'Excellent,' replied Werrimen. She checked with the Condonan pilots to confirm that they'd achieved all the checks they needed. 'Right, Matt, why don't you take the ship in to land? Sean will sit on one side of you and an experienced pilot on the other.'

Jemma was surprised to see Matt grin. Despite his earlier fear and his desire not to be away from Dana for too long, he seemed to be enjoying the exercise. He'd definitely perked up when Sean had backed his idea to take charge of the factory. Nik was still in the navigator seat, but Jemma and Dan were free, so they stood behind Sean until the craft had landed.

Jemma wasn't sure who started it, but once they were safely on the ground, a loud cheer went up and then all of them danced around the control centre floor. It seemed that Pritchard hadn't destroyed their day or their belief that they were about to head home. She edged closer to Sean to listen as Werrimen leaned in behind him.

'I said you could do it,' murmured Werrimen.

'Yep, got this one covered,' he responded, laughing. 'What's my next challenge?'

She rubbed his shoulders and smiled. 'I doubt you want to know.'

'Jesus, that bad,' he muttered.

'Of course. You rose to this challenge and didn't fall too far. The next one has to be harder.'

*   *   *

Preparation for the final flight through the transport zone was stepped up over the next week and Jemma moved from counting down the days to counting down the hours. She marvelled at the specialised chair that was set up for Matt's wife and met the medical crew who were allocated to accompany Dana. They were all introduced to the crew that was to accompany them from Condona to set up the spacecraft factory on Earth. Everything seemed to flow smoothly although everyone, including Werrimen, became increasingly anxious given they hadn't heard from Pritchard.

The day before the big flight, Werrimen advised that Lena and ten other people from Anders would be joining them on their journey to Earth. Each would have a permanent IPL guard with them. The Trustees who had been attempting to determine what had happened to the people from Anders, believed they'd discover the nature of the manipulation. Werrimen had asked the Trustees to start the process to undo the damage, although she wasn't sure how successful they'd be. If the victims' real memories had been destroyed, it would be like dealing with a global amnesia.

'If everyone is comfortable, we should go to the Condonan Council's farewell dinner,' said Werrimen. 'I don't want anyone to stay too late, though, as we will need to be alert tomorrow. Our departure time is 10 am, but I would like you all at the terminal by 7 am please.'

Everyone agreed and had started to go their separate ways when Jemma's communicator sounded. 'Oh no!' she cried when she saw who it was. Fortunately, Werrimen and her team all heard and turned back.

'Good evening, Jemma,' said Pritchard. 'I understand you still plan to leave tomorrow.'

She took a deep breath to steady herself. 'That is correct.'

'I did tell you not to do that,' said Pritchard.

'What is it that you want?' Jemma stood very still as she waited for his answer.

'Are you alone?'

'No,' replied Jemma.

'Kindly ask others to leave and we will talk.'

'No.' She felt Sean's hand on her arm as she worked hard to sound calm and in control. 'I will no longer acquiesce to your demands. We will be leaving tomorrow. Eleven of your people will be with us.'

'You do so at your peril,' snapped Pritchard.

'Then your people will be at the same peril,' replied Jemma, calmly.

'No, they will be removed from your custody before you leave.'

'That will not happen.' Jemma shut down her communicator and turned to Werrimen. 'Do you think he's bluffing?'

'Probably, but we will not take any risks,' said Werrimen. 'Two hundred IPL Trustees landed here this morning to help Condonan security. Fifty of them will be coming with us. Are all of you packed?'

'Yes,' said Jemma, and the others nodded. 'Not that any of us have much to pack.'

'Good,' said Werrimen. 'Given this latest threat, I think we should all move to the security accommodation tonight. Matt, you may stay with Dana and Susan at the hospital. I will send a group of IPL Trustees to increase your security. Are Merrilam and her daughter still happy to come with us?'

Matt nodded. 'Merrilam doesn't want to leave Dana until she's well. Emilrad said she could always come back to Sidlow later, but she doesn't seem to think she'll choose to do that. Susan and Lexie, Merrilam's daughter, are excited about the big trip too.'

'Excellent,' said Werrimen. 'As soon as the farewell is completed, you will return to your accommodation and collect your belongings. You will each be accompanied by a Trustee contingent. It is a shame to have to do this on our last night here, but I feel it will be safer.'

Jemma clung to Sean's hand as they made their way to the dinner. She'd have preferred to run and hide rather than enter the big reception centre. It looked like half the population of

Condona were there. All were seated at large tables arranged in concentric circles and when someone noticed Jemma and her group, people rose and began to clap and cheer. Four tables, two on each side of the room, were occupied by Sidlowns and she assumed they were the Trustees who were to go with them the next day. The next two hours passed quickly. Dinner was not the food cubes to which they'd become accustomed but fresh fruit and vegetables and something that looked like rissoles, although she doubted that they contained meat. Once they'd finished eating, they all stood to mingle with the crowd.

Jemma was enjoying the pleasant exchanges, some of them with people she barely knew, and was disappointed when Werrimen tapped her on the shoulder to indicate they should leave. She looked around for Sean and had just turned to head over to him when a man came up close behind and clamped a hand on her arm.

'Come with me.'

'Jesus, let me go,' exclaimed Jemma. 'Who the hell are you?'

'Come with me. Now. There are several weapons aimed at your husband. My people will shoot if you do not follow my instructions.

'No.' Jemma raised her other hand and shouted into her communicator. 'Help.'

Most nearby people turned to look but had to jump out of the way as Trustees descended on Jemma's position from every direction.

She yelled to Sean, 'Drop down.' To her surprise, he did.

Trustees shouted instructions at the man who'd accosted her. They subdued and removed him within seconds, but Jemma still struggled to breathe. If Sean hadn't raced over to her and held her up, she thought she might have fainted.

'Are you alright?' called Werrimen, who was slightly behind the other Trustees.

Jemma nodded, still unable to speak.

'She will be,' said Sean. 'She just needs some air.'

Werrimen signalled to all the Earth travellers. 'Trustees will accompany each of you to your dwellings. Collect your belongings and go straight to the security building. I will meet you there.'

Too shaken to argue, Jemma leaned on Sean as he led her from the room, surrounded by at least a dozen Trustees, including Dragile. When she finally looked up, she saw that Dan and Nik had a similar group with them. Matt had his own contingent.

When they got to their house, neither Jemma nor Sean spoke as they grabbed their gear and did a quick check of each room to make sure nothing important had been left behind. Equally silently, they followed the Trustees to their overnight accommodation. It wasn't until they were inside their room that Jemma broke.

'Jesus, Sean. That fellow said there were weapons trained on you from every direction. Ninety percent of me said "give in to him" but the other ten percent said, "if I do, this will never end." I didn't know what to do.'

'Come here.' He folded his arms around her, planting a

kiss on her forehead. 'I think what you did was perfect. You held your nerve, called for help and managed to warn me there was a problem.'

She gulped, then forced a smile. 'I'm not sure what stunned me more, the man's demand or when you obeyed my order.'

'I could see that when I looked up,' said Sean smiling. 'Part of leading is knowing your people. And I know you very, very well. When you spoke, I knew it was serious.'

'Let's hope tomorrow's uneventful,' said Jemma. 'I've had enough.'

'Agreed. I doubt we'll sleep much, but I think we should give it a go.'

Jemma tossed and turned all night, eventually giving up well before first light. She headed to the hot drink machine for a cup of target. While the drink brewed, she decided she'd have a shower. She had to try and clear her head before they got to the spaceship. Her first job was the safety check and that would need all her concentration. Sean was first to be pilot, so he needed to be alert, too.

She walked out rubbing a towel through her hair, expecting to find Sean pouring the target, but was surprised to find him sitting on the side of the bed. He held his head in his hands and was groaning. She ran to his side and gently raised his head to look at her. 'What's wrong?'

'I haven't had a drink for months, but I feel like I'm seriously hungover,' he said.

'Oh hell. Why don't you get in the shower and I'll fix you a target?'

'Don't know if I can.' He ran for the bathroom and she heard him throw up.

Alarmed, Jemma stared at the bathroom door. Their task this morning was too important to risk, so she picked up her communicator to contact Werrimen and fill her in.

'Oh dear. Dan and Nikola are the same. I have medicals going to them. I will ask them to come to you also. We must sort them out. We cannot delay this flight.'

When they arrived at the spaceship, Sean, Dan and Nik all looked seedy. Jemma wondered how she'd missed out, given they'd all eaten the same things. The medicals seemed to believe that Sean had been poisoned. Perhaps the man who'd accosted her had somehow put something in their food.

At least Matt looked okay. He was already in the space-ship, fussing over Dana and checking on Susan, Merrilam and Lexie. She heard one of the medicals advise Werrimen that they'd given him a mild sedative, which would calm him soon, and probably make him sleepy.

Jemma left them to it and took up her position to start the pre-flight safety checks even though it was still an hour before flight time. Given Dan was so sick, she'd have to get through it herself.

One of the Sidlown pilots joined her and she thought he must have been reading her mind when he said, 'We'll do this together. I have no doubt you can do it by yourself. My role is to help you, and hopefully make it less stressful for you.'

'Thanks. That does take a load off my mind. When do we start?'

'As soon as everyone is on board. I believe we are waiting now for the last of the IPL Trustees. Werrimen will close the entry and notify us.'

Dragile was next to enter. He smiled at Jemma. 'I have heard about Sean's illness. How are you?'

'I'm fine,' said Jemma, 'but Nik and Dan are ill too.'

'Oh dear.' Dragile reached out and drew her into him. 'Emilrad and I decided last night that we will not be coming with you. My family needs time with us given everything that has happened. I will miss you.'

'I'll miss you, too,' said Jemma, 'but I understand. Family come first.'

'Thank you. I sincerely hope that we will meet again,' said Dragile. He headed back to the blue light and was gone.

Jemma stood, staring after him. She was sad to lose Dragile but didn't have time to think about it. Her current task needed all her focus. She repeated the safety list over and over in her mind until the pilot joined her and told her to proceed. She was grateful that he stood behind and allowed her to take the running although she was quite sure he was double checking everything she did. He did openly check that all the entries were fully secured, after which he advised the lead Condonan pilot that all was clear. Jemma was surprised to see Sean sitting beside the pilot.

'They gave me something to settle the symptoms,' said Sean, in response to her frown. 'I still feel like shit, but I can keep going.'

'Are you sure?' exclaimed Jemma. 'I can take over from you.'

'I can do it,' said Sean. 'You rest for a while. You'll be needed soon enough.'

Although she did as he asked, she didn't think he looked well enough to be there. She decided to wait in the pilot's lounge where she would see him if he had to leave.

CHAPTER 9

Sean used every technique he knew to avoid thinking about his churning stomach, although it was hard to ignore. Deep breaths; slow his breathing; focus on the task. When the lead pilot instructed him to commence the pre-flight checks of the equipment, he had to force himself to keep his mind on the task at hand. Everyone was anxious, but it was up to him now to ensure that the flight started smoothly, and he was damned if he was going to let anyone down. Dan and Nik also looked green, so if they could keep going, so would he. Jemma hadn't been struck down, but much as he knew she loved him, he wasn't prepared to have her fill in for him. She'd be busy enough when her shift came.

Nik handed him the coordinates to direct the craft. He secured them into his console while she sought permission to lift off. Once he had the go ahead, he directed the computer to commence their journey. It all proceeded smoothly, and he forgot all about his sick stomach when the Condonan pilot advised that they were beyond the gravitational pull of Condona. They really were on their way home. When Werrimen tapped him on the shoulder, he gazed up at her, exchanging a look that defined their shared triumph.

'Jemma will take over now,' said Werrimen. 'The poison you ingested has been identified and the medics are waiting to treat you. Fortunately, we have the antidote on board because it is quite a common poison.'

'What about Dan and Nik?'

'You go first. I am organising relief for them, then they will join you.'

He waited until Jemma was seated, impressed by how easily she slotted in, immediately commencing a discussion with the pilot. Walking behind Werrimen, he again became aware of just how sick he still felt.

In the medical rooms, he was told to sit on a large reclining chair while the antidote was administered. A Trustee placed a small bar on his arm. It was about fifteen centimetres long and two centimetres wide. A row of spikes on the underside was placed against his skin. It stung for an instant, then he was barely aware of it. A small fluid filled box which he was told contained the antidote was attached to the top of the bar.

'This will take around twenty minutes to get into your system,' said the Trustee. 'You can move around if you need to do so, but otherwise rest as much as you can. I must warn you that you will feel worse before you feel better.'

'Thanks,' said Sean, 'I think.'

A few minutes later, he again had to race to the bathroom. Clearly, the Trustee had been right.

Werrimen arrived just as he thought he had nothing left inside. She patted his shoulder. 'Better out than in. Dan and Nikola are being treated now. You'll all feel better soon.'

As she walked away, Sean felt marginally guilty that he didn't much care about Dan's or Nik's welfare at this point. He was happy to leave it to the Trustees to manage them. He simply couldn't recall ever feeling so ill. A Trustee guided him to a bed and told him to sleep for a couple of hours.

When a gentle touch from Werrimen jolted Sean upright, his head swam and he felt disoriented, unable to focus his eyes.

'Sit quietly for a moment,' said Werrimen. 'This will resolve soon. I am about to wake the others. Jemma will join us shortly. There is something we need to discuss.'

'Okay,' he muttered, and sat back on the bed, wondering how to get the jackhammer out of his head. Although still unsteady, he rose and walked to a table at the front of the room where he assumed Werrimen would gather the others to talk. He did his best to smile when Jemma ran in.

'Are you feeling better?' asked Jemma.

'Nothing a few days sleep wouldn't fix.'

'I keep wondering why I didn't go down,' said Jemma. 'Matt didn't either. It's just the three of you.'

'Don't know.' Sean sighed. 'I suspect it was carefully targeted. I'm pretty sure that fellow intended to grab you. It was only your quick thinking which stopped him. Maybe he thought we'd be designated too sick to fly and be left behind on Condona.'

'Oh, my goodness. Did you just give me a compliment?'

'Don't make me laugh,' he groaned, resting his elbows on the table and holding his head in his hands. 'I'm regularly impressed by you and I've often told you that.'

'I'm sorry,' she said, leaning over him and kissing his cheek. 'Werrimen told me that you'll recover fairly quickly now.'

'God, I hope so.' He did his best to hold himself up as Dan slid into a chair beside him and Nik slumped onto a chair on the other side of the table.

'Bloody hell,' muttered Dan. 'What the hell did we do to deserve this?'

'I do not think you did anything,' said Werrimen, taking a seat at the head of the table. 'I believe they were trying to disable you. They weren't worried about Matt as he isn't part of the flight crew. And they didn't intend Jemma to leave Condona. We have outwitted them, but we do have a problem. A Trustee contingent left ahead of us to ensure that our passage would be clear. Unfortunately, it is not.'

'Pritchard, I presume?' exclaimed Jemma, shaking her head.

'Probably, although at this stage we do not know for sure. We will find out when we get close. This craft is currently being managed by the Condonan pilots and I have asked them to maintain a holding pattern until more Trustee ships arrive to investigate. It won't take long, but it does give all of you a bit more time to recover.'

'I think that's useful,' said Jemma. 'I'm perfectly healthy though. What would you like me to do?'

'Would you head back to the control room and work with the pilots, please? I am going to send Matt up also. He had a sedative earlier, but it has worn off now. Dana is resting comfortably and Merrilam is perfectly capable of looking after the girls. Please do not be too sympathetic with him. It is time that he became more active. Dana is no longer at any risk.'

'I know,' replied Jemma. 'I just feel for him.'

'Jem, listen to Werrimen,' said Sean. 'Matt has to overcome his demons. He's struggling and if we don't push him some, that struggle might overwhelm him.'

'I understand, and I'll do as you both ask. I'm just aware how hard it is for him.'

Werrimen waited until Jemma had left before she again addressed Sean, Dan and Nik. 'You must realise that Jemma is also suffering. Her confident attitude is bravado.'

'She's tough.' Sean sighed. 'Our best way to help her would be to get rid of Pritchard and give her a chance to rest and recover.'

'Get rid of Pritchard, yes. Rest and recovery are not, I think, going to be available.' Werrimen stood. 'Alright, the three of you should rest for a few hours. Once we are cleared to proceed, you will all need to be alert and ready to go.'

*　*　*

Jemma leaned against the wall outside the medical centre. She'd been so confident this morning that they really were on their way home, but with Pritchard out there she was no longer so sure. The Condonan pilots insisted that Pritchard could not possibly intercept them in the transport zone, but he was working with the Zants. They knew as much, if not more, than the Condonans about these zones. Was it possible that they had found a way? She pushed herself away from the wall and headed back into the control room where she eased in to sit beside the senior pilot.

'What would you like me to do?'

The pilot smiled. 'Swap seats. You can take over, but given the circumstances, I'll stay here beside you.'

'Thanks,' said Jemma, forcing herself to smile. 'I don't fancy trying to tackle someone firing on us if I'm on my own.'

'I very much doubt that will happen. The extra Trustees will be here in another hour. They will take a couple more hours to get to the problem area. I feel confident they will resolve the problem and allow us to proceed.'

'God, I hope you're right.' Jemma settled in and adjusted the screens, but she was disturbed by a number of objects she could see in the distance. 'Is that a meteor shower? It couldn't be someone firing on us, could it?'

The pilot smiled. 'No, your first guess was right. It is a meteor shower. Do you remember what to do?'

'Yes. Put up the shields once the first of the objects is within ten minutes of us. Keep a close check on the largest objects and, as much as possible, avoid those.'

'Well done. I'll leave you to manage this one then.'

'You're not going anywhere, are you?' exclaimed Jemma.

'No, I'll still be here. Stay calm. You can do this.'

It felt good to know that he believed in her, but she'd always previously had at least one of her team with her and usually Werrimen or Emilrad standing behind. Being alone meant taking more responsibility although it was also a great opportunity to learn. Reminding herself how to turn on the shields, she asked the navigator how far the objects were from them now.

'About an hour away,' he replied.

'We're currently in a holding pattern,' said Jemma. 'If I have to avoid them, which direction should I take? Do I head back towards Condona, or continue in the direction we were going?'

'Neither necessarily. I'd most likely aim for ninety degrees from the object in question, depending on what else is around. Sometimes, we just have to remain stationary and let the shields deal with them. Relax now, I will be watching too.'

'I'll do my best,' she muttered, although she couldn't believe how calm he was as the objects approached. Was he really so confident in her abilities, or was a meteor shower so common that it just didn't bother him?

A few minutes later, the navigator advised her the objects were now close enough that it would be appropriate to engage the shields. Once she'd fixed them in, she focussed on the screen. All the meteors were small, and she was advised to maintain her holding pattern for the two hours they took to pass. She'd only just sat back and begun to relax when Sean, accompanied by Werrimen, arrived back in the control room.

'How are you?' asked Jemma, not sure if she'd managed to cover the anxiety in her voice from coping with the meteors.

'Yeah, good. Still a bit tired, but I'll get over that. Werrimen wants me to join you for a couple of hours. The others are resting. They'll take over from us then.'

'Are you okay to continue a little longer, Jemma?' said Werrimen.

'Yes, I'm fine. Have you heard from the Trustees whether we can proceed?'

'No,' said Sean. 'The Trustees have arrived at the point where several craft have formed a barrier. They're all Zant ships. We should know within the hour what's happening once they've fully assessed the situation.'

'Okay,' said Jemma, grinning. 'I've just managed my first meteor shower. With help of course.'

'Not much,' said the pilot.

She laughed. 'Thanks, but you did a lot more than you're admitting to. Werrimen, I'd like to know if you would support me to become a full-time pilot?'

'No.' Werrimen paused.

Jemma knew Werrimen would be choosing her words carefully, so she did her best not to react.

'I will support you to spend most of your time on Trustee training and piloting is a good proportion of that,' said Werrimen. 'However, we must wait until we get to Earth. I believe a great deal has happened there, although I do not have details. Earth's needs might dictate what we all do.'

Jemma wasn't happy with the answer, but she accepted she'd have to wait and see. Turning back to the screens, she felt Sean's hand on hers.

'Give it time,' said Sean. 'I think the general will support you because you're so keen. Hopefully, everything's peaceful down there.'

'Hopefully.'

The next two hours passed without incident and, given that she'd now been nearly eight hours in the pilot's chair, Jemma was ready for a break when Werrimen told them to swap teams. She gave her report to Dan who was to take the pilot's chair and accompanied Sean to go down on the disc to the lounge area nearest their accommodation where they could get a hot drink. She offered one to Sean, but he declined, preferring to let his stomach rest.

'Werrimen said we should aim for a six-hour break now because we'll be busy once we enter the transport zone,' said Sean. 'Happy to sit and chat for a bit but then I think I need to try for some sleep.'

'Still no better?'

'I'm heaps better, but the fatigue's overwhelming,' said Sean. 'Werrimen said it would resolve within a few hours, so I'm hoping. Don't like feeling like this.'

'Why don't you go and sleep now? I'm happy to sit here for a bit, then I'll head in for a rest too.'

The crew accommodation on the ship was basic. Tiny rooms with a single bunk that could only accommodate one person, so they each had a separate room. She hoped the apartment they'd had back on Earth would still be available and in good order. It was a far cry from the house she'd once envisaged as her permanent home. Still, it would be heaven compared to this.

'No, I don't want to rest yet,' said Sean. 'I'd like to chat for little while. Might get some sense of normality that way.'

'Okay.' Jemma reached across and took hold of his hand. 'Chat away.'

'Have you noticed Werrimen's now teamed us together? She did everything shy of building a brick wall between us before when it came to work.'

'Maybe she's realised we can work together,' said Jemma. 'Don't think I'll argue. It's nice.'

'Yeah, it is,' said Sean. 'I'm a bit worried the way she keeps on saying things like, "we'll work that out when we find out what's happening on Earth." It's as though she knows something that she's not telling us.'

Jemma nodded. 'I heard that too. I thought I was being paranoid. But you think there's more to it?'

'Maybe. It could just be she doesn't want to commit to anything until she knows but, I don't know, it feels like there's more.'

'Sean, I don't know how to say this, but ...'

'Just spit it out Jem. Whatever's wrong, we'll find out soon enough.'

'I know you're the boss when we get there, and you'll slot back into that role without any difficulty,' said Jemma. 'The problem is, I don't know where I belong. I'm really not military although the general says I am, and I'm not a Trustee although Zadrus says I am. I'm going to need your help.'

He reached across the sofa on which they sat and drew her into him. 'That's a given. You know that. In an emergency, I might have to throw orders. Other than that, I'll be in there fighting for you. I need you to keep telling me what you want to happen, and when you're unhappy or feeling like you can't do something. I'd like them to let you be a scientist again, but I just don't think it's going to happen any time soon.'

'No, neither do I.'

Sean smiled. 'I dream about eventually getting our own place, plenty of space, a couple of kids, a dog, maybe even a horse.'

'Vegies, chooks, sheep, cattle and a big river bordering one side of the property,' said Jemma, laughing. 'It'd be so good. Maybe one day.'

'We can only hope.' He sighed. 'I've got to go get some sleep. I'm sorry, Jem, but I need it.'

'You go.' Jemma wriggled back onto the sofa. 'I'll stay here for a bit, then I'll do the same. I think it might be pretty hectic when we get back.'

'Yes, particularly if there's some argy-bargy from Pritchard and his Zant cronies going on.' He leaned across to kiss her, then pulled himself up and left the room.

She was concerned as she watched him go. He usually held himself tall, but right now he was bent forward as though standing straight was too hard. Hopefully, a sleep would get him back to normal. She finished her drink and headed to her own cabin to wait for the call to return to the control room.

As soon as she lay down, she was asleep and was unaware of anything else until her communicator sounded. As she sat up to reach for it, she looked at her watch. She'd been gone from the control room for less than five hours.

'Jemma, pick up please.' One of the pilot's was on the screen and he looked worried.

'Sorry. I was asleep.'

'Yes, I understand, and I apologise for waking you, however, we need you up here. Sean has also been alerted.'

'What about Matt?' asked Jemma.

'No, we won't call him for the moment.'

'Okay, I'm coming.' She stretched as she stood. No way was she leaving the room without at least cleaning her teeth. As she made her way to the tiny bathroom, she wondered why they hadn't called Matt. It had to mean there was trouble ahead. She brushed, then splashed water on her face until she felt a little more human. With a sigh, she opened the door and headed out.

Sean met her in the hallway. 'You got a call too?'

'Yep. Are you feeling better?'

'A lot better, thanks. Guess there's something going on up there.'

'I'd say,' said Jemma, 'and they don't plan to involve Matt, so I doubt it's good.'

'No. We'll see when we get there.' Sean sighed. 'I really don't know how hard to push Matt. I know Werrimen's worried about him, but I'd rather wait until we get home. Once Dana, Merrilam and the girls are settled, it'd be easier to push him into a routine. What do you think?'

'I agree,' she said, taking hold of his hand as they walked together towards the control room. 'On Earth, he'll have a lot more support to pick himself up.'

'That's pretty much the way I'm thinking,' said Sean. 'I think I'll focus on backing Werrimen off on this one.'

'Well, here we are,' said Jemma. 'Time to face the music. Find out what the latest trauma is.'

Sean smiled. 'Buck up, sweetheart. We're going home. We can get through anything so long as it gets us there.'

'I know. Here we go.' Jemma stood behind Dan, Nik and the two Condonan pilots, all of whom were staring intently at the screens.

'There,' called Nik.

'Yes, I see it,' replied one of the pilots. 'Engage the shields please. Everyone be seated. Sound the alarm.'

Dan went to work on the shields while Nik activated the emergency alarm which would tell everyone on the ship to strap themselves in. Jemma followed Sean to the seats behind the pilot's chairs which were intended for spare crew. Werrimen sat beside them.

'What's happening?' said Sean.

'We were advised by the Trustee craft to move forward which we did about two hours ago,' said Werrimen. 'The barricade of Zant ships is stopping us from proceeding to the transport zone coordinates. It is odd because we are still two days out from the transport zone entry. It may be that there are others closer to the zone, or maybe they are just arrogant enough to think they will be able to turn us back. Whichever it is, we have to get past them. We are surrounded by Trustee craft and they will fire on the other craft if they must. I would prefer to leave Dan and Nikola in place, but I thought you should know what is happening which is why I had you called. It is one moment at a time now, so be prepared to do whatever you are called on to do.'

'What did they see that worried you?' asked Sean.

'A Zant ship that is behaving differently from the others,' replied Werrimen. 'I suspect it will have Pritchard on board. And I also suspect he plans to make contact.'

'What next?' exclaimed Jemma. 'Does he think he can beat the might of the IPL?'

'He may be that arrogant,' replied Werrimen, her face grim as she stared at the screen.

'Would it be better if I left the control room?' asked Jemma.

'No, he would turn to someone else to make his demands,' said Werrimen. 'What I would like you to do is remain here, be ready for his demands and stand up to him.'

'I'm not sure if I can achieve that,' said Jemma. 'He's the worst kind of bully.'

'You can do it,' said Werrimen. 'You already have. And, I believe you have spent time working with Dragile on how to handle Pritchard.'

'I have, but it's one thing to talk about it,' said Jemma. 'It's quite another to actually do it.'

'Just remember that most bullies are cowards at heart,' said Werrimen. 'He will insist we turn back, possibly demand to have you transferred to his ship. He might expect your colleagues to go with you and will almost certainly demand you disassociate from us.'

'He's made all those demands before,' said Jemma. 'So far we've managed to resist, but I haven't done any of the negotiating. What are your thoughts on how I counter those demands?'

'Do you remember what you said to the man who tried to take you from the farewell dinner, last night?'

'Yes, of course.'

Werrimen motioned to Jemma to sit and took hold of her hands. 'His threats will most likely be baseless. Tell him that you will no longer give in to his demands. Ask him nicely to remove his ships and ensure our safe passage. Advise him that if he does not, the IPL will force him to do so. Can you do that?'

'I'll try,' said Jemma. 'It sounds easy when you say it, Werrimen, but truthfully, I'm terrified of what he might do to us if we resist him.'

'I know, and there is little more I can say to reassure you. Just keep in mind what he might do to you, and to those you love, if you surrender to him.'

Jemma stared back at Werrimen. 'I don't want to be the one to sign our death warrant.'

'And I cannot guarantee that will not happen. However, I do believe that the risk is very, very low and most of what he says is bluff.'

'Honey,' said Sean, leaning across Werrimen to touch Jemma's arm. 'One thing I am sure of is that if you give into him now, you will have to keep on doing that. He will just keep on increasing his demands until we have nothing left to negotiate. We have to trust Werrimen, and the IPL, that they know how to deal with criminals like Pritchard because we are so far out of our league here.'

'I know you're right, both of you.' She withdrew her hands from Werrimen and sat up in her chair. 'Alright, if it's going to come down to me, I can do this. That bastard is not going to destroy our lives forever.'

'Go girl,' called Dan, looking over his shoulder.

'I'm with you, cuz,' said Nik, laughing. 'Do you want me to stand beside you? I'm in the firing line too.'

Jemma smiled. 'Damn right you can stand beside me. Dan and Sean can stand behind us. At least then we present a consolidated front.'

'Now you're thinking,' said Sean. 'Don't take any crap from him.'

It was nearly an hour before the ship that Nik had identified reached them. Jemma and Sean had been about to swap places with Nik and Dan when Pritchard's face came through on the main screen. Two Condonan pilots stepped in to enable the team to stand together.

'I told you to turn back. You have failed to do so. If I do not see evidence that you are changing direction within the next five minutes, my people will attack.'

Jemma stepped forward. 'I have rejected your demands. We will not be turning back. It would be in your interests, as well as ours, for you to remove your ships from our path. Should you fail to do so, I will not be responsible for the outcome. Neither I, nor the IPL, wish to do you harm, but understand that we intend to continue forward and will use whatever means necessary to ensure our safe passage.' She leaned forward and touched the pilot on the shoulder. 'Would you shut down the communicator please.'

'Yes, ma'am,' he responded, a broad smile on his face. 'Well done.'

Pritchard's face was almost purple, and he had started to curse before the screen shut down.

Slumping back against Sean's waiting arms, she turned to Werrimen. 'What now?'

'We wait,' replied Werrimen. 'The Trustee commander was linked into that message. I expect to hear from him any minute.'

'God, I don't think I'll ever get used to this.' She slipped into the navigator's seat, ignoring the look Sean gave her as he slipped uncomfortably into the pilot's chair. Dan hovered for a while, but she waved him away. Whatever happened now, there'd be nothing any of them could do and Dan and Nik needed some rest. Both had been as sick as Sean this morning, and none of them looked fully recovered even now.

Their direction had been set towards the coordinates of the entry to the transport zone and, apart from Pritchard and his cronies, there were no immediate hazards, so there was little to do other than watch and wait. She checked the screen that showed the rear of their craft and saw a line of Trustee ships. She checked and found a similar pattern above, below and to either side, but she couldn't see any in front.

In response to her frown, one of the Condonan pilots leaned across and flicked to another screen. 'They are there, but much further in front than you are expecting.'

'Oh, okay. Thanks,' said Jemma.

Yet another hour passed before Werrimen returned to tell them she'd heard from the Trustee commander. 'The craft which we believe held Pritchard has fled. One of our people fired on another craft, disabling it.' When Jemma gasped, she added. 'It fired first. It was helped by others in their fleet, and they have all pulled back. That is reassuring, but I do not want you to let down your guard. It is possible that we will find other hazards ahead.'

But there were no other hazards, and two days later, they reached the coordinates for the transport zone.

Jemma was thrilled to be pilot as they entered the zone, even though the Condonan pilot sat very close, almost touching her hands as he explained what to do. Once they were fully into the zone, he told her that the zone itself largely controlled their movement now. Her only role was to try to manage turbulence by keeping the ship upright and on a steady keel.

Crews changed over every six hours or so, as intended, and were expected to rest between shifts. There was no socialising. They left as soon as their replacements arrived, headed to the control floor lounge for some food, then to their own rooms for rest. Timing was irregular as their watches didn't work accurately, but when the crew on duty became fatigued, they'd call for the resting crew to take over.

When the call finally came that they'd emerged from the

transport zone, Jemma ran to the disc and up to the control room. She estimated by the number of crew changes, and her own sense of time, that they'd taken around two days to get there.

The pilot smiled at her as she burst in. He pointed to something on the screen. 'Earth.'

And there it was – tiny and still a long way off, but it was definitely Earth.

Nik and Dan were in the pilot's seats. They were holding onto each other, both fixated on the screen.

'I gather you've seen it,' said Werrimen, smiling as she joined them.

'We're almost home,' said Jemma, looking up at Werrimen. 'Thank you so much.'

'I didn't have much to do with it. The Condonans built the ship. You learnt to fly it.'

'As if …' Jemma laughed as she lifted her head to look Werrimen in the eye. 'As if any of this would have happened without you.'

Werrimen smiled as she stroked Jemma's cheek. 'It will be at least a day before we touch down on Earth. When you are not required here, I suggest you prepare yourselves to land. I expect to be busy once we arrive.' Werrimen bowed her head and walked away as quietly as she'd arrived.

CHAPTER 10

Jemma stared at Werrimen's retreating back. They'd been
through so much in the last few weeks. Would the general
really expect them to get straight back into it? She wanted to
yell at someone.

'What the hell does that mean? demanded Nik, standing
with her hands on her hips as Sean joined them. 'Busy once
we arrive? We need a break!'

Sean sighed. He drew Jemma in close to him and rested
his head on hers for a moment. He kissed the top of her
head and turned to face the others. 'Straight after we got
out of the transport zone, I spoke to General Hunt. They
saw us break through and he was so pleased to see our ship
he contacted me to welcome us home. I don't think he was
going to say anything until I stupidly asked him how it's been
going down there. I was just trying to make conversation,
and I didn't expect the answer I got. It sounds like they've
been doing it rough too. He needs all hands on deck to get
it sorted. I don't think he meant to unload, but once he
started, it all came out.'

'So, what's the problem?' asked Jemma.

'Sabotage, theft, assaults,' said Sean. 'He's not had enough

160

experienced people to help him, so as soon as we land, we're into it. Best everyone realises that.'

'No break,' muttered Nik.

'No.' Sean dropped back into his chair. 'The next few weeks are going to be tough. I'm tired of it, and I'm tired of the risk to Jemma. And to you, Nik. But that's the way it is, so we'd better all get ready to leave.'

Jemma followed him to his cabin, waited for the door to close behind them and then nestled into his arms as he turned to her. 'I love you, Sean. You, me, Dan, Nik, we're family. We need to pull together.'

'I know, but I also know that I've got to get a bit of distance. Much as I hate it, I don't have much choice.'

'Maybe we should run away,' said Jemma, smiling. 'Find a safe area to hide.'

Sean laughed, although Jemma could hear a bitterness to it. 'I don't think they'd have much trouble finding us. We've got implanted trackers remember. Sweetheart, they're about to start up the first group at the academy.'

'To do what?' Jemma gripped Sean's hand as she leaned forward.

'I'm to lead a course to bring all of our military people in the settlement up to speed. That includes Matt's people as well as ours. Dan and Matt are to be the instructors.'

'That doesn't include me.'

'Yeah, it does. You and Nik are the next most senior people we have. You will be designated team leaders.' He put his arm around her. 'They're not going to give us any time to ourselves.

I'd hoped for a few days, just the two of us. My problem is that I can't let the others see how I feel.'

'You can, Sean. They're military too. They understand, and they care about you.'

'I guess you're right,' sighed Sean. 'When we land, I'd like us to walk out together. We need to try to look happy and confident, even though neither of us feels that way.'

'Of course, I'll walk out with you,' said Jemma. 'How could you ever doubt that? I suspect the general will see through any show of confidence though.'

'Probably, but I don't want to give anyone room to criticise us or think they can push us around. I've got to go and check on what's happening next. Are you alright by yourself for a bit?'

'Of course,' said Jemma. 'You do whatever you have to do.'

When the call came to disembark, Jemma stood with Sean. He took her bag from her and placed her arm through his, then headed towards the exit. She said nothing even when she saw Hunt waiting on the landing pad.

'Stay calm,' said Sean, so only she could hear. 'Whatever he plans we'll work through it together.'

When Sean put his arm around her, she rested her head on his shoulder, sighing as she felt his body relax against hers.

Hunt waved when he saw them, but his gaze seemed to pierce through her self-control. She kept a tight grip on Sean's hand and did her best to maintain her composure until a scream from somewhere around the head of the craft made her jump. Delighted to see Mary and Erin running towards them, her attempt to look calm and professional disappeared as Erin threw herself at Sean, and Mary grabbed hold of her.

'Oh my God,' cried Erin. 'I wasn't sure this day would ever come. Let me look at you.'

Mary was a bit more subtle, as she hugged Jemma. 'It's so good to see you. I've heard about some of the things that have happened. Are you okay?'

'Yeah, I'm fine, but it feels good to be back on terra firma.' She noticed Dan and Nik standing awkwardly behind them about the same time that Erin looked up.

'Dan, Nik, come here,' exclaimed Erin, her arms wide and welcoming. 'Don't think you're going to get away without hugging me.'

But it was Erin's next move, after she'd finished hugging and kissing Dan and Nik, that surprised them all. She took hold of the general's arm, and led him to Matt, who was standing just outside the blue light, looking lost, as he waited for Werrimen to bring Dana and Susan down to him.

'Your mum's pretty chummy with the general,' said Jemma.

'I noticed,' replied Sean. 'I guess we have to assume life went on while we were away. It's been nearly a year since I was taken, and you left a few weeks after that.'

Hunt left Werrimen and Erin to organise Dana and Susan and brought Matt over to join the rest of the group.

'Head to your apartments now,' said Hunt. 'We'll all meet at 0600 tomorrow morning. Bellamy, would you stay behind please.'

'Oh, okay,' said Sean. 'Sorry, Jem. I'll let you know when I'm free.'

'I'll help with the bags,' said Dan. 'She'll be right. You go.'

*   *   *

'Is there a problem?' asked Sean, once he and Hunt were alone.

'Nothing specific,' replied Hunt. 'I just wanted to fill you in before I include the others.'

'Okay.' Sean shrugged. 'Shoot.'

Hunt smiled. 'I'd rather not, but you need to know what's been happening. I'm so very relieved to have you back.'

'Thanks,' said Sean, 'I think.'

'After you left, we weren't sure if the Zants were gone,' said Hunt. 'So we concentrated all our resources on the army. My first task was to build a suitable facility. I won't go into the details now, but we were confronted with sabotage, theft, explosives and attacks on our people. I assumed it was the Zants, but Zadrus wasn't as sure. Given what you've all had to cope with on Condona, I think we now have to accept that our friends from Anders Major are also involved.'

'Probably,' said Sean. 'Have you seen any Zants?'

Hunt nodded. 'On a couple of occasions, but we haven't succeeded in intercepting them. We're hoping the extra IPL resources who came with you might be able to help.'

'Have you heard if any Zant craft followed us through the transport zone? We hadn't seen any by the time we landed,' said Sean.

'Not so far, but Zadrus expects they will,' said Hunt. 'The IPL is watching closely.'

Sean sighed. 'Expect he's right.'

'Yes, and despite all the attempts to stop us,' said Hunt, 'the academy building is now complete, and it is heavily guarded. Our first group of recruits is ready to start the day after tomorrow. Liam Cleary has taken most of the running with Ciara McMurtry's help, at this stage. I have promoted both to officer status. Their hard work and perseverance have enabled the course to go ahead.'

'I'm sure it'll be good if Liam's involved,' said Sean. 'I don't know Ciara at all.'

'I'm aware,' said Hunt. 'And I am sorry to do this to you, but you need to meet with them today. You've got to be able to hit the ground running the day after tomorrow.'

'Shit.' Sean stared at his boss.

After leaving Hunt's office, Sean spoke to Liam and organised to meet after dinner, then headed back to their apartment. Even just an hour to sit with Jemma and feel like he was back in his own home would help, but he was surprised by Jemma's greeting. It was as if she hadn't seen him for a year.

'Is everything okay?' she asked, leaping into his arms.

Sean laughed. 'It is. Well, as much as it can be. We're about to be busy.'

'Come and have some dinner,' said Jemma. 'You're going to need some decent nourishment to keep going.'

'Thanks.' He sat opposite Jemma at the table. When he'd finished, he leaned back in his chair. 'I'm a bit shocked by the general's expectations. I'm going to have to manage a recruit course that I know nothing about. I've had nothing to do with developing the content. I haven't met the participants and have no information on their backgrounds. Liam has my utmost respect, although I don't know Ciara. Even more importantly, I don't think either of them has ever run a training course. Presumably, the general's been guiding them.'

Jemma reached out and covered his hand with hers. 'God. I'm so sorry, Sean. I've been so focussed on my own woes, that I hadn't really thought about how hard all this is for you.'

'No, don't be sorry. Your situation is difficult and ongoing. Mine is temporary, but I'm worried about letting something go ahead if it isn't good enough, and I've got twenty-four hours to work that out and fix it, if needs be.'

'I'd rather see you rest tonight,' said Jemma, 'but if you feel you need to meet with Liam and Ciara, I'll understand. God, what a mess.'

'Yep, mess is a pretty good word. I think I do need to meet with them. Suspect I'll spend all day tomorrow bringing Matt and Dan up to speed as well. I just have to work out what I'm bringing them up to speed with.'

'Can I do anything?' asked Jemma. 'I'll feel guilty putting my feet up while you're hard at work.'

'No, you rest. Who knows what tomorrow will bring?'

CHAPTER 11

When the alarm sounded at 05:00, Jemma groaned, but Sean slept on. Aware that he hadn't come to bed until well after midnight, she got up quietly, had her shower and organised breakfast and coffee, a murky liquid made from some kind of bean, the whitener from a different bean. She roused Sean with half an hour to spare before their meeting with Hunt, happy that, for once, the tables had turned, and she could do something to help him. Once they'd finished, they walked briskly to the gym, arriving seconds before Hunt who was accompanied by Liam and Ciara. Dan and Nik were two minutes behind them, but Matt was almost ten minutes late.

'Do I have to begin with a lecture about timeliness?' growled Hunt.

'No sir,' said Dan and Nik together.

'I overslept, I'm sorry,' said Matt, looking directly at Hunt. 'It won't happen again.'

'Good, follow me. I want to show you the Academy buildings.'

It was an impressive setup. Staff and recruits were to be housed in a secure accommodation block that was halfway between the gym and the main Academy building. It had its own swimming pool and Jemma was surprised to see tennis courts alongside several basketball courts. She hadn't previously seen either type of sporting venue before in the new settlement.

Hunt had stopped beside her. 'I thought it useful to encourage sport. Everyone has been too focussed on survival to worry about recreational activities.'

'I think it's great,' said Jemma. 'Are you going to allow non-military people to use it?'

'Possibly. We'll see. Now, come on. There's a lot more to look at.'

The main complex was made up of three buildings, arranged around a large central courtyard. Like the rest of the settlement, all were constructed from red brick. They were simple buildings, rectangular, all with four stories and verandas front and back on every level. Behind the buildings were three large, flat paddocks which she assumed were sporting fields.

Hunt led them to the first building and into a large foyer. 'Does anyone have any questions?'

Nobody spoke so Hunt continued. 'I'm aware that I'm asking a great deal of all of you, particularly those of you who have just returned to us. I'm currently finalising the structure of the United Earth Army. It is not my plan to change a great deal from our traditional armies. However, I know that you come from a variety of different background and eras, so I would appreciate your opinions before I put the final seal on it.'

Jemma looked at Sean. He nodded, and she guessed he was trying to encourage her, but why would they listen to her? She hadn't been particularly impressed by the military system in her own era, and these people all had that old system ingrained into every aspect of their being.

'Say what you think, Jem,' said Sean.

'Okay,' she said quietly, pausing to see how Hunt would react, but his expression remained passive. 'You need to rethink your military concept. As an outsider looking in, I see several issues. The "officers versus others" system that most armies traditionally used was a legacy of medieval feudal times. It evolved from the disparity between the British upper and lower classes. Almost all armies throughout the world were influenced in one way or another by the early British forces. You have the chance to change that, to develop something more mature, possibly take everyone in at private level and then at the end of the course slot them at whatever level they best fit. That way people could be promoted in response to their achievements without a false class barrier trapping them between sergeant and lieutenant.'

Sean looked at her with a broad smile on his face.

Hunt looked at her quizzically. 'Go on.'

'You wouldn't even have to keep the same ranks,' she continued, not sure if he was listening or trying to work out how to prove she was wrong. 'Maybe you could start with four bands, each with three levels, or something similar. It seems to me that you're about to develop something entirely new.

Why allow yourself to be bogged down by the old ways, particularly when they didn't work well even then.'

'Okay, I'll take it on board. Now the content of the course: drill, weaponry, combat, strategy.' Hunt stared directly at Jemma. 'Should we throw that away too?'

'You shouldn't throw anything away,' replied Jemma with a sigh. 'But you should question everything you do. People in other countries will have done things differently. If you're going to impose your ways on them, you'd better be damned sure you can justify everything you require. Otherwise, you'll have dissent and internal conflict, and that could build resentment and lead to the process of war between nations all over again. Just my thoughts, mind you.'

Sean now laughed openly. 'Have you ever considered applying for the position of general, Jem?'

She shuddered. 'Can't think of anything worse. You asked what I thought, and that was it.'

No one else suggested anything, probably too intimidated by recent events, so Hunt went on. 'Denis, Jemma, you will be team leaders which means that you will each manage a group of around twenty people.'

'Yes, we know,' said Jemma. 'Is there a timetable, or anything specific we have to do out of hours?'

He smiled as he handed her a folder of papers. 'The timetable is in there. All I need you to do is make sure they're all in the big meeting room, which I'm about to show you, well before 0800 hours.'

'I'm sure we can do that,' said Jemma, trying not to show

her relief that she didn't have to have them marching across from their accommodation.

'Good.' He led them through a door and into a large room with rows of desks and chairs. 'This is the assembly room. I suggest you spend the day meeting the participants and help them settle in. Most will be staying in the accommodation block for the duration of the course.'

'Okay,' said Jemma. 'Is it alright if I go for a run first? I've been couped up so long I need to stretch out.'

'That's fine. Meet me at noon in the Administration Building training room. Do you remember where it is?'

She laughed. 'I believe so.'

'Go on then.'

Outside, Nik took a deep breath. 'I'm not looking forward to this.'

'Me either,' said Jemma. 'Coming for a run?'

'No, I'll go see who we'll be working with. They'll either make the situation bearable or a bloody disaster.'

'You're right. I'll be back soon and join you there.' Jemma slipped onto the track that ran right around the settlement. It was occasionally used for foot patrols, but at the moment there was no one around and that suited her perfectly. She headed east to the furthest end of the factory precinct, then turned south towards the dam, the place where she knew she'd feel most at peace.

As she broke through the bush and laid eyes on the large body of water which gleamed in the sun, it was so inviting that she couldn't resist kicking off her boots and sitting at the edge. The dam wall had obviously been repaired after the Zants had drained the water. Small birds twittered through the nearby bush and a family of ducks swam towards her, giving her the sense of peace that she'd craved for so long, and that made her irritation worse when she heard a male voice behind her.

'Good afternoon.' The voice was familiar, but she'd not heard anyone approach.

Jemma swung around, stunned to see Ryan standing in front of her. 'What the hell are you doing here?'

'Following you,' said Ryan.

Jemma shook her head. 'We left you on Condona. How did you get here?'

'I was on the ship with you.'

'No,' said Jemma, evenly. 'I'd have seen you.'

'You did see me,' said Ryan. 'You spoke to me several times.'

'I'd have recognised you.'

'I didn't look like this. I removed my disguise. Sean chatted to me for some time too.'

'Then why don't you remove it now so we can talk openly and honestly?' snapped Jemma.

'Because I can't risk being identified,' replied Ryan, with a sigh. 'I must speak with you, Jemma. My people are becoming anxious about your presence.'

'What do you expect me to do? I live here,' said Jemma.

Ryan shook his head. 'You are too close to Anders here. We must shift you somewhere that is safe for you and from which you cannot travel to Anders, where those who would re-establish the ruling houses will not find you.'

'And where would that be?' asked Jemma.

'There are many places. I am trying to ensure your safety. Would you come with me now?'

'No,' Jemma said quietly. 'I would not.' She picked up her communicator. Before Ryan could stop her, she said, 'Sean.'

'Where are you?' Sean's worried look made her sigh. She hadn't meant to cause him any grief, but she didn't have a choice.

'I'm at the dam,' said Jemma, quietly. 'With Ryan. He says you know him.'

'On my way.'

'That was a foolish move,' said Ryan. 'I wanted to save you, but Drick will find another way when he arrives. You cannot return to Anders.' He took off, running through a bush track at the eastern-most edge of the dam.

Sean ran through from the western edge just seconds later. 'Where is he?'

'Gone.' She stood, with his help, and looked around. 'I have no idea if he's alone or if there's a whole gang of them, but he threatened me again.'

He drew her into him. 'Relax now. I doubt they'll try anything with me here. So far, he's only approached you when you're on your own. We'd better go back. You're vulnerable here.'

'What do I do?'

'God, I don't want to say it,' replied Sean, 'but you can't be by yourself.'

Jemma was startled by the sound Hunt made as he emerged through the bush.

'Fill me in,' said Hunt.

Sean gave a brief summary, explaining that Ryan had also approached her on Condona.

'Can you recall sitting and chatting to a man on the flight here?' asked Hunt.

'Yeah, I spoke to quite a few,' said Sean. 'Most of them were prisoners with me, so I knew them quite well. There was no-one who looked like the image we have of Ryan.'

'He said he was in disguise,' said Jemma. 'It must have been pretty good if you didn't recognise him.'

'Alright,' said Hunt, as he turned to walk away. 'Let's go back. We'll talk in my office.'

Jemma stood for a few minutes staring after Hunt, then at Sean. 'I don't know how to deal with any of this. I'm scared, Sean. I can't see how I'm ever going to be safe.'

'I know,' said Sean. 'Together Jem. We'll get through it together.'

She sighed as she turned back to walk, with Sean, to Hunt's office. She couldn't fight these Anders people, or the Zants, on her own.

'Come in, Jemma,' called Hunt. 'Have a seat.'

She slipped into a chair and Sean sat beside her.

'I'd hoped you could be free to move around as you please, but I don't think we have that luxury,' said Hunt. 'From today, whenever you are outside a building, you are to have someone with you, an army member, or a Trustee. Is that clear?'

'It is,' she sighed. 'Although, I doubt they'd approach me in the main part of the settlement. I think I'm safe close to the buildings.'

'Probably, but we won't take that risk,' said Hunt. 'I spoke to Zadrus on the way back here, and he would like to speak to you, too. You may go.'

She opened her mouth to say something, but a look from Sean told her to zip it. 'Okay,' she murmured.

*   *   *

Zadrus welcomed her into his room, but he stood so close she had to crane her neck to see the extent of concern on his face.

'General Hunt tells me that this man, Ryan, accosted you,' said Zadrus. 'He did not harm you?'

'No, I'm fine. He threatened me but he didn't do anything.'

'That is still concerning.'

'It seems the people of Anders aren't going to stop,' said Jemma. 'And he was clear that Drick, or Fredrick Pritchard as I knew him, is on his way here. Presumably the Zants will come with him.'

Zadrus waved her to a chair, 'We anticipated that. Tell me what else he said.'

She recounted the whole conversation and that she'd called Sean for help, and most importantly, that Ryan had claimed Sean knew him without his current disguise.

'I see. I will talk to Sean later and see if we can work out who he might be. Now, we have a lot to talk about. This is our first chance to talk since your return. We knew each other quite well on SCARF, but a lot has happened since then. Do you still trust me now?'

'You know I do,' she replied. 'But I think everybody is forgetting that I'm a scientist, not a fighter.'

'Unfortunately, fighting is something you may not be able to avoid. It is best if you are prepared.' He squatted in front of her. With his height, even in a squat, his eyes were level with hers. 'I feel I must show you why.'

With no idea what he planned to do, her anxiety skyrocketed. She thought back to how Hunt had responded when the terrorist shot his shoulder and then his knee. He'd sat, giving no indication of the terrible pain he must have felt. She'd try to emulate that. Zadrus moved behind her and placed his hands on her shoulders. She concentrated on looking as though she was perfectly calm.

At first nothing happened, then suddenly vivid images shot through her mind. Norellian spheres flew over a place she didn't recognise. She saw her parents, although they looked very young, run into a large building. They carried a baby. That had to be her. The spheres were firing on people. Many were hit. She felt the pain as each one went down, and the anguish of others watching them. One of the spheres landed. A couple of Zants and a dozen humans emerged. They used some kind of stick, which must have been the equalisers Sean had told her about. They looked like a cattle prod, but he'd said they produced an electric shock and injected some kind of toxin. People fell, screaming, then they were dragged into the spheres. She felt their pain and their fear.

Zadrus stood back, and she stared at him.

'I take it that was Anders Major?' murmured Jemma.

'Yes.'

'I wasn't there when they were attacked.'

Zadrus's voice was controlled, as he answered, 'Your parents risked their lives, and the lives of all those who helped them get you to safety. They paid the ultimate price. Your reluctance to be fully involved with the fight is dishonouring their sacrifice.'

'I'm not dishonouring it,' exclaimed Jemma. 'If I could change what happened there, I would.'

'Then let me show you what could happen here.' She saw the Norellian spheres again, this time above the East Australian settlement, firing on people below. They ran, screaming. Many were shot. She felt their fear and their physical pain. Then she saw people in Trustee and military uniforms walking through the dead and injured, trying to help. She seemed to be walking with them, until she came on General Hunt, dead. Not far from him, Werrimen picked someone up. It was Sean. He wasn't dead, but he was screaming in pain. Werrimen yelled, 'Follow me,' as she ran towards the hospital. Sean was covered in blood, both his legs hanging at a peculiar angle.

Jemma heard herself cry out, 'No. Stop. No more.'

Zadrus removed his hands. 'We have much to discuss.' He pulled a chair close to her, his knees resting on the outside of hers, as he told her to extend her hands palm down and place them on his so he could transmit his energy to her, which he felt she needed at this moment. As usual, she felt the warmth seep through her body. It was calming and made her feel good about herself, not something she'd felt for several months now. When she looked up at him, he smiled.

'I plan to develop your intuition and hope we can form a bond of total trust in time.' He touched the same spot on the back of her neck Emilrad had used when she went to talk to Lena, to ensure she was telling the truth. She must have started slightly as he gave her an odd look, but it felt like an electric shock running from his fingers through her neck.

'I won't lie to you,' she said.

'No, I don't expect you to, but this removes any doubt. What did you feel as I did that?'

When she explained, he nodded as though it confirmed whatever it was that he'd been thinking. He put her hands back in her lap and stood. She felt herself tense up again after he removed his hands. Before she could ask, he said she would feel some change after he ceased contact.

'I think we have finished.' Zadrus walked with her to the door and took both her hands in his. She felt the same sensation of calm as he did so, and he smiled.

'The fact that you feel this, assures me I am right. Most people would not experience anything other than holding my hand. Go and see General Hunt, and we will meet again tomorrow after your physical training session.'

CHAPTER 12

Shocked by the images Zadrus had shown her, Jemma walked along the hall until she was out of sight of his office before stopping to take a deep breath. He'd made it clear she had a responsibility both to her current community on Earth and also, for her parents' sake, to her home planet, Anders Major. But what the hell could she do about that? She had no means of getting to Anders, and even if she did, why would they accept someone as their leader who'd never known any planet other than Earth?

Hunt had often told her that when she was in trouble, she should look for a positive slant. She guessed she'd now have to do just that. And thinking of the general, there was only one minute left before twelve o'clock when she was supposed to meet with him.

Aware that she needed some fluid before heading into a workout, if that's what Hunt actually intended, she detoured to a fridge which she knew was always filled with fresh water bottles. A man was busy restocking the shelves, so focussed on counting what was there, she didn't like to interrupt. When he finally looked up and saw her, he jumped, then apologised profusely and handed her a bottle from the crate.

After thanking him as politely as she could manage, given her need to get to the training room, she ran to the stairwell and dashed down. Hunt was waiting outside the door, but she was surprised to see her husband step out from behind him. Sean wrapped his arms around her, pulling her into a bear hug, before demanding to know if she was alright.

'I'm fine,' she replied, with a sigh, before easing out from Sean's embrace, wondering what they'd expected Zadrus to do to her.

Hunt's eyes glistened as he returned her gaze, and it hit her how much both men were worried about her. Hunt wrested her from Sean, so he too could hug her. It was a couple of minutes before he released his hold, gently easing her out to arms-length so he could look directly into her eyes. 'No problems between you and Zadrus?'

'No. He's just worried about Ryan and how I'm going to cope with the threat from Anders. He didn't demand anything else.'

'Good.' He playfully pushed her towards Sean. 'Say goodbye to your lady, Bellamy. She and I have a lot to talk about. Bring O'Leary, Denis and Matt here at 13:00 hours. Time to assess everybody's fitness and get serious with senior officer training, including the recalcitrant Dr Anderson here.'

Jemma groaned. She gave a mock salute to Sean, then followed Hunt into his training room. He pointed to the floor and sat himself down tailor fashion. She followed suit but said nothing.

Hunt seemed to be trying to formulate what he needed to

say, and several minutes passed before he broke the silence. 'I want this hour with just you and me, so if there is anything you need to resolve we can talk without interference from anyone else. If there's nothing, then we can train. But today, we need to talk.'

She studied the floor. The hug she'd had from him outside the door had brought home how much she valued him and made her realise how much he cared about her. In many ways, he was like a father to her, a pretty damned strict one, but still important. She'd lost her father when she was eighteen. Hunt, over the last two years, had begun to fill that void. Difficult though it was to admit it, she wanted him to be proud of her. There was no doubt it would take a lot of hard work to get there.

'I've already promised both you and Sean I'll do whatever you want me to do,' said Jemma. 'I'm not going to live in fear, though. I'll question things, and sometimes disagree with you. You'll tell me I'm cheeky and I guess you'll be right, but I'll follow your orders.'

'You've always been cheeky, and I have no desire to break you. I value your independent thinking and your capacity to look at things differently. Now, tell me about Zadrus.'

'He showed me what happened to my parents when they left Anders Major, and what could happen here if I don't fight back.'

'That's putting a lot of responsibility on your shoulders,' said Hunt.

'I think it's already there. He's not suggesting I have to do anything by myself, just that I have to be at the forefront.'

Hunt nodded. 'How do you feel about that?'

'Terrified, but like everyone else, I want the crap to stop,' said Jemma. I know I have to step up, I just don't know how to do it.'

'Fair enough.' Hunt leaned forward and rested his hand on her arm. 'Jemma, that's a huge step forward. I know how much you rely on Sean. I want you to feel you can come to me too. Will you keep that in mind?'

'I've always known that,' said Jemma. 'I just don't see myself as military.'

'Understood. Did Zadrus indicate his plans for you?'

'He wants to continue training me as a Trustee. I had a few sessions with Dragile on Condona, but we didn't have time for much. Despite everything, Zadrus seems convinced I've got what it takes.'

Hunt smiled. 'I expected that. Well, we'll see what comes of it.'

They talked about her time on Condona, learning to fly, finding Matt's wife and her encounters with Drick. Hunt pointed out to her how much she'd learned and the extent to which she'd been involved in solving problems. She realised, as they spoke, that she had played a major role in getting back to Earth without always relying on Sean, even though she was much happier when he was by her side.

Surprised by the arrival of the others, she checked her watch and discovered they'd been talking for nearly an hour. She followed Hunt when he stood and moved towards Dan, her usual training partner.

Hunt shook his head. 'You can team up with Matt today. Show him what you're made of.'

'Yes, boss,' she muttered, as she walked past Hunt.

He put his hand out and barred her movement. 'What did you call me?'

'Boss, boss.'

'Perhaps I should team you with me and teach you some manners.'

'Would you prefer "Dad"?' Her voice was too quiet for others to hear, although she did see Sean shake his head.

'Really,' replied Hunt. 'As the dad of a ten-year-old brat, perhaps I should ground you. Permanently. Would you like that?'

'Nope. I think that's a very bad idea.' She ducked as he took a pretend swing, then she ran towards Matt.

'Oh, and Jemma,' said Hunt. 'Welcome back. Just don't take it too far.'

She grinned. 'As if I would do that.'

Matt shook his head as she joined him. 'You've got a death wish.'

'I've had to deal with him for three years,' muttered Jemma. 'I know how far I can go.'

Matt chatted to her about his expectations for the next few weeks. While she was happy to continue talking, she periodically felt the general's eyes on her, even though he appeared to be focussed on Dan, his current training partner. Sean worked with Nik, and she suspected Hunt was trying to build the team, but she jumped when his voice resounded behind her.

'I sent you two over there to work,' growled Hunt. 'Now you can start. Both of you drop down. Give me a hundred push-ups.'

No point arguing, Jemma murmured, 'Sorry.'

Matt shook his head. 'No, my fault.'

She picked up the water bottle she'd grabbed on her way down to the training room and downed most of it before dropping to the floor to do the general's bidding. Matt looked anxious, so Jemma did her best to encourage him, 'Relax. We'll take a steady pace. Let me count it out.'

At the count of eighteen she winced when a sudden sharp pain stabbed through her abdomen. Determined not to give in with Hunt watching her, she forced herself to keep going. She could only manage two more. She fell down, pulled her knees up and clutched her stomach, crying out in pain. Thirty seconds later she was barely conscious, her limp body stretched out on the floor.

Hunt reached her first.

She heard him call her name, but the pain was so overwhelming she couldn't respond. Aware of Sean as he skidded to his knees beside her, she reached up her hand but was unable to speak to him.

'What the hell happened?' demanded Hunt. 'She was fine a few minutes ago.' He pulled Sean away from her. 'Bellamy, call Zadrus and ask him if he has any idea what could have caused this.' He scratched his head, then yelled, 'Her drink bottle? Where is it?'

Matt reached for it and handed it over just as Zadrus ran

in the door. She was vaguely aware of Sean picking her up and running for the door, then nothing more.

* * *

'The medical centre is two floors down. Take her there,' said Zadrus.

Sean raced towards the disc. A nurse waited to help carry Jemma into the small emergency room and onto the nearest bed. Sean squatted beside Jemma, stroking her forehead. He didn't look up until Werrimen ran through the door, accompanied by a woman dressed in the uniform of a doctor.

'Check the vitals,' said the doctor. 'I want blood and urine samples. You're the husband?'

'Yes,' said Sean.

'Help me get her clothes off.'

Before he could think about it, he heard himself saying, 'Yes ma'am.'

'Roll her towards you,' ordered the doctor. 'I need to check her spine and look for things like bites or needle marks.'

Zadrus walked in as they rolled her back and pulled up the bedclothes.

'I'm taking these to the lab,' called the nurse, holding up the blood samples.

'Take this too.' Zadrus handed her the drink bottle. 'I suspect this contains some kind of poison.'

The doctor nodded. 'Vitals are good. She's breathing without assistance, but she's still unconscious. No sign of anything untoward on her body. General bloods, so far, are fine. Nothing out of the ordinary on imaging.'

Sean stared at her. 'So, why's she unconscious?'

'Don't know. Have to hope the scientists can shed some light on that. You go,' she said to the nurse. 'He's expecting you.'

'Oh shit,' exclaimed Sean. 'Anthony's the chief scientist, Mary's son. Jemma and Anthony grew up together. He'll fall apart when he finds out who the patient is.' Grabbing the samples and the bottle from the nurse, he tore up to the lab. In a way it was good to have something to do rather than sit by the bedside and imagine all the worst possible outcomes.

Anthony's cheerful greeting suggested he hadn't heard.

'Mate, these samples are all from Jemma. She collapsed a few minutes ago. It happened straight after she drank from that water bottle.'

'Don't be daft. I spoke to her a couple of hours ago. She was fine, and she's fitter and healthier than anyone I know.' Anthony frowned at Sean but took the samples and started to prepare them.

'She's not ill, mate,' said Sean. 'We think she's been poisoned. We need you to work out what the poison was.'

'Jesus. Yeah. Yeah, of course I can do that.' Anthony carefully placed his prepared tubes and slides in the analyser, but he gave Sean a sideways look as though not quite sure whether he should believe him. He took several samples from the water bottle and placed them alongside the blood tubes.

Once all was set, he looked up. 'Should have a result in a few minutes. Can I go see her?'

'Let's do this first,' said Sean. 'Then we can go together.'

'Okay, I'll let Mum know,' said Anthony.

'Good idea. Guess I should let my mother know, too.' The next few minutes felt like hours to Sean, although filling in his mother helped him hold up while he waited.

The samples gave finish signals within seconds of each other. Initially, Anthony and Sean stared at each other, but then Anthony jerked himself away and ran for the analyser.

'It's a plant toxin.' Anthony shook his head. 'Itrasoma. I've not heard of it. Give me a minute, I'll see what I can find.'

'Me either,' said Sean. 'Does it come from Earth?'

Anthony didn't answer for a moment as he flicked through some screens on the large communicator. 'Bloody hell. No, it's not found on Earth. Only two known planet sources. Guess what? One of them is Anders Major. There's an antidote, but we don't have it. No reason to assume we'd ever need it. Zadrus will have to get it, or identify something else that will work,' he yelled over his shoulder, as he dashed out of the lab.

Sean took off after him and reached Jemma's room ahead of Anthony, who moved slowly. He'd never fully recovered from the virus spread by Fredrick Pritchard.

'We know the toxin, but don't have the antidote,' called Sean.

Zadrus took the printouts from Anthony when he arrived. 'By the stars. Who could have obtained this? One of the fleet ships should have the antidote. Do not worry, I will find a solution.' He walked away speaking into his communicator.

'Jesus, I hope so,' muttered Sean.

'Where is she?' cried Erin. She ran headlong into Sean as she rushed into the room.

Sean pointed to the bed, then placed a chair next to it.

'Oh darling, what has happened to you?' cried Erin.

'We're waiting for the antidote, mum,' said Sean. 'She's holding her own, so if they can get it quickly Zadrus says she'll be okay.'

'It is on its way down,' said Zadrus on his return. 'Half an hour. Jemma is stable, so we must wait now. I am at a loss to explain how this could have happened, but it may change the way we have to operate here.'

From his peripheral vision, Sean saw Hunt edge in closer.

'Change the way we operate?' asked Hunt, quietly. 'What does that mean?'

'Please do not be worried,' replied Zadrus. 'Until I have more information, I do not have the answer to your question. I suspect all our protections may have to be improved.'

Erin called them back to Jemma's bedside, where she sat holding her daughter-in-law's hand. 'Help's arrived.'

Mary tore into the room beside the Trustee who carried the antidote. It was contained in a metal cylinder much like the one that had been used on Sean after he'd been poisoned on Condona. It was around twelve centimetres long, two centimetres wide, and one side was flattened with multiple rows of tiny spikes along its length. The bar was placed on

Jemma's thigh and the spikes pushed into her skin. As Sean stood back, he bumped into Nik. She'd been standing as far out of the way as they could, Dan and Matt alongside. Erin and Mary sat on either side of the bed, each holding one of Jemma's hands. Nothing happened for a while and Sean feared that his worst nightmare might be about to come true.

Suddenly, Jemma took a deep breath. Then she groaned. Her eyes fluttered, and she appeared to be trying to speak. Her eyes slowly opened as though she had to fight to make them respond to her. Tears washed down Sean's face as he knelt beside her, stroking her forehead, telling her not to move.

She looked up at him and a small frown crossed her face as she whispered. 'Why are you crying?'

'Because you're alive, you goose,' said Sean, choking back his sobs. 'You scared the shit out of me.'

Jemma took a deep breath, then whispered again. 'What happened? Did a spaceship land on top of me?'

'Just about.' Sean felt his smile broaden. Whatever she needed to recover, she'd have, no matter what he had to do to get it. And if she needed greater protection, as Zadrus seemed to think, that's what she'd get. From here on in, he'd wrap her in cotton wool if necessary. She'd probably be just as annoyed about that as she was with Hunt and Zadrus, but too bad.

Zadrus sat on the end of her bed, his hand on her feet. 'You have been the victim of a poison. The antidote will have neutralised it, but you will take some time to recover.'

He turned to Hunt. 'There will be no physical exercise for several weeks. Even then, she must rebuild slowly.'

'I don't care about that. So long as she's going to be alright.' Hunt's eyes narrowed as he waited for Zadrus to respond. 'There's something else, isn't there?'

'Yes.' Zadrus turned to Sean. 'The man she was accosted by at the dam, Ryan. Do you have any idea who he is?'

'No,' said Sean. 'He told her he was in disguise, but that, without the disguise I knew him well. I just can't think who it could be.'

'I think finding Ryan must be our primary focus now. He is either the perpetrator here, or he will know who is,' said Zadrus.

'Is that poison a killer?' asked Hunt.

'Yes, it is,' said Zadrus. 'I suspect her level of fitness has saved her.' He sighed. 'She was clearly the intended target, not an innocent victim, which means they have escalated. This was an attempted murder. We must suspect either Ryan or someone close to him.'

'Yeah, I got that,' muttered Sean. 'But how the hell do we stop them?'

'That has to be our priority. Werrimen is organising a delegation of IPL Trustees she will take to Anders Major to investigate. There have been previous investigations there, but they had all reported that the situation had calmed.'

'While we wait, I'll increase Jemma's security,' said Hunt. 'She won't like it, but we've failed her far too often.'

Jemma's eyes followed Hunt. 'I'm groggy,' she whispered,

'but I'm not deaf.'

'Fair enough,' said Hunt. 'We're just trying to determine what protection we should offer you, and how to resolve this problem.'

'What was that about finding Ryan?' asked Jemma.

Zadrus leaned forward. 'That has to be our first task. He seems to be the key threat.'

Jemma shook her head. 'Ryan wasn't the man who gave me the water bottle.'

'We can't be sure of that,' said Hunt. 'We know he's a master of disguise. I don't want you to worry about it now though. He told you that Sean knows him well, so we'll sit down together and go through every possibility.'

'I'm having trouble moving my arms and legs,' gasped Jemma as she tried to shift.

'That is the poison,' said Zadrus. 'You had a large dose, I think. You must rest for the moment and allow the antidote to go to work. The doctors will test you in a couple of hours.'

'I don't want to go back to sleep.'

'It is the best thing for you to do,' said Zadrus, stroking her forehead.

'I mightn't wake up,' muttered Jemma.

'Oh, I see,' said Zadrus. 'I will have a nurse sit with you.'

'No, I'll stay,' said Erin and Mary, simultaneously.

Hunt laughed. 'Perhaps you could take shifts.'

Two hours later when Jemma again woke, Mary and Erin were both still sitting by her bed, each holding one of her hands. She groaned as she tried to move her arms. There was no response. She could feel them, she just couldn't shift them, and she cried out.

'What is it, darling,' exclaimed Mary, jumping up.

'Can't move.'

'Zadrus warned us that might happen,' said Mary. 'They want to check your nervous system, then they'll start physio, or whatever they call it nowadays.'

'I'll call Sean,' said Erin, 'let him know you're awake.'

'Thanks. And thank you both for staying with me.'

'Why would you thank us?' exclaimed Mary. 'Now that your mother is gone, that is my role, and Erin is your mother-in-law, so it is also her role.'

Tears streamed down Jemma's face. 'I'm scared.'

'I know, darling,' said Mary. 'We'll get through this. Zadrus is very clear that so long as you regain full consciousness you will recover, but it may take time.'

Mary stood aside to give Sean her seat when he ran in. 'How are you, sweetheart?'

'Can't move,' said Jemma.

'Zadrus is confident she'll recover,' said Erin, taking hold of Sean's hand. 'We all have to stay strong for her, if we are to help.'

'I know that,' he snapped.

'Your mother's trying to help,' Jemma whispered.

He looked at Jemma, then up at Erin. 'I'm sorry, Mum. It's not your fault. I'm just so worried.'

'We all are,' said Erin. 'I think Mary and I should go and find some morning tea and leave you two alone for a while.'

'Thanks,' he replied. 'I'm really grateful for everything you're both doing.'

'I know,' said Erin, stroking his cheek.

Over the next few days, Jemma was tested and retested until she was heartily sick of it. Her progress was slow, yet she was making progress. First, she managed to wriggle her toes, then some movement in her fingers, then her knees and elbows, but it was all so very slow. She wondered if she would ever find a time where her life would flow smoothly.

*   *   *

When the delegation Werrimen had taken to Anders Major returned to the East Australian settlement, Peetha, the leading Supreme Trustee on the mission was the first down and Sean, with Hunt and Zadrus, waited at the landing zone to welcome her.

Peetha greeted Zadrus with a broad smile, but her tone was brusque. She clearly wanted to go inside and discuss her findings.

'Where is Werrimen?' asked Zadrus, when they reached his office.

'She'll be down shortly. She has a few things she wants to organise. We agreed it was best for me to come down and fill you in as quickly as possible.'

'Thank you,' said Zadrus. 'What have you found?'

'I will give you a broad outline now,' said Peetha. 'For your information General, Colonel, Anders Major has for centuries been a technologically advanced, resource rich planet populated by peaceful, law-abiding humans. That was also their problem. They had no history of defending themselves from attack, and so when the Zants invaded they had no skill to adequately repel them. By the time the IPL discovered their problem, it was too late, much the same as Earth, and the damage was already extensive. The Zants manipulated the rebel group on Anders into joining forces with them. Not surprisingly, once they'd outlived their usefulness, the Zants turned on them. Many were abducted as they were young, strong and healthy. Most were destined to become slaves. I understand that you already know about the slave trade. The Zants had no qualms in altering memories, which may well be what was done to the people who confronted Jemma on Condona.'

'Excuse me,' said Sean. 'One of them, Ryan, has confronted her here. He claimed to be in disguise and that he came through on the flight with us.'

'I am aware,' said Peetha. 'That is troubling. Many people on Anders did manage to evade the Zants, including some from the ruling houses. Perhaps he was one of them. They fled to the hills and lived off the land after the ruling houses collapsed. We have been trying to help these people fight back, although it has taken more than a hundred years to drive the Zants out and allow civilisation to be re-established on Anders Major. People have now returned to their homes and attempts have begun to re-establish the ruling houses.'

'We were told on Condona that the rulers treated ordinary people like slaves,' said Sean.

'I do not believe that to be true,' said Peetha. 'People were all provided with houses and had ample food and clothing. That was all due to the management of the last Supreme Ruler of Kilkinan.'

'That is true,' said Mary, who had just appeared in the doorway. She bowed her head to the fleet commander. 'Mary of Kilkinan, madam. I am Jemma's guardian.'

'I am pleased to meet you Mary of Kilkinan. I see you are a Supreme Trustee. Please join us. You may be able to provide information.'

'We have to think about what to do from here,' said Zadrus. 'If anyone from the ruling houses of Anders should find out that Jemma is here, they may try to take her back. To some extent, that applies to all of the group with her.'

'And this is in conflict with the ideology of the rebels that have allied, willingly or not, with the Zants,' noted Peetha.

'We belong here,' said Sean. 'None of us know Anders Major. All any of us have ever known is Earth.'

'You must make your own decisions on that,' said Mary. 'I would like Jemma to see Anders for herself. I don't believe the people of Anders would attempt to take her, but I have not been there for a long time, so I am not the best judge.'

'We must protect her right to choose,' said Zadrus. 'You may all want to investigate where you come from, even return there once you have more information. Jemma must make her own decision, and that applies to everyone in your group.'

Peetha nodded, 'Yes, agreed.'

'If it weren't for the attack on Jemma, I'd say why don't we just ignore it? But I suppose we have to accept the poisoning was deliberate,' said Hunt.

'Yes,' said Peetha, 'and until we identify who poisoned her, we must work on the premise that all of you are at risk.'

'We need to identify this person,' said Zadrus, 'before he has a chance to do something else. Have you had any ideas regarding Ryan, Sean?'

'No, and there were about fifty refugees from the Zant prison who came through with us. I think our only hope is to sift through every one of them.'

'Right, then,' said Hunt, 'let's get started.'

'Sounds easy when you say it like that,' said Sean, although he was very aware that none of this was going to be easy.

CHAPTER 13

It was now almost a week since the poisoning and Jemma was frustrated by the amount of effort it took to walk just ten steps to the small ensuite in the corner of her hospital room. Sean had barely left her side since her collapse, only leaving if Hunt badgered him to do something else. She loved Sean's company, but it was often a struggle to stay awake to talk to him, so when he was called to a meeting with the delegation who'd gone to Anders, it was a relief, but that made her feel guilty. But she needed the time to herself, to get up and try to walk again if she was ever going to rebuild her strength. Nobody pushed her. To the contrary, almost everyone insisted she rest, but she knew that if she gave into that she'd never regain her strength.

Having just managed the trip to the bathroom and back, she'd fallen into bed and was doing her best to get her breath back when Zadrus, Hunt and Sean arrived, and she wasn't encouraged by the looks on their faces. Zadrus sat on the bed beside her and took hold of her hands as he told her about Peetha's findings on Anders Major and, in particular, how they'd been invaded by the Zants. The energy he transmitted kept her calm and enabled her to listen.

'Jemma, we must accept that you are the person most at risk because of the status you would hold if you were to return to Anders Major,' said Zadrus. 'I should have done much more to protect you and I am sorry that I have failed.'

Jemma closed her eyes. When she opened them again, Hunt was staring at her, his forehead formed into tight lines, probably worried how she'd respond. She knew he'd push her hard as soon as she was able, and she was okay with that. That was just physical exertion. But it was getting her head around the rest of it and clearing her mind to think that was almost impossible. With a sigh, she raised her head and looked Zadrus in the eyes. 'I doubt there was anything you could have done. We all use water from that cabinet.'

'You are right, but I think there are a number of things I can do now to increase your protection.'

She shook her head. 'I'm so tired.'

'I understand that, and we will work within your capacity,' said Zadrus. 'Werrimen has told me you would like to focus on developing your skills to fly spaceships. I am happy with that, but there is much more you must learn.'

This was too much to take in. 'I need to sleep. I can't think.'

'There is something else that concerns me,' said Zadrus. 'General Hunt has told me he wants to promote you to the first level of General, Sean,' said Zadrus. 'That will make you his second in command. Dan, Nik and Matt will also be promoted, and he plans a high rank for Jemma.' He shook his head as Jemma began to protest. 'That is between you and the general. However, from my perspective, that means five out of the top seven or eight people in Earth's Army are from Anders Major. Do you see how vulnerable that makes each of you, and your capacity to defend this settlement?'

Sean went to answer, but Hunt beat him to it. 'It's worse than that. Liam Cleary is also from Anders as, of course, am I.'

Zadrus stared at him. 'Yes, I am aware.'

'I've recognised the problem for some time, but what can we do about it?' replied Hunt. 'We all feel that we belong to Earth, not to Anders Major. And while I would be prepared to promote others, I don't have anyone with adequate training or experience.'

'I understand, but many on Anders will see you as citizens of their planet, so we must be ready should they try to intervene. I can offer you skills and knowledge that you currently do not possess. Jemma's development is my top priority, but the rest of you are close behind, particularly Nikola.'

'Okay then,' said Hunt. 'I'll call a meeting and we can discuss it.'

After they'd gone, Sean sat beside Jemma on the bed, holding onto her for several minutes as though she might disappear if he pulled back. When he did finally ease away, she slumped back on the pillows, but this time she didn't fall straight to sleep.

'The medical people all assure me that you're doing well,' said Sean, brushing the hair from her eyes. 'But please don't go pushing too hard and exhaust yourself, sweetheart. The general and Zadrus can wait. If it takes an extra month or two, so be it.'

'I know, but I feel so vulnerable. And I'm so damned angry. How could those Anders rebels have done this to me? I've never deliberately hurt another living soul.'

Sean shrugged. 'I wish I had a rational answer.'

'The problem is,' said Jemma, 'I don't think any of it is rational. How do you fight something where logic isn't a factor?'

'Spoken like a true scientist,' said Sean, laughing.

Jemma didn't have a chance to retort. Hunt returned to call Sean to join the meeting.

Hunt stayed with her after dismissing Sean, and his smile seemed genuine. 'They can wait a few minutes for me. How are you feeling after all that?'

'Confused.'

'I'm not surprised. Day by day. Are you feeling any better otherwise?'

'I'm weak and tired, but I think I'm improving,' said Jemma. 'I can walk a few steps now although my legs feel like jelly. Zadrus says I have to retrain my central nervous system. And then all my blood cells have to recover. He predicts at least two months.'

'Fine, we should be able to start training in a couple of days then.'

'Sure, twenty k run next weekend.' Jemma rested back on the bed.

'Thirty k.'

She laughed. 'If I thought you meant that I'd demand an IPL guard who's twice your size. But seriously, I am worried.

I wasn't at peak fitness when this happened, but I was okay. I don't understand how to *retrain my central nervous system,* and I don't want to be an invalid, but I've got no strength at all. I'm scared.'

Hunt moved forward and perched himself on the edge of the mattress. 'I know you're frightened. I might sound like I'm making light of it, but it's because I want you to stay positive. Whatever it takes, we'll get you there.'

'If you say so,' muttered Jemma.

'Damn right I do, and as soon as you've recovered, you're going to pay for scaring the shit out of me.' Hunt had a broad grin on his face as he pulled the sheets up and leaned forward to kiss her on the forehead. 'Now, go to sleep.'

'Scaring the shit out of you,' she muttered, sliding back down into the bed. 'You should have tried it from my side.'

It was dark when she woke again. She could see two people sitting just inside her door, one of them a Sidlown. Security had been stepped up and she knew there'd be guards outside the door. But there was someone else sitting in the chair beside her who now stood. A Sidlown woman. The darkened room coupled with her blurred vision made it hard to make out who it was. Then it dawned on her. She cried out, pushed the bedding back, and did her best to straighten herself up on the bed. 'Werrimen, you're back. Oh my God, you're back.' Tears rolled down Jemma's cheeks.

Werrimen held her until she settled. 'There, there, it can't be that bad. Zadrus has kept me up to date with your progress.'

Jemma sat back down again on the bed. 'God, it's good to see you.'

'It's good to see you too, my dear. So much has happened to overwhelm you. I love you as I would if you were my daughter and while I live and breathe, I will not allow anyone to harm you again.'

'I doubt you can stop them,' said Jemma. 'I'm so confused.'

Werrimen smiled. 'That will pass. Now give me a hug.' Jemma felt herself rocked back and forth until she felt calmer than she had since the day of the poisoning. She drifted off to sleep.

When she woke again, the room was pitch black. She raised her hand but couldn't see it. Something was wrapped around her. It was soft, but the wrapping was tight. She freed her arm and pummelled on the sides of a box-like structure that surrounded her. She could hear the sound of her fist hitting the wood.

Even as she struggled, she heard heavy footsteps. Someone running. A man called her name. Strong hands reached in and grabbed her around the shoulders.

She screamed with every bit of energy she could muster.

The man pulled her up. There was a glimmer of light. Then a bit more. Her vision was still blurred. The sides of the box now seemed fuzzy.

A man in a security uniform stared down at her. He said something.

She had to force herself to listen.

'Jemma,' said the man, 'what's happened? What's wrong?'

'I couldn't move,' she whispered, still shaking. She was so cold. 'There was a box. It was solid timber. I could feel the sides. I could see them.' Her chest felt tight, her lips and fingers tingled, she struggled to take a breath.

'You had a nightmare,' said the man. 'There's nothing there. I'll turn the lights on, and you can see.'

'No, don't leave me.'

'I'm not,' said the man. 'I'm right here. A bit of light will help.'

Before he reached the light switch, shouts sounded outside. Then more people running. Zadrus's voice. He demanded information. Werrimen ran into the room. Hunt was just behind. Someone must have hit the panic button.

'It's alright, sir,' said the guard. 'She had a nightmare.' He told them about the box and how Jemma had described feeling trapped inside.

Zadrus leant over her, gently telling her to slow her breathing. 'Have you had such a dream before?'

Jemma nodded. She knew it only too well. 'Many times, when I was little. It's less frequent now, but it still happens. I don't usually see the actual box as I wake though.'

He stood back, although still watching her. 'A trustee from Anders Major will arrive here tomorrow. I hope he will be able to shed some light on this, although I have a feeling that I already know what is behind it. Try to get some sleep. I'll leave the light on if you like.'

'Don't worry,' said Hunt. 'I'll stay with her. It's almost five o'clock, and I normally wake by this hour anyway.'

'Where's Sean?' asked Jemma, quietly.

'I took him off the alarm list,' said Hunt. 'He needs sleep. I can call him if you would like.'

'No, you're right,' said Jemma, shaking her head. 'He does need sleep.'

'Jemma, I'll be back in a minute,' said Hunt. 'I need a word with Zadrus and Werrimen. Won't be long.'

After they'd all left, Jemma raised herself out of bed. The guards were still there, but they remained discretely in the doorway of the room, and it felt good to not have to worry about what other people wanted. She needed to stand and stretch, to be absolutely sure she was no longer confined. Although still shaky as she pushed herself up, she waved away a guard who ran to help her.

'I have to start doing things for myself.'

He nodded and walked back to his post but continued to watch as she teetered in her first steps.

She walked to the bathroom door, then turned and headed across the room. Getting her legs to move where she wanted was a major effort. Yet, she had to do it. When Hunt returned, she'd changed direction again, aiming herself back towards the bed. She'd only taken thirty steps, yet she could feel the sweat dripping from her face. Hunt smiled when he saw what she was doing but, unlike everybody else, he didn't rush to assist. When she reached the bed and fell onto it, he helped her lift her legs onto the mattress, and tucked the sheets around her.

'Excellent,' he said. 'When you want to do that again, I'll walk with you.'

'Fabulous.' She glared at him when he laughed. 'One of the guards told me you'd found the man who tried to poison me?'

'No, not yet. Zadrus has a team going out to investigate a sighting. I'll check back with them shortly. We'll get to the bottom of it. Now is there anything you want, anything I can get for you?'

She shook her head. 'All I really want to do is go to sleep, and when I wake none of this will have happened.'

His face turned serious for a moment. 'I know, and if I could make that happen for you, I would. Work with me and I'll find a way to get us all back to doing what we want to do. But that's going to take time, and you have to give me that time.'

CHAPTER 14

Before leaving, Hunt had given her a couple of projects to do during the day. They were relatively simple, not much more than delving into her feelings about particular events. Presumably, his aim was to just get her focussed on something, but try as she might, Jemma was unable to resist her overwhelming need for sleep. Zadrus had explained that her body was trying to heal, so sleep was the best remedy and she should give in to it. Having dozed off at least a dozen times as she tried to do the first of his projects, she was surprised to find Hunt sitting beside her when she opened her eyes.

He spoke in as gentle a tone as she could ever remember from him as he helped her to sit up. 'Do you want to try another small walk? You don't have to.'

'You mean I get a choice about something? That's new.'

Hunt shook his head. 'God, you're cheeky. Yes, or no?'

'Yes, I want to get moving,' replied Jemma. 'Don't look at me like that. I appreciate the help, but I'm frustrated.'

'I know. Come on, hop up. Let's get moving.'

With his assistance, she managed to stand. It was then one foot after the other, and she had to think with every step about how to move her body. Towards the bathroom first, then turn and head for the other wall. Halfway through, sweat poured down her face and her legs trembled. God, it was only a few weeks since it would have taken a twenty kilometre run to make her feel like this.

'Do you need to stop?' asked Hunt, bending forward to assist her.

'No. I can't afford to,' said Jemma, shaking her head. 'It was thirty steps last time; it has to be thirty-five this time.'

'Don't overdo it.'

'Yeah right, you've changed your tune.' She saw him suppress a smile.

'I think you forgot something at the end of your sentence,' said Hunt.

'Hmm, what would that be?' Jemma grinned. 'Oh, I know, I've heard Sean say it. Cur. That's what you're after, is it?'

'I can't wait until you're well. I think we're up to around five thousand push ups now. That's after you've done your daily thirty k runs.'

'If only.' Dropping the sarcasm, she looked him in the eyes. 'I'll be so happy when I can run with you again.'

'I know. How many steps now?' Hunt straightened up but she didn't miss the moistness in his eyes.

'Twenty-five,' she muttered, then looked up at him and laughed. 'It's not just about the number of steps. Counting it makes my brain do something and it's been a real struggle to get to the point where I could keep a consistent count.'

'We'll find the bastard who did this to you, Jemma. And God help him when we do.'

'I don't want him hurt,' said Jemma, 'but I do want to understand why. I haven't done anything to these people, yet they'd happily kill me. There's got to be more to this than just hating my grandfather.'

'That's possible. Focus on your walking for now. The rest can come later.'

The last ten steps took ten minutes. Several times, as she struggled to move her feet forward, she thought Hunt might pick her up and put her back on the bed. He was certainly strong enough to do that in her weakened state. But he didn't, and for that she was grateful. She was sure he wanted her to achieve the goal she'd set herself as much as she did. Once she reached the bed, he made sure she was comfortable, then took his leave, telling her to sleep.

* * *

Sean tore up to the interview rooms in the Administration Building as soon as Zadrus notified him that Ryan had been detained. He'd have loved to question Ryan without anyone else present, but he held back and waited for Hunt to finish with Jemma. It made him feel sick inside to see Ryan sitting comfortably on a lounge chair, sipping tea, as though this were a social occasion. It took all Sean's self-control not to rush in and thump the bastard.

'Stand down, Sean,' murmured Hunt, when he arrived.

That pulled Sean up, more than anything because Hunt never used his first name. 'Yeah, I know,' he muttered. 'But that's the arsehole who tried to kill Jemma.'

'We don't know that for sure, yet. We need to wait for Zadrus and Werrimen. Ah, here they are now.'

Sean growled as he strode into the room beside Hunt, but both men were stopped short by a loud screeching noise.

The man, Ryan, swung around. 'I knew about Sean. But the other one as well?'

'That is correct,' replied Zadrus, turning to Sean. 'He is using an electrometer.'

Although Sean nodded, he willed Ryan to attempt an attack and give him the excuse he needed to drop the bastard. Werrimen must have sensed his anger. She steered him to a chair at the far end of the lounge setting.

'We must get any information we can,' said Werrimen, quietly. 'Then this man, and anyone else we can find, will be transferred to the nearest IPL court to be tried and sentenced.'

Sean wasn't sure what he'd have done if Werrimen hadn't been there, but he knew he couldn't stand up to Werrimen and Zadrus together if they tried to stop him, so he complied. It had been more of an order than a request, anyway.

'You claim to have returned from Condona on the same transport zone craft that brought us here,' said Sean. 'You informed Jemma you were wearing a disguise, and that I know you well. Would you please remove the disguise and show me who you are?'

'Don't suppose it matters now,' he replied, with a shrug. He leaned forward and rolled a layer of something that closely resembled skin from his face.

'Good lord,' exclaimed Sean. 'Flamek. You were Lena's friend. We were on good terms. Why would you do this to us?'

'Flamek claims that the ruling class on Anders was weak and selfish, and failed to drive the Zants out before they destroyed their planet,' said Zadrus. 'He believes they have to ensure that no-one from the ruling class remains alive. They must be stopped from doing any more damage.'

'You weren't alive at the time the Zants invaded,' said Sean. 'How could you possibly know what the ruling class was like?'

'Don't throw that garbage at me,' shouted Flamek. 'I know. We all know.'

'How?' Sean did his best to stay calm.

Flamek whirled his head around towards Werrimen. 'Don't you see? He's just like all the rest of them. Arrogant and selfish. They're trying to restart their houses and they're only interested in looking after their own kind. They can't be allowed.'

Flamek's response took Sean back to his first encounter with the Zants when so many people had been manipulated into what they'd called the Rescue Earth Group. That group had believed the IPL was the enemy, yet they had no good reason for their belief. Something must have been done to brainwash Flamek and his colleagues too.

'It is true,' said Werrimen, calmly, 'that some of the ruling houses are attempting to re-establish, but from what I could see it is with the blessing of the people. I think you and

Jemma were right, Sean. Someone has been manipulating these people and we need to get to the bottom of it.'

'There's plenty of us here on Earth,' Flamek said, defiantly. 'It won't matter what you do to me, there's plenty more to replace me. We will win.'

*   *   *

Late in the evening, Jemma was sick of sleeping. The hospital was deathly quiet and all she could think about was how much she wanted to go for a run. She'd managed forty steps after Sean and Hunt had gone off to question that man. Now it was time for forty-five steps, but the door opened just as she was trying to stand and steady herself.

'I thought I was your walking partner,' snapped Hunt.

Several smart answers sprang to mind, but she let them go. She was actually glad to have someone beside her. Getting herself moving again was hard work, harder than anything she'd ever done before, despite Hunt's best efforts at making her life hell when she'd first met him.

'Evening, General. You'd better get over here, if you're planning to walk with me.'

She heard him mutter, 'Cheeky bugger,' but he had a smile on his face as he crossed the room.

After the first step, she felt herself teeter but managed to regain her balance by grabbing his arm. Every step was a struggle, and she wondered why she'd decided to keep putting up the number of steps. That was all her own doing. She couldn't blame anyone else. Hunt chatted away as she took each step, mostly about nothing of any importance, which was good, as she couldn't concentrate on what he was saying. It was a useful distraction though, and she appreciated it until he asked how she'd fared with her projects.

'Sorry, I haven't done much. I have tried but each time I start, I fall asleep. I can't seem to control it.' She paused for breath and looked up at him. 'I know, I know, it'll be three projects tomorrow.'

He returned her glare with one of his own, then his face softened into a smile. 'I know you're struggling, and I'm proud of how hard you're trying, so you can have one more day. I do want you to get your head around doing something, so I'll expect some progress tomorrow morning.'

The bed was only five steps away now, so she concentrated on getting there before answering. He said nothing as he helped her onto it, but he continued to look at her, obviously expecting a response.

'I'll try,' said Jemma. 'I think I am feeling a bit better, but it's up and down.'

'You know what I'm going to say,' replied Hunt.

She laughed, and in the deepest voice she could manage said, 'In my army you don't try, you succeed.'

'You've got it. The Trustee from Anders Major is due about ten tomorrow morning. I'll come back to meet him with you. Why don't you show me how much you've done then?'

'Gee, I'll try.'

He picked up the pillow he'd been rearranging and threw

it at her. 'Maybe I should double your workload.'

She laughed and tried to toss the pillow back at him, although it fell miserably short. 'I will do my level best. I can't promise better than that because I can't control the fatigue, it hits me out of the blue.'

'We'll see how you go.' As he left, he threw the pillow back at her.

She knew he'd expect her to have done something by the time he returned, and she had a couple of hours before Sean was due to visit, so it was the perfect opportunity to get started with the projects, but she dozed off.

It was morning before she woke again, disappointed that she must have slept through Sean's visit. He wouldn't have tried to wake her, preferring to let her rest and recover. She had to get her head around what was about to happen this morning. She wanted to be alert and thinking when the Anders Trustee got here. There were so many questions, so she picked up a notebook, intending to jot some of them down, then took a look at Hunt's instructions, but her head slipped forward, and she slid down the bed.

The grey, slushy fog inside her brain made it hard for her to open her eyes when she woke. Before the poison, she'd have woken bright and alert, ready to jump up and get on with her day. Now, it was like her brain and body were separate, and disconnected, entities. She slowly became aware of Zadrus leaning over her, gently caressing the side of her head, but she couldn't work out where she was or why he'd be with her. Accepting his help to sit up, she rubbed her eyes. The fog always lifted after a while, but it never entirely left her. She gradually worked out she was in the hospital, and then remembered why.

'I have someone I want you to meet, Jemma,' said Zadrus.

Still struggling to clear her mind, she looked at him, then at the other man who stood behind him. The same black uniform, the same gold crest, but he was human, not Sidlown. There must have been a frown on her face as Zadrus, who still supported her to sit, whispered, 'Relax, my dear, this will pass.'

She had no idea if that were true, but she had to get her thoughts together and attend to whatever Zadrus wanted. 'I'm sorry, it just takes a while to focus.'

The man behind Zadrus spoke for the first time. 'Please do not apologise. I have been told what happened to you.'

Zadrus relaxed his grip and introduced Kinbret, a Supreme Trustee from Anders Major. 'He is here to tell us about their history, your history, and what he thinks of recent events. Ah, General Hunt, welcome. We were just about to start.'

'Would you mind waiting a moment? Bellamy is on his way,' said Hunt. 'He needs to hear this as much as Jemma.'

An awkward silence followed, but Jemma was thankful for the break which gave her time to collect her thinking. Hunt sat on the bed behind her, and she leaned back onto him.

'You okay?' His voice was low, just loud enough for her to hear.

She nodded, there was nothing anyone could do, she just

had to concentrate as much as she could. When Sean arrived, he checked on her, then sat on the end of the bed, leaving Hunt to support her.

Kinbret told them a story of greed and deceit. His people had been a peace-loving, law-abiding society. So, when the Zants arrived and offered the people wealth and power beyond their wildest imaginings, most lacked the capacity to recognise the manipulation. As people began to follow the Zants, their society splintered. Most citizens, though, did back the ruling houses and, he believed the Supreme Ruler had done everything he could to protect his people. But the rulers of all the houses lacked experience with aggression and violence and their intervention was largely ineffective.

A rebel group of Zant followers formed. When the Zants let them down, they blamed the ruling houses for the loss of the gifts the Zants had offered. He couldn't say if they'd continued to work with the Zants, or if they had gone on to pursue their own aggression. The whole event had taken place more than a hundred years earlier, so there was no way to find out now.

Those loyal to the ruling houses had either fled to the hills, as Mary had said, or joined the spacecraft evacuations. Jemma's family, and he suspected most of the others, had been caught up in those evacuations.

'Hang on,' said Jemma. 'Ryan, who we now know is Flamek, and Drick have rekindled their link with the Zants. They seem to be working closely with them now. At least, that's what we saw on Condona.'

'Yes,' said Kinbret. 'And we have also seen signs of that on Anders.'

'We believe they're here on Earth, too,' said Sean.

Zadrus nodded. 'One of their craft came through two nights ago.'

'Jesus,' exclaimed Hunt. 'That's information I need to know!'

'Yes, I agree, and I apologise,' replied Zadrus. 'It slipped my mind because the craft did not stay here. It headed in the direction of Anders.'

Kinbret gave a soft cough and all heads turned towards him, although Jemma thought that Hunt still looked annoyed.

'Jemma, Zadrus told me about your nightmares,' said Kinbret. 'I believe I may have an explanation. We know more about your history than most others because of your high status.'

'I'd appreciate anything you can tell me,' whispered Jemma.

'I understand. It must be hard since your parents told you nothing. When you were evacuated, you and each of your family were transferred in disguise from the Kilkinan castle to the spacecraft. In your case you were placed in a wooden box, the type commonly used to carry fresh produce. You'd have been given a sedative, but I suspect it wore off. When you were evacuated, you were less than a year old, not old enough to understand, but probably old enough to form a memory which has troubled you since that time.'

'Why didn't my parents, or my guardians, or any of our parents or guardians, tell us about this?' demanded Jemma.

'I don't know why,' said Kinbret. 'But I suspect it was to do with protecting you.'

The door to Jemma's room opened again. Another man stood just inside the door. 'I can tell you why.'

'It can't be,' Jemma cried, as the man stepped into the room. She gasped for breath.

Hunt's arms firmed around her. Sean stepped forward so he stood between her and the man, clearly ready to react.

Jemma couldn't think. Her brain wouldn't process what she saw. 'You died! Just after Mum and Dad. The police said you were dead.'

The man walked into the room and stood at the end of the bed. 'No, I went over a cliff, but a small transporter was waiting for me, and we took off after dark. The police insisted you had drowned, along with your parents. I was then informed that your sister was missing, presumed dead. Without you, I had no reason to stay. I would never have left if I'd had any idea that you were alive. I'm so sorry, I just had no idea.' He reached out for her, and she pushed Hunt away, sinking into the man's hug, sobbing, even as he tried to soothe her.

As she sat back, she saw a look on Sean's face that suggested he hadn't bought the story. He'd moved closer, still looking like he was ready to spring.

'Sean, this is my Uncle Kevson.'

'I gathered that,' replied Sean. 'What I want to know is why you didn't make sure she wasn't alive? Her sister too. They both needed you.'

Kevson swung back to Jemma. 'Dear God, Thera survived too?'

Jemma nodded.

'When I heard you were here, Jemma, I was devastated that I'd left. The police insisted there was no chance. They said they knew you were in the car, they had witnesses, all your belongings were still in the car, and there was no chance anyone could have survived the crash. I was overwhelmed with grief that I'd lost my family. It just didn't occur to me that the police could have it so wrong. The Trustee who was our minder at the time said I was now at risk and had to go. He insisted, and I was in no state to argue. He arranged for me to join one of the IPL flights. So, I moved forward in time eighty years, just as you did.'

'What do you want from her now?' snapped Sean.

Kevson's eyes narrowed slightly as he looked from Jemma to Sean. 'I'm not the enemy, son. I made a terrible mistake. I can't undo it, but I can try to do something about it now. All I am interested in is Jemma's welfare.'

Jemma considered stopping Sean's questions, but decided against it. Sean was highly intuitive. If he doubted Kevson's story, she wouldn't deny him the chance to resolve his concerns.

'How do you plan to look after her welfare?' demanded Sean.

'I'd like to take her back to Anders Major where I can ensure she has excellent security.'

'And what makes you think your security would be better than ours?' growled Sean.

'She was poisoned here.'

Sean shook his head. 'By your people.'

Kevson looked at his Trustee. 'Yes, that is true. We can prevent their access.'

'Now that we know they exist; we can too,' said Sean. 'Perhaps you could help us here to weed your criminals out of our society.'

Jemma looked from Sean to Kevson. The police had been so clear that he was dead. Could it be possible that this was someone else made up to look like Kevson? Sean had been fooled by Ryan when he'd worn a disguise. But this man didn't just look like Kevson; he sounded like him, moved like him. And she was sure that Werrimen would have checked him thoroughly.

Kevson's eyes narrowed but he remained focussed on Sean. 'We will of course help you get rid of these undesirables, but Jemma is my priority.'

'She's also my priority,' said Sean.

Jemma sensed a stand-off looming between Sean, who she loved more than anyone, and Kevson, who had been so much a part of her childhood, and still meant a great deal to her. 'Sean is my husband.'

'Oh, I see. My invitation of course extends to you too then, Sean. Is your sister here too, Jemma?'

'No, but we know she survived. We found out about her after we arrived in this settlement.'

'Dear God, I should never have left,' muttered Kevson.

Zadrus didn't wait for anything further. 'I think we all

need time to discuss our options. Jemma must make her own choices, and I will assist her to do that.' He turned to Kinbret. 'Jemma and Sean are now also Trustees. They have the full might of the IPL to support and protect them.'

Kinbret bowed his head. 'I am pleased to hear that. She is very important to the people of Anders Major, but that means she is at risk from our rebels. I would ask you to invoke every protection you can.'

With a slight bow, Zadrus indicated to Kinbret and Kevson to follow him from the room.

Sean waited until he heard the door close. 'Sir, before you say anything, I need to get something off my chest. The hairs on the back of my neck bristled as soon as Kevson entered the room. I don't know if my suspicions are valid, or if I'm just responding to my instinct to protect Jemma. I need to know what you thought. And yes, Jemma, I need your thoughts, but I think it's probably harder for you than for anyone to determine his intentions.'

'Can I say something?' Jemma sat on the edge of the bed with her hands on her hips.

'Of course, my love,' replied Sean, laughing.

'Right.' She slapped his arm, then had to take a breath to steady herself. 'I know Kevson better than anyone, and I don't believe he would harm me. I think he genuinely believes that I would be better off on Anders Major. What I don't know is if he will try to force me to go if I say no. I suspect that to him I'm still a child.'

'Hm, to me too,' said Hunt, ducking out of the way before

she could slap him. 'Jemma, you want to believe in Kevson. I understand that, and you may well be right, but I'm not sure. We were all uneasy. Sean, I saw you bristle immediately. I suspect there's some jealousy there, you've always had Jemma to yourself, so a family member turning up is a bit disconcerting. But I'm uncomfortable too, and I've got a lot of questions. If a spaceship was waiting to pick him up, his disappearance was pre-planned. If the Trustees of the time were suspicious, why didn't they do something to protect everyone's safety? We can't deny now that there were multiple murders, including Jemma's parents, my parents, Bellamy's father, O'Leary's guardians and Denis's guardians, and presumably others. Why didn't they return and deal with their rebels, remove them from Earth, or at least let local police know about them? There seems to have been too much self-interest at play here, and I'm not happy with it. So, I have to ask, is it in his self-interest for you to return to Anders Major? Or is he genuinely interested in your welfare?'

Jemma stared at him thoughtfully. 'I believe he would be genuinely interested in my welfare, but it will have to be his way and he will not see that I should have a choice. Both of you have really good instincts, so if you're uncomfortable, then there's something wrong.'

'Question is,' said Hunt, 'what do we do about it?'

Werrimen walked through the door as Hunt was speaking. 'Perhaps I could offer my thoughts. Jemma, you're very special to us, and they know it. The Trustee, Kinbret, will obey me, but like you I'm not sure about your Kevson. I feel he is arrogant enough to believe if he demands something it must happen.'

'He always was pretty arrogant,' said Jemma, 'There's something else that's nagging at me. I remember a night when I was ten years old. We were at Kevson's farm, and they all thought I was asleep.'

'Recalcitrant even then,' muttered Hunt.

'Yeah, yeah. Kevson was telling Mum what to do as usual, when she raised her voice and said, "No, this is what we'll do." Kevson bowed to her, and said, "Your servant, Madam," but I didn't think he really meant it. There was also a person there dressed in black, which didn't mean anything to me at the time. He bowed and said the same thing. I understand now that Mum was the boss and they had to defer to her, but the thing that's bothering me is that I think the man in black might have been Kinbret. Is it possible he moved forward along with Kevson?'

'Very possible,' replied Werrimen. 'What's worrying you about it, my dear?'

'Well, if Kevson believes he's entitled to take me back, can we be sure Kinbret doesn't think the same way? If you're right about Kevson's self-interest when he took off, Kinbret must have supported him. In other words, can we trust either of them?'

'I've got another question.' Sean looked pensive, and at the same time, quite worried. 'Is he the real Kevson?'

'I'm confident he is,' said Jemma. 'He looks the same, the

attitude's the same, his voice is the same. I'm not in doubt, but I am worried about what he's up to.'

'You may have good reason for that fear, Jemma,' said Zadrus, as he joined them. 'He considers you have a duty to return to Anders Major.'

'The problem is, I don't agree with them,' said Jemma, 'but I'm too tired to work out how to fight them.'

'I understand,' replied Zadrus. 'Please leave Kinbret and Kevson to me today. I will do my best to work out if we can trust them.'

Sean stayed with her until well into the evening when she insisted that he go back to their apartment and try to get some sleep. She was desperate for sleep herself, and while she didn't want him to leave, she suspected it would be best for both of them.

CHAPTER 15

Jemma woke to the sound of a voice, but she couldn't clear the fog in her brain to make sense of the words.

'Jemma. Wake up.'

It sounded like Uncle Kevson. But they weren't at the farm. She rubbed her eyes. The farm probably didn't even exist now. No, not the farm. The hospital. After the poison. It all came flooding back. Kevson came in this morning. He'd flown in from Anders Major.

'Wake up.' Kevson shook her arm. 'We have to move. They won't wait much longer for us. We still have to get your cousin yet.'

Her cousin. Was he talking about Nik? Why would he need to get her at this hour of the night? He wasn't supposed to be here alone. The guards shouldn't let anyone through, not without checking.

She shook her head, just couldn't clear her vision, but she knew something was wrong. She vaguely remembered Werrimen giving her instructions on what to do if he bothered her. If only she could make her brain work. It was something about the bracelet on her wrist. She didn't normally wear a bracelet. That was it. Werrimen had put the bracelet there.

Told her to squeeze it if anyone bothered her. She forced her left hand to move across to her right wrist and onto the bracelet, not at all sure that she had the strength to do as she'd been told.

'Don't touch that.' Kevson tried to take hold of her left hand. 'You don't want to make a noise.'

Her vision had started to clear. Although Kevson's face was still blurred, his nervousness told her that he knew he was doing something wrong, and she wasn't in any condition herself to handle it. She trusted Werrimen, but she didn't know if she could trust Kevson. She took a deep breath, then focussed all her energy on squeezing the band of the bracelet. It didn't make a sound, so she wasn't sure if it had worked, but Kevson ran for the door and that, in her mind, sealed his guilt.

He called back, 'Jemma, baby, please. I just want to help you. I love you, sweetheart. We're family.'

Within seconds, Werrimen, Zadrus and Hunt rushed in, almost colliding with each other in the doorway. Sean, Dan, Nik and Matt weren't far behind, but as they began to speak, Jemma stared at the clock until it cleared enough for her to see it. At three o'clock in the morning, the crowd in her room felt quite bizarre, although it pretty much described her life nowadays. It was all so confusing.

Jemma had no doubt Kevson's motivation would be to look after her, and she was sure he would believe he was doing the right thing, but that was the problem. Her views would not enter into the equation. Yes, Kevson was family, and they'd been close when she was a child, but her own mother had, at times, spoken quite harshly to him, as though she had to put him back in his place. She was sure her mother had trusted him, but there was always a little bit of antagonism there. Maybe it was sibling rivalry. Her mother had been, after all, the ruler's heir. Kevson was second in line, although Jemma and her sister had probably made him fourth. Sean thought he might see her as a threat to his desire for the top position, but even if that were true, she didn't for a minute believe that he would harm her. She hated being this helpless, having to trust others to work it out for her.

A heated argument on the other side of her doorway made her swing her legs over the edge of the bed, ready to react it necessary, although she doubted that she could get far.

Kinbret shoved past both Sean and Hunt to get into her room. 'Please tell me what has happened.'

'As if you don't know,' muttered Sean.

'No, I swear to you, I do not know.'

Werrimen answered. 'Kevson just attempted to take Jemma away from us. Her guards are now missing.'

Kinbret vigorously shook his head. 'I don't believe Kevson would harm Jemma. He was bereft when he discovered she was alive. He made himself ill while we waited for a spacecraft to be ready to bring us here. This looks bad, but until I speak to him I can only guess at what he was thinking.'

'It is a strange way to act if he does care about her.' Werrimen responded to her communicator, then turned towards the door. 'They have found Kevson. I am going to join Zadrus now to question him. General, Colonel, would you stay with Jemma for the moment? I will return as soon as I have some information.'

Sean sat in the bed beside Jemma, frowning. 'Once we find the guards, we should have enough information to work out if Kevson's motivation is genuine or not. If he's hurt them, we'll know he's bad news. But we'll wait and see. More importantly, are you okay?'

Jemma nodded. 'I am now. It took me such a long time to get my mind into gear when he came in. I couldn't work out who he was at first, or where I am. But as I came around, I knew something was wrong, and eventually I remembered Werrimen had given me the bracelet. God, it was hard to make my hands work so I could use it.' She clung to Sean until she realised that Werrimen was still standing in the doorway, watching them.

'You did well, Jemma,' said Werrimen. 'I may want you to join us later, depending on what Kevson tells us. I have more guards coming. Some of my people. I am sorry, General, but I have no way of determining if human guards are from Earth or Anders Major just by looking at them.'

Jemma sighed. She understood only too well and thought both Hunt and Sean would too. The two men, along with Dan, Nik and Matt, did their best to comfort her after Werrimen left, but she remained tense. It was a relief when, in just under an hour, the call came to go to Zadrus's office. She'd have preferred to walk, but Hunt and Sean both growled. Under normal circumstances their actions would have made her dig in and demand to go under her own steam, but she knew they were right, and she lacked the energy to argue, so she flashed each of them a dirty look and slumped into the chair.

Zadrus was waiting outside his office. 'I believe Kevson's behaviour was a misguided attempt at caring, Jemma. I am satisfied he is the real person, but we will continue to question him until you and Sean are also satisfied. I'd like something more to verify his identity. Would you please ask him some questions from your childhood? Things that only he would know.'

'Okay, there's a few possibilities.'

It tore Jemma apart to see Kevson, sitting on the sofa, his head in his hands.

His body trembled as he looked up at her. 'I'm so sorry, Jemma. I thought if I could get you out of here, I could make you safe.'

Jemma jumped when something slammed onto the table behind her. Kinbret stood there, fury written across his face. Clearly it was his fist that made the noise. He shook his head.

'How the hell did you think you were going to get her out of here?' snapped Kinbret. 'I control that ship. My crew would never have agreed to do your bidding without my orders.'

'I told them we'd be coming, and you wouldn't be far behind us,' said Kevson. 'I'd planned to convince you I was right once you joined us.'

'It didn't occur to you that I would discuss the matter with my IPL colleagues?'

'No.'

Kinbret's increasing frustration made Jemma intervene. 'Zadrus asked me to ask you a couple of questions, is that okay?'

'Of course,' said Kevson.

'You had two house cows when I was a child, what were they called?'

He smiled. 'Yes of course. You named them, Maisy and Daisy. I wanted to call them T-bone and Sirloin, but you told me there was no way we could eat either Maisy or Daisy.'

The laughter that followed seemed to lighten the atmosphere.

'Always cheeky,' whispered Hunt.

'Damn right,' she shot back. 'Now, you gave me a birthday present when I was ten. What was it, and what happened to it?'

'Oh, that's a bit rough,' said Sean. 'I wouldn't remember every birthday present I gave to a kid.'

'The real Kevson would remember this one,' said Jemma.

'I do indeed. I gave you a horse, a beautiful, gentle palomino gelding. You called him Ginger, which I didn't much like, but he was your horse. Three days later, he was bitten by a western taipan. There was no hope, he died within minutes. We were all devastated.'

'I've no doubt you're the real Kevson,' said Jemma. 'I just don't understand what you want. You said you were here to help me, then you try to kidnap me. Even you'd have to see that doesn't look like someone who's here to help.'

'Probably not,' replied Kevson, with a sigh. 'I just wanted to take you home.'

'Against my will?' she exclaimed.

'I thought you were too unwell to make your own decision,' replied Kevson. 'And if you wanted your husband with you, I'd have come back for him.'

'You have to understand that I am home. Earth is my home.' Jemma had no doubt that would be difficult for him to comprehend. Like her mother, he'd come to Earth as a refugee, so Anders Major was home for him. But she couldn't remember Anders, and neither her mother, nor Kevson, had ever indicated that she was born anywhere other than Earth.

Jemma shifted her chair to sit beside Kevson. She took hold of his hand and was surprised to see a reaction from him as though he had felt something from her touch. 'Kev, before I'd even consider visiting Anders Major, I need more information. And you have to understand there are a lot of people here who will be included in any decision. It's not just me.'

For several minutes he stared at her, then he spoke quietly. 'Let me tell you my story, then you might trust me.'

'After what you did this morning, it'll take a bit,' replied Sean.

'I understand. Sean, Jemma, my part of the outback was very flat. My farm and the outbuildings were set on higher ground, so I brought all my neighbours in for safety when the weather turned bad all those years ago. We were all set to ride it out when I got the call on my satellite phone to tell me that you and your parents had drowned. The police were so definite that you could not have survived the accident, it never occurred to me to try to contact you.'

'I wasn't in the car,' said Jemma, quietly.

'I know that now, but the police at the time insisted you were. I was devastated. I contacted Kinbret and passed on the information. He had been informed that several other people from Anders Major had died in tragic circumstances, and not just in Australia but other countries too, mostly European. Thera was with her guardians in America. When she disappeared later that day, the guardians here on Earth believed that I was the only person left from our Supreme Ruler's family. Your cousin's guardians had hidden her so well that we had no idea where she was, or indeed if she was still alive. A message was put out by the rebels on Anders confirming that our entire family was lost. Stupidly, we never doubted them. Kinbret and the other Trustees and Guardians decided it was too dangerous for me to stay on Earth, and I was in no state to argue. Kinbret found all those he could and arranged to have us picked up. It was easy for me to stage a disappearance. I said I was riding out to check on stock and made it look like I'd drowned after falling off a cliff.'

'That's what is was told,' said Jemma, 'that you'd drowned.'

'I realise that now. Even then, I could have sought more information, I had no reason to doubt the police, so we thought it best to head back to Anders, but we soon learned that Anders still wasn't safe, so the IPL took care of us. They provided refuge on one of their ships, and we worked with them for several years. We were finally transferred to another ship which planned to move forward in time. They offered us other options, but we all agreed we had no reason to stay where we were. We began our journey later that month. We arrived on Earth and then we were transferred to Anders Major. We were shocked by the devastation. The Kilkinan castle was a disaster, but it was structurally sound. We found a few family members, with the help of the IPL, and set about restoring our home. I've been living there now for over a year and we've begun to re-establish law and order.

'When I was informed you were alive, Kinbret again requested IPL help. Jemma, I had no idea about anything that had happened to you, or that you were married. When we arrived, my electrometer alerted me to someone else from Kilkinan, and I requested a search. I had a younger sister, your aunt, who died in the original massacre on Anders Major, along with her husband. They had a daughter. The child's guardians grabbed her and fled. We never knew where. She was a few months younger than you.'

'We know about her,' said Zadrus, looking towards the door. 'Her name is Nikola Denis. Her guardians were killed not long after Jemma's parents. Werrimen has gone to get her.'

Jemma followed Zadrus's gaze to the door and saw Nik standing there, glaring at Kevson.

'Come in Nikola,' said Zadrus. 'Let me introduce your uncle Kevson.'

'I wasn't aware I had an uncle,' said Nik.

Kevson stood, looking pale. 'I am so pleased to meet you. The guardians claimed they didn't know where you were. If I'd suspected otherwise, I'd have wrung it out of them. I'm so sorry for the pain that my generation from Anders has caused all of you.' He fell back onto his chair, his head again in his hands.

'It sounds to me like there were too many people withholding too much information,' said Jemma. 'Everyone thought they knew best, so no one communicated with anyone else.'

'There have been many mistakes, I feel,' said Zadrus. 'We must now try to right the wrongs. I would like a meeting of everyone we've identified as originating in Anders Major. You know who they are, General Hunt. We have to decide what to do next.'

'May I join you?' said Kevson.

'Let him,' said Kinbret. 'I will be his shadow. He will not misbehave again.'

Zadrus held up his hand when Sean began to argue. 'Jemma will have impenetrable protection within the hour. I hope you have learnt a lesson Kevson. You may join us but be aware that we will not tolerate any further risks to Jemma, or anyone else.'

*   *   *

Sean held Jemma tightly to him as they waited for Hunt to round everyone up for Zadrus's meeting. He apologised and eased back when she looked up at him and winced. He hadn't realised quite how angry he was, and he wasn't prepared to forgive Kevson yet. Information had come through that the guards had been found, sedated but uninjured, and Zadrus seemed satisfied that Kevson was acting recklessly rather than with any bad intent so, for the moment, he'd work with Zadrus's view. He'd continue to do his own investigating, though, until he was absolutely sure. Decisions were about to be made that would affect all their futures, but in particular Jemma's future, and he was determined to ensure that she would have control. Whatever she decided to do, he would be there.

He looked up when Werrimen returned and ushered in a group of Sidlowns. All were Supreme Trustees. Their leader, who had nine stars on his crest, introduced himself as Yonkan. 'Hello, Jemma, Sean. I believe that I and my staff will be attached to you for the foreseeable future.'

'Pleased to meet you, I think,' said Jemma.

Yonkan picked up her hand and laughed. 'Your security is now my utmost priority. You are a very important person.'

'I'm not so important,' snapped Jemma. 'I wish people would stop saying that.'

'You're wrong, sweetheart. Even I've come to grips with that … Your Majesty.' Sean only just managed to duck out of the way as Jemma slapped at his arm.

'Alright you two, listen to Werrimen.' Hunt glared at Sean in particular.

'Sorry, sir,' muttered Sean.

The Trustees stood in a line a metre behind Werrimen, mostly with their heads bowed slightly. Zadrus was the only one who stood close, but even he had his head down. There could be no doubt looking at them that Werrimen was their superior, and it was obvious that she wore that as a heavy load as she addressed the group assembled in front of her.

'I have reached the conclusion that every person in this room is at risk,' said Werrimen. 'That includes you, Kevson, and I don't think it matters whether you are here or on Anders Major. I have spoken to Kinbret and other Trustees there. They all tell me there are still two or three rebel events every week. We must develop a plan, one that will protect all of you whether you are here or on Anders Major or anywhere else. Zadrus or I will speak to each of you before the day is out to discuss your next step.

'Kevson, you will be assigned a new Trustee guide. You have flouted Kinbret's authority so it will be someone else.'

'No need,' snapped Kevson.

'It wasn't a request,' replied Werrimen, quietly.

Kevson opened his mouth to say something else, but Kinbret squeezed the top of his shoulder, and he stopped.

The arrogance was still there, and Sean's suspicion that the man hadn't seen the error of his ways was heightened. But, for the moment, he'd leave that with Werrimen. He had to focus on helping Jemma. She needed him most right now.

CHAPTER 16

For the next month, Jemma worked closely with both Hunt and Zadrus, always shadowed by Yonkan. Despite their demands, her focus remained on re-developing her capacity to walk. She'd been provided with a personal mobility device, a PMD, which was similar to the aerial scooters she'd seen on Condona except that it was in the shape of a chair. Picking times when she knew that most would be hard at work in the academy, she used her PMD to head down to the athletics track, the only place she could find a flat, even surface to walk. At first, she could only manage a few metres, but she slowly increased her distance until the day that she was able to make it the whole way around the four hundred metre track without assistance and without stopping. Determined to prove to herself that her achievement wasn't a fluke, she repeated the exercise the following day, not realising that Yonkan had called both Liam and Hunt to watch.

'Well done,' said Hunt. He smiled but said nothing more as he walked away with Liam.

The next day, Liam was at the track waiting for her. He suggested a light jog. It was clearly a small change-up to him, but to Jemma if felt like he'd just asked her to leap across a massive chasm.

'No, I'm not ready,' she said, although she suspected her voice gave away her fear. 'I need a few more days.'

'I think you are ready, Jem,' said Liam. 'Putting it off isn't going to make it any easier.'

'No.' She vigorously shook her head. For weeks now she'd been pushing hard, and had achieved far more than Zadrus, or any of the medical staff, had thought possible. She wasn't ready to jump another hurdle, and by the time the General arrived, she'd begun to hyperventilate.

'Come on,' said Hunt. 'Over here and slow your breathing.'

'Can't,' she wheezed.

'You can. Come on.'

She walked with him to the edge of the track and sat as instructed.

'A few more minutes to get your breath back,' said Hunt. 'Then we'll start.'

'No, please. I'm really not ready.'

Hunt sighed. 'Jemma, what you've achieved since you collapsed has been phenomenal. I'm incredibly proud of you. I understand your reluctance, but I'm not going to let you put unnecessary barriers in your way. This is well within your reach. Come on, up you get. I'll do it with you.'

'That's such a comfort.' Expecting a growl, Jemma was surprised by his smile. Yonkan who had, as promised, stuck to her like glue, bowed his head slightly towards Hunt. It was clear that he knew precisely what was going on and would back Hunt if she sought his help, so she didn't bother. Somehow, she had to overcome her fear, but right now her legs felt like jelly. Taking a deep breath, she held her head high and walked to the track where Liam stood waiting for her.

'I can't do it.' She turned back and started to move off the track.

Liam put his hand on her shoulder. 'Yes, you can.'

She dropped back to the ground and shook her head. 'No, I can't.'

Hunt squatted beside her. 'You can.'

She shook her head.

'You're going to do this.' He gently pulled her up and turned her face to look at him. 'Easy way or hard way, you pick.'

With a few deep breaths, she shook him off and walked back onto the track, not sure if she could even remember how to jog.

Beside her, Hunt started forward. 'Walk first, then when you settle down, we'll pick it up.'

Her anxiety slowly subsided until she felt Hunt pick up his speed just a little, but to her relief she had no trouble keeping up with him.

Hunt put his hand through her arm. 'I'm about to pick it up. Just relax and go with me.'

If she tried to pull away, she had no doubt he'd increase his grip, so she didn't. It was a light jog, and so far she'd had no difficulty, although not knowing how far he'd go she remained tense. With just ten metres left on the track, he broke into a light run. He still had a firm hold on her, so she had to increase her pace to match his. Back at their starting point, Hunt pulled her off the track and sat. Her legs felt strained as she sat in front of him, but otherwise she felt okay.

'So, why do you think you found that difficult?'

They both knew what had happened, so why did she have to say it? 'You already know. I was scared.'

'Still?'

'Some.'

'Okay then we need to keep going,' said Hunt. 'I want you to jog just once right around the track. Still with me beside you. Come on.'

'Hang on, if I'd said I wasn't scared would you have let me stop?'

'Yep.'

'Damn.'

'Come on. Up and at it.'

Now she was annoyed. He didn't hold her arm this time, and she moved out in front of him, still fuming. At the end of the track, when she pulled up, Hunt was laughing. Even Liam had a broad smile on his face.

'So that's the secret,' said Hunt. 'I'll remember that.'

'I'll bet you will,' snapped Jemma.

'Feel up to a couple more rounds of the track?' His tone was innocent, but the expression on his face was anything but.

She swallowed her retort. If she sounded scared, he'd make her do it. If she sounded cranky, he'd probably make her do it too. But she genuinely didn't feel ready to do more.

Her legs were aching, and she'd started to feel nauseated. He stood quietly beside her, clearly waiting for an answer. Thankfully, he didn't push.

'No, I don't think I can. My muscles feel too strained.'

He stared at her for a moment, as though determining what to do next. 'Alright, we'll go for a gentle walk around the academy to cool down.'

'I've never understood why you spend so much time with me,' said Jemma. 'It's more than this whole supreme ruler thing.'

'Come on. Talk while we walk,' said Hunt. 'You know that Sean is very important to me, I've known him since he was ten years old and he's more like a son than a subordinate, but it's also due to the relationship that you and I have developed. I feel some guilt that we weren't able to stop all these attacks on you, although Werrimen thinks it unlikely we could have done more. We've all been manipulated one way or another. I believe you have extraordinary talent, Jemma, despite the fact that you are the most difficult and ornery person I've ever tried to train.'

'Really?' exclaimed Jemma. Her turn to feign innocence now. 'I think I've actually been amazingly cooperative and compliant given everything you've put me through.'

'Careful, I'll start running again,' said Hunt, grinning.

'As if that would surprise me.'

Hunt laughed. 'Go on. Have a rest. Lots to do later.'

Yonkan escorted her back to her apartment where Sean was waiting.

'I'll be just outside when you're ready to go out,' said Yonkan.

Jemma smiled at him. 'Thanks. I need to rest for a while. I'll call you when I get up.'

'Well,' said Sean, once she was inside and had shut the door, 'I heard about what happened this morning. How are you feeling?'

'Pretty exhausted, but I'm okay. He's just going to keep upping the ante though, so I'm going to have to rest every chance I get.'

'Suspect you're right,' said Sean. 'There's a meeting this afternoon and I understand we're all going to be allocated to permanent roles. I don't really know what that means, but I think the general, Werrimen and Zadrus have got their heads together and have made some decisions. Werrimen told me that they're keen to normalise our lives. Whatever that means. The general won't let me in on his plans for you. All I can say is you should be ready for whatever it is. Sorry, that's not much to go on, but I don't have anything else.'

'I'm pretty used to having to deal with it now.' Jemma sat on the side of the sofa. She'd have liked a shower but was too tired to get herself in there.

'Okay, you've got a couple of hours,' said Sean. 'I'll leave you to rest.'

After he left, Jemma remained on the sofa, curling up on the soft cushions. She wasn't planning on going to sleep, but she was so tired she drifted off. She woke to the sound of Yonkan's voice on her communicator. Although she was normally able to rouse herself more quickly now, it still took a few minutes for her mind to clear.

Yonkan's voice became more insistent. 'Jemma. Answer me please.'

She picked up her communicator. 'I'm sorry, Yonkan. Have you called me before?'

'Yes. Are you alright?'

'I am,' said Jemma, unable to stifle a yawn. 'I was asleep. It took me a while to come around.'

'That is fine. I was worried when I could not raise you. General Hunt has requested your presence at a meeting. I am outside your door.'

'Okay. I'm coming. Thank you.' She raced into the bathroom to wash her face. Getting her brain to work was harder than she could ever have imagined. She grabbed her gear, including the alien weapon she now always carried. It stunned, rather than killed, but even so it would provide her with the time to get away from an attacker. She ran from the apartment, and in her haste, almost ran into Yonkan.

'Slow down. They will wait for us.'

As she followed him to the disc, it struck her how much her life had been changed by the poison. Before that day, she would never have taken the disc, she'd have run down the stairs at the end of the building, but now the stairs were too much effort. Irritated, but recognising she couldn't change it, she walked with Yonkan to the administration building, doing her best not to worry about what Hunt planned to throw at her. As they entered the room, all eyes turned towards her. And that was another irritation. She'd become a curiosity since the poisoning, but there was nothing much she could do about it. Hopefully, time would resolve all.

'Have a seat, Jemma,' said Hunt. 'We'll begin as soon as Zadrus and Werrimen get here.'

Sean picked up a chair and placed it, so she'd be sitting next to him. 'Feeling okay?'

'Yeah. I overslept and scared Yonkan because I didn't answer the communicator when he first called.'

'He looks happy enough now,' said Sean.

'Yeah, he relaxed once he knew I was alright. I still feel guilty that I scared him, but I honestly couldn't do anything about it.'

'I'm sure he understands that,' said Sean.

'Everyone, listen up,' said Hunt, when Zadrus and Werrimen entered his office. 'All of you have played a role in getting the army up and running, with the exception of Dr Anderson, who has been holidaying in the hospital.'

'I wish,' she muttered.

'I'm going to reveal the new military structure now and the roles each of you will assume. I have taken on board your preferences and all the various suggestions that I've received. Rather than take on the old ranks, we will have four bands, each with a different colour insignia. Each band will have up to three stripes on their epaulettes. Recruits will all have one red stripe. My purpose in doing this is so that anyone from any band can take the courses and apply for promotion to the next band. There will be no false barriers between officers and non-commissioned ranks.

'Band one, the bulk of the service, will be orange and comprise the old ranks of private, corporal and sergeant. We may change the names of all the ranks as we proceed.

'Band two, the supervisors, will be yellow and will include first and second lieutenants and captain.

'Band three, the managers, will be green and will include major, lieutenant-colonel and colonel.

'Band four, the executive level, will be blue and will include three levels equivalent to general.

'I have taken the role of commander of the United Earth Army for every settlement and Zadrus requested that I wear a different colour, so I have adopted a purple epaulette. Any questions, so far?'

When no one answered, she suspected most were more concerned about where they were to be placed in this structure, than anything else, but she did smile to herself at his adoption of her suggestions.

'Alright then,' said Hunt. 'Bellamy, you are my deputy both with this settlement and across all other settlements. You will have three blue stripes.'

Sean gaped. 'That's equivalent to a lieutenant-general.'

'Yes and no. It's all different now. I'm asking a lot of you and your rank has to reflect the demands we'll all make. O'Leary you will have three green stripes and will take overall charge of both the army and the academy.' He didn't give anyone time to respond. 'Cleary and McMurtry, you will both report to O'Leary. You will each have one green stripe. Cleary will take charge of the training academy and general fitness.

'McMurtry will take general charge of the army, in this country to start. Those roles might have to be expanded as we proceed. It will be up to each of you to prove whether or not you are up to expanding with them.'

Both Liam and Ciara stared at him, mouths open, as though trying to form words, but nothing came out. Jemma smiled. Neither of them had been officers in the old army, and Hunt had just given them a rank equivalent to a major. Even more, he'd hinted that promotions could be available. All they had to do was prove themselves, which made her groan, because she knew exactly what that meant.

'Matt, you will also have three green stripes. I understand that you expressed an interest in taking over the factory that will build the new spaceships and have already been involved with the set up over there.'

'Yes, sir, I have.'

'Good, you can keep going with that, but I need you to stay on top of the alien technology too, so you will take both roles. I also want an organised investigation unit to identify both internal and external threats. Time will tell how we deal with each, but I would like you to get that organised. I know that you have already done a lot of work there.'

Hunt turned to Nik. 'Denis, I believe you also expressed an interest in the spaceship factory. You will have one green stripe and will be Matt's deputy. I also want you to maintain your role with the alien technology and the investigation unit.'

He then turned to face Jemma. 'Jemma, you will have two green stripes.'

She shook her head.

'Problem with that?'

'You know I do,' sighed Jemma.

'Time to come to grips with it, then,' said Hunt. 'You will work with Zadrus to take charge of Trustee training within the army. That does not mean you will conduct the training, at least not yet, but you will organise those who are involved with it. That will include flight training as you have expressed an interest in learning to fly the large craft. You will have to work closely with the Condonan pilots, and those setting up the factory. You will also remain involved with the alien tech, and probably have a role in the investigation unit. We will talk more about that later.'

She shook her head. She had no idea how to do any of that. 'Are you stark raving mad?'

'Nope, and neither are you, so all is good.'

Jemma didn't hear much else as he allocated tasks to others in the room. She whispered to Sean, 'Did you hear who I'm to report to? I think I missed that bit.'

'He didn't say. I suspect it'll be directly to him which is how it is now. He won't let you report to me or to Dan, and your role is different from Matt's.'

'Bloody hell,' said Jemma, sighing.

*   *   *

After two further months of daily training with Hunt, Jemma felt she was almost back to normal. She still fatigued more quickly than she'd have liked, and had the occasional dizzy spell, but her movement and strength had recovered well. Zadrus had insisted that regaining her health was paramount before tackling the Anders Major problem further, so days consisted of physical workouts, rest period and then study and training to come up to speed with her military role. She'd become so busy that the short snatches of time she managed to spend alone in her office were as precious as gold. After carefully securing her office door, in the hope that nobody would realise she was there, she wasn't happy when Yonkan, who was still her shadow, requested to enter.

'Good morning, Jemma,' he said when she released her door.

She took in a deep breath. 'Good morning.'

'Zadrus has asked me to retest your flying skills since you have been out of action for some time,' said Yonkan. 'I thought we might do that this morning.'

What Jemma really wanted was a break from Hunt's intensive training so she could do some research to work out her new role. Her days had been filled with lessons from Dan and Matt on how to handle her newfound rank. Sometimes even Hunt involved himself. Still, she loved flying, so a morning out there clearing out the cobwebs with pilot practice, which was to be a major part of her role anyway, might be just what she needed. 'When do you want to start?'

'Now is as good a time as any,' said Yonkan, smiling.

'Okay, I'll just have to notify the general that I'm going out.'

'No need. I have already done that.'

She followed Yonkan to a transporter parked on the roof of the Administration Building. As soon as they stepped inside, he threw questions at her about the engine's anti-gravitational system, the navigation system, safety checks and the pre-flight program. Werrimen, Dragile, Emilrad and the Condonan pilots had trained her so well, that she rattled off the answers, although it surprised her how clearly her mind processed the tasks, given the way her brain had been since the poison.

'Gravity pulls things down to the ground,' he said. 'If you can overcome the force of gravity, you have to go up. You don't need to know the mechanics, only that to go up you counter gravity, and to come down you allow it to take back over.'

He said, 'Forward,' then asked for a map and she laughed when the computer grumbled, 'Would you make your mind up? Do you want to go forward or look at maps? If you don't decide soon, I'll shut back down.'

'Be quiet and do as you're told,' responded Yonkan. 'Take no notice of it, Jemma. All these craft have cantankerous computers.'

Much to Jemma's amusement, the computer continued to grumble but the craft started to move forward.

They were a little over a hundred kilometres from the settlement, but still within the transparent energy membrane that they called the TEM, when they noticed a small township. Smoke rose from several chimneys, although they couldn't see any people. Yonkan told Jemma to take the craft lower, while he watched for any other sign of inhabitants. She was pleased he was confident to let her do it until something flew past her window, small but moving fast.

'By the stars!' yelled Yonkan. 'Craft, secure the force shield. We are under attack. Rise up.'

'Alright, alright, I'm getting there. Why did you come here anyway? Should have known better. I expect something better in the quality of my pilot.'

'Good Lord,' said Jemma. 'I think you need to reprogram your computer.'

'I wouldn't be rude, lady. Unless you want to walk home.'

'Be quiet, you stupid computer,' snapped Yonkan. 'Is the shield in place?'

'Which do you want? Quiet or answer?'

'Answer,' yelled Yonkan, 'right now!'

'Keep your pants on. Shields are up. We're hovering at two thousand metres. Should be above the range of their missiles.'

Something hit the rear of the craft. Jemma felt a thud, then saw a flash of light.

'We're okay,' Yonkan called to her. 'The shield will deflect any missile, but we need back up. Use your communicator and tell Zadrus what has happened, then advise your general.'

Within minutes, several other transporters joined them. A quick conversation between Yonkan and Zadrus followed, and it was decided two transporters would land with shields deployed and they would attempt to negotiate.

'We will stay up here,' Yonkan said to Jemma. 'We don't

know who these people are. They may present too big a threat to you.'

'You're not serious,' exclaimed Jemma. 'Aren't I supposed to be an active member of this army?'

'Yes, but you are still learning.'

She threw herself down into the co-pilot's seat. 'This is bloody ridiculous.'

Yonkan turned back to her and took hold of her jaw, lifting her face up to look at him. He was not gentle. 'Do not lose your temper with me. I will not tolerate it any more than Zadrus would tolerate it. You are a Trustee now. This behaviour is unacceptable.'

More than anything she wanted to yell back at him. Trouble was, he was right, her response had been childish. With a sigh she stood back up. 'I'm sorry. What do you want me to do?'

'For the moment, nothing,' replied Yonkan. 'None of us want you to suffer, Jemma, but you must learn some self-control. Zadrus and I both thought you'd come a long way.'

Was he really saying he believed she hadn't learnt anything? She didn't think she could achieve the control exhibited by most of the Sidlowns. They showed no emotion most of the time, although she had seen some angry outbursts from Zadrus.

'I don't know what to say,' sighed Jemma. 'Everything has been so confusing for me, and I get such mixed messages. It's like I have to put everything into learning skills for both the army and Trustees, but when it comes to any sort of problem, I can't use those skills. I shouldn't have answered you the way

I did, but that's what was behind it. I am trying very hard to be everything everyone wants me to be.'

He sat beside her. 'Perhaps you should just try to be who you are. Put your hands on mine, take my strength, and listen to me. I need you to do everything I tell you to do. This has changed from a training flight to a mission under fire. Our lives may depend on your responses to me. Can you do that?'

'Yes, of course. I can do that.'

For the first time since her short meltdown, Yonkan smiled. 'Good. I want to focus in on what is happening down there. I will get the viewing screen working, then I want you to watch and advise me of everything you see.'

It took less than a minute for him to clear the image of the scene below.

'A transporter just landed,' she said, still watching. 'It's Zadrus. He's walking towards the people.' Zadrus wore a suit of a type that Jemma hadn't seen before. General Hunt and Sean stood behind him. They wore the same suits, although they looked rather big on them. They'd obviously been designed for the Sidlown figure. 'There's another transporter. It's Werrimen. Dan and Matt are with her.' They also wore the suits.

People emerged from the houses. Several held old-fashioned rifles which they trained on the transporter crews.

'Zadrus said something, but I can't make it out,' said Jemma, as she tried to adjust the controls.

Yonkan leaned over her and fiddled with the equipment until the speech became clear.

'We don't believe you,' shouted one of the residents. 'We've seen you bastards before. You're not here to help. Get back in your craft. We will shoot.'

*   *   *

Sean whispered to Zadrus that he'd like to try a more personal approach. When Zadrus nodded, Sean removed the headpiece of his suit and stepped forward. 'Ladies and Gentlemen, the aliens who are with us saved all our lives. Without them most of us would be dead. We have established a settlement with their help and can provide for all your needs, including medical assistance.' He pointed towards a woman who struggled to walk. She had no walking aids of any kind.

The first man waived his gun. 'Get out of here, we don't need your help.'

Zadrus called to Sean to put his headgear back on, which Sean did just in time to avoid being shot. Thankfully, the bullet bounced off his suit. Sean moved forward again.

'Sir, my suit will protect me from your bullets. I am Colonel Sean Bellamy of the Australian Army. We have come across many communities such as this one before. Every time people look at our settlement, they accept our invitation. They recognise they will be much better off. I would like to invite a delegation from here to come with me to have a look. If you like what you see, we can help you to move. If you don't, we will not interfere with you.'

'Bugger off,' said the first man.

A woman walked behind him and grabbed his shirt. 'I will go,' she said.

'I will go with her.' Another man stepped out from behind them. 'If they are lying to us, they might kill us, but we are barely surviving here. I'm prepared to take the risk.' Several others moved forward and indicated they would also go.

Sean held up his hand. 'May I suggest we start with two people? I will bring them back and they can tell you if we can be trusted. May I ask how long you've been here?'

'Around ten years,' said the woman. 'We've not seen another human being in all that time. But we have seen a few of those spaceships. They've shot at us several times.'

'How long since you've seen one of those?'

'About ten minutes,' muttered the first man.

'Before ours,' said Sean.

'Several months,' said the woman, 'maybe six.'

Zadrus touched Sean's shoulder. 'We should go. The sooner we leave the sooner we will get back to find out what these people need.'

As they headed towards the craft, Zadrus asked the volunteers to leave their weapons behind.

Both people looked at Sean and faltered.

Sean nodded and pointed to the ground. 'We don't allow that kind of weapon on our craft. They're too dangerous. We can provide you with alternative weapons if you wish.'

Both of the volunteers complied, although neither looked particularly confident.

Sean smiled. It wasn't so long since he'd had much the

same experience. He'd do for these people everything Zadrus and Werrimen had done for him, explain the craft, show them around the settlement and, by the look of them, offer them a better meal than they'd had in a very long time.

* * *

Yonkan patted Jemma on the shoulder. 'We can leave now. They have defused the situation down there. What is our first command?'

She figured she'd better not get this wrong, Yonkan was already annoyed with her. 'I have to state the destination, then tell the craft to move forward.'

'Something else first.'

If he'd told her before, she couldn't remember. Perhaps he wanted a safety check. She'd try that.

'That is right,' said Yonkan, 'but can you recall what I said when we began this flight?'

'No, I'm sorry,' murmured Jemma.

'Don't panic, I am not annoyed with you. You are right about safety. We check doors and ensure passengers are seated. But we also check the engine and ask the computer for a technical safety check which it can do without us. I will teach you later how to do a manual safety check if the computer ceases working.'

'Okay. I'm not really panicked,' said Jemma. 'I don't want to let you down again.'

He squeezed her shoulder. 'Focus only on what you have

to learn, not me. I am here as much for your safety as to teach you, and for that reason, I have high expectations. Let us go home.'

When they landed, Zadrus was waiting. He didn't believe the people they'd found had anything to do with Anders Major. He planned to ensure they had their bloods checked before he took them back but was not concerned about them.

Jemma felt strangely disappointed that these people weren't from Anders. She'd been hoping they might have some useful information. It frustrated her how well the Anders people seemed able to meld into the settlement. They moved freely in and out of buildings which did make sense given they were human, except that security right through the settlement was tight.

Legitimate residents were registered for the bead entry to any building that they were entitled to enter. Records were kept for facial recognition, retinal scans and DNA. Yet Anders people, such as Ryan, who couldn't have been registered, somehow managed to evade all those security measures and find their way into places they should not have been able to enter. Given she'd now been allocated the investigation role in the new setup, that seemed as good a place as any to start.

She ran to catch up with Zadrus. 'Do you have any idea how these people are getting into our buildings given they haven't been scanned for our beads?'

'No. They have found a way around it. We have not yet identified how.'

'So,' said Jemma, 'when a bead allows someone to enter a building, there's a record kept isn't there?'

Zadrus nodded. 'Yes, your CIG computer keeps a full database of all entries and exits.'

'Is it possible to disable the bead? Or copy someone else's records?'

'Technically, yes,' said Zadrus. 'But it would require very advanced knowledge of our systems.'

'Which, the people from Anders Major would have,' replied Jemma.

'Yes, you could be right.'

'If they disabled the bead, there'd be a glitch in the database, wouldn't there?' asked Jemma.

'Yes, you'd be looking for a missing time period,' replied Zadrus. He was now smiling, and she assumed he'd figured where she was going with her questions.

'And if they'd duplicated someone else's records, the computer should show the owner of that record entering the building twice without having left. I'm thinking that if we could isolate the images captured by the bead at the time, we should be able to identify both people who've used those credentials, the legitimate user and the imposter.'

'I see your point,' said Zadrus. 'I will have one of our technical people assist you to look into it. You should discuss this with Matthew.'

Jemma left Zadrus feeling more than a little pleased with herself. Keen to pursue the idea, she decided to look for Matt straight away. When she found him, he was deep in conversation with Nik about the setup of the spaceship factory. As she listened to them discuss all the technical obstacles that faced them, she began to think her idea might be too trivial to bother Matt now. She was about to discreetly leave when he spotted her.

'Afternoon, Colonel,' said Matt, grinning. 'What can I do for you?'

She started to bare her teeth, but she needed his help, so in the sweetest voice she could muster she filled him in on her conversation with Zadrus.

He nodded several times. 'Good thinking. Nothing much more I can do here at the moment. Let's go see what we can find. Hopefully, Zadrus will remember to send one of his techs down.'

Zadrus had remembered and the three of them spent several hours extracting data. Jemma was happy to find she'd been thinking along the right lines, but shocked by the level of sophistication as they slowly unravelled the system used by the intruders. As they meticulously distinguished between legitimate users and imposters, thirteen people were identified who appeared to have entered the Administration building twice without having left. A small square box-like device was held behind the genuine resident as they stood under the bead. Jemma presumed it copied the ID. Once the owner of the ID was inside the building, the intruder held the box underneath the bead. The door then opened. Simple as that.

Matt broadened the search, asking the computer to check

the records for every person registered within the settlement. He specifically asked if anyone was registered twice in any building at that current time. He also asked it to identify anyone currently registered in two different buildings. If the black box had stored the credentials, it was logical that the intruder might be able to enter another building.

While the computer continued its analysis, Matt set about organising staff who could be sent out to intercept both parties involved with the suspect ID.

'Good thinking,' said Jemma, and she was genuinely impressed.

'That's why I've got three green stripes and you've only got two.'

'And that's two too many,' muttered Jemma.

Matt laughed. 'Come on. Let's go tell the boss what we've found.'

'For God's sake, don't let him hear you call him that.'

'Oh, what's that I hear?' said Matt, cupping his hand behind his ear. 'Are you about to start calling your superior officers "sir"?'

'I guess that depends on your definition of superior,' replied Jemma, smiling sweetly.

He shrugged and pointed to his shoulder. 'Three stripes.'

She ignored him and started to head towards Hunt's office, not surprised when Matt nipped past to make sure he entered the office first. Both were laughing when they stood in front of the general and, to Jemma's amusement, Hunt looked up at them, one eyebrow raised.

'Morning, sir,' said Matt. 'Spare a moment?'

'Of course.'

'We've been working on an idea raised by a more junior officer, Lieutenant-Colonel Anderson.'

'All right. All right,' said Hunt. 'Cut to the chase.'

Matt was instantly serious which made Jemma shake her head, as he filled Hunt in.

'Well done,' said Hunt. 'Between you and Jemma, I might be able to retire sooner rather than later.'

'Just say the word, sir,' said Matt, grinning. 'Happy to jump in whenever you wish.'

'Pleased to hear it,' said Hunt. 'Just don't bury me while I've still got a pulse.'

'I'd never do that, sir,' said Matt, earnestly. 'Far too much paperwork. I'm sure we could find a nice aged care facility for you.'

Hunt picked up a hand towel from his desk and threw it at Matt.

Jemma did her best to appear serious. 'Would you like me to help you arrest this upstart, General?'

'I believe I can manage that by myself,' said Hunt. 'Now, enough of that, let's talk strategy. Don't pounce on the imposters when you find them. Have your people follow them. Find out where they go. Identify their base, where they live, and how they're surviving without any input from the IPL.'

Matt nodded. 'And when we find all that out, what do you want us to do?'

'Bring them in. Disable their craft. I'd like to work with

you to interrogate them. That's if you don't think I'm too feeble, of course.'

'Certainly, sir,' said Matt. 'I'll let you know when the dementia progresses too far.'

'No bloody wonder you and Jemma get on so well. You're as cheeky as she is.'

*   *   *

Hunt was still smiling when he turned back to his desk after Matt and Jemma had left. If his son and grandson had been anything like Matt, he'd have enjoyed watching them grow. Perhaps he could gain some of that from watching Matt and his daughter. Dana was a delightful great granddaughter-in-law, although she still had a long way to go to recover her health. Yet the precarious balance between being Matt's boss, and something approaching a father figure was sometimes hard to achieve. It wasn't all that different with Jemma. He wondered how the late, great Lieutenant-General Gerard Hunt who Matt spoke about with such reverence would have managed Matt, and what he'd have thought of Jemma.

Hunt started when Werrimen interrupted his thoughts. She moved so damn quietly. 'You and Matt seem to be enjoying your interactions with each other.'

He suspected by the way she stood with her arms folded across her chest that she had something more important to discuss, but he'd play it cool and restrict himself to answering her question. 'He's a fine young man. Mind you, I'd like to know whose silly idea it was to team him with Jemma.'

'I believe it was yours, General,' said Werrimen, smiling.

'Damn, I should have thought that one through a whole lot better,' said Hunt, laughing. 'Alright, you obviously want to discuss something. Out with it.'

'I know how fond you are of both young people.' She stopped and stared at him, a slight frown on her face.

Hunt waved her to a chair. 'Don't hold back. What's the problem?'

'Jemma got herself into some minor trouble with Yonkan this morning,' said Werrimen.

'Oh no.' Hunt sighed. 'They seemed to be getting on so well. What did she do?'

Werrimen shook her head. 'Do not worry. It was not serious. Jemma reacted badly to something he told her to do. I would not have mentioned it, except that she said something to him that concerned me.'

'Oh Lord.' Hunt leaned back in his chair. 'What was it?'

'She apologised after the incident and then tried to explain herself,' said Werrimen. 'She said that she has to train to protect herself, but as soon as anything happens, she's not allowed to be involved. She doesn't want to be treated like a queen bee.'

Hunt nodded. 'Okay. Since we've found out about her heritage, we've all been focussed on protecting her. Perhaps we've gone overboard. Sean told me once not to wrap her in cotton wool, she'd rebel.'

'Yes, and I understand that,' said Werrimen. 'But we cannot allow her to be at too much risk, either.'

'Can't we? I took her on in the first place because I saw something very special about her. Before we left the Earth of 2020, she fought off a terrorist with her bare hands. She saved all our lives. I'm just as guilty of forcing her to sit back as anyone else. But it may not be in her best interests.'

'Zadrus agrees with you, I believe,' said Werrimen. 'But I have promised her I will not allow any harm to come to her. How can I do that if she is at the forefront? She is the main target.'

'Yes, I know.' Hunt sighed. 'It's a delicate situation. Let me talk to her, see if we can find a solution.'

Hunt was interrupted in his attempt to call Jemma by Matt's return. 'It didn't take long, sir. My crew noticed one of the people we'd identified as an intruder leaving the administration building. Nik and I followed her while Jemma set up surveillance to track us. Their site isn't far away, but it does seem to be underground. I'd like to establish a team to investigate.'

'Well done,' said Hunt. 'Get Bellamy. He needs to be involved. Then round up O'Leary, Denis and Jemma. We all need to discuss our next move. I'm not usurping your authority, Matt, but with something this important we need to work as a cohesive team.'

'I'm good with that,' said Matt.

Hunt wasn't convinced that Matt was actually good with that, but it didn't matter. This was the way it was going to be.

CHAPTER 17

Sean attempted to hide his annoyance that Matt hadn't let him know there was an operation in progress when he made his way to Hunt's office and rapped on the door. 'Sir, Matt said you wanted to talk to me.'

'Did Matt fill you in?' asked Hunt.

'He did,' said Sean.

'And you're pissed he left you out?'

'Yeah, a bit.' Sean shook his head. 'No, not really when I think about it. It's going to take time to settle down the hierarchy.'

'Agreed. If it helps, I didn't know either,' said Hunt. 'Jemma had an idea. She discussed it with Zadrus and then approached Matt. I don't think either of them expected a quick result. We'll discuss management roles later. Right now, I want a strategy meeting. I've sent for the team, but you should run it.'

'Have you included Jemma and Nik?'

'I have, and there's something else you need to know.' Hunt relayed Jemma's conversation with Yonkan that morning. 'I had a quick chat with Mary. She tells me that both Jemma's grandfather and her mother were leaders of their army. As was Kevson. If Jemma were to return to Anders, she would be expected to be a warrior.'

Sean sat back and closed his eyes. 'Are you saying we have to let her take a more active role?'

'I am.' Hunt shook his head. 'No, don't get your hackles up. We can ensure she has good back up, but I think for the sake of her self-esteem we have to let her be more involved. We've demanded she learn how to defend herself, then when it comes to the crunch we step in and defend the damsel in distress. She's better than that, Sean.'

'Christ.' Sean rubbed his face. 'I know better than anyone how capable she is. I still hate it.'

'I feel the same,' said Hunt. 'But after talking to Werri-men, I think we've become the problem. We're protecting her out of our own fear. She needs us to value her, not treat her as the little woman who needs us to look after her.'

'She means everything to me,' said Sean, quietly. 'I can't bear the thought of anything happening to her.'

'That I understand, and that really is the essence of our problem,' said Hunt. 'Now we need to try and see it from Jemma's perspective and allow her to be who she is.'

'I know you're right. It doesn't help.' Sean stared at the ceiling for a minute. 'Alright then, I'll open the meeting, but we need to remember that Dan is the leader of the army. Matt has done his investigation, and now for something this important, the army should take it from here.'

'Hmm. Interesting times. You're right. Matt should have a key role though. He needs to be out there given all he's been through. Jemma and Dennis should each lead a team. I'll leave you to work that through with O'Leary.'

'Christ almighty,' exclaimed Sean. 'They're the two most vulnerable people in the settlement. I accept I'm over-protective, particularly of Jemma, but it's not just that. It's Jemma and Nik that these bastards want to kill.'

'I know,' said Hunt. 'That means they have the highest stake and every right to be out there. Brief O'Leary, then return.'

'Should we involve Liam and Ciara?'

'I'd say you'll have to because we'll need people from the academy to form the teams.'

'Okay.' Sean took Dan aside when he arrived for the meeting and quickly filled him in. When they returned to Hunt's office, Sean congratulated Matt and Jemma on their discovery, then appointed Dan to command the operation. He didn't miss the dark look on Matt's face, as he handed over to Dan, but thought it best to ignore it.

When Dan had finished, Jemma asked if he wanted her to take surveillance. She didn't appear annoyed. It was more a resigned acceptance that she wouldn't be allowed to actively participate.

'No, it's time you showed us what you can do,' said Dan. 'Matt, our most vulnerable area is to the East. It's a sheer cliff face. I want you to take the blue team. Start at the south of the area and head north, staying as close to the east as possible. Jemma, you'll lead out with the white team, from the west and head north-east,' said Dan, using a map that Hunt had organised onto the screen on the wall. Nik, you'll lead the red team, starting at the north of the mapped area and head south-east.'

'Any idea where they've gone?' asked Sean, doing his best not to take any notice of the surprised look from Jemma.

'Behind that clump of trees,' said Matt.

Sean shook his head. 'They couldn't all hide there.'

'No, but they haven't come out in the open anywhere,' said Jemma. 'They must have gone down somewhere. We couldn't see an opening, so we assumed it must be directly behind that clump.'

Sean desperately wanted to speak to Jemma, tell her about precautions she should take, instruct her not to take any risks, but he knew that she was already aware of all of that, so he helped Dan organise the people from the academy into the teams. Once it was organised, he accompanied Dan to the site, being careful to stay well behind and let Dan take the running, although he remained close enough to intervene if needed.

The teams moved out on Dan's command. Jemma's team was first to reach the clump of trees. Sean swore at himself when he realised that he was tense and plotting what to do if anything went wrong.

'Nothing here,' said Jemma, through her communicator.

That pulled Sean back to focussing on strategy. He had to be ready to respond to Dan if he needed assistance.

'Oh, hang on,' called Jemma. 'Liam just pulled on a sapling that looked different from the others. Something moved on the ground in front of us.'

'What have you found,' yelled Sean, not waiting for Dan to respond, as he saw Jemma start to edge forward.

'It's a cavity,' called Jemma, her voice tinged with excitement. 'There's a set of stairs here. We're going in.'

'No, stand down,' bellowed Sean. 'Wait till we all catch up. That's how I was caught last time.'

'I was about to say that,' muttered Dan.

'I know,' said Sean. 'I'm sorry. I just had to stop her.'

Jemma interrupted. 'There's no-one here.'

'Follow orders,' snapped Dan. 'It could be a trap. That's how the Zants got us.'

'Fine,' said Jemma.

Dan didn't respond to her. 'All teams proceed to white team's position. Come on,' he said to Sean.

When they reached Jemma, Dan allocated Ciara with four of her people to remain above ground and act as lookouts. Then, with Sean close behind, he led the way down the stairs into a large void that opened out into something that looked like a massive underground landing bay. It was dark, and there didn't appear to be any natural lighting other than from the opening they'd just come through.

'Looks like one of the old Zant hideouts,' said Sean, as he looked into the cavity.

'Sure does,' muttered Dan. 'Everyone, keep your eyes peeled. Stay in groups. Nobody goes in alone.'

Matt and a couple of others had light sticks, small cylindrical devices not much bigger than a graphite pencil which, once activated, gave off an intense light.

'Look at that,' said Jemma. At the eastern end of the cave a transporter was parked. It was the type used by the IPL, not a Norellian sphere or a Zant craft as Sean had feared.

'Yeah, I've seen it,' murmured Sean. Then he raised his voice. 'Stop. Everyone stay where you are. I'm sending images to Zadrus and the general.'

It only took a few seconds for Zadrus to appear on Sean's communicator. 'Do not approach. I am on my way. Please go back outside.'

'You heard the man,' said Dan. 'Everyone outside.'

Jemma threw him a dirty look.

'Problem, Jemma?' said Sean.

'No, it's just the same old story.' She looked back as she sighed. 'Not allowed to do anything.'

'I understand how you feel, but we don't know what we're dealing with here,' said Sean. 'So, we wait for Zadrus and Werrimen. I have no desire to be a victim of the Zants again.'

'Oh God. I'm sorry,' murmured Jemma. 'I should have realised that. You don't really think the Zants are here, do you?'

'No, but I think they have been, and we know they're working with the Anders rebels, so they could be anywhere.'

'You're assuming the Zants are still on Earth,' said Jemma.

'There's plenty of evidence that they could be,' replied Sean. 'We know they've got orbiting ships and they're so tricky, we can't assume they're gone.'

'I guess I was just hoping they had,' said Jemma.

'Don't assume anything,' said Sean. Something in Zadrus's

tone of voice had bothered Sean more than his words, so he wasn't surprised when Zadrus arrived that he had Yonkan, Kinbret and Jemma's uncle Kevson with him.

'I believe this is an Anders Major craft. Kinbret is here to identify it,' said Zadrus, as he walked towards Sean. 'Anders has access to IPL transporters. There should be several small identifying marks.'

'I'll go with him,' said Kevson.

Zadrus, Yonkan and Kinbret simultaneously said, 'No.'

But Kevson insisted. 'I know I'm at risk, but if I can help to remove these people it's worth it.'

'I'll go too, then,' said Jemma. 'It's me they're after. Let's confront them.'

'Let's all cool down,' replied Sean. 'One or two people alone in there could easily be overpowered. Almost everyone here has an Anders Major connection, not just the two of you. If we're going in, we do it together. There's power in numbers. That makes it harder for any of them to gain the upper hand.'

Zadrus stared back at him, and Sean thought he was going to say no, but he seemed to think better of it. 'That makes sense, Sean. You and Jemma lead the way. Liam can take charge of Jemma's team and follow behind us along with Nikola's team. Kinbret, Kevson, Yonkan and I will go next. Matt's team take the rear. Watch for anyone following us. Kinbret, see if you can identify the craft. Determine if you can disable it externally. Everyone, remain alert. Be ready to deal with whatever happens in there. Weapons ready.'

Sean waited for Dan to check each team, then Sean led

out with Jemma beside him. He was pleased to see that she was neither excited, nor frightened, just watching in much the same way as he did himself. When they neared the craft, he motioned to the others to fan out around it. Zadrus moved directly behind Sean while Yonkan moved in close to Jemma. She gave him an irritated look to which he smiled and patted her shoulder. To Sean's relief she didn't react. She maintained her vigil on the craft as she was supposed to do. Satisfied that everyone was in place, and after a quick word with Dan, Sean waved Kinbret forward.

'It is an Anders Major craft,' whispered Kinbret as he edged past. 'I should not have any difficulty disabling it.' He fiddled with something under the craft, then stepped out and nodded to Sean to indicate he'd accomplished his task, but before he could return to the group a man ran out from underneath the craft and grabbed Kinbret around the neck, pushing his arm up behind his back.

'One false move from anyone, and I will kill him,' shouted the man.

'Steady mate,' said Sean. 'We just want to talk.' The fellow wasn't large, and under other circumstances, either he or Dan could have taken him down easily. But there was a crazed look about him. Sean chose to err on the side of caution.

'Talk? I don't believe so,' snarled he man. 'While you support this trash from my planet, I don't believe we have anything to talk about.'

Zadrus shook his head. 'Perhaps we can help you resolve your problems. It is not our wish to support either side.'

From the corner of his eye, Sean saw one of the IPL Trustees edging around the outside of the group towards the craft. The man must have seen him too.

'One more step, and I'll kill this one.' The Trustee froze, as he saw the man push something closer to Kinbret's neck. The object was round, maybe five centimetres in diameter, and thin, less than a millimetre in height, but the look on the faces of all the Trustees convinced Sean it was dangerous.

Zadrus held up both his hands, palms facing the man. 'I am unarmed. May I come a little closer to you so we can talk.'

The man nodded, but when Zadrus was within two metres, he ordered Zadrus to stop.

'For the benefit of those who don't know,' said Zadrus, 'I will explain that this object is an incendiary device. I do not understand why you would murder an innocent person. We have not threatened you, nor have we attempted to detain you.'

'You protect them,' said the man.

Zadrus shook his head. 'We will not stop you from returning to your craft if you allow my Trustee to go, unharmed. If you harm Kinbret, you will not leave here alive.'

He shrugged. 'We can all die together then.'

'I will not have anyone die on my behalf. It is not Kinbret you want, it is me.' Kevson stepped forward towards the man. 'I am Kevsondi of Kilkinan, ruler of Anders Major. I will come forward if you let Kinbret go.'

To Sean's dismay, Jemma went to say something, but Yonkan stepped in front of her and told Kevson to stay back. They would not permit any more killing. Yonkan gave the slightest nod towards the Trustee who had tried to skirt around Kinbret before.

Sean was aware that all the senior Trustees had their weapons pointed at the man. The Trustee near Kinbret used the slight distraction and fired, immobilising the fellow. As the man started to fall, Yonkan ran forward and grabbed the device before it could hit the ground. Kinbret simultaneously turned and rolled the man over, pinning both arms behind his back.

'On his side,' said Yonkan. 'Make sure he can breathe. He must tell us precisely what is going on. Kinbret, what did you take from the craft?'

From his shirt Kinbret pulled something that looked like a sheet of plastic. 'Without this, they have no power, their computers cannot work.'

'Can you get us inside?' Sean walked towards the craft. 'There might be others there. It'd be ideal to round them all up.'

'Yes, I agree,' said Yonkan.

'Please come behind me with weapons,' said Kinbret. 'I'd prefer not to be held hostage again.'

Sean moved forward, his weapon ready.

Kinbret stepped beside him and held up something that looked like an old-fashioned credit card. He placed it against the side of the craft. 'This is where the door should be. Ah yes, here it goes.'

The outside had appeared seamless, but now a panel slid

back. Kinbret pulled down a ramp and jumped up inside. Sean followed him, then Jemma, both with weapons set and ready to fire. Six people stood together at the far end of the craft, two men and four women. Two of the women were shackled and almost naked.

Zadrus hauled himself in. He gave a loud sigh. 'I know what is going on here. Jemma release the two ladies and take them with you. They have obviously been held prisoner, and I am sure they will feel safer with another woman. Yonkan will go with you. Give them clothes and take them to the hospital. We will interrogate the rest of these people.'

As they left, Sean noticed Jemma frown as she took a last look at the craft from Anders Major. He'd have to wait to ask her what that was all about until the prisoners were settled.

CHAPTER 18

Jemma gently questioned the women on the way to the hospital. Both stated they were residents of the East Australian Settlement, and although she planned to verify it later, she believed them. One of the women said she'd gone to bed as usual but had woken up in the transporter. She had no idea how she'd got there. The other woman agreed but dissolved into tears as she tried to recall anything else. Jemma was relieved when both women made it clear they hadn't been raped, although she wondered if that were just a matter of time.

Aware that her questioning was causing distress for both women, Jemma left them in the care of a nurse she knew well, then headed back to Zadrus's office. She was convinced that he and Werrimen knew more than they were saying and she wasn't prepared to let them withhold any more information. It was time for everyone to come clean and give her the facts that she'd need to stand up to these Anders people. When she arrived, Sean was deep in conversation with Zadrus, but she wasn't in the mood to be polite and wait for them to finish.

'Zadrus, what was it about those two women that had you so worried?' demanded Jemma.

'Of course,' said Zadrus. 'Sean, would you ask General Hunt to join us? Jemma, are the women alright?'

Jemma sat on the sofa. 'They will be, but they couldn't tell me much. The thing that concerned me most was that neither could remember being taken.'

'I see,' said Zadrus. 'I believe that verifies our belief that the Zants are again working with the Anders rebels.'

Werrimen sat beside Jemma on the sofa. 'My dear, you will probably not like what we have to say, but please hear us out.'

Kevson sat on her other side as they waited for Sean and the rest of the team. He looked like he wanted to reassure her, but she was tired of being told that everything was okay or that she shouldn't jump to conclusions. It seemed to her that there was an enormous amount of criminal activity going on, and none of it was okay.

Werrimen stood when Hunt arrived. She waved him to a seat and fiddled with the base of her shirt for a minute, then cleared her throat and began. 'Earth was traditionally seen by other planets as a prison planet.' She paused. 'Thousands of years ago, several planets dumped their convicted felons here, but there were free settlers too. Everyone who came here knew they would have to learn to hunt for their food and build their own shelter. I do not suggest that the prison image is fair, but that has long been the pervading attitude. Some planets, like Anders Major, saw humans from Earth as inferior to them, largely due to that image. Paradoxically, if they needed someone as a helper, or even a spouse, they'd send a crew to Earth to find a suitable candidate. Sean's mother, as you know, was one of them.'

'We knew they took people from Earth,' snapped Jemma, shaking both Kevson and Sean away as they tried to calm her. 'But what we've learned today is that they're still doing it.'

'Yes, we did know,' said Werrimen. 'And, like you, I thought it had ceased. Clearly, it hasn't.'

'How could they have thought kidnapping people was okay?' exclaimed Jemma. 'Then or now.'

'The leaders of Anders' ruling houses humans were arrogant rather than cruel. They saw themselves as superior, but their problem was that the ruling houses were becoming inbred. They needed fresh blood.'

'Kidnapping and forcing people into any kind of service is cruel, even if they treated their victims well afterwards,' said Jemma.

Kevson took her hand in his. 'Jemma, Werrimen is trying to gently let you know that our family history is littered with these abductions. I don't know if you are aware that your grandmother, my mother, was an abductee from Earth, as was my grandmother. Do you understand what I'm saying? My mother was from Earth, and my father was half Earth human. So, I'm three-quarters Earth human, as was your mother. Your father was at least half Earth human too.'

'So, more than half of me belongs on Earth?' exclaimed Jemma.

'Yes, and that applies to most of those here with Anders Major blood,' said Kevson.

Jemma shook her head. 'So, why do the rebels from Anders Major see us as such a threat? We genuinely do belong to Earth.'

Werrimen sighed and took her hand. 'My dear, those in power on Anders Major believe that you belong to them. It will be outside their comprehension that you could choose to stay somewhere that they see as inferior. People like Kevson were raised in the belief that they had been rescued from an inferior place, which was Earth. We must …'

Everyone was startled by a voice on Sean's communicator. All heads turned his way.

*   *   *

Sean excused himself and left the room. The voice belonged to Matt and he was speaking so quickly that Sean couldn't make out what he was saying.

'Slow down mate,' said Sean. 'Try that again.'

'I met Dana on my way back,' whispered Matt. 'We were accosted by 2 people with weapons, just a few metres from the Administration Building. I pulled my weapon and managed to scare them off, but I saw a Zant run behind the building. I need to give chase, but I can't leave Dana.'

'Stay where you are. I'm on my way.' Sean ran back into the meeting. 'Zants at the back of this building. Matt's there with Dana.' He didn't wait for a response but headed to the rear stairs and ran down at speed. By the time he got to the back exit, Dan was beside him.

'Others are coming,' yelled Dan. 'How do you want to play it?'

'Someone should escort Dana back into the building. Not Matt. The rest of us fan out and try to find them. If there's one Zant, there'll be more.'

Jemma and Nik tore out of the building together. Dan went to direct them to look after Dana, but Sean, remembering his earlier conversation with Hunt shook his head. 'Fan out. Jemma, Dan on my left,' said Sean. 'Matt, Nik on my right. As soon as someone arrives to take care of Dana, we move.'

Werrimen, Zadrus and Hunt came next, and Sean was pleased to see Hunt automatically move in beside Dana.

'I have sent a transporter up,' said Zadrus. 'Our best chance is aerial surveillance. I also have a heat detector with me. We will try that too.'

'Which way, Matt?' called Sean.

'The one I saw was heading towards the factories.'

'What about the humans who stopped you?' asked Sean.

'Same direction.'

'Alright, follow me.' Sean yelled again to fan out as others joined them. They moved in a line toward the factory precinct. There were so many possible hiding places. Thick bush between the general settlement and the factories was aimed at stopping noise and reducing visual pollution. Some spots were dense enough to camouflage a small transporter, and probably make it impossible to spot even from the air. The Zants were so brazen they may well have parked somewhere in the open and be heading towards it now.

'Movement,' called someone from the northern flank. 'Behind that clump of trees. The ones that are covered in white flowers.

'Everyone, maintain your line.' Sean ran to the area in question. A small child cowered behind a low-lying bush. Sean picked the child up and pulled a young man out from the line. 'Take the kid back to the general. Tell him what's happened, then return here, unless the general says otherwise.'

'You realise people refer to you as the general now,' murmured Dan, when Sean re-joined the line.

'Shit,' muttered Sean. 'Let's just keep our minds on the job at hand.' That concept hadn't previously occurred to him although he supposed it was inevitable. But he didn't have time to think about it when Jemma raised her hand and yelled.

'Zant transporter,' called Jemma. 'Hundred metres, direct east, behind the water tank.'

'I'm on it,' shouted Zadrus. He used his communicator to tell the IPL transporter to block the Zant's departure.

Seconds later, Sean spotted at least a dozen IPL transporters racing towards them.

'I requested back-up,' said Zadrus.

Most of the transporters formed a barrier, but two zoomed down and landed. Yonkan stepped out of one, Peetha, the other. Both walked underneath the Zant craft. When Yonkan emerged, he held up a plastic sheet similar to the one the Kinbret had pulled from the IPL craft they'd disabled just a couple of hours earlier. Peetha placed a small device on the rear of the craft. There was a loud explosion.

'Oh my God,' cried Jemma. 'Did she blow it up.'

'No,' said Zadrus. 'She has blown a hole in the wall at the rear. No one would have been hurt, but it will give the Trustees access so they can extract the Zants inside and anyone with them.'

'What do we do now?' asked Sean.

'Let's find out who is there, then we can decide,' replied Zadrus.

Peetha climbed in through the hole, followed by two other Trustees. Shortly after, three Zants emerged, then two humans.

'Now we have a problem.' said Sean. 'We don't have a prison.'

'That's not quite right,' said Zadrus, smiling. 'When we designed the academy building, we decided to include a small complex that could be secured to hold prisoners if necessary. They will be taken there. My people will question them. I suggest we head back to my office now and continue our earlier discussion.'

Sean sent most of the search team back to the academy, calling the rest of them to return to Zadrus's office. Hunt had already escorted Dana back to her accommodation, so Matt was free to join them.

*　　*　　*

The events of the last few minutes had clarified in Jemma's mind what she must now do.

'Sean, General, the events of today have clarified in my mind that I can no longer sit back and hope the Anders Major rebels will go away. If I'm to have any chance to take charge of my future, particularly now that we know these abductions are still happening and the Zants are still here, I no longer have a choice. I have to go to Anders and meet the people there. Maybe I can also do something to help them. I'm well enough now to do what I have to do.'

Sean went to protest, but Jemma held up a hand. 'I've repeatedly been told that the whole problem is due to criminal elements, rather than the ruling houses or the general population, but I have to judge that for myself. The criminals have to be stopped, not just for my sake, but because I suspect they are doing harm to their own people. I'm coming to the conclusion that the ruling houses are not just arrogant, but they're also naïve, although probably not criminal. My home is on Earth. I doubt anything will change that, but I will keep an open mind.'

'That is fair,' said Kevson. 'And wherever you decide you will live is where I'll stay.'

'No, I don't agree,' said Sean. 'It's too dangerous.'

'I understand your fear, Sean,' said Werrimen. 'But I also believe Jemma is right. If we are to resolve this problem and secure Jemma's safety, we have to tackle it directly.'

'I have to do this, Sean, and I want you with me,' said Jemma. 'I'd like Dan and Nik to come too.' She looked directly at Hunt. 'I'd like you to be with me too.'

'I'm with you, cuz,' said Nik.

'Me too,' said Dan.

'Sean?' Jemma watched him open his mouth, then stop, but she didn't jump in. More than anyone else, she wanted him by her side, but she wouldn't force him.

'Of course I'm with you.' He sighed and moved closer to her. 'I don't think it's the right decision, but there's no way you're going without me.'

Holding him close, she turned to Hunt. 'Will you come?'

Hunt nodded. 'I think it is the right decision, and yes of course I'll be with you. Matt will have to fill in for me here, backed by Ciara and Liam, which is asking a lot of all of them.'

'You can communicate easily with them from the space-ship, General,' said Werrimen. 'It is not the same as it was when we were on the other side of the universe.'

'Right then,' said Hunt, 'you'll have to train even harder, Jemma. And we'll need an agreement that whichever Trustee is with you, you will obey them without question.'

'Zadrus already has that agreement,' she retorted. 'And I know that I'm asking much more than I should, but I would like both Zadrus and Werrimen to come with me.'

'Can we work that out later?' said Werrimen. 'One of us will come with you. Perhaps Yonkan could join you too. We need a lot more information from Kinbret and the other trustees on Anders Major to plan our mission. But you will have our support.'

* * *

It took over a month to organise the trip to Anders Major, and Hunt more than doubled Jemma's physical training while they waited. Yonkan demanded intensive sessions for both Jemma and Sean on transporters and spaceships. He also insisted on regular practice with the alien weapons, while Hunt rounded up each day with a strategy session, every one of which started with 'What should you do if your enemy is ... behind you, in front of you, scattered, hidden ...'

On the day they boarded the spaceship to head to Anders, Jemma muttered to Sean, 'I think I'm going to Anders to have a rest.'

'I heard that,' said Hunt. 'From the minute we enter their airspace, you need to be on full alert. Don't let me down.'

She couldn't hold back the laugh. 'How often have I heard that? But the truth here is, you need to *not let me down.*'

He growled something, but she chose to ignore it as she headed to her seat to prepare for the flight.

'What do you think you're doing?' Yonkan sat in the chair beside her. 'You are a pilot. Take your seat at the control panel. Our journey will be at least two weeks. All pilots will take turns.'

Although she chose not to let Yonkan see it, she was thrilled to have something to do rather than sit and wait through the journey. She jumped up, ready to follow, stopping long enough to kiss Sean's cheek and then headed to the front of the craft.

Yonkan was already setting up in the pilot's seat, so Jemma sat beside him and began the pre-flight checks. When she'd finished, she spoke to the ground crew, then walked around to ensure every entry, including cargo holds and the blue light were secured. Once she'd finished, she reported back to Yonkan that he was clear to go.

Werrimen, who was the official flight commander stood behind them. 'Are you sure, Jemma?'

After a couple of seconds of panic, Jemma went back through the list in her mind, counting off the ten points using her fingers. 'Yes, I'm sure.'

'Good,' said Werrimen, a broad smile on her face. 'You may proceed, Yonkan.'

Jemma grinned as she turned back at the controls. Werrimen had been testing her, but she'd immediately assumed she'd forgotten something when she was questioned. Time to start believing in herself again.

She felt Yonkan's hand on hers. 'You did well. Werrimen was teasing.'

'I know, but I've made so many mistakes I just seem to assume now that I've done something wrong.'

'Oh.' He looked at her, but this time there was no amusement in his look. 'We will have to work on that. I believe in you and so does Werrimen. We must put the past behind us. It has been difficult, but your future is ahead of you, and I believe you will make the right decisions.'

'Thank you,' said Jemma, smiling. 'I'm grateful to you and to everyone else from the IPL. It's time to find me again now, I guess.'

He squeezed her hand, then turned back to the controls,

motioning to her to do the same. They were about to enter the space junk zone, and it would take all their skill to avoid being hit. If it became too bad, they could put the shields up, but that took so much energy. Yonkan preferred to get through without them.

CHAPTER 19

Four hours into the flight, Werrimen asked Sean to relieve the current pilots. He reluctantly walked through to the control room and was surprised to find Peetha in charge. After sliding into the co-pilot's seat to replace Jemma, he commenced his practiced routine of safety and propulsion unit checks. He adjusted the screen at the front and called up the rear viewer.

'What's that?' said Jemma who was still standing behind him. 'It wasn't there a few minutes ago.'

Yonkan leaned over her shoulder and looked to where she pointed. 'Another spaceship. Too far away to identify. Sean, try to communicate with it. Peetha, I will notify Werrimen.'

Suddenly, a section of the front screen lit up and a man appeared mid centre. He was human, but he spoke a language Sean didn't understand. Peetha turned on the translator in the control panel and asked the man to wait until Werrimen joined them.

'We do not recognise the IPL,' said the man. 'I will speak to you.'

'No,' replied Werrimen, as she strode in. 'You will speak to me.'

'I repeat, we do not recognise the IPL. You will heave to and wait for us to board. We will take charge of your ship.'

'Identify yourselves,' said Werrimen.

'I am Trenoa, President of the new Anders Major. You have at least five of our people on board, and we require their return.'

'No, if you wish to speak to them, you may do so when we land on Anders Major.' She looked down at the rear viewer in front of Sean and nodded. 'You will notice that you now have an IPL escort which will remain with you until we arrive at our destination.'

'We take your escort as a declaration of war.'

'Our escort is as much for your protection as ours. If, however you commence aggression, we will retaliate.' Werrimen shut down the communicator and turned to Peetha. 'Are there other ships nearby?'

'Two others will be here within the hour. There are three more we can call on should you consider it necessary.'

'Good,' said Werrimen. 'Before this happened, I was coming up anyway to advise you about the Zant ship that was in orbit around Earth. It left there a couple of hours ago and, I am told, is heading in our direction.'

'By all the stars!' said Peetha. 'We need all the backup we can get.'

'Agreed,' said Werrimen. 'Mobilise everything available. I do not fully know what we are dealing with here, so we will activate all emergency precautions. Jemma, Yonkan, remain here as back-up crew. At the end of this four-hour shift, you will go for an eight-hour rest. The current crew will then become back up to the third crew, and you can keep rotating that way. I will speak to Kevson and Kinbret to see if they know this Trenoa.'

Sean was comforted by Jemma's hands resting on his shoulders. They couldn't prevent the Anders Major craft from firing, so the best he could do would be to stay focussed and identify any action as it occurred. He'd only have a split second's notice to activate the shields, so he was pleased to have Jemma and Yonkan watching with him, although it would be an even bigger relief to land on solid ground.

Nothing happened, though, and eventually Sean allowed himself to relax. By the time Werrimen returned with Kinbret, he was fired up and ready to demand answers. 'Ma'am, I understood Kinbret was a Trustee and that the IPL was well established on Anders Major. So how could all this have been happening without his knowledge?'

'I am a Trustee,' replied Kinbret. 'We are established there. None of this has been without my knowledge. Trenoa is the rebel leader. He claims to be president. Although he has no status, we cannot ignore him. He is both dangerous and unpredictable. The IPL presence on Anders Major is to be increased before we land, and I agree with Werrimen's order to bring in any other craft that are nearby. I believe Trenoa is less likely to attack if he realises that he cannot win, although I am unable to guarantee that.'

Werrimen nodded. 'It is my intention that Trenoa will be taken into custody when he lands. I have requested all members of the IPL Supreme Council to travel to Anders Major, so we can meet and help you determine what must be done to resolve this problem.' She turned to Kinbret. 'You will, of course, have a significant role in that meeting.'

'Thank you,' said Kinbret. 'I appreciate the offer. I have not wanted to admit that we need outside intervention, but I think pride must be ignored now. We clearly need help.'

'Kinbret, I'm still puzzled,' said Sean. 'These people make claims that don't make sense. My understanding is that there hasn't been any input from the ruling houses for nearly a hundred years, yet they're antagonistic. Why?'

'I do not know the answer. When we have detained any of these people, they are vague and confused in their responses.'

'Which is exactly what we've found,' said Jemma. 'They're being manipulated by someone. I know I've asked this before, but could it be something like those bars that the Zants implanted in the old Rescue Earth Group?'

'We have not been able to identify any implanted devices,' said Kinbret, with a sigh. 'But I agree with you that it does appear like their minds have been manipulated somehow. I have not been able to work out how, though.'

'Then, surely that's where we have to focus,' said Jemma.

'Agreed,' replied Werrimen. 'For the moment, we must concentrate on getting to Anders Major in one piece.'

Sean waited for Jemma to slip into the chair beside him, then went through his check of both front and rear screens again. IPL ships flanked the rebel ship, and he could see another ship catching up quickly. The new ship settled into a flight pattern directly above the rebels. Half an hour later another ship arrived, and it took up a path between the rebel ship and their own ship. He pointed it out to Werrimen.

'They are running interference which takes a great deal of energy. Each of the ships will take turns to do that. Then they will fall back into the formation to restore their energy supply. When the other IPL ship arrives, it will set up behind the rebel ship, so it is completely surrounded. We must remain vigilant. If the Zant ship we were advised is heading our way has joined them, then we must expect their tricks.'

'Umm,' said Jemma. 'Can I ask an unrelated question?'

'Of course,' replied Werrimen and Yonkan together. Each smiled and bowed their head to the other, before turning back to Jemma.

'My role in the new army is to manage army members who are learning to fly, so you mentioned something technical that I didn't understand.'

'I will leave Yonkan to answer,' said Werrimen, and she left the control room.

'I don't understand how a ship that has expended all its energy can replenish that energy.'

'Oh, I see,' replied Yonkan. 'If it has expended all its energy, then it cannot. We always make sure that we have some energy in reserve. The propulsion unit works something like your motorcar batteries of the twentieth century. Provided it is able to run normally, it regenerates its own power. A motorcar battery provides energy to start the motor, then takes energy back from the motorcar as it is running. Our ships do much the same, but if the propulsion unit runs out of power, there is no capacity to regenerate. It must use another energy source before it can operate again.'

'So, is that how you can remain in space for weeks and months without having to land for fuel?' asked Jemma.

'That is correct,' replied Yonkan. 'We mostly land to replenish food and water supplies. The ships are checked whenever we land, but otherwise they run themselves, provided we don't do anything foolish.'

The remainder of the two-week trip to Anders Major was uneventful, despite the threat, but as they approached the planet Sean, again in the position of co-pilot, noticed a dozen craft heading towards them. He spoke to the senior pilot, then declared an alert.

Werrimen, whose cabin was next to the control room, ran in first. 'What is it?'

He pointed to the screen. 'Are they friendly?'

'Yes, I believe so. I was expecting a welcoming party from Anders Major. My apologies, I should have told you. They are coming from Kilkinan, the main ruling house and should be welcoming, although I remain cautious. I will organise a replacement for you. When she gets here, come to my office. I will call Jemma also.'

When he walked into the office, he found Werrimen, with Kevson and Jemma on either side of her, engrossed in a conversation with a woman, on the screen, who looked like an older version of Nik.

Jemma beckoned him over. 'My mother and Kevson had a

younger sister. She was Nik's mother, and this is Nik's great niece, Heneker.'

'Shouldn't Nik be here, then?' asked Sean.

'She's been called,' said Jemma. 'Werrimen plans to check her DNA, but Uncle Kevson's certain.'

Werrimen acknowledged Sean but her voice, when she spoke again to Heneker she was terse. 'Thank you. We will await your arrival.' Shutting down the communicator, she stared at the screen then turned to look directly at Kevson. 'All right, what does Heneker have planned?'

'I don't know.' He held up his hand. 'No, don't look at me like that. I honestly don't know. You must realise by now that my sole interest is to protect Jemma, and I will do that against anyone, including Heneker, if necessary.'

Sean stood closer to Jemma and looked from Kevson to Werrimen. Jemma's excitement was obvious, but he saw concern on Werrimen's face and even Kevson frowned. 'What's wrong?' asked Sean quietly.

'I am not sure anything is wrong.' Werrimen sighed.

'But we both feel Heneker is up to something,' said Kevson.

Werrimen nodded. 'I am awaiting more IPL ships to join us. They will have two to three hundred of my people to help us. Heneker may come on board, but we will not land or leave this ship until I have reinforcements.'

When Werrimen left to go to the landing bay, with Kevson by her side, she beckoned Sean, Jemma and Dan to follow. Nik almost collided with them as she ran in. Werrimen stopped to explain the situation, then led the group to the disc which took them down to the safe room in the landing bay. It was sealed to provide a secure place to wait while the external entry door was open for the transporter to dock. Jemma and Nik clung to each other, ready to greet Heneker, but Sean remained on edge, Werrimen's and Kevson's concerns resounding in his mind. The look on Dan's face suggested he also sensed a problem. Sean moved between the two women and made sure he had a firm hold on Jemma, intending to tell Dan to do the same with Nik, but he had to smile when he saw Dan had already acted. Should have realised he'd be thinking the same way.

Once the external landing bay entry was shut and had been secured, Werrimen stepped out onto the main floor. Twenty trustees, who Sean hadn't known were on board, emerged from the disc. All were armed, and their weapons were pointed at the transporter.

Jemma went to step forward too as the transporter's blue light flicked on underneath, but Sean firmed his grip.

She glared at Sean. 'I'd like to speak to this woman, to find out why she's here.'

Nik suddenly broke away from Dan. He reached out to pull her back, but she was too quick and raced for the door.

Werrimen quickly sidestepped, blocking her path. 'Nikola, you will stay in the safe room. Sean, release Jemma. Jemma and Nikola, you will remain here until I advise otherwise. Are you prepared to obey me, or do I have to send you away while this meeting takes place?'

Sean released his hold but remained close to Jemma. To his relief, Nik had also backed down.

'We want to meet her,' Jemma said to Werrimen. 'She's family.'

'You will, as soon as I am satisfied it is safe. Kevson and I will greet her first.'

After they left, Sean was surprised to see several of the Trustees line up outside the safe room. Kinbret and Yonkan remained inside with them but both had weapons drawn.

'Surely you wouldn't use those things on us?' Sean drew Jemma closer to him ensuring that he stood between her and the two Trustees.

Yonkan smiled. 'Of course not, although if Jemma were to run for the door I may be forced to reconsider.'

Jemma scowled, which amused Sean, but he wasn't prepared to waste time talking about it. The underlying message from Yonkan had him worried. While the Trustees looked calm, all of them, inside and outside the safe room, were tensed and ready to react. He recognised the signs from his own experience in dangerous situations. They were considerably more worried than they were letting on, and shouts outside made him draw Jemma closer.

At least forty people, mostly armed, exited the Anders transporter and, as they jumped down, they formed a line on either side of Heneker and aimed their weapons at Werrimen and the other Trustees. When Jemma gasped, Sean tried to mutter some reassuring words, but he stopped when he saw Werrimen take a couple of steps back. She pulled Kevson with her. Heneker followed while her people remained in a line behind her. Werrimen stepped further back. Heneker again followed, increasing the distance between herself and her people. Sean recognised the value of enlarging the gap but couldn't see how that was going to help in the tight space of the landing bay, although he realised the move had to be strategic, particularly when he noticed Yonkan nod.

'Just a few more steps,' Yonkan muttered.

Werrimen continued to step back. Heneker seemed to blindly follow, her face drawn tight as she recklessly waved her weapon and yelled at Werrimen to hand over her family.

'Two more steps,' whispered Yonkan. 'You can do it, Werrimen.'

A transparent hemispheric shell suddenly slammed down over the Anders craft, trapping all but Heneker within it. Sean and everyone around him, with the exception of Yonkan, who'd clearly been expecting it, jumped.

'It is safe now,' said Yonkan. 'We can go and meet your relative.'

'But can't the Anders people fire at that shell thing? Or blow it up?' Jemma stayed close to Sean without his urging now. 'And why did she threaten Werrimen, the very person who brought us here?'

'They planned to take you from us,' said Yonkan. 'Perhaps they don't trust us. I am not sure, but we must find out. Fortunately, we were ready. We will follow Werrimen to her office.'

As they walked past the shell, Sean could see the people from Anders punching at it and shouting. While he'd supported Jemma's need to visit their home planet, he'd never been sure it was the right thing to do. He wondered now if they should just turn around and go home.

CHAPTER 20

Jemma held onto Sean's hand as they walked with Werrimen back to her office, aware that Heneker had been taken ahead by a group of Trustees. She was baffled by what she'd just seen.

As soon as Heneker saw Jemma, she bowed. 'Welcome to Anders Major, my liege.'

'No,' replied Jemma, taking a deep breath to control her shaking. 'I have not agreed to take that role.'

'You do not have to agree. It is your birthright. You and your cousin must come home with me now so that we can celebrate your return.'

'We're not ready,' muttered Jemma. She waited for Werrimen to step in before saying anything more. It worried her that Heneker didn't seem to realise how much she'd antagonised the IPL. Someone at risk of facing an intergalactic court should have been more concerned. Perhaps she had something up her sleeve and simply didn't care.

'Yonkan, take Heneker to a secure room,' said Werrimen, 'and organise a guard please.'

Heneker shook Yonkan's hand away. 'No, I will stay with my great aunts' daughters. They are my responsibility.'

297

'Jemma and Nik are mature women,' said Werrimen. 'They are responsible for themselves and have the support of the IPL to ensure they are allowed to make their own decisions.'

'Heneker. Do as they say,' said Kevson.

'I will stay with Jemma and Nikola,' replied Heneker, as she continued to fight Yonkan.

Jemma saw Werrimen nod when Yonkan looked up. He squeezed his fingers on either side of Heneker's neck, and she fell limp by his side. He picked her up before she could fall, then carried her out the door.

'That was harsh,' said Kevson. 'Perhaps you could give me time to talk to her.'

'Of course, you can talk to her,' replied Werrimen. 'However, I cannot take the risk that she could talk you back to her way of thinking. I will not allow you to be alone with her. Nor will I leave Jemma or Nik alone in the company of any of your people as yet. I take my responsibility to both of them very seriously.'

Kevson bowed. 'As do I.'

The tension in the air fell heavily on Jemma. She couldn't say she trusted Kevson without question, and she knew Sean still had doubts, but she didn't want Kevson or Heneker or any other person from Anders Major to be hurt on her behalf. The only way she'd find out about the planet and its people would be to get down there, and she hoped that would happen soon.

'You have questions, Jemma?' asked Werrimen.

'No, not questions. I'd like to spend some time with my relatives so I can work out for myself if I can trust them. And I need to get down there and meet the people of Anders Major. I understand why you're concerned, and I appreciate it. More than that, I value your opinion. Now I have to work out what *I* think.'

'Yes, I understand, and I agree,' said Werrimen. 'As soon as it is safe, I will take you to meet Heneker. As far as going down is concerned, we must wait for my backup to arrive. They should be here within the next two days. I do not want to proceed too soon and find that we have to fight our way out.'

'No, that's not good enough,' said Nik. 'I want to talk to our relatives too. Heneker behaved foolishly, but I need to meet her and try to understand what is happening too.'

'I do understand,' said Werrimen, kindly. 'That will happen very soon.'

The next two days passed without further incident. Jemma took her turn as co-pilot, always alongside Yonkan, for eight hours each day and spent the rest of the time either exercising or sleeping. She only saw Sean at changeovers because he was either sleeping or working during her down-time. She was careful to ensure that Yonkan always knew where she was, but also who she was with. On the third day, Yonkan met her in the makeshift gym to tell her that one of the IPL ships had arrived and the other ship wasn't far behind. Werrimen had directed that only one of the IPL ships was to land on Anders, and everyone who was going down to the planet was to be transferred to that ship. The rest of the ships were to remain in orbit.

Shortly after Yonkan left, Jemma and her team were called to Werrimen's office. The last IPL ship was close and Werrimen was ready to give them instructions as soon as Sean and Dan were relieved from the pilot team.

'We will all go together,' she said, once they arrived. 'I will be the initial spokesperson, so I will lead, and I will have a Trustee on either side of me observing for any sign of trouble.'

'Do we follow?' asked Jemma.

'Not quite. I want a second cluster behind me. You and Sean will be in the middle. Mary will be next to Jemma. Kevson will walk beside Sean. You will have a circle of IPL Trustees surrounding you.'

'Won't that be read as aggressive?' snapped Jemma. 'We're here to find peace.'

'It should be seen as protective, although I can't guarantee that. We will have to judge as we go. Your safety is top priority. Let me finish my plan, then we can talk about it.'

The mild rebuke stung, but Jemma had no intention of remaining quiet if she thought the plan wouldn't work.

'A third cluster will have Nikola, in the middle, flanked by Dan on one side and General Hunt on the other. Don't glare at me, Dan. You will also have a circle of Trustees surrounding you.'

'This is becoming a major exercise,' said Jemma, her frustration rising, alongside her fear of how the strategy might be interpreted.

'Yes, it is,' said Werrimen, no longer hiding her own frustration with the constant interruptions. 'Yonkan will lead another group of Trustees out next. Is everyone clear on my strategy?'

'This is supposed to be a conciliatory exercise,' said Jemma, 'to see if we can fit in with our past. It's turning into a giant military manoeuvre and, I'll say it again, it's going to be read as aggressive.'

'It *is* a military manoeuvre, Jemma,' said Yonkan, kindly. 'We must start out strongly and then, if possible, back off. It is much harder to increase our strength if we are seen as weak.'

Jemma persisted. 'We don't know how that will be perceived. Shouldn't we test the waters first?'

'How many times have people from this planet tried to kill you or abduct you, Jemma?' said Werrimen, glaring at Kevson.

Kevson glared back at her before turning to Jemma. 'I have to accept that, even though I've apologised multiple times. My intention was to protect you, Jemma, but I didn't really think through what I was doing. Others here will be as keen as I was to bring you back into the fold. Heneker has already made that quite clear. We are best to work within Werrimen's strategy. They will accept my explanation, even if they are angered by our actions.'

'Thank you, Kevson,' replied Werrimen. 'Do you have any further complaints Jemma?'

'I'm not complaining. I just don't see the sense in inciting more trouble.'

'I don't think we will,' said Kevson. 'They will expect the Supreme Ruler to be surrounded by security, but if there is any negative reaction, let me address it. I am sure that I will be able to settle down any concerns.'

'Listen to them, Jem,' said Sean. 'I think we're so far out of our reality that we have to accept other people know better.'

'Much as I hate to be out of control,' said Hunt, 'I have to agree with Sean and Kevson. We must follow Werrimen's strategy.'

'Thank you,' said Werrimen. 'Now we should begin. I, and my team, will start. Please wait until I give the signal for the next line to follow. Are you comfortable now, Jemma?'

Jemma gave a reluctant nod. 'No, but I recognise that I'm not going to be comfortable, whatever strategy we use.'

'Yes, my dear, I realise that.' Werrimen nodded to her crew. An opening appeared in the side of the craft and a ramp extended down to the ground. 'We are using the ramp so that I can see everyone, inside and out, at all times.'

As the ramp descended, the sudden realisation that she was about to see Anders Major for the first time she could remember, slammed through Jemma's brain. This was it. Her chance to determine where she wanted to be and how she was going to live the rest of her life. But what if she couldn't decide? And what if Sean wanted something different? The stark reality of the biggest decision she would ever make left her gasping for air, and she stared up at Sean.

'It's okay,' he whispered, squeezing her hand. 'Remember

our pact. We can get through anything so long as we're together.'

She watched as Werrimen, with her two Trustee companions, descended to speak to a small waiting delegation. There didn't seem to be any animosity. One member of the delegation wore the uniform of a Supreme Trustee, which had to mean something. Werrimen turned back and waved Jemma forward. She forced her feet to move, one after the other, leaning on both Sean and Mary for strength. People lined both sides of the ramp, many calling out to her, 'Welcome home,' or, 'my liege.'

If there hadn't been such a large group with her, Jemma suspected she'd have turned and run back into the transporter. She couldn't understand why these people were so happy to see her. They'd never laid eyes on her before.

'I can't do this,' she muttered.

'Yes, you can,' said Mary. 'It is the only way you will ever find peace. I am here and I will not leave your side.'

As she moved forward, she felt both Mary's and Sean's arms around her, neither of them pushing, just supporting.

'Alright,' she murmured, 'just got to get through the crowd.'

'We've dealt with worse,' said Sean, softly.

She smiled at him. He was so right. A few people in colourful clothing, smiling and waving, hardly compared to Fredrick Pritchard and his virus or the Zants with their evil ways. She raised her head and did her best to smile back at the people who were obviously delighted to see her.

'These people seem pretty genuine,' said Sean.

Jemma nodded. 'They do. It's rather nice in a weird sort of way.'

There were men, women and children lining the pathway between the transporter and the building to which they were headed, and their cheerful greetings made her relax enough to take in her surroundings. The way they were dressed reminded her of traditional Indian costumes, with swirls of bright colours and sparkling sequins, or perhaps gemstones, in all sorts of designs. Struck by their relaxed, happy smiles, she looked to see what was beyond. They'd landed near a large, manicured garden, full of colourful bushes and flowers, most of which she didn't know, yet the overall feel was similar to Earth. Although she hadn't heard what they called their solar body, it shone directly above them and the atmosphere was warm, if maybe a little humid. It was much like home. And that made her frown. Perhaps this was home.

The structure that rose in front of them looked to be four stories in height. It was reminiscent of buildings like Buckingham Palace which reinforced the link that she'd started to recognise had to exist between Earth and Anders. Right from the first time she'd heard of Anders, it had struck her as odd that people like Sean's father and even her own parents had, after fleeing their own planet, arrived on Earth and slotted easily into top government positions. Yet they had, and not only in her country. It had happened in every country on Earth. Could it be that the technological advances on Earth in the latter part of the twentieth century and the early twenty-first century, all of which had happened at incredible speed, had been assisted by people from Anders? Perhaps humans from other planets had been welcomed by Earth's governments too. When she thought about it, what better way for the IPL to advance Earth than to slot humans with advanced skills into the mainstream? If Earth's governments had been open and transparent, and had allowed the IPL to show the way, maybe the war could have been prevented. She sighed. Political stupidity never ceased to amaze her.

'Penny for them,' said Hunt, from behind her and she realised that Werrimen must have called the third line forward.

'Nothing really. Just surprised at how Earth-like this all seems.'

'Yes, I had the same thought.' Sean touched her arm. 'Look over to your right.'

She followed his gaze to a large rotunda in which a group of people with a variety of musical instruments struck up a tune. If she hadn't known better, she'd have thought she was attending a function on Earth. The instruments were almost identical – a keyboard, violins, a cello, drums. No wonder her parents had fitted in so easily on Earth.

'Bloody hell,' muttered Sean. 'They've got a guitar.'

As they approached the doors of the building, a small procession of people, all holding weapons with which Jemma wasn't familiar, formed an honour guard. They were dressed exactly like the guards at many English and European palaces, right down to the red tunic and bearskin hats.

'Dear God,' whispered Jemma. 'This is becoming creepy. Are they trying to make us feel at home?'

'No,' said Mary. 'This is the Anders I remember, although the people seem more subdued.'

Kevson nodded, 'They have been through a great deal.'

'Do you think all the women they abducted advised them on design, or did they advise Earth?' Jemma looked around at those in her party who she thought might know, but she was met with shrugs and blank looks.

Once inside, massive wooden doors swung shut behind them, which startled Jemma and made most of the IPL Trustees place a hand on their weapons.

A man who had been waiting inside to greet them, came forward. 'Where is Heneker?'

Werrimen started to answer, but Kevson stepped forward to stand beside her. 'Do not worry, Geron, Heneker decided to remain on the IPL ship. The Trustees are filling her in on recent events, most particularly the actions of Drick. She will be down shortly.'

Werrimen had remained passive at the mention of Drick's name, the man who Jemma knew as Fredrick Pritchard.

Geron's eyebrows tightened. 'Are you satisfied she is safe?'

'Oh yes,' said Kevson. 'No harm can come to her there.'

'Very well then,' said Geron. 'Shall we begin the ceremony?'

'No.' Kevson's face turned crimson in response to Werrimen's glare.

'What ceremony?' hissed Werrimen.

'We had planned to welcome Jemma and anoint her into

the position of her birthright,' said Kevson. 'Like everyone else here, I assumed that is what she would want. I realise now that is premature but, as you know, I have not had the capacity to communicate Jemma's wishes to the people of Anders.'

'Are you saying she does not want to take up her position?' Geron paced up and down, running his hand through his hair.

'No,' replied Kevson, before Werrimen could intervene. 'Not as yet.'

'What am I supposed to tell her people?'

'Try the truth,' snapped Werrimen. 'Jemma does not have sufficient information to make any sort of decision yet, particularly one that will not only affect the rest of her life, but the entire population of Anders Major. She will need time.'

'Perhaps,' said Jemma, stepping in front of both Werrimen and Kevson to avoid the situation deteriorating further, 'you could say it has to be postponed for safety reasons.'

'What safety reasons?' Geron recommenced pacing. 'My people … our people, have lived in fear for a hundred years. I cannot say there is a safety issue. They see you as their saviour.'

'Oh, dear God, they can't,' said Jemma. 'I'm no saviour, I'm just an ordinary person.'

'You are Jemma, daughter of our beloved Thera,' exclaimed Geron, rubbing his hand through his hair. 'Surely Kevson has explained this.'

'I have, Geron, and like you I assumed she would want to come home but, you see, Anders Major has never been Jemma's home. She did not know we existed until Drick kidnapped her. It is only due to the courage of Sean here, that we have her at all. After speaking with Jemma, I now realise that she must decide for herself whether she will stay here or return to Earth.'

'She must stay here, of course,' said Geron.

'No. Sadly, that is not our decision to make,' said Kevson. 'I suggest you tell the crowd that she is fatigued as a reason to cancel the ceremony. We are both related to Jemma, Geron. Her welfare is our responsibility.'

'Oh, dear me,' cried Geron. 'This is a disaster.'

'No,' said Werrimen. 'Not a disaster. Breathing space for all of you to determine how to proceed. We will take her back to the ship.'

'No, no. Please. She should stay here. We have prepared the Supreme Ruler's suite for Jemma and her partner.'

'Husband,' murmured Sean.

'Husband,' repeated Geron. 'What is that?'

'Partners for life,' said Sean. 'We are committed to each other.'

'Earth humans are monogamous,' said Kevson.

'But that will be a problem,' said Geron. 'This is just one disaster after another.'

Both Jemma and Sean looked at Kevson who dropped his head and took a deep sigh.

'Geron, our people are moving the same way, and that is a good thing,' said Kevson. 'Jemma, Sean, traditionally people on Anders did have one committed partner but they didn't see that as exclusive, shall we say. The war has changed much.

Many practices have changed and can be changed further. It is not something to worry about.'

'Will you at least accept our hospitality while you make your decision?' asked Geron. 'The people will be most distressed if you return to your spaceship immediately.'

Jemma looked to Werrimen. It wasn't a decision that she could make alone and, for once, she didn't think she could rely solely on Sean's advice.

'Geron, if Jemma stays, IPL Trustees must remain with her,' said Werrimen. 'Are you satisfied with that?'

'Of course. Of course.'

'Jemma, what would you like to do?'

'Right now, I'd like to turn tail and run straight back to the transporter,' said Jemma, her hands shielding her face. 'But I don't think that's the best thing to do. We should stay. Mary, General Hunt, will you also stay? I assume there is accommodation for you also.'

'Yes, yes. The guardian of the liege has a suite alongside the liege.' He nodded to Mary. 'General, I understand that you come from the house of the guardians. Would you prefer to stay here or in the guardian house?'

'I also feel a responsibility to Jemma,' said Hunt. 'I would prefer to stay as close to her as possible.'

'Certainly, that is easily arranged. Jemma, Sean, please follow me.'

CHAPTER 21

Walking through the door of the Supreme Ruler's personal suite, Jemma gasped. It was the size of a small house on Earth. A curved window at the side of a cavernous reception room provided a view over a large beautifully maintained garden and across to an expansive body of water beyond, either a bay or an exceptionally wide river. A formal dining room on the right, was big enough to entertain a sizeable delegation. Twenty places had been set and she wondered who she'd been expected to entertain before Kevson had shut the reception down. Beyond, she spotted a kitchen, but it was obviously not intended for royal patronage, because a man and a woman standing just inside snapped a screen door shut when they noticed her. Geron led her through the dining room and into a corridor. The first door opened into the largest bedroom she'd ever seen, complete with a four-poster bed that she was sure would be big enough to accommodate six. Perhaps that was what Geron had been alluding to.

'If you continue along the corridor,' said Geron, 'you will see four smaller bedrooms, traditionally used for the liege's children. There is also a lounge which was used exclusively by the ruler's family.'

'Perhaps we could use that as the Trustee base,' said Werrimen who must have followed silently behind. 'That's if you would be happy with that, Jemma?'

Geron whirled around to her. 'These rooms are for the exclusive use of our liege. They are not for the workers.'

Jemma cringed at his attitude, her thoughts sneaking back to Lena's words about her ancestors' arrogance. Although she'd been assured that Lena was wrong, she couldn't help but think there might be an element of truth in those assertions. 'Werrimen is my family. If it weren't for her, I would not be alive. She and her Trustees will stay with me.'

'As you wish,' said Geron, although it was clear he didn't approve.

Jemma remained standing until everyone had left, then she collapsed onto the bed. 'Oh my God, Sean. What have we done coming here?'

'The right thing,' he said, although he wasn't looking at her as he spoke.

'What's up?' she asked, following his gaze.

'That painting.' Sean pointed to an ornately framed landscape on the wall opposite the foot of the bed. 'If that isn't Surfer's Paradise, I'm a monkey's uncle.'

'Hmm. You don't look like a monkey to me,' she replied, smiling. 'But you're right. That's the southern end of Surfers, almost directly opposite my old apartment. Is it possible that there's a beach just like it here?'

'I suppose, but not exactly like it. I mean, look at the trees. I know those trees and that picnic table. That's where you first saw Drick.' He reached up and carefully prised the painting from the wall, then turned it over to check for any sign of its origin on the back. 'Holy snapping duck shit – look at this.' Sean turned the painting around so Jemma could see what he was looking at. 'Surfers Paradise, 1998. All my love, Thera.'

'I wonder if my mother painted it. She was quite a good artist. Turn it over, see if she signed it on the front.' She bumped heads with Sean as they both bent down to look. 'Look there.' She pointed to a tiny signature in the bottom right corner. 'Catherane. That was her name. She always shortened it to Thera. Well, I guess we have to believe them now.'

'Yeah, guess we do,' said Sean. 'Wonder what else we might find here? It doesn't look like it's been touched in years. Someone's obviously been in to clean, but there's quite thick dust behind the cupboards.'

'I thought the castle was in ruins,' said Jemma. 'Appears it isn't as bad as Kevson suggested.'

'Hard to say,' said Sean. 'They've done a lot of work.'

With a shrug, Jemma bent down to the cupboard underneath where the painting had been and carefully opened it. Inside, she found bedclothes, towels, even face washers that had been neatly stacked, most likely in anticipation of their arrival. 'You know, I keep being struck by how like Earth everything is here. We know they've abducted women from Earth, but have they also been putting people on Earth to set up a society like their own? It's just all too similar to be coincidence.'

'Yeah, I know what you mean. I'm trying not to read it as sinister, but I've got an uneasy feeling. Do they want you here to rebuild their society, or do they want to use you as a conduit so they can move to Earth, or worse, take us over? I might go find Werrimen and talk to her about it. Do you want to come?'

'No, I'll stay here and see what I can find,' said Jemma. 'I feel safe enough, and there are Trustees everywhere.'

Surprised by how many cupboards there were, she began her search with the linen cupboard and moved counter-clockwise. The first couple of cupboards held old clothes which both looked and smelt like they'd been stored for decades. Most other cupboards were empty, and she was losing heart when she came on a large chest of drawers beside the side of the bed furthest from the door. She suspected that had been her grandmother's side. The top drawers were empty, and the bottom two drawers were key-locked. She searched but couldn't find a key. Surely if there was one, someone would have found it by now and checked the contents. Still, she wouldn't know until she got into it. She cast her eyes around, trying to imagine where she would hide a key if she didn't want it found. She crawled under the bed, turned paintings over, ran her fingers under the edge of each piece of furniture, but she couldn't find anything. She climbed up onto the bed, hoping to see something on the top of one of the cupboards, but again nothing. Frustrated, she turned to jump down. As she grabbed the top post of the bed to balance herself, something sharp spiked her finger.

Unable to get her head far enough around to see what it was, she jumped down and pulled the bed out from the wall, which wasn't easy given it was made of a heavy wood that looked like mahogany, but she managed. From behind the bed, she could see a small metal plate. It appeared to be attached to the top of the post. She reached up but it was just a bit too far beyond where she could extend her fingers. Too excited to give up now, she found a stool in the attached bathroom and clambered up onto it. The metal plate moved easily when she pushed on it, exposing a small cavity that held a key which she carefully extracted. She slid it into the slot in the drawers and it turned easily.

The top drawer held dozens of photos – all of them were of her parents, herself and her sister. Most had backdrops of areas she knew well on the Gold Coast. Jemma dropped down onto the edge of the bed and stared at them. It appeared that not only had her mother hidden the truth from her, but she'd been in regular contact with her own parents.

So, why hadn't she ever talked about them? Jemma could only guess at how many other secrets had been withheld.

She carefully pushed the first drawer shut, then opened the other. Numerous leather-bound notebooks were stacked neatly in rows. She picked up a bundle and sat back on the bed, her legs crossed, and laid the first notebook on her lap. Inside the front cover, in very neat lettering, was written 'Jemma O'Shaughnessy'.

At least that was a name she knew. Her mother had told her often of the O'Shaughnessy's and how she'd not seen them since she was a child. All Jemma knew of her grandmother was that she came from Northern Ireland, a little town called

Omagh, and that she'd attended a Catholic school. Although she realised now that everything else that she'd been told about her family was a lie, she suspected that this was the one piece of truth.

Jemma flicked over a few pages and hoped her grandmother wouldn't have seen this as an intrusion. Each page was dated, and the contents were clearly a diary. She turned back to the first page and began to read.

27ᵗʰ November 1968

I have been in this wretched room for at least two weeks now. My captors keep calling it "the spaceship" and tell me we are in orbit outside Earth's atmosphere. I know this is wrong as it is clearly not anything like NASA's rocket ships. There are no windows so I cannot see out. I don't have any sense of movement and there is normal gravity. We are not floating around the ceiling as the astronauts do. There is some kind of odd creature on board. It is small, no more than four-foot, cream-grey in colour, tiny body, but it has a large head with big black eyes. Its arms and legs are incredibly thin. One of the other girls told me to look away if it comes near. It carries a long thin object, and she says that causes terrible pain if you are touched by it.

Jemma was horrified. Her grandmother had been taken by the Zants. She knew that the rebels were in league with the Zants, but if her grandfather knew who'd abducted her grandmother from Earth then the ruling houses were also involved with Zants. Was that possible?

25th December 1968

I should be at home with my family for Christmas. I won-
der if they know what's happened to me. The man they call
the Supreme Ruler is to come and inspect us again today.
One of us is to become his wife. God, I hope it isn't me,
although I don't know what will happen to me if I'm not
chosen. Last time he came to look, they made us strip and
parade in front of him naked. It was so humiliating. At least
he didn't touch us. In fact, he looked rather embarrassed.

Knowing that her grandmother had become the chosen
one, Jemma read on to find out how she'd reacted when she
was told.

28th December 1968

They made me put on this gawdy skin-tight dress with slits
right up to the waist and a neckline that only just covers the
tips of my breasts. My mother would have called it a slut's
outfit, but what can I do? They threaten us with that stick
thing those tiny creatures used. I'm too afraid to say no. At
least the creatures aren't here. They stayed with the space-
ship when we arrived and made sure they weren't seen.

I'm the chosen one it seems. The others are to be my
attendants. Why couldn't he have chosen one of them?

Jemma continued to flip through, devastated at how
they'd treated her grandmother but curious at the same time.
It was a relief to see that her grandfather hadn't raped her.
He'd told her that he wanted her for his, but he was prepared
to wait until she wanted the same. A little further on she was
informed that as the chosen one she was to have a baby, but

it didn't have to be naturally conceived; the sperm or even a full embryo could be implanted.

That was as far as she'd read when Sean burst into the room. 'Come and join us. Mary can tell us quite a bit about how things were.'

Jemma held up the diaries. 'Oh Sean. You have no idea. My grandmother was abducted by the Zants.'

Sean's eyes widened. 'What? That can't be. We know the Zants teamed up with the rebels, but if that's right they were here *long* before the war.'

'I can show you in her diaries. She doesn't actually name them, but the way she describes them there's no doubt.' She took the hand he held out and walked with him to the formal lounge, convinced now that Anders Major could never be her home.

Mary led her to a sofa and sat beside her. Sean sat on the other side, Werrimen opposite while Dan, Nik, and Hunt stood behind Werrimen.

'Before we start,' said Jemma, 'I need to tell you I've found my grandmother's diaries. She was brought here by the Zants.'

'No,' said Mary. 'The Zants were never here. I'd have known. Dreadful though the practice was, it was our own people who were sent out to find brides for the Rulers.'

Jemma shook her head. 'She describes them in such detail there can't be any doubt.'

'Sweetheart, I'd never seen a Zant until we found them on Earth,' said Mary.

'Then they must have been working with your kidnappers,'

replied Jemma, 'because they were clearly there on the ship that brought her here.'

Mary winced. 'I don't know what to say. If you're right, we were terribly misled.'

'Even if the Zants weren't there,' said Werrimen, leaning forward, 'this was a dreadful practice. How could your people have seen it as right?'

'Most of us didn't,' said Mary. 'But we didn't dare disagree with the Supreme Ruler. He wasn't a bad man, but his decisions were absolute.'

'I've heard you say that before,' said Jemma. 'But kidnapping and forcing women into marriage and having babies is unspeakably cruel. I realise he was my grandfather, but even so, I think he must have been a very bad man.'

'We had started to change,' said Mary, with a sigh, 'but we had a long way to go. Over the millennia, many of our brides came from Earth, and we placed many of our people in royal and powerful positions on Earth. It was accepted here as normal, but in the years leading up to the war there had been many changes. Even though you despise your grandfather's actions, he was progressive. He brought about many of the changes we needed. He made sure that all our people had decent housing, good food and clean water. He reduced rents to a minimum and excused people from paying at all if they were if a difficult position.'

'That doesn't excuse kidnap and rape,' snapped Jemma.

'No, it doesn't, but I know he didn't rape her. I first met her when I was a child. I was around the same age as your mother, and we played together. As we grew up, your grandmother seemed happy, and she and your grandfather were very close. It wasn't until they planned to send someone out to find a bride for Sean's father that she talked to us about it. She told us that she'd learned to accept her fate and make the best of it. By that time, she and your grandfather were husband and wife in every sense of the word. The first baby, your mother, had been conceived by artificial insemination, but after that her other babies were natural.'

'Artificial insemination, against someone's will, is still rape, surely,' snapped Jemma.

'I don't think it was against her will. The way she spoke, she was happy to go ahead with it. I wasn't there, so I don't know how she felt at the time.'

'No,' said Jemma, sinking back in her chair. She felt extraordinarily weary. 'Her diary suggests she was devastated. My God, Mary. How would you feel if someone ordered you to have a baby and then implanted the embryo?'

'I think "devastated" is a good word,' said Mary. 'All I can say to you is that she adored her babies, all three of them, and she never lost contact with your mother, even after she was sent to Earth.'

Jemma gripped Sean's hand tighter. 'I saw a lot of photos. I'm not questioning my grandmother's integrity. It's my grandfather and the people of Anders Major I'm questioning. Lena told me they were debauched and arrogant. I'm thinking that might be right and, if that's the case, I certainly don't want anything to do with them.'

'It is too soon to make that decision,' said Werrimen. 'I think we should try to meet some of the people here and look at how they live. It may be that you could do some good if you were to stay, but you must have the facts before you reach any conclusion.'

'Jemma,' said Mary, quietly. 'I'm not happy with my own people. I'd always thought I wanted to return here to my home, but when we rescued Sean's mother I realised just how cruel the regime on Anders had been. I'll say it again, your grandfather was bringing about change and if your mother had lived to return, I think Anders would have become a very different place. Speaking to Kevson and to Geron, I suspect the people here are confused. They desperately need leadership.'

'Yes, they do,' said Kevson, who must have quietly joined them during their conversation, although Jemma hadn't noticed him.

'It doesn't have to be me,' replied Jemma.

'No, I accept that, and wherever you go, I go,' said Kevson, 'but I would ask you to think about it. I have been saddened by the disintegration of this society. Like Mary, I would not like it to go back to the way it was, but there is a very great need for strong leadership, and you may wish to provide it. I accept now that that will be your decision, and yours alone.'

'I don't know the first thing about leading an entire planet,' said Jemma.

'That is not true, Jemma,' said Werrimen. 'You are a natural leader. Keep in mind that if you decide to stay, the IPL will be alongside you, be it Zadrus and myself or someone else.

You will not be alone. Now, we must work out what you need to see in order to make that decision.'

Hunt had remained silent throughout the discussion but now he placed a hand on Werrimen's shoulder. 'May I add something here?'

'Of course, General.'

'Jemma, I had a look at the crowd that is waiting to catch a glimpse of you,' said Hunt. 'They were excited to finally see you. I think you should go out there and speak to them, acknowledge their presence at the very least. The ruling junta here, or whatever it is, has built the people up to expect something extraordinary, which is a bit awkward, but I think you could put some hope into these people's lives.'

'But what if I don't stay?' exclaimed Jemma. 'It's false hope.'

'Not necessarily,' said Hunt. 'You and the IPL might be able to put something else in place.'

'I'm not their Supreme Ruler.' Jemma stared at Hunt. 'I don't even know what that means; to be a Supreme Ruler. What would I say? How do I act?'

Hunt smiled. 'Be yourself and tell the truth. Say something from your heart. Explain your situation and tell the people you'd like to meet them. It doesn't have to be much, but the people here are hurting just as much as the people on Earth. We've both had wars and we've both lost most of our population to violence.'

Sean and Werrimen were nodding when Jemma dropped her eye contact with Hunt.

'I feel so lost. Will you all come with me?' asked Jemma.

Werrimen shook her head. 'Sean must be by your side, and Mary. Kevson must also escort you. The rest of us can stand in the background for support, but you are the most important person.'

Jemma stood, not at all sure that her legs would hold her, but she understood Hunt's suggestion and agreed that it was the right thing to do. Holding Sean's hand, and with Mary on her other side, she followed Kevson to the balcony. It was so like Earth's royal families, yet they always looked composed, and she was anything but.

The crowd cheered, and all the beautiful colours of their gowns swayed in the breeze as they waved to her, creating quite a spectacle. She held up her hand and the people were instantly silent, which made her gulp.

Doing her best not to stutter, Jemma began to speak. 'My friends. I hope I may call you that.' Another cheer resounded. 'I must tell you a little about my story before we go on. I understand that I was taken from here to the planet known as Earth when I was a baby. I remember nothing of it and grew up on Earth believing that I was born there. My mother should have succeeded my grandfather as Ruler, but she died when I was eighteen years of age. I did not learn about my heritage until I was kidnapped by the person you know here as Drick.'

Gasps and murmurs rose from the crowd, followed by horrified looks.

'Drick attempted to prevent me from returning here, but as a result of his actions I found out that as the daughter of

Thera I could now claim the position of Supreme Ruler on Anders Major. But, you see, I know nothing about Anders Major or what you would need from me. I must find out everything I can before I decide if I am the right person to lead you forward. I will not be lured by power or wealth to take that position unless I am convinced that I can do you, the people of Anders, justice.'

Suddenly, a woman rose on a vehicle that looked to Jemma like a flying motorcycle. She flinched but forced herself to look at the woman.

'It is alright,' said Kevson. 'People use those here to stand out so they can be heard.'

'We were led to believe that you wanted to return here,' said the woman. 'But hearing your words I understand that you have also suffered. I'd like to say, however, that you have convinced me that you are absolutely the right person to lead us. I speak for myself, but I suspect others here are with me when I say, welcome home Jemma of Kilkinan. I hope you decide to stay with us. You will make a wonderful ruler.'

There were many shouts of, 'Agreed,' and, 'Yes, yes,' as Jemma stepped back from the balcony.

'I have to go inside before my legs give way,' murmured Jemma.

'Of course,' Kevson waved to the crowd, then led her through the doors to some lounge chairs.

Hunt was laughing as she sat. 'I knew you could do it. That was a damned fine speech.'

'No, it wasn't. I just said what I felt.'

'The crowd loved you,' said Sean. 'I haven't said anything to this point, but I think you need to get out there and meet the people. See how you feel. Don't make your mind up yet. All you've really seen is your grandmother's diaries, and if you were to stamp out those appalling practices, you might find you'd be happy here.'

'Will you stay if I do?'

'Oh, Jem. You should know by now that you can't get rid of me,' said Sean. 'Besides I might enjoy that power and wealth you scoffed at out there.'

Jemma slapped his shoulder. 'You're no more like that than I am.'

But could she learn to love this place? With her parents gone and most of Earth shattered, was Earth any more home than Anders might be? She had no idea how to make that decision, but the message that everybody seemed to be giving was get out there and have a look, meet the people and see for herself whether she could fit in.

CHAPTER 22

Geron called to say a meal had been served, which made Jemma realise she hadn't eaten since the night before, so she was happy to follow him to the dining room. But, at the sight of the crowd that awaited, she again lost her appetite.

Kevson, who now stood next to her, whispered, 'Would you like to leave? This has to be one of the events Geron organised before we arrived. I'm sorry, I did tell him to cancel, but he obviously didn't understand I meant everything.'

Jemma shook her head. 'No, if I'm going to come to grips with this place, I might as well start now. Who are these people?'

'They're key members of each of the ruling houses,' said Kevson. 'I'd say the security house, Bellear, will attempt to get close to Sean because he is the rightful heir there. The same might happen for General Hunt.'

'So, I take it Geron's the boss of Kilkinan now?'

'No,' replied Kevson, laughing. 'In fact, I am.'

'So, you organised all this?' exclaimed Jemma.

'Yes,' replied Kevson. 'Again, I apologise. I set it all up before I came to rescue you from Earth.'

'Okay,' said Jemma, with a sigh. 'Let's get on with it then.'

The banquet that had been laid out was enough to feed an entire village, but her immediate concern wasn't so much the potential waste, although that did bother her, it was that she didn't recognise most of the meats or vegetables. Platters had been laid out much the same as they would have been on Earth, but that didn't help. The only familiar item was bread and even then she wondered what it was made from.

Everybody was standing patiently, looking at her. Jemma smiled back until she realised that they were waiting for her to start, so she picked up a plate, checked with Kevson how to proceed, then took a small amount from each platter. By the time she was done, her plate was overflowing, but that's what Kevson had advised her to do, anything else would be insulting to whoever had produced that dish. Well aware that she couldn't possibly eat it all, she did her best to sample everything so that she'd know what to choose next time, but even then, while it was all delicious, it was far too much.

Given there wasn't a table with enough chairs to seat every-one, she presumed that she was meant to remain standing and mingle as she ate. Several people chatted to her and three men, at separate times, made it clear they would like to meet her in a more intimate setting. When a fourth man sidled up to her and suggested that they retire to another room, pref-erably her bedroom, she put her plate back on the table and faced him. 'Do you not understand that I am married? Sean, over there, is my husband.'

'Yes,' said the man. 'He looks like a decent fellow. I'm not suggesting that we make a child.'

'But you are suggesting sex?'

'Well, yes. It's a good way to get to know each other.'

'Sean is my husband. I don't sleep with anyone else.'

'How quaint. *Sleep with*. I don't want to sleep; I want to be actively involved. Surely you are not sexually exclusive with him.'

'Yes, I am. On Earth, that's what marriage means.'

'But ...' the man faltered. 'Don't you have a pregnancy preventer in place?'

She thought back to her miscarriage, now so many months ago, after which Werrimen had inserted an alien form of birth control to keep her safe until she decided to again try for pregnancy. 'I do, but I'm afraid I don't see things the way you do. If you'll excuse me.' She tripped as she turned and only just managed to right herself so she could walk swiftly from the room.

Kevson caught up with her before she reached the Supreme Ruler's suite. 'Something's happened. What's wrong?'

'That was the fourth man to tell me he wanted sex. No strings of course.'

'Oh dear,' said Kevson. 'They have a different view of many things here. It is slowly changing. Most of the people outside the ruling houses don't approve of this behaviour. I was doing my best to change it before I came to find you, but they have been resistant. Please don't judge us on this.'

Jemma shook her head. 'It seems I have to put an awful lot aside in order to not make a judgement. We know that they're still kidnapping women.'

'I made a decree before I discovered you were still alive that all of that was to stop,' said Kevson. 'Despite what happened just before we left Earth, that is something that I will work towards if we stay. Don't forget that your grandmother was my mother. I felt her pain all my life, and I vowed from a very young age to change it. I'm not sure if your mother agreed with me. There is a pervasive view here that Anders offered a more advanced way of life than Earth and so abductees were far better off here.'

'I can't credit my mother would have thought any of this okay, but I'm not really sure that I knew her at all now. She told me nothing Kev, not a thing. My grandmother had photos that Mum obviously sent to her. Why didn't she let me meet my grandmother? I was named after her for God's sake.'

'You did meet her,' said Kevson, clearly surprised. 'Your mother brought you back here twice to meet her. Don't you remember?'

Jemma stared at him, gasping as she began to digest the implications of his statement. If she had been back to Anders, then her mother, or someone else, must have wiped her memory. Of course, her mother would have wanted to make her own mother happy, but she was stunned to think that they could have taken her to Anders then so cruelly violated her trust by removing any recollection of it. Now she didn't know what to believe. 'I need Mary.'

'I understand,' replied Kevson. 'She is still at the reception, I believe. I will bring her here.'

Jemma walked up and down in the large room outside the

reception hall while she waited. She wanted Sean to hold her, to reassure her, to keep her safe, but she couldn't rely on Sean to solve everything. He'd always be there, and be her strength, but she had to work this out for herself. If her mother had been prepared to do something like this to her, even if she believed it was for her own good, then what else had she with-held? And why would she want anything to do with her past if they'd been so happy to wipe it from her memory?

Mary had barely entered the room when Jemma swung around to her. 'Tell me it isn't true.'

'Kevson told me,' said Mary. 'Yes, my beautiful girl, I'm afraid it is true.'

'Then who altered my memory? Was it Mum? Was it you?'

Mary shook her head.

'Who then?'

'Do you remember meeting General Patrick Harris, just before the terrorist attack? Before you were removed from Earth?' asked Mary.

'Did he do it?'

'He did. Your mother fought against it, as did I, but he wouldn't listen. He said security was his domain and he forced your mother to comply.'

Although not sure she wanted to hear the answer, Jemma pushed for more. 'How did he force her?'

'He threatened that he would have you removed from her care if she didn't comply,' said Mary.

'But Mary, Mum was the Supreme Ruler's daughter. Why couldn't she just tell him where to go?'

'Because he was following the Supreme Ruler's instructions.'

Jemma stared at her. 'My grandfather ordered him to suppress my memory of the visits. Are you serious?'

'Yes, I am,' said Mary, sighing. 'We couldn't fight it. But you have the chance now to change everything.'

Jemma shook her head, holding up her hand to stop either Mary or Kevson from following her. She couldn't understand how her mother could have so cruelly betrayed her trust or been so dominated by Harris that she complied with his orders. Still, it gave her a small amount of comfort that it hadn't been her mother's idea, and that Mary hadn't approved. She walked back through the master suite to her grandmother's bedroom and pulled out the diaries. She needed to know more.

Flipping through the pages, she came on the section where her grandmother had written with delight about the visit of Thera and her two children; Jemma, who was then fourteen, and Thera junior, who was twelve, and how she'd taken many images. Jemma searched through the bundle of photos until she came on one in which she was smiling up at an older woman she didn't recognise. She took a deep breath and looked again, hoping for even a grain of recognition. There was none, but the older woman on one of the photos, handed her a teddy bear, a big chunky brown thing which she knew well. She'd called it Gerry. Perhaps that was short for one of Geron's ancestors. She'd kept it until the day she had to flee from Fredrick Pritchard, or Drick as they called him. Her hands shaking, she picked up her communicator. 'Werrimen.'

'Yes, my dear, what is it?'

'Could you come to me, please?' whispered Jemma.

'Of course. Where are you?'

'In my suite.'

As soon as Werrimen arrived, Jemma launched into her story. 'The thing is, I actually met my grandparents, but I can't recollect anything about them. I can look at my grandmother's photo, but it could be anybody. How could they have done that to me?'

'I have no answer,' said Werrimen. 'The Supreme Ruler here was a dictator and I guess they were afraid to refuse. It is possible that I might be able to recover your memory. I cannot guarantee it, but if you would like me to try, I will.'

She stared at Werrimen for several minutes before she nodded. 'I would.'

'I will try then. Perhaps Sean should be here to help you through this, in case you do not like the memory you find.'

For the first time since Kevson told her she'd been here before, Jemma smiled. 'That had occurred to me. Mary seemed to think it was a good visit though, so I'd like to try.'

Werrimen waited for Sean to arrive and for Jemma to explain to him what had happened. He sat beside her on the sofa and held her hand, his eyes not leaving hers which helped her relax enough to begin.

Werrimen touched the back of her neck as she had many times before to help her relax, but this time she seemed to go deeper, and she could see the family farm as clearly as if she were standing there. A transporter was parked behind the house, and Kevson stood beside it looking around as though he was afraid someone might see it. Then the image changed, and she was floating up in the blue light, her mother beside her. She responded with the wide-eyed innocence of a teenager to Werrimen's questions. She described the transporter which took them up to the larger ship, the flight to Anders, the landing and how they were hurried inside to avoid any exposure to the rebel forces. The lady in the photo waited just inside, roughly where Geron had met them earlier. A man stood beside her. He looked regal and spoke with a commanding tone. He told her mother that this visit was not wise and that he had not approved it.

She could hear her mother's voice so clearly that it hurt. 'I know, Father. However, I believe that Jemma and Thera have a right to meet their grandparents, so they are here. We will not stay long. Given the situation, I wonder if Mother should come back with us.' Jemma's mother had adopted an almost imperious tone, obviously attempting to sound like she was in charge, but Jemma could hear the slight tremor in her voice that she always got when she was nervous.

'Your mother's place is with me,' he snapped. 'Perhaps it is time for you to return too.'

'Perhaps,' replied Thera. 'We will talk about that as the week progresses.'

Jemma felt Werrimen's hands shift, and the images faded, but she now had a clear picture of her grandmother and, more than that, she could feel her grandmother's body against her as she was pulled in for a hug. A soft, sweet scent filled her senses, one that she knew would now stay with her forever.

Jemma smiled. 'Thank you.'

'My pleasure,' said Werrimen. 'What did you learn?'

'I think my grandmother was a beautiful woman, but I think my grandfather was a tyrant. My impression so far is that the ruling houses should be disbanded. Either that or there needs to be massive change, maybe an elected leader.'

'Too soon to reach that conclusion,' said Sean, 'but I have to say I'm getting a fairly bad feeling too.'

'Yes,' said Werrimen. 'I agree that it is too soon. However, I am pondering the need for IPL intervention. I need to work out where Pritchard fits in, whether the Zants are still here, and where the rebel force are still active. If so, we must determine if they have a legitimate reason to continue their fight.'

'Werrimen, I'm just a simple scientist from Earth,' said Jemma. 'How can I make any real difference here?'

'There is nothing simple about you my dear,' Werrimen replied, smiling. 'However, we are yet to determine what you can do, or if you want to be involved at all. Now, you have had a harrowing day. I am going to suggest you have a rest and I will take Sean with me. Together we will outline a plan of attack to help you make those decisions.'

'Can I lock the door so no-one else can get in?' asked Jemma.

'Yes, my dear,' said Werrimen. 'I will reprogram it to you, Sean and myself only.'

*   *   *

Sean was about to slam his fist against the wall when his hand was firmly grasped from behind by a much larger one.

'I want to smash something,' he snarled.

'I know,' said Werrimen. 'I am not far behind, but it will not help. Let us go and find General Hunt and Nik and Dan. I have asked Yonkan to join us. Do you feel we can trust Mary and Kevson?'

'Mary, yes. She's more embarrassed than anything about how these people behaved. Kevson, I wasn't so sure, but I think now that we can.'

'Would you prefer I left Kevson out for the moment?'

'No,' said Sean. 'What's the old saying? "Keep your friends close, but your enemy closer." If he's safe and he really cares about Jemma, I want him close. If he's not her friend, then I want him as close as I can get him because if he does anything to harm her I will kill him. No, don't glare at me. I'm tired of the amount of harm these people have done her, and the number of times she's only just escaped with her life. I want it to stop.'

'I agree,' replied Werrimen. 'But thoughts of killing someone will do you harm. I need you to clear your mind and focus on the strategy.'

Sean remained resolute. 'I'm focussed. You have to understand that I'm determined to bring all of this to an end.'

'I understand. We will find the others.'

Sean clenched and unclenched his fists as he followed.

Until he'd met Jemma, he'd been confident that he could tackle most situations and get through unscathed, but now with all the different aliens, some of whom were as human as he, he wasn't at all sure of how to proceed.

'One step at a time, my dear.' Werrimen cast an amused look over her shoulder.

'Sure.' Damn it. How was it that she always seemed to know what he was thinking?

Werrimen stopped in front of him. 'I have organised Yonkan to act as her bodyguard again. She will listen to him. I think she is a little afraid of him, which at the moment might be a good thing. Between us, we will make the right decisions.'

Sean shook his head as he looked back at her and wished he could keep at least some of his thoughts to himself. The woman could read his mind, he was sure of it. Relieved to find Hunt, Nik and Dan in Mary's suite, he threw himself on a chair and recounted Jemma's experiences while Werrimen stepped out to find Yonkan.

Mary had tucked herself into a corner, looking like she would happily slide through the wall if she could.

'I don't understand any of this, Mary,' said Sean. 'It seems like just about everyone in Jemma's life has betrayed her, including those closest to her.'

'No, not betrayed,' sighed Mary. 'We did as we were told. I can look back now and think that was the wrong thing to do, but at the time we all thought we were acting in Jemma's best interests. None of us ever contemplated the possibility that her parents would be murdered, or her grandfather for that matter. It all just seemed so logical, yet the consequences have obviously been disastrous. I'm sorry. I don't know what else to say.'

'Can we trust Kevson?' demanded Sean.

'I believe so.' Mary sighed. 'This has been so hard on all of us. Kevson's attempt to drag Jemma out of the hospital and bring her here was, I believe, about trying to look after her. I'm confident he has now realised that she is an adult who can think for herself, and I also believe that he does not really like much of what he has seen of Anders. We all accepted it when we were young because we knew nothing else. Both our views have changed.'

When Werrimen returned with Yonkan, Sean wasn't surprised to see everyone in the room quietly turn to look at the aliens. This world was foreign to all of them, even to Mary and Kevson. The culture of their day had been an autocracy which they both now seemed to reject, yet would the ruling houses accept any other approach?

'I think we need to get out there and meet the people,' said Sean, 'the ordinary ones, not these arrogant toads.'

Mary flinched.

Sean noticed her reaction but chose not to respond. 'If we find they are more like us than the ruling classes, that might give Jemma something to work with. But if their attitudes reflect those we've found here, I don't think there's much hope.'

Well over half of Jemma's heritage was from Earth. Her parents and grandparents had deceived her. Worse, they'd left her dangerously vulnerable to the likes of Pritchard without the knowledge or the resources to fight back. He could see Werrimen waiting patiently for him to focus again, but he'd already decided on the bones of his strategy. They had to meet the people, but they also had to meet the rebels and find out if they genuinely had something to rebel against.

'I have asked Yonkan to stay close to Jemma,' said Werrimen.

'Damn it, Werrimen, I'm tired of Jemma needing protection,' snapped Sean.

'As are we all,' said Werrimen. 'This is not just about protection, though. As a Trustee, Jemma has connected with Yonkan, and I believe he can help her find her way.'

Sean let out a deep sigh. 'I'm sorry. I appreciate everything you've done to help her. And Mary and Kevson, knowing how much you love her, I don't understand how you could possibly see this place as good for her.'

Kevson dropped into a chair beside Mary and took hold of her hand as tears streamed down her face. 'You must understand, Sean, that we grew up here. We knew no different until we went to Earth. It wasn't perfect there by any means, but the concept of a democracy was astonishing to us. We talked about it often, and we thought we could bring those ideas back here and create change. I believe we still could, but not if it will harm Jemma.'

Patting Kevson's hand, Mary raised her still watery eyes to Sean. 'I don't blame you for being angry with us. We should have handled so many things differently. I wish we could go back and change it all. We both love Jemma and feel responsible for her. All I ask is that you let her make her own decision, whatever that may be. I don't want her to have regrets.'

'There are already regrets, Mary,' said Jemma who'd slipped soundlessly into the room. 'My decision will be influenced by all of you, most particularly Sean, and I don't have a problem with that. What's disturbing me is that everybody who mattered to me as I grew up deceived me.'

'I'm so sorry, sweetheart,' said Mary, dropping her head down again.

Kevson shook his head. 'We can't change the past. We made mistakes, big ones. All we can do is try to help you now.'

CHAPTER 23

Having made up her mind to meet the people of Anders Major, Jemma didn't want to wait for an IPL contingent to be organised for her protection. She left Werrimen to call in all those nearby, then insisted on heading out. At Jemma's request, Kevson led the way, on foot, through the gates of the Kilkinan Palace grounds, into Kilkinan Town for an unannounced visit. She wanted to see the town as it was, without adornments, and without time for the people to hide anything they may not want her to see. Sean walked by her side, while the rest of the Earth humans, including Mary, walked in a line behind. She counted ten IPL Trustees, all Sidlown, who formed a semi-circle covering both sides of the group and the rear.

It fascinated her that there were no high-rise buildings and nothing even slightly resembling a shop, yet there must have been somewhere for people to purchase food, clothing and other supplies. Kevson laughed when she questioned him.

'The factory town is well away from any living areas. People use their communicators to order what they want and then it's delivered to them.'

'How do they pay?' she said.

'It's the same as the new Earth. Everyone works and all their needs are supplied.'

'I don't understand,' said Jemma. 'Lena claimed that the people paid exorbitant rent.'

Kevson nodded. 'Yes, they did, but it was your grandfather who was trying to bring that under control. Before he died, he'd begun to experiment with the concept of everyone works, no-one pays. I suspect he was advised by the IPL, and the people seemed to like it.'

'Then why did they turn against him?' exclaimed Jemma.

'Most didn't. It was a small group that started the trouble. You see, without an economy no-one owns anything, but everyone's basic needs are catered for. Many people who'd been living on the streets in poverty suddenly had a roof over their heads and food in their belly. The problem was with those who'd owned the houses. They'd suddenly lost their properties. Hence they also lost their accumulated wealth and power.'

'So, are you saying the whole thing was about greed?' asked Jemma.

'To a large extent,' replied Kevson. 'The people had been unhappy for a long time. My father was doing his best to address it. Most people respected him for it, but some resented losing the things that they believed they had a right to keep.'

'Hang on,' said Jemma. 'Lena told me they had to revolt against the ruling houses because they were corrupt, but it sounds like the rebels were even more corrupt.'

'That's probably a reasonable conclusion,' said Kevson. 'The rebels didn't want change. Some of the ordinary people were frightened of change too, and afraid it would harm them, so they were easily manipulated and misled by the power-mongers. Lena's family may have come from that group.'

Not so different from Earth, thought Jemma. Political self-interest and greed had led to the destruction there too. But she wanted to focus on Anders Major. As they'd flown in, she'd seen a lot of houses spread over a very large area. The population of Anders, despite the ongoing conflict, was still around ten million and she'd been told that this city alone housed more than one million, but at street level it felt like she was walking through a small rural village. Houses were arranged in clusters, separated by laneways. All were unfenced and appeared to back onto a communal area, many of which had firepits, bench seats and children's activity centres just like a backyard on the Earth of her era. A woman walked out her front door as they approached. She started at the sight of the procession.

Jemma turned towards her, 'Hello. I'm sorry if we disturbed you.'

'No, no. It's no trouble.' The woman stared at her. 'Oh my … you're Jemma. I'll just … oh my … I'll go back inside.'

'No, please don't do that,' said Jemma, holding out her hand, although she wasn't sure if the people of Anders actually shook hands. 'I'm here to meet people. What's your name?'

The woman stopped, then tentatively extended her own hand. 'I'm Relba. It's lovely to meet you, my liege.'

'It's lovely to meet you, too,' replied Jemma, swallowing the urge to object to being called *my liege*. 'I'd like to know what life is like here, on Anders Major. Would you be prepared to talk to me?'

Relba nodded her head towards Kevson and explained that since he'd returned and restarted many of the programs initiated by Jemma's grandfather, life had improved no end. She spoke of terrible turmoil and fear with no certainty for the future, but now they had hope.

Jemma sneaked a look at Kevson. Clearly, he'd won some hearts, and she wondered if his desire to stay would make him pressure her to do the same, even though he'd said otherwise. She thanked Relba and moved on. Within minutes, people appeared on the front doorsteps of almost every house.

'Looks like the bush telegraph has made its way here,' muttered Jemma.

'What is the bush telegraph?' asked Werrimen, quietly.

Jemma hesitated, and looked at Kevson.

'You started it,' he said, smiling. 'You explain it.'

It was something that had been ingrained in her from childhood, but she'd not had to explain it before. 'I guess you'd say it's the way people communicate in country towns. It means you can't keep a secret because everybody knows everybody, and they all talk. Information spreads like a bushfire. Fast.'

'Oh, I see,' said Werrimen, although Jemma wasn't at all sure she'd explained it adequately.

The procession stopped to allow her to talk to several more people as they continued up the central laneway, but she was distracted by an increasing number of small aerial craft overhead, much like the one that had risen above the crowd she'd addressed the day before.

Kevson must have noticed her frown. 'They're called aerial ride-ons.'

'They look like flying motorbikes. They had something like them on Condona and called them aerial scooters there.'

'I think you'd find them throughout the universe,' said Kevson. 'They only go up twenty or thirty metres. They're designed for one or two people to get around quickly.'

Just ahead, a large open stretch of land was packed with people, hundreds of them. How on Earth had they gathered that fast? She smiled at herself. No, not on Earth. She turned, with the intention of walking towards the gathering.

Werrimen held her arm out and told the procession to stop. 'It is far too dangerous for you to risk being entangled in that crowd.'

'I have to talk to the people,' snapped Jemma. 'How else am I to make a decision?'

'I understand, but we have to find a safer way,' said Werrimen. 'Perhaps if we stop here, we could bring small groups to you. That way I can keep control.'

Jemma felt Hunt and Sean close in on either side and desperately wanted to push them away, but she knew they were right. Anybody could be hidden in that crowd, and there was no way to distinguish between a loyalist and a rebel. She dropped back between the two men and waited for Werrimen to organise her people. What followed was a very pleasant couple of hours talking to people and discovering that her grandfather had been held in high regard and Kevson was seen in much the same light. Yet the rebels were still antagonistic. When she raised that with several of the people, she reached the conclusion that they didn't see the rebels as their allies either.

Large numbers of aerial ride-ons had remained overhead, but now they'd moved closer. Without warning they parted down the middle to form a V pattern and one ride-on moved forward. The man astride the vehicle sent a mock salute in Jemma's direction. She almost fell into Sean's arms, and the IPL Trustees surrounded her so tightly that she couldn't see daylight.

'Dear God in heaven,' she cried. 'It's Pritchard!'

'Drick,' snapped Kevson. 'The scourge of our people for over a century. This time we have to get him.'

'I got him last time,' growled Mary. 'Some fool released him. I know the bastard. You have to let me help.'

'We will,' said Werrimen. 'First, I want everyone into the transporter I've called. We will regroup in the palace and decide on our strategy.'

Her vision beyond her group on ground level blocked, Jemma looked up to see a transporter making its way down. She felt a surge of movement, as the Trustees guided the group towards the craft. Surrounded by the blue light, relief flowed through her and, safe in its protection, she floated up. Falling into a seat, she let out the breath she'd been holding and for the first time noticed the anxious look on Sean's face. She reached out and took his hand. 'Safe now.'

'Yeah, but for how long?' exclaimed Sean.

'We must move outside our fear,' said Werrimen, brusquely. 'He is flesh and blood. Mary has captured him before, and we will again. But we must remain focussed if we are to do so. Mary, tell me what you did last time.'

'It is quite a long story,' said Mary. 'You see, Drick owned over a hundred houses and half the food distribution factories. He had a stranglehold on this city, on most of the cities for that matter, because if he cut off the food supply everyone would starve. Jemma, your grandfather was very aware of that and it worried him. That's why he was experimenting with ways to change. The trouble began when he made all land titles void. So, no-one owned anything. Including the palaces, I might add.'

'So, grandfather lost all his wealth too, I guess,' said Jemma.

'Exactly, but he thought that was right and proper. Drick didn't. Your grandfather took a group of people out on a walk, like the one you just did, similarly surrounded by IPL Trustees. About half a kilometre along the road, someone noticed an incendiary device. We pushed our Supreme Ruler out of the way, but the people at the front were killed when it went off. Many were injured. My arm was broken as I fell, but it had been set. Then I was angry.'

'Drick,' murmured Sean.

'Yes,' said Mary. 'Two weeks after the attack, I asked to lead the unit who were searching for him and was given permission.'

'But your arm wouldn't have been healed,' exclaimed Jemma.

'Healed enough. I wasn't going to let that get in the way of stopping that mongrel.'

'So, what did you do?' asked Werrimen.

'First, we took the decision that the heirs to the ruling houses and other important people should be evacuated,' said Mary. 'Earth was willing to take us on. Eric and Anthony went with Jemma and her family. Sean's family had already been there testing our welcome. Then I went after Drick. We had an idea where he was living, but by the time we got there, he'd gone. Many of the people outside the ruling houses joined us. They were just as angry. One of them stumbled on a secret rally and pretended that he was meant to be there. No-one argued, so he slowly infiltrated. After a while they accepted him as one of their own. He advised us of the location of the next rally, so we all dressed in similar clothes to those Drick's people wore, and with weapons hidden we went along to the rally. We did get some suspicious looks, but we had our strategy in place. Before anyone realised who we were, we had him surrounded and captured.'

'Did his people not at least try to fight back?' said Werrimen.

'They did, but I had a transporter standing by. Within seconds they had us surrounded by the blue light and then safe. Their weapons could not penetrate the light.'

'That must have taken months, if not years,' said Jemma.

'Indeed. It was two years before I was able to join you

on Earth. I relaxed then because with Drick imprisoned we should have been safe. But then some do-gooder decided he was reformed, for Christ's sake.'

'We must not dwell on that,' said Werrimen. 'I doubt we'll find someone to infiltrate quickly this time. Kevson, do you know how many of these rebels there are?'

He shook his head. 'No, we don't have numbers. We know they've found places to hide in the hills behind Kilkinan and they have their own spaceships. I suspect they live in the ships most of the time.'

'It shouldn't be hard to locate spaceships,' said Werrimen.

'We've tried, but we haven't succeeded.' Kevson led them to a table and sat, his head in his hands. 'I realise now that Anders is not safe for Jemma and will not be safe until we get rid of Drick and stamp out the rebels.'

'Hang on. I'd like to have a say in this,' snapped Jemma. 'I think I had already concluded that I don't belong here but, whether or not you come with me, Kev, I feel I need to ensure that my grandfather's legacy is respected and enshrined before I leave.'

'My beautiful girl,' sighed Kevson. 'Now that I know you're alive, I will not leave you. If you go back to Earth, then so do I.'

'Alright.' Werrimen stood. 'There are three main things to do then. First, we must develop a plan to capture Drick and disband his organisation. Secondly, find a way to get this civilisation set back up to run as Jemma's grandfather had intended. Thirdly, we must transport Jemma out of here, safely.'

'I agree with all of that,' said Sean, 'but I think that Dan and I and General Hunt would like to have a look at the place of our heritage, first. Jemma and Nik have seen theirs and, while it is grand, neither of them is interested in staying.'

'Are you thinking you might like to stay?' said Jemma.

'No, but I would like to have a look,' said Sean. 'I agree with your thinking, but I'd like all the information that's relevant before we finalise our decision.'

'Fair enough. Werrimen, how do we organise that?' said Jemma. 'I'd like to see those places, too.'

'I understand,' said Werrimen. 'Logistically, we will need to use separate transporters. Jemma and Nikola in one with me, perhaps Kevson can go with Sean and Dan, and Mary with General Hunt. Each transporter will have a unit of IPL Trustees with them. You can look at the places together, but I think travel separately.'

'But, given Jemma's the main target, shouldn't we all be with her for her protection?' said Sean.

'No. Three transporters makes three targets. Even if they have electrometers, their devices will not be able to penetrate the walls of a transporter, so they will not know who is in which craft. And there will be several other transporters travelling with you. I may even use a strategy I have learned from General Hunt and place decoys who look like each of you to be seen entering other craft. That might even draw the rebels out.'

It took several hours for Werrimen to get enough transporters in place, and then a couple more to mould facial features onto some humans who'd volunteered to help. They all had features that were close to the person they were to impersonate, but not quite close enough for Werrimen's satisfaction.

Jemma held onto Sean as though she might never see him again. She saw Dan and Nik doing the same. Everyone, including the Sidlown Trustees, wore a cape with a hood that covered their head. As they walked to the transporters, they kept their eyes fixed on the ground. The decoys were instructed to, at some point, look up. When they did, the Trustees shouted at them and ordered them to pull the hoods further forward to cover their faces. She couldn't credit that the rebels would be so easily fooled, yet she'd seen it work before when Hunt had done it, with much less sophistication.

Sean's house, the Bellear Palace, was on the other side of the planet, so Jemma sat quietly, looking out over the breathtaking landscape and sparkling blue ocean, and was almost disappointed when they touched down. Bellear was not as grand as the Kilkinan Palace but was probably larger overall as it had multiple small buildings in its grounds.

As they entered the palace and were introduced to Biloda, who they'd been informed was the current ruler of Bellear, Jemma was struck by his similarity to Sean and Dan, but not just in build. He was a big man, and he exuded a presence that made it clear he was in charge. So very like both Sean and Dan. His welcome though was rather cool. Perhaps he thought Sean wanted to step in, but he should have realised that Sean would become part of Kilkinan with her if they stayed, although she supposed that would make Dan the heir. Still, Sean and Dan didn't seem to notice as they wandered around the various rooms, most fascinated by the one that their parents would have occupied prior to leaving for Earth. Unlike Kilkinan, in which the Supreme Ruler's suite had been left untouched, Bellear had been extensively redecorated, so it was harder to get a sense of how it would have been. Afternoon tea had been laid out and they sat in the gardens which were far less grand than Kilkinan, although pleasant. The back garden rolled down to the edge of the ocean and a private beach.

It wasn't long before Werrimen called them all back to the transporters. 'We should go to Xander, the guardian's house, then decide what you all want to do from there.'

The guardian's palace was different again. The ruler there was Hunt's great-niece, and she was much more welcoming. Like Bellear, it was large, but its decorations were in keeping with a female occupant, softer colours and more thoughtful placement of furniture and other items. They were again offered refreshments and while Jemma thought it would be rude to decline, she wondered if she might have to waddle back to the transporter.

'I would like to stay overnight,' said Hunt. 'Then I could see more.'

'Certainly,' said Werrimen. 'Your IPL unit must also stay, and I will ask Mary to stay with you.'

Hunt nodded, but Sean looked more thoughtful as he spoke to Werrimen. 'I'd like to stay overnight at Bellear too.'

'Yes,' said Dan. 'So would I. Could we go back there?'

'We could,' said Werrimen, 'but, Jemma and Nikola should return to Kilkinan. There are more Trustees there for their protection.'

Jemma opened her mouth, but before she could speak, Sean intervened. 'Although I'd rather have you with me, Jem, I think Werrimen's right. Dan and I need to do this, but I don't want to put you at any more risk.'

Although not happy to be separated from him, Jemma did understand. Dan had been taken from Sean's parents and placed with his father's cousin just after birth, supposedly for his safety. They had only learned that they were brothers after Jemma was abducted by Drick. The two men had bonded long before they were made aware of their relationship, but for something like this, it was probably right that they pursued it together, and her presence would be an added pressure as they would both feel the need to protect her.

Leaving Hunt behind they headed back to the transporter. When they stopped at Bellear, Jemma again hugged Sean, but she and Nik remained in the transporter which quickly lifted off as soon as the men had left, to take them back to Kilkinan. Even though it was now dark, Geron hurried them inside. He seemed flustered, even as the women followed his instructions. More refreshments waited in the dining room although this time, thankfully, they were light, but Geron urged them to be seated quickly.

'Is there a problem, Geron?' said Werrimen.

'I don't know. There might be.'

Werrimen sat beside him and placed her hands on his, which seemed to take the edge off his distress. 'Tell me please.'

'I have received threats,' said Geron. 'A parcel was thrown into the grounds from a ride-on, not long after you left. It had a letter inside that said if Jemma has not left here by tonight, they will attack. It may be idle nonsense, but I can't ignore it. I don't know what to do. Jemma, nothing would make me happier than for you to stay with us, although I will understand if you choose not to do so. In the short-term at least, I do not think it is safe for you here.'

'No,' said Jemma. 'I don't know what to do either, but if I am placing others at risk then I should probably leave. Do you think that you would be safer if I were to go?'

'I have no idea.' Geron rubbed his temples as though even thinking about it hurt. 'But I am not interested in my safety, only in yours.'

'Thank you,' said Jemma, smiling. 'But I am interested in your safety, and I need to be sure that I'm not endangering it. Werrimen, what do you think?'

No-one had a chance to answer before Werrimen's communicator lit up and Sean's face appeared on the screen. Dan was beside him.

'We're under attack,' said Sean. 'Can you send reinforcements?'

'Immediately,' said Werrimen. 'Tell me the nature of the attack.'

'From the air. Ten … no twelve, transporters and twenty or thirty ride-ons. We've enclosed everyone in the castle, and they tell me security shields are in place, but I can see people climbing the fences. They've bombed some of the outlying houses in the castle grounds.'

'What type of transporters?' asked Werrimen.

'Mixed,' said Sean. 'Mostly Norellian Spheres, but there's also a couple of Zant transporters that I can see.'

'Stay inside. I am on my way,' said Werrimen.

CHAPTER 24

Sean turned to Biloda. 'It's us they're after, not you. Do you want us to take a transporter and leave?'

'No, they would shoot you down, and I don't think they'd back off now that they've started, anyway. It would be easy for me to say that your return has brought this on, and it might have hastened it, but I suspect it was only a matter of time. It would be best to wait for the IPL reinforcements to arrive, then we can decide together what to do.'

'Right,' said Sean. 'Do we need to do anything more to secure the castle? Are there people still in those houses that we need to bring in?'

'No, the castle is secure,' replied Biloda. 'When the first transporter appeared, a signal went to every house. I believe everyone is safe. My people are checking to be sure as we speak. There is nothing more we can do. I have resisted seeking IPL help but now I have to accept that we need it.'

'I'm pleased to hear you say that,' said Sean. 'It seems to me that it's quite a small number of people causing all the trouble.'

'No, not small,' said Biloda. 'They number in their thousands, although we don't know exactly how many. The problem is they have massive resources, and they're cunning. They seem to know when to attack and how to undermine us.'

'If Drick's at the helm, that doesn't surprise me,' said Dan, turning away from the window. 'There's some new transporters. I think it's the IPL.'

Biloda joined him. 'Yes, it is. The spheres and Zants are retreating, but they'll be back. They've probably just gone for reinforcements of their own.'

'Two transporters have landed,' shouted Dan. 'The others are still circling. Werrimen's jumped out. She's heading this way. Can we get her in?'

'Yes, of course.' Biloda ran to the entry, where a small screen showed Werrimen racing towards them. He pressed his hand on the screen as she reached the door and it opened. Once she was in, he pressed his hand on the same spot and the door slammed shut.

'Are we secure?' asked Werrimen.

'I believe so,' said Biloda.

'The guardian's palace is also under attack,' said Werrimen. 'I have sent a unit there, but I believe this might be a ploy to have us leave Kilkinan unsecured, so I have left several units there, and I have called for more. Jemma and Nikola are secured inside, and I am satisfied they are safe for the moment. Is there somewhere private we can talk?'

Biloda led the way to a side room. He closed a heavy wooden door behind them. 'I don't believe anyone can hear us in here. The walls are reinforced, and I have signal blockers in place.'

'Good,' said Werrimen. 'My suggested strategy is two-fold. First, we evacuate Jemma and all who came with her. That may settle things for the moment, but I do not believe it will end the turmoil and end it we must. I would like to bring in as many units as necessary to weed out your rebels and restore law and order. Would you accept that?' She focussed on Biloda.

He sighed, then slowly nodded. 'I thought we could resolve it ourselves, particularly after Kevson returned. Tensions increased when he left to find Jemma, and I blamed her, all of you, for making it worse when you got here, but of course that was nonsense. I agree with the evacuations, although I hope they will only be temporary. Werrimen, we will not only accept your help, but we will welcome it. I would like all of my people, not just the ruling houses to feel safe and secure on our planet.'

'Thank you,' said Werrimen. 'I will commence organising my forces. We have no desire to take over. Once you are secure, we will reduce our presence until, hopefully, we are no longer needed. However, I think we should always maintain a small presence so that if we are needed again, we will know and be able to intervene, quickly.'

While Werrimen and Biloda discussed the details, Sean contacted Jemma, not convinced that the rebels could be successfully held back from infiltrating Kilkinan.

'They're here, but they haven't done anything,' she said. 'Heaps of IPL transporters have also arrived. God, I hope there isn't going to be a battle play out around us, like the one in the factory we endured on Earth.'

'Hopefully not. We've all got to stay where we are for the moment. Werrimen's bringing in reinforcements, but she was worried that attacking us might have been a diversion. Sweetheart, we know you're the real target. Promise me you won't take any risks.'

'I promise, and I can hear Dan making Nik promise too, but honestly, Sean, you've got to trust me to be able to look after myself.'

'I do trust you, but we're so far out of our realm of understanding that we have to also trust the people who belong here.'

'I won't do anything silly,' said Jemma. 'We've all got to get out of this alive and I'm praying that no-one else gets hurt because I'm here.'

*   *   *

As she closed the communicator, she noticed the concern on Geron's face. 'The IPL will flood us with reinforcements soon. We just have to sit tight.'

'I know, but I am concerned for you,' said Geron. 'If the war recommences, I fear that I may never see you again.'

'That's a possibility,' said Jemma. 'We all have to get through it. I don't think the IPL will allow war to restart. Most people on Anders don't support the rebels, so if the IPL can weed them out you might be able to achieve a permanent peace.'

'The way you say *you might*,' said Geron, 'I presume you don't intend to return.'

'I don't know,' replied Jemma. 'I think that I'm not good enough to be your Supreme Ruler. Perhaps Kevson is. I'd like to think that I could come back and be of some use, but it may be that we will decide to live on Earth. I just don't know.'

'I accept that,' said Geron. 'For now, all I care about is your safety and I have to accept that getting you off the planet is the best way to do that.'

After leaving Geron, Jemma and Nik sat on the Supreme Ruler's bed clinging to each other until well into the night when Nik gave in and fell asleep. Jemma walked into another room, leaving the door open between the two, and fell asleep herself, but she was woken early by Mary, on her communicator.

'Are you safe?' asked Mary.

'Yes, we are,' replied Jemma. 'What about you?'

'Yes. For the moment,' said Mary. 'Have the extra IPL craft arrived?'

'I haven't looked. Give me a minute.' Jemma raised herself from the bed, walked back to check on Nik, then looked out the big gable window. 'I can see about twenty IPL transporters out there, and no Norellian spheres or Zant craft. I don't think there were that many here last night.'

'I'm going to try to get to you,' said Mary.

'No, no, please don't,' cried Jemma. 'Wait until Werrimen tells us it's safe.'

'Don't worry about me, sweetheart,' said Mary. 'I won't do anything foolish, and I'll have permission before I lift off.'

'Mary, I love you,' said Jemma. 'If anything happened to you, I don't know how I'd cope. Please stay where you are.'

'I love you too,' replied Mary. 'My place is with you, and I will get there somehow. Just trust me.'

'Of course, I trust you.'

Jemma felt Nik's arm around her as she sank into a chair by the window.

What a mess.

She'd hoped by coming here she'd be able to stop all the trouble, but it seemed she'd made it worse, and she didn't think there was anything she could do about it.

'Come on,' said Nik. 'Let's go see if we can get some breakfast. It's going to be a big day. We need to be fuelled and ready to go.'

Jemma smiled. It was just like Nik to focus on the bright side, yet she suspected she had good reason to worry about Mary. The guardian's role was to be with her charge and that's the way Mary would be thinking.

'You can't do anything about her,' said Nik, taking hold of Jemma's hand and pulling her to her feet. 'Mary will do what she thinks no matter what you say. So, come on. Breakfast.'

As usual, Geron had the table laid out with far too much food. Perhaps that had been the Supreme Ruler's way so he could pick and choose what he wanted, and to hell with the waste. If she did stay, that would change. She sighed. What was she doing thinking about staying?

There was no way she could bring about adequate change here. The rebels had been causing trouble for more than a century, but that made her think about her future. Her role as a Trustee should enable her to keep an eye on Anders, even when she was based on Earth. Hunt had been easing her in the Trustee direction anyway. It was reassuring to think that, even from Earth, she might be able to do some good here. She smiled at Nik, then tucked into her breakfast which drew a suspicious look but explaining her thoughts would have to wait. It wasn't appropriate to talk about it in front of Geron.

Satisfied she'd reached the right decision about her future, she was startled by her communicator.

Hunt appeared on the screen. 'Jemma, is Nik with you? We have a problem.'

Nik moved in beside her. 'Yes sir, I'm here.'

'Good. Mary just took off. She used the distraction of the extra IPL craft arriving and shot out of here. Someone in the house must have helped her get to a transporter. She's trying to get to you. Look out for her and get her inside as fast as you can.'

'Damn it,' said Jemma. 'I told her not to do that.'

'She's a lot like you,' said Hunt. 'She does her own thing. Mostly I'd admire that, but I think this was foolhardy.'

'Very funny,' said Jemma, but she wasn't laughing. 'We'll be watching. Thanks.' She turned to Nik. 'God, could this get any worse.'

'I suppose,' said Nik, 'but not much.'

They walked to the window where Geron had already stationed himself and prepared to wait.

'I imagine she will come to the back,' he said. 'The front is too open, although I have asked one of the Trustees to keep an eye on it.'

Several chairs were near the front door. She suspected they'd been there for the welcoming party to sit as they awaited her arrival from Earth. She dragged one to the window beside the big wooden doors and sat with Geron to look. There was little else she could do until Mary appeared. Half an hour later, a transporter raced towards them, weaving its way through all the other craft. Presumably it was Mary. Jemma prayed that the IPL craft had been notified so they knew not to shoot it down. As the transporter came into land, there was a loud explosion which seem to bounce off the craft. The shields must have been in place. Mary zipped down through the blue light and started to run towards the palace, a distance of about fifty metres. Jemma held her breath, but when a ride-on appeared, seemingly out of nowhere, she cried out. The ride-on dived in towards Mary and fired. She fell. Jemma held her breath, willing Mary to move, but she remained still.

Jemma screamed as she saw blood pouring from the right side of Mary's chest. 'I'm going out.' She jumped up to disarm the door's security which she knew had been programmed to take her command.

'I'm coming too,' said Nik.

'No, stay here,' said Jemma. 'We don't both have to put ourselves at risk.'

'Geron's gone to organise his people,' snapped Nik. 'There's only us and you can't carry her by yourself. I'm coming. Deal with it.'

'Alright, no time to argue. Let's go.' Jemma ran as fast as her legs would carry her, zigzagging as Hunt had taught her, in an attempt to avoid any stray bullets, although she had no idea if it was bullets that they'd used.

Mary still hadn't moved. Jemma threw herself down as much to protect Mary from further shots as to find out how badly she was hurt. She had a pulse, and she was breathing, although it was ragged. Jemma looked around for any other risk, and saw that Nik had her weapon out, covering them.

'Nik,' said Jemma. 'It'd be quicker to get her back inside the transporter. We can decide what to do from there.'

'Shit, Jemma. We've got no idea who's out there or what they might do.'

'I know, but Mary was fine until she landed. We both know how to fly this thing and I'd say the shields are already up. If not, we can fix them. Getting Mary to the spaceship is probably her best chance for survival. We can call for help as we go.'

Nik looked around as though hoping someone might emerge who could tell them what to do. 'You're right. We're probably going to be safer there than out here. Let's go.'

Mary groaned as the two women picked her up, but she didn't regain consciousness as they took her up through the blue light. They laid her across two of the chairs.

'I'll get this thing going, if you can find a blanket or something for Mary,' said Jemma.

'Sure,' said Nik. 'Make sure the shields are in place.'

'Will do.' Jemma set about her safety check, knowing that's what Werrimen would expect even though they were in such a precarious position. She started the propulsion unit, got the navigation screen in place and checked that Nik was ready for her to lift off.

'Yeah, we're good,' said Nik. 'What do you want me to do?'

'I'll fly it, at least first up. Do you want to take comms and contact the ship to let them know we're coming? We need its coordinates.'

'You just want me to be the one to get into trouble,' groaned Nik.

'Now you've got the idea. Okay, I'm lifting off.' Jemma found a gap in the transporters and shot through it, aiming to head straight up into the atmosphere, and hopefully out of the range of the Norellian spheres and the ride-ons. She was fairly sure she'd shaken off the ride-ons when she heard Werrimen shout at Nik.

'By all the stars in the universe, what do you think you are doing?' cried Werrimen.

'Um,' said Nik, 'we had to rescue Mary.'

'Swap,' said Jemma, quite surprised when Nik did exactly as she said. She then stood in front of the communicator to make sure Werrimen could see it was her. 'It was the safest thing we could do. If we'd tried to run back to the palace, we'd have all been shot.'

'Did it not occur to you to call some transporters down to rescue Mary, rather than put yourselves at risk?' exclaimed Werrimen. 'Geron was almost seizing when he contacted me.'

'I know how to fly this thing,' said Jemma, evenly. 'We're okay, but I need urgent medical attention for Mary. I don't have the coordinates for the spaceship. How do I get them?'

'Do you have the shields up?' snapped Werrimen.

'Yes ma'am.' Jemma though it best to show Werrimen some respect. She knew that she should have called for help, but in the panic of the moment it hadn't really occurred to her to call the transporters down. She'd acted on instinct.

'Continue to head straight upwards,' said Werrimen. 'Yonkan is on his way to meet you. He will guide you in. You can explain yourself to me later.'

'Ouch,' said Nik when the communicator shut down.

'It was my decision,' said Jemma. 'She can get into me.'

'Oh yeah, right. Did I tell you to stop?'

Jemma smiled. 'No, but I didn't really give you a chance.'

'I'm as guilty as you are,' replied Nik, shaking her head. 'In fact, probably a bit more. I couldn't think in the moment. You stayed cool and calm, and I left you to make all the decisions.'

'I don't see it that way, but it doesn't matter now. We have to remain calm to get ourselves to the spaceship.'

'Not sure that's going to be plain sailing,' said Nik. 'There's a Norellian sphere to our right and slightly above us.'

'Okay,' replied Jemma. 'With the shields up, is there anywhere that the transporter is vulnerable?'

'I don't think so, but if there is, I suspect Drick will know about it, so hopefully that's not him in that sphere.'

'Yeah, best thing is to keep going upwards,' said Jemma. 'There'll come a point where he can't follow.'

'Hope you're right.'

Seconds later, and without warning, there was an ear-shattering bang at the top of the transporter. Jemma grabbed the edge of the control console to keep herself upright as all the lights went out, leaving them in total darkness. A loud voice sounded although she didn't know where it came from. 'Attention. Attention. Upper deck compromised. Evacuate all personnel from the upper deck. It will be sealed at the count of ten.'

'Nik, where are you?' There was no answer, as she waited for the countdown to get to zero, praying that the lights would come back on then.

'... Zero. Upper deck is sealed and secure. Navigation system is compromised. Propulsion and all other systems are intact.'

The lights were restored enabling Jemma to look around. She searched frantically for Nik and found her lying on the floor behind the seats on which they'd rested Mary. She was still and looked to be unconscious. Jemma raced over and checked for a pulse, then charged back to the communicator. She was clearly on her own.

'Jemma, report.' It was Yonkan's voice.

'Yonkan!' she yelled. 'We need help!'

'Stay calm, Jemma. I am not far from you. I can see a Norellian sphere above you. I saw it fire. Tell me what has happened.'

Jemma took a deep breath to steady herself. 'There was a loud bang. The upper deck is damaged and sealed. Navigation isn't working.'

'Is the propulsion system working?'

'The voice said it was,' said Jemma.

'Good. You can trust control to have checked it properly. Can you manage the craft otherwise?'

'Yes, I can,' said Jemma.

'Where is Nikola?'

'Unconscious.'

'And Mary.'

'Also, still unconscious,' said Jemma, although her voice caught as she looked over at the two women.

Jemma heard another loud bang, but this time she didn't feel anything in the craft.

'I have disabled the Norellian sphere,' said Yonkan. 'It will be able to get back to land but will not give us any further trouble.'

'Okay,' said Jemma. 'How do I navigate?'

'Pull the manual controls out from underneath the panel,' said Yonkan. 'I know you have been trained in this. Calm your mind and allow yourself to remember.'

Easy for you to say, thought Jemma, but she forced herself to concentrate. She touched the small screen, that she had learned to use on a training flight and prepared to key in the coordinates. 'Yes, I have it.'

'Good, now copy the figures exactly as I say them.'

Jemma wanted to shout at him for talking down to her but realised that she'd brought this on herself by not thinking through her options when Mary was hit. She read the figures back, then waited.

'Good,' he said, after a pause. 'Your craft is shifting direction and is headed where we want it to go. Place it back on automatic. It will continue on the path you have now set. Then I want you to have a look behind the panel to see if we can fix the automatic navigation.'

'Done. There's a thing that looks like a cable lying on the floor,' said Jemma.

'Describe it to me,' said Yonkan.

'About a centimetre in diameter. It is yellow with a red stripe down each side.'

'Good. That is the cable we need,' replied Yonkan. 'Does it have a black fitting on the end?'

'Yes, it does.'

'See if you can find a black slot. It will be on the floor behind the control panel. I think the cable has just come loose from the jolt. If you can put it back in, getting into the landing bay will be much easier.'

'Yes,' muttered Jemma. 'I've seen this before. Emilrad taught me.'

'Do not be too hard on yourself, Jemma. This is your first real crisis in a space craft.'

Jemma was too busy looking for the slot to answer him, but she suspected he'd just given her a compliment of sorts. 'Yes, I've found it.' She almost asked him how to pick if the automatic navigation was working again, but remembered that Emilrad had also taught her that, so she stood and closed off the manual control panel, then checked the lights on the automatic panel which were now all green. 'I think it's fixed. Everything is green.'

'Well done. Don't relax,' said Yonkan, firmly. 'We still have to get you to safety.'

'I know,' muttered Jemma, 'but I have relaxed a little. I feel more confident I know what I'm doing now.'

'Good. Have you set everything to automatic again?'

'Yes,' said Jemma.

'Go and check on your patients.'

She went first to Nik who had started to groan. She had a lump the size of a hen's egg on the back of her head, but she opened her eyes to Jemma's voice.

'God, what happened?' whispered Nik.

'We were hit,' said Jemma. 'I'm okay up here. I've got Yonkan guiding me. I'll help you to a chair, but I want you to rest.'

'No, I should be helping.' Nik shook her head and groaned.

'Uh uh,' said Jemma, smiling. 'You need to recover, and until I know how badly injured you are, I don't want you doing anything. My biggest concern is to get help for Mary. She hasn't regained consciousness at all. Maybe you could watch over her. That would give me some relief.'

'Okay, I'll do that. I'm sorry, Jemma,' said Nik.

'What for?'

'I've been absolutely useless to you today.'

'Don't be ridiculous,' exclaimed Jemma. 'I couldn't have dragged Mary in here or got off the ground without you.'

She turned back to the communication screen once Nik was settled, and described the injuries to Yonkan, explaining that she'd told Nik to rest. The rest of the trip passed uneventfully until they neared the spaceship. Getting into the landing bay had her worried. She'd done it several dozen times before, but she had no idea of the extent of the damage to the top of the transporter. Yonkan's calm instructions helped, and she felt her body almost collapse under her as the transporter touched gently down. The outside door of the landing bay closed and Yonkan instructed her to release the blue light to let someone else in, which she did. A Trustee jumped up beside her and moved her transporter forward, while another trustee checked Mary. Jemma was told to remain inside while the outer panel of the spaceship opened again to enable Yonkan to enter. Once everything was secured, several other Trustees rushed in and carried both Nik, to her disgust, and Mary, out. One of the Trustees told Jemma to lean on him and he gently helped her out of the transporter to where Yonkan waited below.

'Come with me,' said Yonkan. He led her to a small lounge, sat her down and gave her a hot drink.

'I'm sorry,' she said. 'I thought I was doing the right thing at the time. I didn't think we could make it back to the palace without being shot. All I could think to do was get in the transporter and get the hell out of there.'

'I am not angry with you,' said Yonkan. 'You have acted courageously and probably saved Mary's life. There was one other thing you could have done, though,' he said. 'Can you think what that might have been?'

'I've been trying to work that out all the way here. The only other thing I can think is that maybe when we got in the transporter, I should have called Werrimen then. But I think I would still have had to take off.'

'Possibly, but we could have given you an escort, perhaps even transferred someone in to help you.'

'Okay,' said Jemma. 'How angry is Werrimen?'

'She is more worried than angry. I have notified her that you are safe. She now has to evacuate the rest of your group. That is her most pressing issue.'

'Of course,' said Jemma. 'I shouldn't be thinking of myself with everybody still down there and at risk.'

He held out his hands. 'Come, take my energy. As soon as you have settled, I will take you to see Nikola and Mary.'

CHAPTER 25

Sean stood beside Werrimen, too worried to do anything else. She'd been glued to her communicator since Jemma had taken off in the transporter. He'd tossed around every aspect of Jemma's actions in his head and, while he was terrified for her, he didn't think he'd have done anything differently under the circumstances. He suspected Werrimen thought the same. When Yonkan advised that the transporter had docked on the spaceship and Jemma was safe, Sean collapsed to the floor, unable to collect his thoughts for several minutes.

'Jemma is now safe, Sean,' said Werrimen. 'We must focus on rescuing General Hunt.'

'I know. Give me a minute.' Hunt was still trapped in the guardian house, and Sean knew that Werrimen was trying to formulate a plan, but in reality, no matter how much they strategised, the only way to rescue Hunt would be to land a transporter at the back of the palace and extract him.

'Could I fly a transporter across to get him?' asked Dan.

'No,' she snapped, then turned back to her communicator to continue what sounded like a frantic conversation with another Trustee who neither of the men recognised.

Sean and Dan exchanged glances as she turned back to them, but both remained silent.

Her voice softened as she began to speak. 'I am sorry. My frustration is with this morning's events, not with you.'

'Do you mean Jemma?' asked Sean.

'No, not really,' said Werrimen. 'I'd have preferred her to contact me, but otherwise no. She did well to get Mary out safely. It is the behaviour of those rebels. We are sending a fleet to get General Hunt. They will return here to Bellear once they have him.'

'Won't the rebels shoot at them?' exclaimed Sean.

'Probably, but their shields will protect them, and they will form a group above the transporter that goes into land. There is risk but we will minimise it. We must now wait.'

'Then there's something else I'd like to discuss,' said Sean. 'The rebels must have been told by someone that we were coming out here. I suspect they were also informed about Jemma's walk through the town. That's the only way they could have been in either place so quickly.'

'But who knew, other than us?' said Kevson. He gasped when he looked at Sean. 'Oh, my Lord. You can't mean me?'

'If not you, then someone close to you,' said Werrimen. 'You are right, Sean. It was all too fast.'

'No, I can't believe it,' said Kevson, and he seemed genuinely shocked. 'No-one at Kilkinan would work with the rebels.'

Sean had to push the glimmer of guilt at suspecting Kevson, to the back of his mind. 'Who knew what we were doing?'

'All of us,' said Kevson.

'Hang on,' said Dan, who'd been standing at the back of the group. He stepped forward. 'Geron was there for every discussion.'

'No,' exclaimed Kevson. 'I've worked closely with Geron since I returned. He is somewhat anxious, but he's fiercely devoted to the Supreme Ruler.'

'Could there be anyone else who overheard?' said Sean. 'Perhaps someone close to Heneker?'

'Heneker is still in the IPL spaceship,' said Kevson. 'Besides, she is not a traitor. She is hot-headed. Her actions on the spaceship were due to excitement that Jemma had returned. Like me, she had no concept that Jemma might not want to stay. She genuinely believed that the IPL were holding Jemma prisoner.'

'Who then?' said Sean. 'There has to be someone.'

'Any number of people,' replied Kevson, with a sigh. 'I have no idea how to work it out.'

'Could anyone have been blackmailed?' asked Sean.

'Possible.' Kevson glanced at Werrimen, then flicked his eyes to Sean, as though something had just dawned on him. 'I haven't seen Geron's child since we've been back. So much has happened that it didn't occur to me before.'

Sean whirled around to Kevson, but Werrimen's raised hand stopped him from saying anything further.

'That will be our starting point when we return to Kilkinan,' she said. 'I believe General Hunt's craft is about to land. The whole fleet that went there to retrieve him will now provide us with cover to get to a transporter, then we will all return to Kilkinan. We will stay there until they arrive, and I am able to hand over to their Commander.'

Sean stood just inside the door and watched the transporter come down at high speed. Multiple craft, too numerous to count, hovered a few metres above. 'Are we ready to go?' he said impatiently.

'We wait until the unit leader notifies me that he is satisfied.' Werrimen stood beside Sean, her hand on his shoulder, and he knew not to move once she had given the order.

Her communicator lit up and the man on the screen said one word, 'Go.'

Sean followed Werrimen out with Dan alongside. Kevson was a bit slower, but he did his best to keep up, and Dan dropped back to help him. Once they were secured inside the craft, there was again a single order and the transporter lifted vertically up at speed. When they arrived at Kilkinan, the Palace was surrounded by Norellian Spheres, all sitting just outside the line of IPL craft. Higher up, Sean could again see two Zant transporters. They appeared to just be observing, but he wouldn't rule out anything when it came to them.

Many of the craft that had escorted Sean's group in now peeled off and, one-by-one, intercepted each of the Norellian spheres. Sean jumped down through the blue light and ran with the others to the Palace door.

Geron pulled them through and slammed the doors shut behind them. 'I'm so glad you're safe.'

Before Sean could stop him, Kevson had pushed Geron

up against a wall, his hands pinning Geron by the shoulders. 'Where's your daughter?'

Geron stared at him. 'What?' he stammered. 'What do you mean?'

'Your daughter, god damnit,' shouted Kevson. 'Where is she?'

Werrimen stepped between the men, lifting Kevson's hands away. 'We suspect you may have been compromised,' she said, kindly. 'Have they taken your daughter?'

Geron sank to the floor. 'Just after Heneker left. Word got out that she was heading up to meet you. My little girl went into town to play with a friend. Neither came home. She's only ten years old. I had to do whatever they demanded. I'm so sorry.'

Kevson threw a cup he'd picked up, smashing it against a wall. 'Why the hell didn't you tell me? I'd have moved heaven and Earth to find her.'

'They said they'd kill her,' said Geron. 'She's not on Earth, she's here somewhere.'

'I didn't mean Earth … I meant … Oh, never mind, it doesn't matter. You listen to me, now. We'll find her, Geron. Whatever we have to do, we'll find her.'

Sean helped Geron up from the floor. 'Drick abducted Jemma a couple of years ago. Tried to kill her. He also took Nik, threatened to kill her too. We got both back with the help of the IPL. Now we have to retrieve your daughter. The IPL can do it, Geron, I promise. Work with them. It's your best hope.'

'All we want is a peaceful planet for our children to grow up,' said Geron. 'I will do as you say.'

'I understand.' Sean hoped with all his heart that the IPL could work the same miracle and find Geron's little girl, but there was one thing of which he was certain. Doing nothing would definitely not find her. He stopped and looked away from Geron when he heard Werrimen on her communicator.

'Are you sure it is Kilkinan?' Werrimen shook her head towards Sean as he started to question her. 'Geron, does your daughter have a tattoo that is sensitive to an electrometer?'

'Yes, she does,' he said excitedly. 'Have they found her?'

'Is it a Kilkinan specific tattoo?'

'Yes,' cried Geron. 'Please. Tell me.'

Sean also couldn't hold back any longer. 'What have you found?'

'Our ships had previously identified three localities which are most likely rebel hideouts,' said Werrimen. 'Transporters have just flown over each of them. One is registering a Kilkinan tattoo. We cannot be sure it is Geron's child, of course.'

'Do they have a plan?' said Sean. 'We can't just charge in there.'

'No, we cannot,' said Werrimen. 'The Laniakea fleet has arrived, though, so we have increased resources now.'

'Good,' said Sean, not quite sure what else to say. He was aware that both Earth and Anders were located in the Milky Way galaxy, which was part of the galaxy supercluster, Laniakea. Yet, it remained beyond his comprehension that the

IPL controlled an enormous spaceship fleet that Werrimen could so easily mobilise within Laniakea.

'I have asked their fleet commander to pepper the skies with transporters. That should unsettle the rebels,' said Werrimen, 'although it will take a few hours. I also have three Anders Trustees who have volunteered to infiltrate.'

'I'd like to join them,' said Sean.

'No.' Werrimen smiled. 'Even though Anders people are, on average, taller than Earth humans, you still stand out. You will assist me to organise.'

Despite his irritation, Sean didn't waste his breath arguing, but he did want to get on with it. Every minute that child remained with the rebels increased her risk. 'Okay, what do we do?'

'We wait,' said Werrimen. 'The Trustees who are about to arrive here will infiltrate the rebel camp. They are Kinbret, who you know, Durilda and Wandine. The signal that was heard was close to Bellear. They will travel to the nearby town where they will pretend to be lost and will drift towards the rebel site. Sean, you will liaise with Kinbret. General you will take Durilda. Dan you will work with Wandine. Kevson, I want you to stay with Geron. Learn everything you can about his daughter, in particular, find something the Trustees may say to his daughter to convince her they are there to help.'

Sean stole a glance towards General Hunt. He was not a man used to taking a back seat, but his face was impassive, and he stood with his hands behind his back, his eyes fixed on Werrimen.

'They are here,' said Werrimen, after speaking into her communicator. 'I do not wish to waste time. You will each greet your relevant Trustee and then we will move out. We can develop plans on the transporter.'

'Move out?' said Sean.

'We will go in the transporter to support the Trustees.'

Now he understood. She'd allocated Kevson to Geron because he was the best to keep Geron under control but, in her kindness, she didn't want to leave Geron behind. She would want to reunite father and daughter as quickly as possible. As soon as he'd greeted Kinbret, Sean followed Werrimen to the transporter. Dan sat beside him, clearly ready to hold him up if he panicked. He wouldn't. He'd been in enough of these things now to accept he was safe, although that didn't mean he had to like them.

Werrimen encouraged the Trustees to eat something from the servery as they travelled. She had no idea how long the campaign would last or until they would again have access to food. Sean was impressed by how calm each of the Trustees appeared. Before a mission, he was always a bundle of energy, pacing or speaking to his team, as much to get his own focus as theirs. As they got closer to the site, the number of patrolling transporters increased until they were so thick, he wondered how their pilot would find a way through. The craft slowed, but Sean had to admire the way the pilot threaded through the tiniest spaces, eventually heading down to a park-like clearing on the edge of town. Sean and Kevson checked their communicators and, as soon as the others had done the same, Werrimen cleared the Trustees to go down.

Geron rushed towards the blue light, but Kevson and Werrimen, who'd obviously been anticipating the move, blocked his way, and the pilot locked the exit from the control panel once the Trustees were out. Kevson eased Geron into a chair as he dissolved into tears.

'Please find her,' cried Kevson.

'They will,' said Sean, and they didn't have long to wait as Kinbret's voice came through.

'I think we've found their camp.' He advised his coordinates. 'The rebels haven't made any attempt to hide where they are. The people of Bellear must know about them.'

'Shit,' snapped Sean. 'Does that mean they're supporting the rebels?'

'No, I don't think so,' said Kinbret. 'The site looks like an itinerant camp. Most town people would stay well away from it. Hiding in plain sight is a good strategy.'

'Okay, what are you going to do?' said Sean.

'We'll head in,' said Kinbret. 'I'm going to turn my communicator off, so they won't work out who I'm talking to if I'm captured. You'll still be able to hear me through my tracker, but you won't be able to communicate with me.'

'No, don't do that,' cried Sean, but it was too late. Kinbret had already gone. When he felt Hunt's hand on his shoulder, he looked up. 'Damn.'

'Would you have done anything differently?' asked Hunt.

'No, probably not, but Jesus, we can't warn him of anything now,' said Sean.

'We have to accept what he's done,' said Werrimen, 'and wait.'

Sean moved to the front of the craft and sat with the pilot. Perhaps he could learn something given the extraordinary way the pilot had manoeuvred through the large number of transporters and was still doing so as they moved around them. He baulked when asked if he'd like to take the controls, but a quick glance towards Werrimen told him he should do so.

'I've seen a couple of Zant craft around,' said Sean. 'But they appear to be just looking on. Any idea what they're up to?'

'No,' replied Werrimen, 'but we are watching.'

'They must still be working with the rebels,' said Sean. 'But what would they be getting out of that?'

'It is hard to say,' said Werrimen. 'There will be some kind of material gain. Geron, any idea?'

'Not really,' said Geron. 'We have always presumed that Drick has offered them something, but we don't know what.'

*   *   *

Kinbret pulled his fellow Trustees into a laneway. He needed to ensure that they were all thinking the same way. 'They will have the child somewhere central, a small building probably, not one of those huts.'

They could see the campsite from where they stood, essentially a shanty town with huts built from old, discarded materials cobbled together. They were probably quite solid, but he thought that the residents wouldn't really care so long as they provided protection from the elements. They wouldn't be concerned about safety. Nobody here would attack or rob another resident. If they had some criminal intent, they'd head into the village and do whatever they'd planned there.

'The children must be terrified in a place like this,' said Durilda. She shuddered as she looked around. 'We can only hope they have not already been harmed.'

'Agreed,' said Kinbret. 'I think there will be enough fear of how the IPL would respond that they will not have hurt the girls. It is our own safety we must manage now, or we will be of no use to the children.'

'Yes,' said Wandine, also staring around as he checked his weapon. 'Kinbret is right. However, I do not believe that Drick is sane, and from Werrimen's description of the behaviour of these people, I doubt we can rely on them to be rational.'

Kinbret nodded. 'I suspect you are right. We should stay together. If one of us has to peel away for some reason, the other two should not be parted.' He adjusted his shirt which was frayed at the hem and had a large hole over the right shoulder. They'd all dressed in scruffy clothes, and their weapons were hidden underneath equally frayed jackets.

'We must act like we belong,' said Durilda. 'They've not taken any notice of us yet, but as we get close to wherever they're holding the girls, they may become more suspicious.'

'Possibly,' said Kinbret. 'Durilda, I feel I must say this.

These are not good people. If you were caught, you would probably be forced into their beds, and I cannot predict what else. I must offer you the opportunity to withdraw. Once we go further in, it will be too late to turn back.'

Durilda's eyes narrowed as she glared at him. 'Are you saying I am not as good as you? We are both Supreme Trustees, Kinbret.'

Kinbret sighed. 'I am not saying that at all. As leader of this team, I am responsible for the welfare of every member. I feel you are most at risk. I apologise if it sounded like I was casting a slur on your competence.'

'Accepted,' said Durilda. 'I am close to both Geron and his wife. I will not turn tail and run. Do you trust me to back you up if we find ourselves in a tight situation?'

Kinbret smiled. 'I absolutely trust you, Durilda. Right, we will move out.'

As they moved further into the campsite, the few scattered huts gave way to more concentrated clusters, and considerably more people. Most were poorly dressed which enabled the Trustees to move through without anyone looking sideways at them, until a large man in well cut, clean and pressed trousers and shirt, blocked their path.

'Where are you from?'

Kinbret did his best to sound like he was grovelling, while Durilda edged behind him, acting fearful. He didn't dare look around for Wandine, just hoped he'd found somewhere behind one of the other huts to hide. 'Our home is near the edge. Back there.' He pointed in the direction they'd come.

'Where's your security pass?'

'Oh dear,' said Durilda. 'I put them in the wash with our clothes. I left them in the house to dry. Should I go and get them?'

'No need, pretty lady. Your man can go. We'll get to know each other while we wait.'

Before Kinbret could come up with a distraction, he saw Wandine sneak towards them from behind the man. Wandine raised a small black cylinder, around ten centimetres long, and half a centimetre wide and slammed it onto the man's neck. The fellow started to swing around, raising his weapon, but fell as he did so. By the time he hit the ground, he was unconscious.

'What the hell was that?' asked Durilda.

'Just a bit of sedative,' responded Wandine. 'It won't hurt him, but he'll be out for a few hours. Help me hide him.'

'By all the stars.' Kinbret stared at Wandine for a few seconds before shooting forward to help him. Once the fellow was safely stowed inside a derelict looking hut, Kinbret motioned to the others to start moving forward.

'They are going to be around here somewhere,' said Durilda. 'That fellow was not like the others. He is hired help, and they are not going to have someone like him just wandering around anywhere.'

'Right, and he is not going to be the only one here,' said Kinbret. 'Stay alert.'

'Just a minute,' said Wandine, after they'd walked further towards the centre of the settlement. 'Over there. Guard on the door. Two more at the front of the hut.'

'Good spotting,' said Kinbret. 'I cannot see any guards at the back.'

'No, neither can I.' Wandine edged behind some trees and closer to the back of the building. He waved them forward. 'No one there. Suspect they are inside though.'

'We will check.' Kinbret led the group from tree to tree until they had a full view of the back wall. 'I am going closer to see if there is a way in.'

'I am with you,' said Durilda. 'I know the girls. They will trust me.'

Kinbret wanted to say no, but Durilda had a point and the last thing they needed was for the girls to panic. 'Right then. Wandine, stay back and keep watch. Durilda, come with me.' He used the cover of trees as far as he could, but there was an open space directly behind the hut, and no option but to cross it.

'We are going to have to go out in the open,' said Durilda.

'Yes, we are.' He waved to Wandine to join them. 'I will go first. Wandine, watch from here. Once I am close to the hut, Durilda, you can follow me.' He didn't wait for an answer, as he sprinted across the open space. It was only fifty metres, but it might as well have been a couple of hundred, it was so exposed. He looked back for Durilda who seemed to fly across the ground to him, then checked in every direction for anyone who might be watching. Wandine signalled all clear, so Kinbret slowly raised himself up to look through a small window. Both girls were inside, sitting on the floor, and it looked like they were drawing. To his surprise a young woman sat with them, one of her wrists chained to something on the floor.

Kinbret drew back as a man walked into the room, although he managed to maintain a partial view of the children. The man carried a stick-like weapon that they all recognised – a Zant equaliser.

'Here,' said the man, reaching down to unlock her wrist. 'Put this on. The boss will be here soon. You're his tonight.' He threw something made from a bright green fabric into her lap, then he dragged her up, gripping her breasts as she stood. Leering at her as he ripped at her clothes, he forced her to strip everything off, then he turned her around for a better look. 'Go on put your dress on, you're scaring the girls. I can wait, you're mine tomorrow, once he's finished with you.' He threw back his head and laughed as he walked out of the room.

Kinbret dropped down. He wanted to vomit, but he had to keep himself together if he was to save the children, and now also this young woman, whoever she was. 'We have got to find a way in,' he whispered to Durilda.

'I went underneath while you were watching. The floor is poorly constructed and there is a weak patch to the left of the children. If you can watch for anyone else to come into the room, I will go to work on the floor.'

'Good. Do that.' He stood again and looked back inside. The young woman was in tears and both children were doing their best to comfort her. He knew Durilda would do the job and get inside, but standing here, he felt so helpless. Wandine was still in position and given he hadn't signalled any trouble, Kinbret was sure there was no one around, but it would only take one person to see them and raise the alarm, so when Durilda's head popped through the floor, it was sheer relief. He continued to watch as she encouraged each of the children to drop through the hole, then motioned to the older girl to follow, but the hole was too small. The two women frantically worked to pull back the boards, but they were stuck.

When he heard her say, 'Leave me, get the children to safety,' he dropped down and scurried under the floor to help. There was a loud crack as one of the boards gave way, but it was enough to get the young woman through. 'Come on. They might have heard that. Hurry.'

Durilda led the way out with the children beside her. Kinbret followed with the young woman. Together they ran to the trees where Wandine was still hiding.

Kinbret didn't waste time looking back. He pushed others ahead of him. 'Keep going. It will not be long until they discover what we've done.'

They were only a few metres into the stand of trees when he heard a shout.

'By all the stars,' muttered Kinbret. 'Move!'

'Through here. I know a place.' The young woman ran behind a derelict-looking hut and peered inside. 'Quickly. There's no one here. We must stay very quiet until they are gone.' She huddled with the girls, reassuring them, then looked up at Kinbret. 'Thank you. I thought my life was over.'

'Who are you,' he whispered.

'Althera. My father is Ruler of Bellear.'

'Pleased to meet you Althera,' said Kinbret. 'Quiet now, everyone.'

Shouting, followed by people running in every direction, continued for some time. When all was again quiet, Kinbret checked on everyone, then raised his head to peer out a window. There didn't seem to be anyone outside. 'I think we should try to get to the village. Then we can call a transporter in to retrieve us.'

'You are right,' said Durilda. 'I will help you get there. Then I will return. I am going to get Drick this time or die trying.'

'No, Durilda,' said Kinbret. 'We will send in an army of Trustees. He cannot get away now.'

She shook her head. 'He is too smart for that. If we don't take him now, he will slip through again.'

Wandine held up his hand as Kinbret went to argue. 'I am with you Durilda. We will go after him together. We will ensure that Kinbret and the girls are safe, then we will return here and work up a strategy.'

'I know a way through to the village,' said Althera. 'I have used it before. They took a friend of mine. I came in looking for her.'

'Is that how they got you?' asked Durilda.

'No. They tricked me when I stopped to help someone I thought was injured. Next thing I knew, I was waking up in their transporter.'

'Good lord,' said Kinbret. 'Did you find your friend?'

'No, they retrieved her body a couple of weeks later. I'd like to stay and help you fight them.'

'That is not a good idea,' said Durilda, gently. 'You are not trained, and you have your whole life ahead of you.'

'I belong to Bellear. I have been training all my life. Yes, I do have my life ahead of me, and I don't want to live it under the constant threat of someone like Drick.'

Durilda stared back at her. 'I feel I should not agree, but I do understand your need to fight. Alright, we need to get out of here first. Althera, lead on.'

Although the girls were slower than Kinbret would have liked, Althera's route enabled them to get back to the city quite quickly. He slipped into an alleyway and pulled out his communicator. 'Werrimen, can you hear me?'

'Go ahead, Kinbret.'

'Pick me up please. You will have to track my coordinates. I have both children.'

'We are on our way,' said Werrimen. 'Be prepared to run under the blue light. Are the girls unharmed?'

'Yes, they are fine. We will be waiting.'

Sean, with the pilot's help, zoned in on Kinbret's position although he was anything but confident that he could manage the rescue.

'May I take the controls?' said the pilot.

Sean laughed. 'Yes, please. I'll do my best to guide you in.'

'Everyone be seated,' said the pilot. The transporter ducked and weaved through other craft, then suddenly dashed down at breathtaking speed. 'Kinbret, blue light is now available.'

Seconds later, Kinbret with Geron's daughter and her friend were sucked up into the craft. As soon as they were in Sean secured the blue light entry, but he didn't have time to check on the girls before Geron snatched them from Kinbret. Hugging them close to his chest, Geron collapsed to the floor, caught between laughing and crying.

'Where are Durilda and Wandine?' asked Werrimen.

'They chose to stay and go after Drick. I could not dissuade them. There was another young woman with the children, Althera of Bellear. Both the Trustees and Althera have remained behind.'

'Oh God,' said Sean. 'I overheard talk that Althera was missing when I was at Bellear. She'd been missing for a couple of days. It didn't really mean anything to me then because I didn't know who she was. Is she alright?'

'She is unharmed,' replied Kinbret. 'I believe we got her just in time. They had lined her up to pleasure Drick tonight.'

'It gets worse by the minute,' muttered Sean.

'This is not good,' said Werrimen. 'But we must go. I will redirect some other IPL transporters to back them up.'

Sean was relieved to see the Kilkinan Palace as they neared, but then everything seemed to progress at lightning speed. The children were reunited with their families. Kinbret was asked by Werrimen to stay and help Geron. Hunt, Dan and Kevson, along with Sean, were rushed back to the transporter which took off vertically, again at lightning speed, Sean's worst nightmare.

CHAPTER 26

Jemma waited in the safe room on the landing bay of the spaceship, desperate to see Sean. Although Nik and Mary had both recovered well, Yonkan had insisted on at least another twenty-four hours observation in the medical centre before he would be prepared to clear them. She sighed as she waited, alone, for the landing bay to be secured. All she really wanted was to settle down in a nice apartment with Sean and live her life without interference. As soon as she was permitted, she ran to the base of the transporter to wait for him to descend through the blue light. She flew into his arms and stood clinging to him for several minutes.

Werrimen smiled and moved aside a little until they'd separated, at which point she led them to the disc and up to the control floor conference room, securing the door once they were all inside. 'We must talk. Those of you who were with me have not eaten for several hours. Take what you wish, then join me at the table please. We can speak while we eat.'

'I need to see Nik,' said Dan.

'Yes, of course,' replied Werrimen. 'Would you stay with us for a few minutes to discuss what we must do next, then I will take you to her.'

Dan nodded, but he was obviously still anxious as he took a plate and filled it with food.

'Werrimen,' said Jemma, as she sat. 'I have a few things I need to say to everyone. May I do that now?'

'Certainly. We do need to debrief but you may start.'

Jemma took a deep breath and, holding Sean's hand, she looked between General Hunt and Kevson. 'I have made my decision. I will not be staying on Anders Major at this time. But, having learned a great deal about my grandfather and what he was trying to achieve, there are things I want to do before I leave.'

'I thought that would be your decision,' said Kevson, his eyes reflecting the sadness in his heart. 'What do you want to do about your grandfather's legacy? Remember, you can't go back to Anders until we weed out the rebels.'

'I think I can do what I need to do from here, with your help,' said Jemma.

Kevson shrugged. 'Alright, I'll do what I can.'

'My grandfather was trying to improve life for all his people, not just the wealthy. There were obviously still problems with the way he lived his life, particularly his infidelity to my grandmother and the way she was brought to him in the first place. Having said that, I believe that he was doing his best to right a corrupt culture. I'd like to see that continued and Kevson, that's where I need your help.'

'As I said, I'll do what I can.'

'Thank you,' said Jemma. 'I would like you to support the IPL to weed out the rebels and shut them down for good. My impression is that the Ruling Houses have, for a very long time, abused their power, and that also needs to be stopped. I know you were working towards that, and I would like to see an elected government, but none of that can happen overnight. I thought we could start with an elected council of advisors to the Supreme Ruler and the Rulers of the other houses. They could advise of the people's needs and express their wishes. Over time, that council would take on a stronger management role. They could still maintain the ruling houses, but with less power. Kevson, the key to making that work will be your presence. I'm asking you to return to Anders, at least in the short term, until you have someone who can take over from you, someone who will continue our philosophy to make life fairer for all.'

'I see.' Kevson was silent for several minutes, everyone else at the table watching him. 'If that is what you want, I will stay so long as it is short-term. Werrimen, is Heneker still here?'

'She is,' said Werrimen. 'If you are considering her as a successor, I must say that I am concerned about her attitude.'

'I understand, but I would like to talk to her,' said Kevson. 'If I can make her understand what Jemma is trying to do, and that it is for the good of the people, she may be able to take over from me. Geron is not strong enough, although I believe his daughter is, but that would be a long time to wait.'

Jemma nodded. 'Once the IPL gets the rebels under control, particularly if they can capture Drick, we would be able to visit each other. That brings me to my second decision.'

'Yes,' said Werrimen, smiling. 'I am pleased you have made decisions.'

Jemma fixed her gaze on General Hunt this time. 'I have never wanted to be part of an army. I still don't.'

Hunt sighed. 'Jemma, we've been through this so many times. Zadrus has said you will be.'

She stood and placed herself beside Werrimen. 'Please hear me out.'

Hunt grinned. 'Certainly, my liege.'

'Oh, shut up,' snapped Jemma. 'Werrimen, I enjoyed learning to fly the spacecraft while we were on Condona, and I want to continue with that. I've watched both you and Yonkan develop strategies that you've subsequently implemented with amazing calm and determination, and I would like to develop that capacity. I know that I have discussed this with you before, but now I understand a lot more about what I am asking. I would like to train full-time to become a Trustee and learn everything I can from your scientists.'

'We must discuss this with Zadrus. He is your guide,' said Werrimen.

'I believe Jemma is suited to such training,' said Yonkan, which made Jemma jump. She hadn't realised he'd joined them. 'But I must say that in most planets with a situation like the one on Earth, those who've joined us have also been part of that planet's military both in rank and in training.'

'Oh Jemma,' said Hunt, outwardly laughing now. 'It looks like you're going to have to work with me after all.'

'I've never had a problem with that,' snapped Jemma. 'But I want to focus on Trustee training.'

'We will see what Zadrus says,' said Werrimen. 'Now, there is something else that I wish to say. I have been in discussion with the IPL Supreme Council. They have made two decisions. First, I will tell you about Kinbret, although he is not here. He is to be awarded another star for his bravery and cunning in rescuing Geron's daughter and her friend. He is also to be appointed Supreme Trustee Commander for Anders Major.'

'That's excellent,' said Kevson. 'He is a wonderful man. I would not be alive without him.'

'I'd also like to say, and this is purely my suggestion,' said Werrimen, 'that if Geron's child is as strong as you say, we should commence her training sooner rather than later.'

'Certainly,' said Kevson. 'I will discuss it with them as soon as I return.'

'Now, the IPL council gave me another direction,' said Werrimen. 'Jemma, while I was bothered that you did not communicate with me when Mary was injured, I acknowledge that you did not have many options available to you. The council has directed me to award you your first star and promote you to senior Prehling.' She handed Jemma a small case with a gold star crafted from metal, possibly gold. 'The star will be embroidered onto your uniform, but we all receive an actual star with our award, and we treasure them. Congratulations, my dear. All that I ask is that you wear it with pride.' She reached out and wrapped her arms around Jemma who suddenly felt very small and humble beside this great woman.

'I don't know what to say,' said Jemma. 'Of course I'll wear it with pride, and I'll never forget how you've helped me.'

'I know what to say,' said Sean. 'That's fan-bloody-tastic. You absolutely deserve it.'

'Hear, hear,' said Hunt, clapping as he stood. 'But don't get too big-headed. It doesn't get you out of the army.'

'No,' she replied, laughing, 'but you need to remember that I've got a star and you haven't.'

'You have,' said Sean. 'But we've got these flash stripes on our shoulders.'

'I've got stripes, too.' Both Sean and Hunt were grinning, but Jemma felt the need to make them understand. 'You earned your stripes. I didn't. But I did earn the star.'

'Oh Jem,' said Sean, wrapping his arms around her. 'There's no question that you earned your star. I'd argue that you also earned your stripes.'

She shook her head. 'You're missing my point. This star makes me a part of the IPL. I really am on my way to becoming a Trustee.'

'Yes, you are. And I'm really pleased for you.' Sean still looked puzzled.

'Don't you see? The IPL has a presence throughout the universe. This star means that I'm accepted by the IPL. I'm now a part of something much bigger than either Earth or Anders. Through them, I can now have my own presence on both planets.'

'I think I get it,' said Sean. 'You can be on Earth, but still go to Anders and make sure things are progressing.'

'That's right,' said Jemma. 'I no longer have to feel torn between the two planets.'

FROM THE AUTHOR

I do hope you enjoyed *Torn In Exile*.

If so, I'd appreciate a review on the site from which you
purchased this book.

And, of course, tell your friends.

If you would like to know more about me,
have a look at my website. **https://almcdonnell.com**

If you would like to hear from me when I publish the next
book in the series, sign up to my newsletter and I will send
you my free anthology – *Behind the Exile*.

ALSO BY THIS AUTHOR

Books 1 (*Abandoned*) and 2 (*Stranded*)
of the *In Exile* Series.

Available from Amazon, Booktopia, Book Depository
and other online booksellers.

www.ingramcontent.com/pod-product-compliance
Lightning Source LLC
Chambersburg PA
CBHW020542120726
47903CB00001B/88